Also by Libby Fischer Hellmann

Havana Lost
A Bitter Veil
Set the Night on Fire

♦

THE GEORGIA DAVIS SERIES:
Nobody's Child
ToxiCity
Doubleback
Easy Innocence

♦

THE ELLIE FOREMAN SERIES:
A Shot to Die For
An Image of Death
A Picture of Guilt
An Eye for Murder

♦

Nice Girl Does Noir (short stories)

♦

Chicago Blues (editor)

WITHDRAWN

from the
MANITOWOC PUBLIC LIBRARY

MANITOWOC PUBLIC LIBRARY

DEC 05 2017

MANITOWOC, WI 54220

DOUBLEBACK

DOUBLEBACK

LIBBY FISCHER HELLMANN

THE RED HERRINGS PRESS
Chicago

Originally Published by Bleak House Books in 2009.

Copyright © 2015 by Libby Fischer Hellmann All rights reserved. No part of this publication may be reproduced or transmitted in any form or by any means, electronic or mechanical, including photocopy, recording, or any information storage or retrieval system, without permission in writing from the publisher.

Cover design by Miguel Ortuno
Interior design by Sue Trowbridge

ISBN: 978-1-938733-85-7
Library of Congress data on file

For Michael, with love

"Go West, Young Man"

Acknowledgements

I am grateful to everyone who shared their time and expertise for *Doubleback*. If any of the information is inaccurate, it's my responsibility—not theirs. For the bank information, thanks to Blair Robinson, Ed Bettenhausen, Liz Taylor, Jeff Cohen, and especially Erich Laumer, who took frantic calls from me with grace and patience. Thanks also to Joel Ostrander, Mike Green, Sean Chercover, Cindy Clohesey, and especially Cara Black, with whom I shared long car rides brainstorming plot. Don Whiteman continues to be a muse of long standing, as is Judy Bobalik. And thanks to Chris Acevedo for her translation services. Brian Gilomen deserves a shout-out for help with the winery.

A very special thanks to Maryelizabeth Hart and author Jeff Mariotte for sharing their love of Douglas, Arizona, and supplying me with information, newspapers, and other local lore.

And special thanks to Michael Dymmoch who read *Doubleback* in manuscript form and provided a very necessary edit. Thanks also go to Ann Voss Peterson, who let me borrow her name. And to Ann Rittenberg, Ben LeRoy, and Alison Janssen, who really is the best editor in the universe.

Finally, these books were indispensable in my research:

Licensed to Kill by Robert Young Pelton, Crown, 2006
Blackwater by Jeremy Scahill, Nation Books, 2007

Doubleback

CHAPTER 1

P anic has a way of defining an individual. It scrapes the soul bare, strips away pretense, reveals the core of the human spirit. It's hard to dissemble when fear crawls up your throat, your heart stampedes like a herd of wild animals, and your skin burns with the prickly-heat of terror. For the six people thrown together in a Loop office building elevator on a hot June day, the moments they shared would reveal parts of themselves they had not known existed.

It was early afternoon in Chicago, the kind of day that made people want to ditch the chill of air conditioning and head to Wrigley Field. The first man who stepped into the elevator on the sixty-fifth floor might have been doing just that. He was a florid-faced, doughy man with gray at his temples. His jacket was hitched over his shoulder, and his shirt gapped between buttons, calling attention to his belly. He moved to the left side of the car and kept his gaze on the floor, as if by doing so, he—and his early departure—might escape notice.

The elevator descended to the sixty-second floor, where two women who didn't know each other got on. One was slender and small, with mousey brown hair pulled back at her neck. She wore a heavy sweater over a flowered dress. She went to the back of the car and leaned against the metal railing, trying to look inconspicuous. The other woman, in a gray pinstriped pantsuit over a sleeveless black tank, wore her hair in a chin-length bob. She positioned herself on the right side of the car and kept her eyes on the car's indicator panel. The faint aroma of coconut shampoo drifted over her.

On fifty-seven a young man got on. Wearing shorts and a ratty t-shirt, he clutched a large manila envelope in one hand and a bicycle helmet in the other. The envelope bore the logo of a prominent Chicago messenger service. He kept shifting his feet, and his mud-caked sneakers left tiny pellets of dirt on the tiled floor.

Three floors below a middle-aged man in khaki chinos entered. His shirt sleeves were rolled up, and he wore his hair in a sparse comb-over. Another man entered the car on the fifty-first floor. Dressed in a suit, tie, and crisp white shirt, he wore wrap-around Oakley sunglasses. He kept one hand in his pocket, but through the shades appraised everyone in the car.

As the elevator descended past the fiftieth floor, it gathered speed. It was one of three express cars from the upper floors; the next stop was the lobby. Both women stared at the overhead panel lights. The messenger squeezed his eyes shut. Comb-over Man hugged the back wall. Florid Face shot the man with the Oakleys a sidelong glance, but whether from envy or trepidation, it was hard to tell.

No one expected the elevator to lurch to a sudden stop.

When it did, the force threw everyone to the floor. The lights blinked out, plunging the car into darkness. One of the women screamed. So did a man. The messenger shouted, "What the fuck?" Florid Face moaned. So did Comb-over Man. The man in the Oakleys kept his mouth shut.

"Please, please, don't let me die," one of the women cried out. It wasn't clear who she was addressing: someone in the elevator? Jesus? God?

"I think my leg is broken!" Comb-over Man screamed. "Help me!"

The messenger tried to get up. The weight in the car shifted. The elevator rocked.

"Stop! No one move a fucking muscle!" Fear thickened the voice of the woman in the pantsuit. "We'll all be killed."

"Doesn't fucking matter," the messenger said. "We're already dead."

"My leg! I can't move!"

"Oh my god… oh my god…" The mousey-haired woman started to hyperventilate. Waves of tension radiated through the air.

"Anyone have a light? A match? Flashlight?" It was Florid Face. He shifted. Again the car rocked.

"I said don't fucking move!" Pantsuit yelled. Her breath came in short little gasps. "Someone push the alarm button!"

"I tried! It's not working!"

Florid Face found his voice. "Oh fuck, oh fuck…" He started babbling. "Holy Mary, Mother of God!"

The car swayed enough that anyone who tried to get up might have lost their balance.

"Father, forgive me for I have sinned…" The mousey woman

prayed in a thin, quavering voice. The smell of fear permeated the car.

"We should try to stay calm," a male voice broke in. "If we were going to die, it would have already happened."

Pantsuit wasn't mollified. "I don't believe it. Where is everyone? Where are the lights?"

"Shit, shit, shit…" Comb-over Man chanted.

Someone made a rustling sound. The elevator rocked again. Bounced a little.

"Who's doing that?" Pantsuit shouted. "Stop, goddammit it! Don't you understand English?"

The messenger said, "I'm trying to climb up on the railing so we can get out, you know, through the roof…"

"Yes, and when the fucking elevator rolls over, we'll be smashed to bits. Stop it asshole!"

"Jesus! Someone help me!" Florid Face raked his hands across the floor tiles as if he was trying to collect something precious from them.

"Look, someone has to know we're in here…" the messenger said. "Try the alarm again. Somebody!"

Pantsuit started to reply. "I had my finger on it for over a—oh fuck! What now?"

There was a lurch and a rumble. The elevator groaned. The lights flashed on. Off. Then on again. They stayed on.

"Oh god! This is it!" The mousey-haired woman gripped the steel railing so hard her knuckles turned white. The man in the Oakleys clutched it too. Mousey-hair looked over, noticed the index finger on Oakley's left hand—or most of it—was missing. She quickly looked away.

The elevator started to descend—slowly, under control—as

though nothing unusual had just happened. But Comb-over Man was still moaning, and Pantsuit's cheeks were stained with tears. The messenger, looking wild-eyed, searched for his manila envelope, picked it up, and clutched it to his chest. Florid Face turned ashen. Rising to his knees, he pulled out a handkerchief and wiped sweat from his face. His hands shook. Oakley picked himself off the floor and stood in the back, looking blank.

After what seemed like eternity, the elevator reached the lobby. The doors whooshed open. Three security guards were waiting with anxious expressions. A crowd of people gathered behind them.

"Are you all right? Is anyone hurt?"

The messenger yanked a thumb towards Comb-over Man, who was still on the floor. Two of the guards hurried in to examine him.

"What the hell happened?" Pantsuit demanded as she stepped out. She was followed by Mousey-hair, Florid Face, and the man in the Oakleys.

One of the guards shook his head. "We're not sure. The power dipped in parts of the building. This entire bank of elevators went out. Probably a brown out. It's really hot out there." He looked at the others. "But we'll find out. If I could just get your names—"

The messenger cut him off. "Not me. Man, I'm never coming in this fucking building again." He ran toward the revolving doors, pushed through, and disappeared from sight.

The guard turned to Florid Face. "Sir, could I have your name?"

The man shook his head. "Just let me out. Right now."

"You sure you're ok?"

Florid Face didn't answer, just turned on his heel and walked away.

"It's a miracle no one else was seriously hurt," the guard said to no one in particular.

Mousey-hair gave the guard her name. Pantsuit did, too, adding she had some serious bruises. Comb-over Man was in the process of being carried out by the guards, who assured him paramedics were on their way. "Just hold on, sir."

"I don't have much choice, do I?" Now that the danger was past, anger was replacing fear. "Watch it, goddammit. That fucking hurts!"

In the commotion no one noticed the man in the Oakleys. Turning away from the security guards, he eased his way through the crowd toward the revolving door. As he pushed through, he slipped his hand out of his pocket and looked at his watch.

"Right on schedule," he thought to himself.

CHAPTER 2

Ellie

I found the used condom when I was changing the sheets in the guest room. Technically, it's not a guest room—it's my office. But there's a daybed against the wall, and, sometimes, when out-of-towners show up, or some of Rachel's friends spend the night, it's put into service. As it clearly was last night.

At first, I didn't know what it was. Crumpled up, an off-white, beigy color, it might have been a used Band-Aid. Maybe one of those footlets they give you at the shoe store. Even an empty sausage casing. I swept my hand over the sheet and scooped it up. When I realized what it was, I dropped it back on the bedcovers, ran into the bathroom, and washed my hands. Then I gingerly picked it up with a pair of tweezers and placed it on a sheet of clean, white printer paper. I picked up the paper and walked into the hall.

"Rachel..."

Her bedroom door was partially closed, but I could hear her

talking on the phone. There was no pause or drop-off in her voice. I called again, louder this time, all the while staring at the condom as if it was infected with Ebola.

I heard a grudging, "Hang on a minute," and in the next breath, "What is it, Mom?" Her voice had that clearly-annoyed-to-have-been-disturbed tone.

"Out here," I snapped. "On the double."

A dramatic sigh was her response. Then, "Call you right back." Rustles and creaks followed as my eighteen-year-old pulled herself off her bed and emerged from her room. Her blond mop of hair, so unlike my dark waves, fell across her forehead. Her big blue eyes that she'd learned to highlight in just the right way with liner and mascara sought mine. As tall as I, and more slender, she wore a red t-shirt and gym shorts, and all her physical attributes were very much in evidence. My daughter had turned into an attractive, desirable young woman.

Evidently, I wasn't the only one who'd noticed.

I held the condom out in front of me. At first she squinted as if she couldn't figure out what it was. Then her brain registered, her lips parted, and a flush crept up her neck. At the same time, she tried to hide her surprise and shot me a look that managed to be both shrewd and defiant.

"Let me guess," I said. "You and your friends were blowing them up like balloons."

Her eyes narrowed, the way they do when she knows I'm onto her and the only possible recourse is disdain. "No, Mother."

"Pouring water into them, maybe."

Her eyes were little more than slits.

"No? Pray tell how this ended up in the sheets."

Her eyes flicked to the condom then back to me. Her shoulders heaved, and she blew out a breath. "All right. I'll tell you. But you've gotta swear not to tell anyone."

"I can't promise that, Rachel."

"Mother, please. You have to. If it gets around…"

"Tell me. I'll decide."

Her face scrunched into a frown. Her lower lip protruded. There was another dramatic silence, and then she said, "It wasn't me. It was Mary. She and Dan were in there."

Mary was her best friend. Dan was Mary's boyfriend. "When?"

"Saturday night."

It was Monday now. "Where were you?" She didn't answer.

"With Adam?" Adam was Rachel's boyfriend. At least on Tuesdays and Thursdays, or whenever she wasn't breaking up with him. Regrettably, she'd inherited my emotional intimacy patterns. Or lack of them.

"We didn't go upstairs, Mom. I swear. We were out on the deck smoking hookah."

My house had become the "go-to" place for Rachel and her friends over the summer. I kept a lid on drinking and smoking, but otherwise left them alone. The newest craze was smoking flavored tobacco in ornate silver hookahs that would do Alice's Caterpillar proud. But teenagers always think they're smarter than adults, and I knew they slipped in some weed now and again. I'd done worse in my youth—I came of age during the sixties—so I pretended not to notice.

Still, sex in my office wasn't my idea of acceptable behavior. "Rachel, this is wrong. It can't happen again. Not in my house."

"Mother, we're not children. Jesus. I'm going to college next year."

"I know. And I can't wait."

"You would say something like that. You never want me around. You don't trust anyone. You always have to be in control." When Rachel goes into attack mode, I cringe. It was a tactic she'd learned from her father, who figured he could wear me down with belligerence. It didn't work when he did it; it wouldn't work now.

"If I were you, I'd button my mouth before I found myself grounded for a month."

She tightened her lips, but her eyes were pools of rage.

Then the phone rang. Her eyebrows went sky high, and she bolted into her room to grab it. Which was fortuitous. We were both on the verge of saying things we'd regret.

"It's for you," she called petulantly.

I poked my head in her room.

"Could you please take it in your office? I need to call Julia back."

"We'll continue this conversation later."

She rolled her eyes.

I went back in my office, put down the condom, and picked up the phone.

"Sounds like another fun morning at the Foreman's." It was Susan Siler, my best friend and possibly the wisest person I know.

"She's full of mother angst right now." I started to tell her about the condom but Susan cut me off. "Ellie, I want to hear about this, but it's got to wait. Something important has come up."

"Go ahead."

Susan rarely makes demands. Of course, her life is perfect. She has the perfect husband, two perfect kids, a perfect house, and a perfect part-time job in an art gallery. We've been friends for nearly twenty years, and I still don't know how she does it.

"I have this friend," she said. "Sort of a neighbor, actually. Christine Messenger."

"I don't think I know her."

"Ellie, her daughter has been kidnapped."

* * *

We live in a peaceful bedroom community twenty miles from Chicago on the North Shore. It's an affluent suburb in which the biggest tragedy occurred twenty-five years ago when a disturbed young woman went on a school shooting spree that killed one child and wounded several others. In fact, our village is generally so safe that, if you believe the rumors, it was once a haven for Outfit families—their children deserved safe neighborhoods, too, didn't they? It stayed that way until the village police chief was caught extorting money from local businesses, after which he and the Mob made a speedy exit.

Christine Messenger's red-brick house, nestled on a block of similar homes, was neat and well-tended, with what had to be a nitrogen-enriched green lawn, a riot of annuals and climbing roses flanking the door. It wasn't that large—three bedrooms, I guessed—but it fit nicely with the white picket-fence theme of the street. I met Susan outside—she lives three houses away—and we trudged up the flagstone path to the door.

Susan is taller, slimmer, and more graceful than I. She's always perfectly coiffed and dressed, and today her light green sun dress and matching sweater complemented her red-gold hair perfectly. Her pearl earrings—studs, of course, nothing too ornate—glowed in the sun. Susan gave me the once-over with a practiced eye, taking in my cropped pants, wrinkled t-shirt, sandals, and hair tamed temporarily with an elastic band. She didn't say a word.

"What did you tell her about me?" I asked, trying not to feel slovenly.

"I told her you were my friend, and you had experience with this type of thing."

I raised my eyebrows. "This type of thing?"

"You know what I mean."

Over the past several years, I've had several encounters with the dark side of human nature. I don't look for it, and don't much like it. I prefer a boring, normal life. But then Rachel is my daughter, Jake Foreman is my father, and Luke Sutton is my boyfriend. Normal is not an option.

"How old is the girl?" I asked Susan.

"About eight."

"When did it happen?"

"Couple of hours ago. After she dropped Molly at camp."

The Park District runs a day camp for kids during June and July, basically a glorified baby sitting service with arts and crafts and the occasional trip to the pool. Rachel had attended when I worked in the Loop.

"Chris took the train downtown as usual," Susan went on. "She was just getting to her office when the call came."

"What did they say?"

"That... well, why don't we let Chris tell you herself?" She stepped up on the porch and rang the bell.

"You know what I'm going to tell her," I said, listening to three perversely cheerful chimes.

"What?"

"That she needs to go to the police. Now. Do not pass go. Do not collect two hundred dollars."

"You can't."

"Why not?"

"The kidnapper specifically said no police. Or he'd kill Molly."

I leveled a look at Susan. She looked back at me. We stood there staring at each other for a long moment.

She blinked. "Don't look at me with those big gray eyes. I'm not asking you to get involved. Just talk to her. Chances are she'll do whatever you say. But she's totally freaked out, and you're the only person I could think of who'd understand."

I sighed.

* * *

Houses give off smells. Some are pleasant, some sour. Sometimes they define the home's personality, and you know at once whether the place is one you want to spend time in or leave as soon as you can. I've never figured out where the smells come from—laundry soap, lingering body odor, dirty carpets—but a stale, briny odor bit at my throat as I entered Christine Messenger's house. I resisted the impulse to flee.

Not that the house was a mess. The décor was well-bred Wasp elegance, with plenty of silk and brocade, an antique or two, and a splash of color that her decorator must have said would "give the room a finished look." But the shades were drawn, and the dim lamplight threw gloomy shadows across the living room.

Christine Messenger closed the door and stood against it, as if she was barricading herself—and us—inside. She would have been attractive, were it not for the fear and misery etched on her face. She had red hair, like Susan, which fell to her shoulders, but hers was darker, almost auburn. Her eyes were green and red-rimmed. Her skin looked pasty, and when I examined her closely, I saw it was covered with freckles that she probably agonized over as a child. Although she looked thin, I couldn't tell for sure. She was wearing bulky sweats, like it was the middle of January. I'd seen it before. Grief can strip body heat away faster than a cold shower.

"Thank you for coming." Her voice was ragged. "Susan said you might be able to help."

"I don't know." It was a brilliant blue-sky June morning, but as I stepped into the living room, my mood darkened. "I'm so sorry."

She nodded grimly and pulled out one of those small packets of tissues from a pocket.

"When did it happen?"

She extracted a tissue and clutched it tightly. "It must have been around seven-thirty this morning. Right after I dropped her at camp."

I could feel her desperation. "Perhaps we could go into the kitchen?"

Christine stared at me blankly, as if her distress had slowed down her reflexes and she needed extra time to process. Then it registered. "Yes, of course."

The kitchen was cheerier, mostly because of a skylight that bathed everything in bright light. I considered it a hopeful sign. We sat in chairs around a butcher block table.

"So you dropped her off at camp..."

"They have the early bird program, you know. She likes making lanyards. Blue and purple. And pink." She fingered the tissue. "I drove to the train station as usual. Got the 7:52 downtown. I was almost at the office when—"

"Where do you work?"

"Midwest National Bank at Madison and Dearborn..."

I nodded. "... when I got a call on my cell."

"Who was it?"

"I didn't recognize the voice. He said..." She took a breath. "They had Molly." She crumpled the tissue.

"He said 'they'?" When she nodded, I asked, "Did he say how much—I mean—what they wanted?"

Christine looked blank again, then shook her head. "No. He said not to call the police. That if I did, they'd... hurt her." She said it slowly, enunciating each word.

"Did they let you talk to her? You know, to prove they really had her?"

Christine's hands began to shake. Susan covered them with her own. Christine gave her a grateful look. "Yes. She sounded... so frightened." Her voice quavered.

"Do you have a picture of Molly?"

She nodded, got up, and brought back a photo she'd obviously had ready. A school photo with the ubiquitous blue background, it showed Molly in a Kelly green sweater over a white collared shirt. She was a fresh-faced kid with flaming red hair tied back in a scrunchy. Her eyes were blue and widely-spaced, her nose tiny, and a flash of silver gleamed behind a pair of reluctantly smiling lips. I could relate. I had braces when I was her age, and I swore never to let them show in pictures. But when the photographer said "smile" or "cheese" or "artichoke" as did Sid, the man who took all our school pictures forty years ago, I couldn't help it. "She's adorable."

It was the wrong thing to say. Christine blinked away tears.

I stood up, my chair scraping the floor. "Did he say anything about next steps? What you needed to do? What they would do?"

"He said he'd call me later. After he was convinced I wouldn't go to the police." She bowed her head. Susan kept her hands on Christine's but looked over at me. I saw a warning in her eyes.

I started to pace. "Christine, Susan called me because she thought I might be helpful." I paused. "But my advice is to go to the police. They have the resources and experience to deal with this. Despite the threats."

Christine looked up. Tears rimmed her eyes. "I can't take that chance."

"I understand."

She looked up. "So you'll help me?"

"I can't. As I said, I really don't have any special knowledge in matters like this."

Her face crumpled. Tears inched down her cheek.

I tried to look hopeful. "But I know someone who does."

CHAPTER 3

Georgia

Money can't buy happiness, but it sure is a start. Hunched over her laptop, Georgia tried to remember who said that. She was in the middle of a search for the title of a vacation home in Galena, Illinois. A couple, one of whom was her client, had been married thirty years but was now locked in a bitter divorce battle. Both parties claimed the property, but even with a subpoena, neither the husband nor the wife—or their respective lawyers—had coughed up enough information to verify the claim. Georgia was slogging through public records on the state of Illinois's website, hoping to find the title to the property, but so far she'd had no success. She was cursing Paul Kelly, the lawyer who'd sent her the job, when her cell trilled.

"Davis here."

"Hi, Georgia. It's Ellie Foreman."

Georgia sat up. She'd known Foreman for years, since she'd been the youth officer on the village police force. She'd counseled

Foreman's daughter, Rachel, through a dark period when the girl was twelve. A year later she and Ellie had found themselves on the same side of a case involving white slavery and the Russian Mob. Foreman was the kind of woman who seemed to attract trouble; it was a small miracle she was still alive. Georgia hadn't heard from her in almost a year, which was a good sign. That she was calling now wasn't.

"Hello, Ellie. Is everything ok? How's Rachel?"

"She's fine. She's a senior now. Applying to college soon."

"No way. I'm not that old. Where does she want to go?"

"We're hoping to cheer on the Hawkeyes."

"Great school."

"It's her first choice. But that's not why I called. I need your help, Georgia. It's an emergency."

* * *

Georgia hung up, went into her bedroom, and opened her bureau drawer. The furniture in her Evanston apartment was still new—she'd had to replace it all after a fire last year—and she felt a sense of satisfaction as the drawer slid smoothly across the metal tracks. She took out a white tank top, then went to her closet and pulled out a pair of beige slacks and a lightweight navy blazer. She had four nearly identical blazers: two for summer, and two for winter. They were all loose fitting and had plenty of pockets. You never knew what you might have to stash in them.

In the bathroom, she peered into the mirror. She normally wore her blond hair in a ponytail, but today she left it down. It softened the sharp planes of her face and made her nose seem less prominent. Her blue eyes were wide and unflinching, but her eyelashes and brows were so light they seemed to disappear on her face. Even so, Pete said that she reminded him of Scarlet Johannson. She smiled at the thought and applied some lipstick, her only concession to fashion. Then she stuffed her wallet, keys, notebook and pen in her pockets and took off.

Driving her red Toyota up Green Bay Road, she thought back to what Foreman said on the phone. Of all the crimes against people, kidnapping was the most personal. And cruel. To steal a child, someone's flesh and blood, suggested a viciousness that was hard to understand. Even if the resolution was good and the child was returned uninjured, the family would bear the scars forever. The parents would always worry about the people who came into their child's life. And if it turned out that one of the parents had taken the child, as so often happened, the other would never sleep through the night again.

Foreman had said Christine Messenger was recently divorced. Had it been ugly? If so, the ex-husband could be involved. He might have skipped town, maybe the country. Fathers sometimes did. Even so, the chances were good no harm would come to the child. Which was oddly reassuring. In the event it was a stranger abduction, the kidnapper probably wanted money. That also usually meant the child wouldn't be harmed, at least until the ransom was paid. The problem was if there was no demand. No communication from the kidnappers. Georgia didn't want to think about that.

Whatever the situation, the police were better equipped to handle it than she. Foreman knew that. Georgia wondered why she hadn't insisted the mother call it in. Foreman wasn't a fool. Maybe she needed a third party to reinforce her advice. Georgia tapped the steering wheel with her palm. Being a good PI meant knowing when to take on a case and when to hand it off. This one practically screamed "hands-off."

* * *

"I don't understand why we have to talk about that now," Christine Messenger said. "The man on the phone was not my ex-husband."

Georgia sat in Christine Messenger's kitchen at the butcher block table. Foreman was still there, but her friend, Susan, had left. "A major factor in child abductions is the relationship between the child's parents. A bitter divorce can be a motivating factor." She paused. "As for the voice on the phone, that could have been anyone: a friend of your ex, a brother, a cousin. Tell me, what was Molly's father's reaction when you told him?"

Christine didn't answer. Then in a small voice, she said, "I haven't."

"Why not?" Georgia knew her voice was sharp.

"You don't understand. Terry's always accusing me of being a horrible mother. Of putting my career before Molly. This— well, he'll see this as the last straw. He'll file for sole custody. I— I couldn't handle that."

"Mrs. Messenger." Georgia tried to keep her voice neutral. "The issue right now is getting Molly back safely. Not whether your husband—sorry—ex-husband—approves of your lifestyle." She looked at her watch. "Molly's been gone for almost three hours. He needs to know. Where does he work?"

"He's a doctor at Rush."

"You need to call him right away."

Christine eyed her doubtfully. "Please. He'll use it against me.

I'm telling you." She dabbed at her eyes with a tissue, though she didn't appear to be crying. Then she took a long breath. "It was a horror show."

A spit of tension thickened the air.

"The divorce?" Foreman asked softly.

The woman nodded. "It's been final less than a year."

Ellie crossed her legs.

"So he's bitter?" Georgia asked.

Christine made an ugly noise, somewhere between a laugh and a cry. "Him? I couldn't say. *I* am."

Georgia exchanged glances with Ellie.

"Why?" Georgia followed up.

"My father died ten years ago. Right after we got married. He left me—and my brother—some real estate. A shopping center in Joliet. It turned out to be pretty lucrative when it was sold. It was clearly an inheritance, but my ex-husband tried to claim it was part of our marital assets. We had to jump through hoops to prove it wasn't."

"I see."

Christine crossed her arms. "No, I don't think you do. I had to waste over a hundred thousand dollars. On top of supporting Molly, since I make more than Terry."

"I thought you said he's a doctor," Georgia said.

Christine's mouth tightened. "He is."

Must be nice to make that kind of money, Georgia thought and looked over at Foreman, who was frowning. Was she thinking the same thing?

"And then, when the lawyers realized they'd soaked us for as much as they could, and made their quota for the week or the month or whatever, they settled the case. In three days. Don't ever mention the word 'lawyer' to me."

Foreman ran a hand down her arm. Her ex-husband was a lawyer, Georgia recalled.

"Was any of your—bitterness—directed toward Molly?"

Christine shook her head. "We tried to keep her out of it. We knew we would probably share custody, regardless of the money situation, and we didn't want to put her in the middle of it. At least I didn't."

Her words sounded scripted. Was she hiding something? "Do you have any reason at all to think your ex-husband took your daughter?"

"I—I don't know."

"Where do you work?"

"At Midwest National Bank. I'm the director of IT."

"Information technology?"

She nodded. "I used to run the computer systems. Make sure they're secure. Make acquisitions. Do maintenance. Facilitate our online activities. Manage the staff. But I was promoted recently. I still have responsibility for IT, but I'm also an Officer in Account Management."

"What's that?"

"Basically hand-holding major customers. Making sure they're happy. Encouraging them to use as many of our services as possible. That kind of thing."

"That's a promotion?"

"That's what they tell me," she said dryly. "Midwest isn't really that big. Despite the building downtown. We..." Her voice suddenly trailed off as if she'd just realized how inappropriate it was to be talking about her job at a time like this.

Georgia persisted. "That's an unusual mix: computer geek and customer service."

Messenger's expression was tight. "I was part of a new business pitch for a customer who requires a lot of online banking. It made sense to have me work with them. But, really, I don't understand what this has to do with Molly."

If Christine Messenger earned more than her husband, a doctor already earning a nice chunk of change, she was a *very* senior level officer. Still. Georgia checked her watch. "Mrs. Messenger, you need to call your ex-husband. And then you need to call the police."

"I told Ellie. No police. They said they'd hurt Molly."

Georgia leaned forward. "Listen to me. The police get these kinds of cases all the time. They know how to deal with them. They'll work the case in a quiet, clandestine way so that Molly is protected."

Christine tilted her head, as though she hadn't considered that.

"And they have capabilities neither Ellie nor I have. Resources and connections all over the country, not just Chicago."

A look of horror shot across Christine's face. "Do you think they took my baby to another state?"

Georgia dodged a direct answer. "As I understand it, there hasn't been a ransom demand yet, right?"

"That's right."

"What, exactly, *did* he say when he called?"

Christine tightened her lips. "Just that he had Molly, and that if I wanted her back unharmed, I'd be here when he called again."

"Nothing more?"

She shook her head.

"Do you have any idea what he might be after?"

"No." Her voice was reticent, even timid.

"Maybe he's trying to figure out how much he can demand," Ellie said.

"Maybe," Georgia said. "Or he's still working on a getaway plan."

"But why Chris? Why Molly?" Ellie looked at Chris. "You have no idea?"

"How many times do I need to tell you? I don't know a goddam thing. All I know is that I want my baby back." Tears welled in Christine's eyes. "Whatever it costs, I'll pay. You need to know that."

Georgia sighed. "I get it. Which is why you really need to bring in the police. They can trace the call when it comes. Maybe bring in the FBI to help. And, by the way, if your ex-husband is involved, they'll know that, too. I can't emphasize it enough. You're doing your daughter a disservice if you don't."

A tear rolled down Christine's cheek. "If you heard the man on the phone, you wouldn't say that. His voice was... so cold. He specifically said that I had to—just—please. Isn't there anything you can do?"

"The longer you hold off, the harder it gets. A trail grows cold quickly. I wish I could help you, Mrs. Messenger, but this is the best advice I have. If you want, I'll call my former boss. His name is Dan O'Malley, and he's the Deputy Chief of Police for the village."

"If I do—call the police—and my daughter is hurt or..." Christine couldn't finish. She slumped in her chair.

Georgia pulled out her cell and went into the hall to call. Waiting for it to connect, she gazed around. Clustered around a window in the living room was a group of plants. Their leaves were thick and shiny. Georgia remembered the flowers outside, growing in gay abandon. In addition to a high-powered career, Christine Messenger had a green thumb. Georgia had bought plants for her apartment last fall. She watered them, fed them, even talked to them, after someone told her it would help. By Christmas, though, they looked sick and weak, and by the end of January, they were dead.

CHAPTER 4

Ellie

"How do you know God exists?" Rachel asked. "How do you know He doesn't?" my father answered.

I was in the kitchen chopping celery and eavesdropping. It had been three days since Georgia Davis and I met Christine Messenger. After Georgia called the police, we waited outside the house until an unmarked drove up. We chatted about Dan O'Malley finally receiving the promotion he deserved, and I thanked Georgia for coming. Then I went home.

I thought about Molly over the next two days, but there was nothing in the news about her disappearance. I figured the police were working quietly. I prayed for her safe, speedy return, but feared that, in this case, no news was bad news. I had to let it go for my own sanity. I tuned back into Rachel's conversation with Dad.

"... want to know what *you* think, Opa."

"And I want to know what *you* think, Rachel," Dad said,

emphasizing the first syllable and adding a throat-clearing sound to the "ch," which was the Hebrew pronunciation.

An exasperated sigh was her reply.

I could relate. My father likes to use the Talmudic method of answering a question with a question. He says it helps define one's thoughts. The problem is that there's never a definitive answer—just more questions, like the endless "why" game kids play. For a garden-variety neurotic like me, who needs the clarity of a concrete answer, it's maddening. Apparently my daughter felt the same way.

She took a stab anyway. "Okay, Opa," she said. "I think natural disasters, like tsunamis, fires, and tornados, plus the fact that we're running out of water, plus the fact that millions of people on this planet still don't have enough to eat, is proof there is no God. Or if there is, He's turned His back on us."

"Maybe we've turned our backs on Him."

"But I thought God—if He exists—is supposed to be generous, all loving and forgiving. Even toward non-believers."

Dad was silent for a minute. Had she stumped him? Then he said, "What about miracles? Do you believe in them?"

"Why?" she asked suspiciously.

I recalled a book called *Small Miracles* that someone had given Rachel when she was thirteen. She read it from cover to cover and gushed to me about the stories, mostly warm-hearted tales of coincidences and seemingly random events that changed peoples' lives. I considered the book vaguely seditious but never said anything. At least she was reading voluntarily.

"Well," Dad went on, "maybe you could take a piece of paper and draw a line down the middle. On one side, list all the atrocities, horrors, and disasters you can think of. On the other, write down all the things you think could be miracles. See if it balances out. Perhaps that will help you decide."

I finished chopping and went into the family room. Rachel was on the couch with a pad of notebook paper, scratching out her list. Dad was in the easy chair, rubbing his chin with his thumb and forefinger. He smiled. I went over and kissed the top of his head. Except for a thin fringe of hair around the base of his skull, he's bald, and his skin is freckled with age spots. He's never been tall, and age has stooped him, but mentally he can still bench press a Cadillac, and when he smiles, everything seems possible.

"I'm hungry," he announced. "When do we eat?"

"I'm throwing the steaks on the grill now."

"Good. Red meat. Hubba hubba." He shot a glance at Rachel and rubbed one of his hands over the other in fast little circles.

She giggled at that—she always does.

Twenty minutes later, we were eating dinner like good carnivores on the deck outside my kitchen.

"So what are you working on?" Dad asked.

I'm an independent video producer—it's how I support myself and Rachel, especially since Barry, my ex-husband, is, at best, "irregular" with child support. Although the video world can be feast or famine, I've been lucky to eke out a living. Sometimes the topics I cover are even worthwhile.

"I'm excited about this one, Dad. I'm working for Voss-Peterson."

"The agricultural processor?"

"You got it." Voss-Peterson is a huge conglomerate that turns crops into soymeal, oil, corn sweeteners, flour, feed, and ethanol. "They've got a new ethanol facility, and they want to make a video about it."

"That's the stuff they mix with gasoline to extend its life, right?"

"Right. It comes from corn. Essentially, it's a form of grain alcohol."

"I didn't know that."

"Neither did I. Anyway, it burns cleaner than gasoline, it's cheap, it's renewable, and it can reduce our dependence on foreign oil. I'm finally working for a company that's on the right side of an issue for a change."

Dad raised his eyebrows.

"In fact, Mac and I are driving out tomorrow to scout locations."

"Where?" Rachel asked.

"Their headquarters is in central Illinois. Between Peoria and Bloomington. We'll be taking a look at some farms out that way, too. We can't shoot until the corn is higher, of course."

"Knee high by the Fourth of July," Dad said. He put down his fork and started to hum.

Rachel looked mystified.

"There's an old saying..." I started to explain then glanced at Dad. He was still humming and his eyes twinkled. I listened more closely. It was the tune of "Wonderful Guy" from *South Pacific*, the song that goes, "I'm as corny as Kansas in August..." I shook my head. Dad's sense of humor still surprises me.

Rachel looked from Dad to me, still puzzled. I was about to explain, but the phone rang. Rachel jumped up and hurried into the kitchen to answer it.

"Oh hi, Becky." Her voice carried back outside. "Yeah. I'm just finishing dinner. Nothing except that my Opa is practicing for *American Idol*..."

Dad smiled, then picked up his knife. His eyes went flat. "So, what do you hear from that—Sutton man?"

Dad still can't accept that David Linden and I broke up. My boyfriend of three years, David and my father had a personal, almost familial connection: as a young man my father had been in love with his mother. But intimate relationships have never been one of my strengths, and David was deficient in that area too. We might still have been stumbling along, had I not fallen in love with Luke Sutton.

Not that it's been easy there. Luke has baggage—serious baggage filled with the repercussions of family secrets that I unintentionally exposed. In fact, you couldn't really call what we have a "relationship." It's more like an IOU, a chit to be surrendered sometime in the future. Still, when he walked through my front door last summer, I remember tingling and blazing like a Fourth of July sparkler. I still do. Susan says it's just hormones. I think she's wrong, but even if she's not, I'm grateful I have enough of them left to fire.

All of which made it difficult to answer my father. "Luke's fine." I finally managed. I felt like an uncommunicative teenager.

It was dark, and long shadows fell across Dad's face, but I could feel him frown.

"Look, I know he's not Jewish," I said. "And I know he's got issues, but—"

"What kind of example are you setting for your daughter?"

"Example? Me?" Irritation scratched the back of my throat. I was tempted to tell him about the condom. Although, in truth, since meeting Christine Messenger, the condom incident just didn't seem that significant. Rachel was eighteen; her grades were good; she had a job as a lifeguard. She might even have been telling the truth: that it was Mary—not she—who'd been partying in the guest room. In the end, though, if it was Rachel, she'd been practicing safe sex, she was out of harm's way, and, unlike Molly Messenger, she was *here*.

I kept my mouth shut.

The wonderful thing about my father is that he doesn't rub it in. As I got up to clear the dishes, he rose too and tried to lower the umbrella that had been angled to block the rays of the setting sun. He wrestled with it, pulling and pushing and finally shaking the pole, but he couldn't straighten it. "I think something's wrong," he said.

Rachel came back out with a plate of chocolate chip cookies. I helped myself to one. Rachel passed the plate to my father.

"Sweetheart, Opa says something's wrong with the umbrella. Can you lift it up and put it away? I'll ask Fouad to look at it next time he comes."

"It's pretty old. Why don't you throw it away and get a new one?" she said.

"I just bought it last year," I said around a mouthful of cookie. "Can you put it away, please?"

"Okay." She grabbed a couple of cookies.

We cleared the rest of the plates and went inside before the mosquitoes made a meal out of us. Dad and I settled in the family room to watch the nine o'clock news.

The program preceding the news ended, and the screen cut to a teaser shot of the news anchor. "Abducted North Shore Girl Comes Home!" she announced breathlessly. "Details Ahead!"

I gasped. Was this Molly Messenger? Had she been freed? I waited impatiently as a series of commercials told me about yet another sale at Macy's, a new car for zero percent financing, and the latest menu addition at Red Lobster. Finally, the news began, and the program cut to a close-up of a little girl in a school photo with a blue background.

Molly.

"Our top story is the return of an eight-year-old North Shore girl to her family. Molly Messenger was abducted three mornings ago. Gerry Rivers has the story." The report cut to B-roll of the park district building, kids getting out of cars, parents walking them inside.

A male voice-over continued. "Molly Messenger's parents have been working with police ever since the girl was kidnapped from camp on Monday. Then, today, just a couple of hours ago, witnesses say, a car stopped at the end of this block." The story cut to a wide shot of the reporter walking down the middle of Molly's street. "The door to the car opened, Molly got out, and, according to witnesses, ran down the block to her house. Her parents say she appears to be healthy, although she will undergo tests at a nearby hospital. Her parents, of course, are exceedingly thankful."

The story cut to a shot of Christine Messenger on her front steps. She still looked pale and haggard, but the tension had drained from her body. Standing beside her was a bald man. He looked handsome and young, forty at the most, so the baldness was probably a choice, not a condition. He wore navy chinos and a red golf shirt. The ex-husband. They stood close together. Trying to put on a united front for the public?

"This is a miracle. My prayers have been answered," Christine said. "I am so very grateful to have my daughter back. She seems to be fine, and she's already asking when she can go to the pool." A wan smile flitted across her face.

The husband cut in. "But, as you might imagine, we have been through an ordeal, and now we need time to heal. We hope you understand our need for privacy."

The report cut back to the reporter who said the family was going into seclusion. "No one appears to have seen the car Molly was in. And, as far as we know, there never was any demand for a ransom. In fact, police remain tight-lipped about the case. Which means the mystery surrounding this bizarre kidnapping persists." The reporter signed off after bantering with the anchorwoman about staying on the story and reporting new developments as soon as possible.

As the program transitioned to a fire in a West Side warehouse, I ran a hand through my hair.

"*Nu?*" Dad asked. That's Yiddish for "well" or "so" or just "what's going on"?

"I know that woman. I—uh—went to her house three days ago."

My father's eyes narrowed and he pointed to the TV. "You met with that woman? I thought you were done with your—meddling."

"I was doing Susan a favor. Christine Messenger is her neighbor. Susan thought I might be able to help."

"And?"

"I told her to call the police. So did Georgia Davis."

"Georgia Davis? How do I know that name?"

"She's an investigator. Used to be on the police force up here. She—"

"I remember. Rachel saw her for a while."

Whoever said elderly people's memories get foggy doesn't know my father. "That's right. And then a couple of winters ago, she and I—well, never mind."

"So, what's the problem? The girl is home. She's okay. It's a happy ending."

I wasn't convinced. Usually the police love to crow about their accomplishments, and resolving the Messenger kidnapping was a big one. So why were they, in the reporter's words, so "tight-lipped?" I'm no cop, but I know that when people decline to talk to the press, it's because they've done something either so shocking or so stupid they're afraid it will be revealed.

CHAPTER 5

Georgia

Sometimes there really is a happy ending, Georgia thought as she drove back from the gym Thursday morning. When she heard the news about Molly Messenger on the radio, she felt relief, elation, then a deep sense of satisfaction. She hadn't especially liked Christine Messenger. There was a remote quality about her, almost guarded. Georgia thought Molly's disappearance seemed to be more of an inconvenience, a disruption to Messenger's carefully planned career, than a gut-wrenching tragedy.

At the same time, Georgia realized she was being uncharitable. People dealt with suffering in all sorts of ways. The woman had been to hell and back. Who was she to pass judgment? She turned off the radio and took a swig from her bottled water. At least one child had been rescued from the maw of tragedy. That was cause for celebration, wasn't it?

Back home she showered, toweled off, put on a clean pair of jeans. A new case had come in, and she was eager to start in on it. A lawyer suspected a dating service was a front for an identity theft ring and wanted Georgia to investigate. One of the lawyer's clients had met with "More-than-Friends" in an out-of-the-way office in Palatine, a suburb about thirty miles northwest of Chicago. The woman hadn't given them any money but did surrender her address and social security number. A week later, her credit cards were maxed out and her bank account emptied.

Georgia Googled the company and checked their website, but other than the address, phone number, and a few "testimonials," she didn't learn much. She went into her kitchen. Bright morning sunshine poured in through the window, and a squirrel was perched on the telephone line. She'd always wondered how they could balance on such a flimsy tightrope. Then it scurried across the line and hopped onto a nearby branch.

She went back to her computer. The best way to get a first-hand look at "More-Than-Friends" would be to see it herself. She thought about impersonating a potential client. She was in her thirties, the right age, and she could act the part of the lonely, desperate woman. She'd been there, not so long ago.

She jotted down the number then clicked to a news website to skim coverage of Molly's return. She wanted to see how the police cracked the case: the communications, negotiations, how it played out. But there was nothing. No statement, no photos, no comment. She went back to the More-than-Friends website but couldn't get the kidnapping out of her mind. Five minutes later, she picked up the phone.

* * *

Thursday evening was a good night at Solyst's, a village tavern with rough-hewn floorboards and neon red beer signs on the walls. Solyst's was a blue-collar haunt, with drinks as cheap as the conversation, but somehow it had flourished. While other places on the North Shore changed hands faster than you could say under-the-table-payments, Solyst's had been owned by the same family for seventy-five years.

Georgia hadn't been inside in a while, but nothing had changed. On one side was the bar, its stools patched with duct tape and, despite the new law, a residue of cigarette smoke in the air. On the other side was a brightly lit room with tables and chairs and a menu of pizza, salads, and surprisingly good fried fish.

The faces at the bar looked like the same ones she'd seen two years ago. In fact, several nodded as though it had only been two weeks since she'd been in. She found who she was looking for at the bar near the dart board.

Dan O'Malley and Georgia had come onto the force at the same time, but Dan had ended up her supervisor. Now he was Deputy Chief. She was happy for him; he was a good cop, honest and smart, and his promotion was long overdue. As for her, she sometimes wondered what might have happened if she'd played the career card as well as, say, Christine Messenger. Maybe she would have been made it to upper management, too.

O'Malley's butt hung over his stool, and he shifted as he nursed his scotch. His eyes had made him look old ever since he was a rookie, but now craggy lines dug into his forehead. At the same time, his carrot orange hair, bristly mustache, and ruddy cheeks made him appear young—even naive. O'Malley used that to his advantage. People always underestimated him.

She slid onto a stool next to him. "Congratulations. Drinks are on me."

He looked up, surprise on his face. She wondered whether that was part of his *shtick*. Act shocked and a suspect might feel obligated to explain. And incriminate himself.

"Thanks," he said.

Georgia waved a hand. "It's the least I could do. Except I had to wait longer than I should have to buy you a round."

"Tell me about it."

She swiveled toward the bar. The bartender lifted his chin.

"Another Dewers for him, Diet Coke for me. With lemon."

The bartender nodded. Georgia swiveled back. O'Malley's face smoothed out.

"You thought I was back on the booze?"

He flipped up a palm.

"You gotta have faith." She grinned. "So, congratulations."

O'Malley cocked his head. "You already said that."

"I mean the Molly Messenger case."

O'Malley looked down.

"Nice work."

He tossed back the rest of his drink, then clinked the empty glass on the bar. "Everyone's a joker."

"What's so funny?"

He kept his mouth shut.

Their drinks came. Georgia pushed his scotch towards him. "So, what's going on? Why so tight-lipped with the press?"

"You noticed."

"Hard not to notice when the force that loves to brag about itself suddenly goes quiet."

O'Mally wiped his sleeve across his mouth.

"Who handled the investigation?"

"Who do you think?"

"Robbie Parker."

Parker had been her partner on the force. He'd never been a particularly thorough cop. Except when he played politics. Which, it turned out, he did better than Georgia. He'd been promoted from patrol to detective a year ago.

"What's the story?"

O'Malley's eyes bored into her. "I wasn't here tonight. Or if I was, we never had this conversation."

"Just buying my former boss a drink to celebrate his promotion."

O'Malley nodded. "What happened was nothing. A big fat zero."

Georgia frowned.

"Parker started working the case. Did all the things you're supposed to. Went to the camp, interviewed the counselors. Canvassed neighbors and relatives. Even tried to talk to some of her friends— 'course, then he had to get the parents involved, and some of them refused, and—"

"I get it." Georgia cut him off. "This is the North Shore."

"Right. Well anyway, we got nowhere. Really. The kid just showed up."

"That's crazy."

"God's honest truth is whoever had her just decided to let her go."

"Come on, Dan. That doesn't happen."

"It did here. We had people with the mother 24-7. Monitored her phone, her email, her cell. Even went downtown with her when she went to her office. No one was more surprised than us when the car pulled up at the corner and the kid jumped out."

"What kind of car? The TV report didn't say."

"We canvassed the neighborhood again. Someone came forward. They think it was a Lexus. Their biggest fucking sedan."

"No plates, I guess."

"You guess right."

Georgia sipped her drink. "Weird."

"You're telling me."

"Do you think someone was negotiating behind the scenes?"

"It wasn't us."

"Maybe the mother was working it herself."

"If she was, we didn't see it. And, in any case, there's nothing we could do. There's no law against trying to rescue your kid."

"Maybe it wasn't a kidnapping to begin with. Maybe the ex-husband just took her for an 'extended' visit."

"Don't think so. His whereabouts are accounted for. He went to work. Then stayed overnight at his girlfriend's."

"Girlfriend?"

"Plenty of people vouched for him."

"You think maybe the mother staged the whole thing?"

"I don't see how. Or why."

"Munchausen's?" she asked. Munchausen Syndrome by Proxy was a form of child abuse in which a mother invents imaginary symptoms of illness in a child that are subsequently treated, sometimes with fatal results. "It could be a variation."

O'Malley shook his head. "No evidence."

"There wouldn't have to be." Georgia said. "Anyone following up with the kid? About her captors, how she was treated?"

"Parker's trying, but the mother won't let us talk to her. Says there's been too much trauma. But we'll keep at it."

Georgia ran a finger around the rim of her glass. "You said your guys went downtown with her?"

"Yeah."

"When was this?"

"Wednesday morning. The kid came back that afternoon."

"Why did she go downtown in the middle of everything? The mother, I mean. How could she work while this was going on? Why wasn't she glued to the phone at home?"

"She said she wanted to pick up a few things. Pictures of Molly, her laptop. She left it there when the kid was taken."

"If my daughter had been kidnapped, and I didn't know if she was alive or dead, I sure as hell wouldn't take time to 'pick up a few things at the office.'"

O'Malley shrugged. "Parker told her we'd get the stuff for her, but..."

"He was obviously very persuasive." She frowned. "And Molly was released that afternoon." She stared at O'Malley.

"Hey, Davis. Our job is over. The girl is safe. We got a happy ending. We move on. We're having a press conference later today."

"Which will thank everyone for doing a great job."

"What do you want from me?" He tapped his glass on the bar again. Then he stopped. "You know Eric Olson is gonna retire next year."

Eric Olson was the village's Chief of Police. O'Malley's boss. "I didn't know."

"I need good officers, Davis. I know you told him no last year. But what if I asked you to come back?"

Georgia propped an elbow on the bar and massaged her temples. She didn't answer for a minute. Then, "Don't go there, Dan. Not right now."

CHAPTER 6

Ellie

One of the things I love about the Midwest is that you really *can* see to the horizon. I've spent time on both coasts and, except for the beach, the cities and suburbs are densely packed and obstruct your sight lines. Here on the prairie, though, the eye sweeps across the landscape, and you can see for miles.

Mac and I were driving through farmland in central Illinois the following Monday. The occasional metal silo and cell phone tower glinted in the sun, reminding me I wasn't really that far from civilization. The ground shimmered with the pale growth of early summer, and when I rolled down the window, an earthy, damp aroma poured in. In a few months, the growth would be thick and sturdy—not quite lush, but our version of it. For now, though, everything was tender and green and very Norman Rockwell.

Mac is Mackenzie Kendall the Third, and he owns a video production studio in Northbrook. He pretends to be an aging hippie, and he rarely changes out of jeans and sandals. A jagged scar down his cheek used to make him look dangerous, but he's older and grayer, and the sharp planes of his face have softened. A year ago he added a silver hoop earring. Rachel, who knows about these things, promptly told him he'd pierced the wrong ear.

Despite his idiosyncrasies, Mac is a talented director and a shrewd businessman. We've worked together for fifteen years. He also employs Hank Chenowsky, one of the best video editors in the solar system. I'm convinced Hank grew up in a dark room with a computer monitor as his only source of light, because he works magic with my shows, making them look like they have twice the budget they do.

"So we're finally going green," Mac said as we cruised down state highway 136 in his Ford Expedition.

"We?" Mac's van probably sucks down gas at the rate of ten miles per gallon. "Speak for yourself, white man."

Mac threw me a look. "Can you spell significant business expense?"

"You're polluting the planet."

"They have these trade-offs, you know. Maybe you've heard about them. You get credits when you do something that conserves energy, demerits when you don't. Linda drives a Prius, so we balance out."

Linda was Mac's wife.

"And what about your new boyfriend?" he went on. "Doesn't he have his own plane? Now there's a real energy saver."

"Don't bring Luke into this. Everyone has to do their part. It's people like you who..." I stopped myself. "I can't believe this."

"What?"

"You've done it." I glared at him. "You've gone and become a conservative when I wasn't looking."

Mac kept his mouth shut.

"My father always said a person gets more conservative when they have something to lose. Are you going to register as a Republican?"

Mac let out a long-suffering breath. "You know, it is possible to accumulate assets without losing one's humanity. Or becoming a hypocrite." When I didn't answer, he added, "It might even be possible to run a business ethically. Aren't we going to scout one right now?"

* * *

"I am delighted that such a lovely woman as you made time to visit our humble operation."

I knew I was in trouble as soon as the words came out of his mouth. Fred Hanover, the man who would be showing us the Voss-Peterson ethanol plant, wasn't much to look at. He had small recessed eyes, a middle-aged paunch, and a smear of a mustache that looked painted on. What little hair he had was slicked back with something that reminded me of Bryl Crème. In fact, with his starched white shirt, striped seersucker suit, and red bowtie, he looked like a door-to-door salesman from seventy-five years ago. But his manners were impeccable, and when he opened a door for me and called me "ma'am," I couldn't resist a smirk at Mac.

"Now, ma'am," Hanover said with a rueful expression, "I am so sorry to muss up that lovely hairdo, but you're going to have to wear this." He handed me a yellow hard-hat. "The ladies hate these," he said as an aside to Mac. I absently touched my hair, wondering who'd told him that—his wife? a secretary?—and put it on.

"Does it fit all right, Ms. Foreman? Because I have another size." He looked concerned.

"It's fine," I centered it on my head. He handed another to Mac and clamped one on himself.

"Well, then. Let's go." He rubbed his palms together and led us outside. We'd been in a utilitarian one-story building set back from the road. Behind it, railroad tracks ran past a series of stainless steel tanks and metal-roofed sheds, all connected with pipes of various diameters and lengths. All the equipment gleamed and looked antiseptically clean, but its unfamiliarity made me think some alien society had somehow jettisoned it from their spacecraft and plunked it down on the prairie late one night.

"You know, you needed top secret clearance before we could let you in here," Hanover said with a chuckle.

Had the man been reading my mind?

"We had to make sure you were on the up and up. Both of you." He glanced at Mac.

"Why?" I asked.

"The process I'm about to show you is proprietary," he said. "Can't let in any industrial spies, can we now?"

"I thought ethanol production was generic—like petroleum refining."

"Not at all. Our competitors are always looking to see what we're doing and how we're doing it. We use a dry milling process, but there's a wet one, too, which is very different. We have to be careful." He grinned. "Then again, if I'd known I would be in the presence of such a lovely woman, I might well be forced to reveal our secrets."

He chuckled and rubbed his palms together in little circles. I smiled painfully. Mac kept a straight face.

Hanover walked us over to the train tracks which led into a small warehouse and out the other side. "Basically the grain comes here in covered hoppers, unless it happens to be trucked in. Then it's unloaded, and transferred to these." He gestured to several tall silos behind the warehouse.

I peered inside. "We could get a great shot from the rail car going into the shed," I said to Mac. "You know. From the POV of the rail car, shooting up."

Mac nodded. Hanover looked perturbed at being interrupted. "The grain is ground into powder and piped into tanks where it's mixed with water and enzymes and forms a mix we call a slurry." He guided us past a group of huge cylindrical tanks. "And this is where the mixture is fermented."

"Like beer?" Mac asked.

Hanover nodded. "We let it sit for forty-eight hours. Then, after it's distilled, which happens here..." Hanover gestured to another group of tanks, "... the alcohol is separated from the solids. At that point, it's ethanol. One-hundred-ninety proof."

Mac whistled. I visualized vats of Jim Beam and Johnnie Walker, and wondered whether they had any place in the video.

"The alcohol is siphoned out the top while the stillage goes out through the bottom for further processing. Then the alcohol mix is dehydrated, where it becomes two-hundred proof ethanol," Hanover turned to Mac. "That'll do some damage, won't it?" He chortled. "Make you as stiff as a board."

Mac pasted on a smile.

I checked my watch. Hanover had been talking for half an hour. I didn't know how much more I could take. As we walked, his hand touched the small of my back. I recoiled, but he didn't seem to notice.

"The finished product—ethanol—is ultimately transported in tank cars to processors that mix it with gasoline," he said cheerfully. "Today we're processing corn, but tomorrow, who knows? Our scientists are working on other grains and prairie grass. Even garbage."

How had Hanover ended up a tour guide flunky? He had to be pushing fifty, a little old for PR. Was he a ne'er do well son-in-law or nephew? The guy they couldn't fire? Maybe they couldn't find any other place for him.

He prattled on about state-of-the-art vats and silos while we walked back to the office. He introduced us to the plant manager, a taciturn man with a bulbous nose and gray stubble, who answered my questions in monosyllables. Hanover seemed to realize the guy might not be a great interview and offered to do it himself.

"We can decide that later," I said, trying to be politic.

"Anything I can do, just ask." Hanover rubbed his hands together again. "Well, I just don't know when I've had a better time on a tour. You are certainly the most charming thing that's been around here for a while."

"Oh, I bet you say that to all the girls."

* * *

A few minutes later we were driving gratefully back upstate through tiny towns like Funks Grove and Shirley. We'd skipped lunch, and both of us were famished, so we stopped at a place whose outdoor sign advertised "home cooking." The menu was on a board above the counter; it featured sandwiches on one side, hot meals on the other, and a Pepsi logo in the middle. Mac went for the pork chops. A tired-looking woman told him it would take ten minutes. Mac said he'd wait and smiled. She smiled back, but when I ordered a tuna sandwich, her smile faded and she pursed her lips. Did I insult her by not ordering a hot meal? Or was she just flirting with Mac?

"I'll probably need to bring in some extra crew to handle the lighting, you know," Mac said as we sat at a small, grimy table.

"Why can't we just go with available light? Everything at the plant sparkles."

"Not inside. And what if it's an overcast day?"

"I suppose."

"I'll also bring in a dolly to get some shots moving around all those pipes and tanks."

"What about a steady-cam?"

"We'll be okay without it. Nothing really shakes that much, except the rail car, and that'll be somewhat contained. But that plant manager wouldn't be my first choice for an interview. I'd rather go with your new boyfriend."

I shuddered. "Unfortunately, he's the right guy. The plant manager, I mean. Why don't we give him a shot, and if it doesn't work out, we'll use Hanover." Our meals came, and I took a bite of my sandwich. It was surprisingly good. "There's a chance we won't have to use either of them. We're going to interview the CEO of Voss-Peterson. Maybe he can give us enough for a voice-over."

"Doubtful." Mac dug into his pork chops. I generally don't eat pork, but the aroma from whatever seasonings they used was seductive. I looked over longingly. He slid his plate closer to his side of the table. I sighed and went back to my sandwich.

We were back in the van heading north on back roads rather

than Interstate 55 when we passed a field with a barbed-wire fence. A sign on the fence said "Restricted Area—No Unauthorized Personnel."

"That's weird," I said.

"What?"

"The sign. You don't see that kind of thing in farm country."

Mac slowed so he could take a look, but a berm at the edge of the field obstructed our view.

"What do you think is back there?" I asked.

"Who knows?"

"Maybe it's some top-secret agricultural facility," I said. "Maybe Voss-Peterson has a super-secret program where they're cloning animals."

"In central Illinois?"

The fence stretched about half a mile, a long distance even for the countryside. Beyond it was nothing for another half-mile except a field of trees and prairie grass. "With my luck, they're probably cloning Fred Hanovers."

That got a smile from Mac.

We were just turning onto the interstate when the opening bars of "Honky Tonk Woman" rang out. Thanks to Rachel, I have personalized ring tones for everyone who calls my cell. Rachel claimed the Stones tune, based on her adoration of Keith Richards. I fished the phone out of my bag.

"Hi, sweetie."

"Hi, Mom. I wanted to tell you I'm going to Iowa for the Fourth of July."

"Excuse me?"

"I'm driving with Becky. We're gonna spend the weekend there."

"Where will you stay?"

"At Becky's apartment."

"We must have a bad connection. For a minute I thought you said 'apartment.' You mean 'dorm room,' right?"

"Mother, you are so retro. Everyone lives in an apartment now."

"You're not everyone. And since the condom incident—"

"I told you it wasn't me. It was Mary."

A stony silence ensued. Then, "It's okay, Mom." Rachel's voice was suddenly honey. "I know how much you're gonna miss me next year. By the way, Luke called. He said to tell you he's coming this weekend. So, you see, it'll all work out. You guys can have some 'private time.'"

I wondered if she could sense me blushing.

"And, oh... I almost forgot. The woman whose kid was kidnapped called too."

I straightened up. "Christine Messenger?"

"She wanted you to call her right away. She said it was important."

CHAPTER 7

Georgia

A stack of storm clouds battled the setting sun as Georgia drove to Christine Messenger's house Thursday evening. Despite the weather, neighborhood kids were still outside pedaling furiously on tricycles, bikes, and toy cars. Two girls glided down the sidewalk on skates. Carefree shouts echoed up and down the street. The cheerful scene tugged at her, but she pushed it away. It was all an illusion. Lurking beneath the surface of the suburbs were demons every bit as dangerous as those in the back alleys of Chicago.

Ellie Foreman was waiting outside the Messenger house, waving away mosquitoes. She looked worried. "Thanks for coming so quickly, Georgia. I appreciate it."

"What did she say?"

"She said she needed help fast. That something bad had happened. She sounded terrified."

Georgia raised her eyebrows. She wouldn't have pegged Messenger as the type to panic.

"Look," Foreman slid her hands in the pockets of her jeans. "I don't know what's going on, and I promised my family I wouldn't get involved. But—if there is something *you* can do..." her voice trailed off. "Of course, that's your decision."

Georgia hesitated. "I'm not sure I'd take the case."

"Why not?"

"Because nothing about this makes any sense."

"You mean the kidnapping?"

Georgia nodded. "We don't have the whole story, you know that. And—I don't trust her."

"Well, maybe that's why she called me. Look, I know you have more pressing things to do, Georgia, but I—"

Georgia cut her off. "Let's just get this over with."

Christine Messenger answered the door. If anything, she looked worse than the first time they'd met. Her skin was ashen, her expression haggard, and her hair looked like she'd been pulling at it. "Thank you for coming—again."

"It's okay," Foreman said soothingly. "We're glad you called."

Georgia kept her mouth shut.

Christine led them into the living room. The approaching storm had lengthened the shadows, and the room looked dark and brooding. She turned on some lamps. "Molly's in the kitchen on her computer," she said. "I keep it there so I can keep an eye on what she's surfing."

Georgia sat on a couch upholstered in blue brocade. Foreman took a matching armchair. Christine put herself in another chair and gripped the arms. Her knuckles were white.

"Something horrible has happened."

"What?" Foreman asked.

"I told you that I work at Midwest National Bank, right?"

"You're the director of IT," Georgia said.

"Right. Well, my boss is the COO. The Chief Operating Officer. He—he died this morning."

Surprise streaked across Foreman's face. "My god. What happened?"

"His car smashed into the back of a truck on the Eisenhower."

"Oh, no. I'm so sorry."

Christine swallowed. "The thing is, well, I don't think it was an accident."

Georgia leaned forward. "Why do you say that?"

"Because he called me at home last night. He told me we had to talk first thing this morning. That it was critical. So I went in early, but he never showed up. And then, when I heard about the accident, well, it seemed too coincidental. I think something else is going on, and I'm scared."

"What do you mean 'something else'?" Georgia asked.

"It just—well..." Messenger looked down at her hands.

"Do you think there's a connection to Molly's kidnapping?" Foreman cut in.

"I don't know," she said. "Maybe."

"What do you want us to do?" Foreman asked.

"I think I need protection. I—I feel vulnerable." She looked at Georgia.

Georgia blew out a breath. "Lady, until you come clean about what happened to Molly, we—I can't do anything."

"What do you mean, 'come clean'?" She looked over, but her face didn't register much.

Georgia frowned. "You may think you pulled the wool over

everyone's eyes, but this—situation—never made any sense. First off, there's no proof Molly was ever actually abducted. You won't let the cops talk to her, and—"

A suspicious look came over Messenger. "How do you know that?"

"That's not important. What is important is that I don't know who you are and why you're doing this. For all I know, you are a sick woman who needs help."

Messenger drew herself up. "You have no right to talk to me like this."

"That may be," Georgia said. "But you have no right to expect me to help you. I'm a private investigator, not a baby-sitter. Hire yourself a bodyguard. As for your boss..." she paused. "Maybe he was on his cell and wasn't paying attention."

Georgia got up and started toward the door. She avoided looking at Foreman; she knew Foreman would be upset, but she knew she was right. The whole thing smelled. She was almost at the door when a little girl ran into the room.

"Mommy, Mommy... Guess what? I just got eight out of eight on a movie quiz! Come see, come see!" She grabbed her mother's arm.

Christine Messenger's countenance shifted from anguish to smiles so quickly Georgia couldn't believe she was looking at the same woman. "You did? What quiz is that?"

"It was on the internet, and..."

The child stopped abruptly as if she'd just realized Georgia and Ellie were there. Georgia studied her. Her red-brown braids were tied with green ribbons. She had frank blue eyes, pale eyelashes, and a button nose. Freckles splayed across a round face, and rosy patches glowed on her arms and legs where she'd been out in the sun. She was wearing a pink tank top and green shorts, which she kept hitching up.

"Sorry, Mommy, I didn't know you had company." The way she emphasized the word made Georgia think Christine had instructed Molly never to interrupt when "company" was in the house. Georgia's own mother, all Southern gentility and courtesy, had done the same thing. "A lady never interrupts," she would say in the soft, lilting voice Georgia could almost remember. She looked away. She hadn't seen her mother since she was twelve.

"Is it that movie quiz on Kids' Facebook?" Foreman interjected.

The little girl's eyes grew wide. "How did you know?"

"My daughter loved that website, too." Foreman laughed.

"You have a daughter?" Molly asked eagerly. "How old is she?"

"Eighteen."

"Oh." Molly looked crestfallen. Eighteen had to be tantamount to fifty in her mind. "I'm only eight."

"I know." Ellie looked at Messenger, but the woman made no move to introduce them. "Molly, I'm Ellie Foreman..." She gestured toward Georgia. "And this is Georgia Davis. We're—friends with your Mom."

"Georgia..." Molly turned to Georgia. "Like the state?"

Georgia nodded. "Ever hear of Georgia peaches?"

Molly looked unsure. "I don't know."

Ellie laughed. "Well, that's just peachy. Just like Georgia."

When Molly giggled, Georgia couldn't help smiling.

* * *

"I'm still not sure what I can do, Ellie," Georgia said.

They were outside a few minutes later. Night had fallen, and the street was now deserted. The wind had picked up, carrying the scent of rain. Crickets chirred nervously.

"Then why'd you tell Chris you'd look into it?"

"It was the kid. She—" Georgia stopped, not exactly sure where she was going. Once Molly had skipped into the room, it was hard not to be taken with her. In fact, the girl had forced Georgia reassess the mother. If Christine had raised a kid like that, maybe she wasn't such a train wreck.

"I get it," Foreman said. "I know you have a thing for kids. Especially girls."

Was it that obvious? She'd spent years building her shell, making sure people couldn't ferret out her secrets. But Foreman knew more about her than most.

"Look, I admit," Foreman went on, as if what she'd said was common knowledge and not even that significant, "the whole thing sounds weird, coming right after the kidnapping. But it's clear Christine is scared. And I keep thinking what I would do if Rachel had been kidnapped." She looked over at Georgia. "You know what I mean?"

Georgia cut in. "You're forgetting something else."

"What's that?"

"The woman didn't offer to pay me. I'm doing this on my own time and my own dime. Don't expect much."

Georgia was being hard. She had to be. Foreman might be led by a soft heart or the pursuit of justice, but Georgia couldn't afford those impulses. She had to make a living.

Foreman's tone cooled. "In that case, Georgia, just forget it. I can make a few calls. I know O'Malley, too." She hiked her bag further up her shoulder and turned towards her Volvo.

Georgia watched her take a few steps, then called out, "Wait."

Foreman spun around.

"O'Malley's not going to know anything. The accident happened on the Eisenhower. It's the Illinois State Police you need to talk to."

Foreman cocked her head.

Georgia blew out a breath. "Shit. I'll call around and see if there's an accident report. But that's it."

Ellie smiled.

"And I probably won't know anything for a few days. When there's a fatal, they do a pretty thorough investigation."

"Thanks, Georgia. You're doing a real mitzvah."

"I'm not doing it for you."

"I know," Foreman said.

A few fat drops of rain spattered the sidewalk. "Go home and give Rachel a hug."

CHAPTER 8

The next day Georgia didn't know much more than she had the day before. As soon as she got home, she filed a freedom of information request with the Illinois State Police. Twenty-four hours later, she had the preliminary accident report on Arthur Emerlich, Christine's boss.

The problem was it was inconclusive. The cops had brought a photographer as well as a reconstruction expert to the scene, but after dozens of photos and measurements, an analysis of the speed and impact of the collision, skid marks, and debris, all they knew for certain was that the brake fluid was low, which could have caused the brakes to fail.

Sure, it was suspicious, but whether someone had drained it, or the deceased—like so many drivers—had just neglected to maintain proper fluid levels, they couldn't say. Without more evidence, the incident appeared to be exactly what it was—a tragic accident. Cook County would be doing an autopsy and a tox screen, which might provide more clues, but those findings wouldn't be back for another week.

The Illinois State police report had redacted most of Emerlich's personal information. Curious, Georgia went to her computer and clicked to the Midwest National Bank's website. There he was on the list of bank officers: Arthur Emerlich, Vice-President and Chief Operations Officer. His bio said he had a wife and two grown children. She Googled his name and learned that he was a member of the Crest Haven Country Club and had won their golf tournament two years running. He was also on the Board of Directors of the West Suburban Theater. He and his wife, Dierdre, lived in Hinsdale, an affluent western suburb. In other words, there was nothing unusual about Arthur Emerlich. He seemed to be a model member of society, a successful executive inching toward retirement.

Georgia filled Ellie in and said she'd call Christine Messenger, but there was no answer when she did. She left Messenger a voice mail saying she'd copy the report and drop it off. Then she checked her calendar. Tomorrow was the Fourth of July, the start of a three-day weekend. Whatever she needed to do, she'd have do today or wait until next week.

She went through her closet, pulled out a sundress she rarely wore and put it on. She applied make-up, something else she rarely did. Then she pulled down directions from Mapquest, got into her car, and set out for More-Than-Friends, the dating service in Palatine that allegedly stole her client's identity.

Forty minutes later she entered a newly built office park with three buildings, two restaurants, and a manmade lake. She was surprised. She'd been expecting a small, sleazy office tucked away in the wrong part of town. She parked in the lot behind one of the office buildings and proceeded into the lobby, a space with marble floors and enormous glass windows with a view of the lake. The building directory indicated that More-than-Friends was on the fourth floor.

She took the elevator up and was surprised again to find a set of glass doors, with the name of More-than-Friends in elegant lettering. Inside was a waiting room with a counter and receptionist's desk, and comfortable looking leather chairs. The place looked like a law firm, corporate office, or any other white-collar business. Not a dating service. Georgia wondered if her client had it wrong.

An attractive young woman behind the receptionist's desk was reading *Cosmopolitan*, but when Georgia opened the door, she slipped it in a drawer. The woman was perfectly made up and coiffed, but her outfit, a dark green suit with no blouse, exposed a little too much cleavage for the office.

"Can I help you?" She asked sweetly.

Georgia rethought her strategy. She'd been planning to pretend she was a teacher who was looking for love in all the wrong places, but given the upscale atmosphere, she'd probably need a more lucrative "career." She cleared her throat, glad she was wearing a nice dress. "I'd—I'd like to see someone about your service."

The receptionist looked her up and down. "Do you have an appointment?"

Georgia felt a tic of irritation. The receptionist was screening her. "I don't."

The woman hesitated, then flashed Georgia a bright smile. "That's okay. I think we can squeeze you in." What did it? Georgia wondered. Her hair? Clothes? Her sad dog expression? She didn't know, but she was pleased she'd passed muster. The receptionist opened another drawer and pulled out a form. "You'll have to fill this out."

"No problem." Georgia took it and sat in one of the chairs. Four pages long, the form asked for her education level, work history, income, significant relationships, hobbies, and about a hundred other things. As she filled out the "relationship" box, a fleeting memory of Matt surfaced. They'd lived together for a year. No. She wouldn't include him. Too close to the truth.

As for a career, she decided she would be a graphic artist. Her friend, Samantha Mosele, was one, and she was raking in a bunch of money developing and maintaining websites. Georgia wrote down her true name and address, but everything else—the degree from Northwestern, graduate work at Loyola, clients, and generous income, was a fantasy. She smiled. Creating a character out of whole cloth was kind of fun. For the relationship box, she wrote that she was recently divorced after seven years of marriage.

She handed the form back to the receptionist, who promptly took it and knocked on a door down the hall. Georgia heard a muffled conversation. The receptionist returned and said to follow her. A whiff of sweet, musky perfume trailed behind her.

Georgia walked into a large, airy office. Behind a desk covered with a mass of papers was a woman with long black hair, pale skin, red fingernails, and a face that was almost artfully made up. Dressed in a casual black pantsuit—also with no blouse underneath—the woman looked like Morticia Addams as played by Angelica Huston. On the wall behind her was a framed diploma from George Washington University. She motioned Georgia into a chair.

"Hello, there. Felicia says you are a walk-in." Her voice was soft but her smile chilly. "Tell me, what made you drive out here without an appointment? It's not as if we run commercials on TV."

Georgia's antenna went up. The woman was already grilling her. She needed to be careful. She shot back with a question of her own. "And you are?"

She held out a hand. "Tracy Alessi. I own More-than-Friends." Her handshake was perfunctory. Another cool smile. Then she scanned the form. "Georgia Davis." She looked up, her eyebrows arched. "Well?"

Georgia remembered a name from the lobby directory. "I—I had a meeting with PRSA Management Consultants. I'm a graphic designer. Anyway, when I was looking for the floor it was on, I noticed your listing. It looked—well—I just thought I'd take a chance."

"I see." Alessi studied her. Georgia knew she was trying to make up her mind whether she was for real. "And what were you meeting PRSA about, if you don't mind me asking?"

"They have a client who wants to redesign their website. That's what I specialize in." She hoped to hell Alessi didn't know anyone at PRSA. Then again, maybe Alessi wouldn't ask. Maybe she figured no one would lie that blatantly. Alessi tapped a long polished nail on her desk. Then she squared her shoulders.

"Well, this is your lucky day. We usually don't take clients over the transom, so to speak. But I didn't have any other appointments..." She looked down at the form again. "I see you were married for seven years. Why did it end?"

"He—he met another woman and fell in love." That was the truth.

"That must have been hard."

Georgia hesitated. "It was."

"I get it. Rejection is probably the most destructive force in the world. It makes you doubt everything. Not just your desirability and your worth—you start to doubt your ability to perform. To make decisions. To get anything done."

Georgia kept her mouth shut.

"I can see it's still hard for you to talk about it."

It was.

"You've been spending a lot of time grieving, haven't you? Mourning the loss. You've probably been doubting yourself. Maybe even hating yourself. Deciding you don't deserve another chance."

Georgia blinked. This woman knew her.

"And you probably think you're the only person in the world who feels so raw. It's a lonely place to be, isn't it?"

Georgia struggled to keep her emotions at bay. That's exactly what she was doing. Keeping everyone, including Pete, at arm's length. Not getting involved. And it was lonely. She blinked again, felt her throat get hot. Then she looked up at Alessi. Her cool smile was still there, but something else was too. Triumph.

Georgia's mood snapped. Her spine stiffened. She wasn't here to relive her break-up with Matt; she was here to investigate a potential criminal. But she'd been reacting exactly the way Alessi wanted her to. This woman was good.

Alessi didn't appear to notice. She folded her hands, still the compassionate therapist. "But now you think you're ready to dip your toe back into the water."

Georgia decided to play along. "Yes," she said meekly.

"But you're still tentative. Afraid you'll make another mistake. Go through hell all over again."

Georgia nodded.

"Well..." A tiny smirk curled Alessi's lips. It was hardly noticeable unless you were looking for it. "Well, I think we can help."

For an instant Georgia felt a swell of pride. She'd been approved. Chosen. Then she realized she was supposed to feel that way. She bit her lip.

Alessi slipped on a pair reading glasses and took out a pen. "Tell me what you want in a partner."

Georgia decided to play her own game. "Someone I can trust." Alessi nodded and wrote something down. When Georgia didn't go on, she looked at Georgia over the rim of her glasses. "And..."

"That's it."

"Surely, there are other qualities you're searching for. Looks, sense of humor, career, hobbies..."

"Nope."

Alessi put the pen down. "I would have thought someone as professional and sophisticated as you would want a partner with similar social and intellectual habits."

"Trust cuts across everything."

"I see." When Georgia didn't volunteer anything further, Alessi seemed to falter. "Well, uh—when would you like to get started?"

"Right away." Georgia smiled. "If we can."

Alessi tipped her head to the side. "All right. Let me tell you the way we work. We'll search our files carefully to find potential partners for you. We do guarantee six dates over the course of three months. We'll follow up with both you and your date afterwards and see if we can cement the match. No pressure, of course. If nothing happens, we'll send you on six more."

"Sounds wonderful."

"Good." She drew out another piece of paper from a drawer. "These are our terms."

Georgia promptly looked for the bottom line. There it was, in the middle of the page. Twelve hundred dollars. She swallowed. That was way more than she'd expected. She'd thought it might be five, six. But twelve? That was two hundred per date. Plus presumably, another two for her "partner." These people were scamming big time. She tried to hide her distaste and scanned down the page. At the bottom was a blank line for her signature and social security number.

Bingo.

She looked up. "Why do you need my social security number?"

Alessi rocked back in her chair but left her hands on the desk. Her nails looked like talons. "To be honest, we need to run a background check. Make sure you're who you say you are. That you have no outstanding arrest warrants. Or criminal record. I'm sure you can understand. You'd want the same assurance about a potential date."

Georgia frowned. "I don't know that I want you to do that."

"Why? You don't have anything to hide, do you?"

"No. Of course not."

"Is it our fee?"

Georgia looked down.

Alessi leaned forward and tapped a finger. "Georgia, how can you put a price on happiness? It's impossible. But, if it seems too overwhelming, I understand. And we do have an installment program. You can pay as little as a hundred a month. Surely you can afford that."

It was Georgia's turn to fold her hands. "Well, actually, I need to think about it."

"But Georgia, if you sign up now, we can get started right away. The longer you wait, the more time we'll need to find you a match. And the longer you'll stay isolated. And lonely. We can end that for you. In a few days, if you sign now."

Georgia's tone was prim. "I'm—frankly—not prepared to spend that kind of money."

"Oh Georgia, don't you remember how good it is to feel welcomed and nurtured and special? You've been searching for this your whole life. You can't let this slip out of your fingers now, just when it's within reach."

Georgia shook her head.

Alessi frowned. Apparently, this wasn't going the way she expected. "Georgia, you came in our door. Without an appointment. We made the time commitment and invested in you. Don't you think you have an obligation to return that investment?"

Georgia got up. "No, I don't."

"Georgia, Sit down. Don't do this to yourself. You deserve another chance."

But Georgia exited the office, leaving Alessi staring after her with her mouth open.

* * *

Although she got what she'd come for, Georgia seethed on the drive back to Evanston. Part of it was the fact she'd been manipulated, but part of it was something else. Whether she knew it or not, Alessi had zeroed in on the truth. Georgia had been dumped, and Alessi had forced her to relive the hurt and shame. She tried to shake it off—she'd put herself in that position by showing up at More-than-Friends in the first place. Still, it wouldn't quite go away, which only fueled more anger, much of it directed inward.

Luckily, asking for her social had been a dead give-away. Alessi probably had some tech in a back room running searches as soon as she got a number. Assuming you knew where to look, you could find plenty of sites that yielded enough information to start stealing identities. Georgia knew—she'd done her own share of background checks on Kroll and Accenture. She gripped the wheel. Creeps like Alessi shouldn't be allowed to operate. First thing next week she'd call her client.

Friday night after the fireworks she met Pete Dellinger at Mickey's, her favorite place in Evanston. Pete was her neighbor and her friend, and while she knew he wanted it to be more, he wasn't pushy. As she walked into the dimly lit bar, she spotted him at the bar, talking to Mickey's owner, Owen Dougherty.

"Here she is." Dougherty was a big man in his sixties with dark coloring and a mustache that made him look like Jackie Gleason, whose *Honeymooner* reruns Georgia had discovered on cable. He snapped the white towel that usually hung over his shoulder. "So, what'll it be, tonight? The firecracker special?"

Pete was nursing a draft.

"Diet coke with lemon," Georgia said.

"How's by you, Davis?" Owen said as he poured her drink. Protocol demanded that everyone go by last names at Mickey's. Except Owen. Georgia decided to buck the system.

"Just peachy, Dougherty," She slid onto the stool next to Pete.

Owen frowned at her breach of etiquette but set down her soda. Pete touched her arm by way of greeting. He had sandy hair, a small nose, and behind a pair of glasses, lively blue eyes.

He wasn't what you'd call handsome—his eyes were too widely spaced, his chin too prominent, and his hair too unruly—but he was interesting.

And nerdy. Pete dressed like he lived in Pleasantville during the fifties. Once Georgia had teased that he must have been deprived of penny loafers and a button-down shirt as a kid, because he always wore them now. When he didn't reply, she realized she was closer to the truth than she'd known. She'd seen him in shorts and a tank top, though, and knew that underneath his Ivy League getup was a great body: broad shoulders, muscled arms, flat stomach. She sighed. If she'd been a different kind of woman...

"You go to the fireworks?"

"Nope. Just got home. I was doing laundry."

"Where were you?"

"Camping in northern Wisconsin with my brother."

"You have a brother? I thought there was only you and your sister."

"Steve's my half brother. Lives in Minnesota. He called a few weeks ago. Wanted to spend some time together. We went fly fishing on the Flambeau river."

"Tents and campfires and all that?"

He nodded. "A little bit of paradise on earth."

Georgia shook her head. "My idea of paradise is a hotel with room service, a minibar, and movies on demand."

"You don't know what you're missing: two stinky men drinking beer for breakfast and lunch, and fishing for our dinner."

Gemma, Mickey's only waitress, came over with menus. "You want over there?" She motioned toward an empty booth.

"We can eat at the bar," Georgia said. "Save you the trouble of bussing."

"Appreciate it." Gemma had three kids and no husband and was putting herself through a CPA program. She'd been moonlighting at Mickey's for years. Georgia ordered her usual: hamburger, rare, with fries. Pete ordered fried fish.

"You didn't have enough last week?"

A flush started up Pete's cheeks. "Well, turned out we didn't quite have the right lures. We ate a lot of pizza."

Georgia laughed. "So much for living off the land. Or water."

"Hey, we had a great time. Lots of brotherly bonding." He took a pull on his draft. "So, what have you been up to?" He was always careful not to get too personal. Giving her space.

She told him about Molly and Christine Messenger. "Then, right after the girl was released, which itself was strange, the mother's boss died in a car accident. The mother is freaked out. Thinks it's related to her daughter."

"Do you?"

"Hard to say. I'm waiting for a tox screen and the autopsy results."

Pete took another sip of beer. "You do have a thing for kids... especially girls."

Funny. Foreman had said the same thing. They probably had a point. First Rachel, Foreman's daughter, then Lauren Walcher, now Molly Messenger. Georgia was drawn to the vulnerable ones, the ones who couldn't defend themselves. But it wasn't just girls. She thought back to Cam Jordan, a mentally challenged kid who'd been railroaded last year for a murder he didn't commit. He'd needed her to fight for him.

It was probably all wrapped up in being abandoned by her own mother. She'd walked out when Georgia was twelve, leaving Georgia with her father, a cop who liked the bottle as well as the strap. Georgia had more or less raised herself. Still, the idea of motherhood terrified her. She started to fidget.

Pete picked up on it. "Hey, that wasn't supposed to make you stress out."

She stared at her drink.

"So what do you think?" Pete tried to change the subject. "About the mother?"

"I can't figure out whether she's on the level or she's the kind of woman who feels entitled to special treatment. The referral came through... well, that's not important. The thing is, I looked into this as a favor. I'm not getting paid. So whatever she turns out to be, my part is over once the screens come back."

"But what if the mother's hunch is right and it wasn't an accident?"

"A hunch is just wishful thinking unless the evidence is there." She twirled her swizzle stick. Enough about Christine Messenger. "Hey, you ever hear of a dating service called More-than-Friends?"

Pete shook his head.

She was about to tell him when the news on the TV above the bar came on. When she heard the top story, she gasped.

CHAPTER 9

Ellie

The flame from the scented candle flickered in the dark. Currents of cool air kissed my skin, but I felt heat in the sweep of his fingers, first tender then insistent. Luke had a way of touching me that made me feel I was the most beautiful, desirable woman on earth. I tried to arch up, but his weight held me down. I felt his mouth hot on my skin. My muscles tightened and my breath caught. His fingers dug into my shoulders, and he entered me, thrusting hard and fast and deep. I rose up to meet him. When we made love, the rest of the world fell away. He claimed not only my body but my soul too, ransacking then refilling it so that all my thoughts and senses were of him.

* * *

I woke up later than usual Saturday morning. Luke sat on the edge of the bed already dressed, watching me. I smiled and reached for him. He buried his face in my neck. I felt his heart beating against mine. Warm. Comforting. He kissed me, then straightened up.

"I thought I'd go for a run."

I nodded lazily. "After all the fireworks last night? You were amazing."

"I know." His eyes twinkled. They were a shade of blue that changed from ocean deep to cloudless sky depending on his mood, and they were his most interesting feature. He had carrot-colored hair on top of his head, gray on the sides, and freckles all over his skin. He wasn't that tall, but he was compact and fit. Most people wouldn't look twice at him, but when his eyes landed on me, frank and guileless, my stomach flipped, and I couldn't look away.

"You sure you want to go for a run?" I remembered the passion we'd shared just a few hours ago. "I do have another idea."

"More fireworks, huh?" He disengaged from my arms. "I'll be back in thirty minutes. We'll negotiate."

I sank back against the pillow. Truth be told, I am not a morning person and I resent the cheerful types who are. For Luke, though, I made an effort. "Go ahead. I'll make breakfast."

"We could go to the pancake house," he said.

"And put back all those calories you burned off?" I shook my head. "Eggs this morning. Maybe egg whites."

"You can splurge on the yolks. We earned them."

When he grinned I felt a twinge of desire. It never quite faded. "You'd better get out now. Or you never will."

He kissed me again, then took the stairs down. The screen door banged. I took my time getting up, threw on a tank top and shorts, brushed my teeth, went down to the kitchen. I got out eggs, milk, bagels, and a cantaloupe that had been ripening on the counter and smelled just right. Then I went out to grab the paper.

It was a perfect summer day: azure sky, puffy white clouds, sunbaked breeze. I could turn off the air conditioning. I was bending over to pick up the paper when an old, battered pickup pulled up to the curb. For an instant I thought it was Fouad Al Hamra, a friend who owns a landscaping company and helps me take care of my garden. But Fouad just bought a new Dodge Ram, and unless he'd entered it in a demolition derby, this wasn't his truck.

Three Hispanic men climbed out. Landscapers are a familiar summer sight on the North Shore, even on a holiday weekend. Most are probably illegals, working long hours taking care of peoples' lawns for minimum wage or less. To them, we are "rich *gabachos*... northerners."

The men gathered at the edge of my driveway and stooped to examine something at the curb. From my vantage point all I could make out was green material. Speaking in Spanish, they gestured excitedly, then looked up at me and smiled. I smiled back. They bent to pick up the object. What they were doing wasn't uncommon—I'd often see people cruising around the North Shore, scavenging perfectly good items other people had thrown away. I couldn't blame them.

Until I realized what they were carrying to the truck. It was my patio umbrella—the one I bought last year. The one I'd asked Rachel to put away a few days ago. Put away. Not throw away. She must have misunderstood. I dropped the newspaper and hurried to the curb.

"Hey..." I waved my hands. "No, no. That's mine. Sorry. You can't have it."

The two men frowned but kept hold of the umbrella.

"The umbrella. *Es lo mi!*" My Spanish is practically nonexistent. "It's new!" What was the frigging word for "new" in Spanish? *Nouvelle* in French. My father was right, after all. He'd told me to take Spanish, but my mother insisted on French. Damn them both. Where was Rachel? She was in Spanish Four.

The men's faces remained impassive. They were gaming me. They had to know, even if they didn't understand the words, that I didn't want them to take it. Still, they looked away and slid the umbrella into the bed of the truck.

I went over to the pickup and grabbed one end of the umbrella. So much for my give-me-your-poor-and-oppressed compassion.

The Mexicans talked excitedly among themselves. One of them turned to me and shook his finger. "*No no, es de nostros.*"

"It wasn't supposed to be thrown away. *Muchacha es mistaken.*" I tried to slide the umbrella out of the truck, but as one end fell to the ground, one of the men snatched the other end and started to pull.

"No!"

Another man shouted at the one who'd grabbed the umbrella. Umbrella man shouted back. From their tone, I knew they were arguing, trying to decide what to do. I couldn't tell whether Umbrella man was trying to placate his buddies or wanted to give me a hard time. I kept hold of my end, and he kept hold of his. A tug of war ensued.

"Come on, give it back!" I said. "*Es mi!*"

He pulled. I pulled. If both of us kept it up, the umbrella might come apart. Thankfully, Luke chose that moment to appear at the end of the street. He slowed as he jogged to the driveway. Confusion swam across his face.

"Luke, help!"

He was breathing heavily, and sweat poured down his cheeks. "What the hell is going on?"

Between tugging on the umbrella and trying to keep my balance, I tried to explain. I didn't get too far, but he must have gotten the point because suddenly his voice rang out, louder than mine.

"Stop. *Dejala ya!*"

Everybody froze, including me.

"This belongs to the senora," he said in a more reasonable tone. "*Dejala, por favor. La sombrilla es de la senora,*" he went on in perfect Spanish.

"*¿Y eso? Porqué estaba votado en la basura?*" The man playing tug of war with me asked.

Luke turned to me. "Why was it on the curb? With the garbage?"

"It was Rachel," I panted. "She threw it out by mistake."

Luke turned back. "*Fué una equivocación.* Her daughter didn't understand. *Su hija se equivocó. La señora no quería votarla.* She doesn't want to get rid of it."

The man at the other end of the umbrella shot me one of those if-looks-could-kill glances but let go. I lost my balance but held on. I started to carry it back to the house.

Luke prattled on in Spanish. The three men started to nod. He spun around and called out, "Ellie, go inside and get them ten bucks a piece."

"Why? They were stealing—"

"Just do it."

I recognized an order and meekly went inside. I came out a minute later with my wallet, peeled off a twenty and a ten, and handed them over to Luke.

"Sorry for the misunderstanding," Luke said. "*Disculpa la equivocacion.*"

The man who'd been holding the umbrella grinned. He was missing a couple of teeth. The men saluted Luke and piled back into the pickup. They smiled at me, then took off.

I planted my hands on my hips. "What did you tell them? Why did they salute you?"

He came over and put his arm around me. "You're something else. Getting territorial over a patio umbrella?"

"It was practically brand new."

"It's not like you couldn't afford a new one."

"Easy for you to say." Luke comes from old Wasp money. Lots of it.

"Don't you think they needed it more than you?"

"Well, yes, but —"

"Next time, let them have it. I'll buy you a new one."

I was loath to admit it, but Luke was right. In the vast scheme of things, fighting over a patio umbrella was not one of my finer moments. My cheeks got hot, and I went to pick up the newspaper, hoping to come up with some pithy response to justify my behavior. But when I saw what was on the front page, any urge to be clever flew out of my mind.

CHAPTER 10

I met Georgia at the village diner an hour later. Tucked away on a side street just off the expressway, the restaurant is the twenty-first century version of the general store, a place where everybody congregates for sustenance, gossip, and a good cup of coffee. During the week the groundswell of traffic outside, plus the machines at the dry cleaners' next door, can make it impossible to hear. But on a Saturday morning, you can actually have a normal conversation.

Georgia was in a booth in the back. I slid in across from her. The naugahyde upholstery felt cool against my legs.

"How long have you known?" I asked as a Hispanic bus boy filled her cup with coffee.

Georgia picked up the cup, took a sip, let it clatter as she put it back on the saucer. "I was out for dinner last night. Saw it on the news."

I shook my head as the guy tilted the coffee pot toward me. I didn't think I could swallow. "Poor Molly... first the kidnapping. Now her mother dies. On the Fourth of July, no less."

Georgia winced.

A waitress tried to hand us menus, but I waved her off. "Have you talked to O'Malley?"

"No."

"The paper says it was a car accident. On the Sheridan Road ravines."

A string of bluffs hugs the shoreline of Lake Michigan from Winnetka to Lake Bluff. Between them are steep ravines that can be treacherous if you're driving too fast. Or if your brakes aren't working.

Georgia stared at her coffee as if the hot liquid could reveal the truth.

"Shouldn't we tell the cops up here about her boss's accident? Make sure they connect the dots?"

"Go ahead."

I frowned. "Will you come with me?"

"No."

"Why not?"

"They're already on it. You know that. Molly was abducted up here, don't forget. Now that her mother's dead, they'd be cretins not to look for a connection."

"So why not help them out?"

"Like I said, you go ahead. It's not my job. I'm not officially working this case."

"But if you were?"

"I'd be all over it. Although I'm guessing there won't be much evidence. If someone is good enough to make a murder look like an accident, they know what they're doing." Georgia leaned forward. "Whoever's behind this knows how to operate in that—netherworld between fact and fog," she added. "That means they're not someone you want to tangle with."

"I wasn't thinking about me."

Georgia's eyes narrowed.

"I'm going to call Molly's father," I said.

"What the hell for?"

"Because he's the only one I can think of who can hire you."

* * *

Georgia

Sunday morning Georgia came in from a run to find a message from Terry Messenger on her voicemail. "Ellie Foreman said you might be able to help me. I'd like to set up a meeting."

An hour later she drove to his condo in the Glen, a self-contained community with overpriced homes, restaurants, and stores. But if you were looking for a place in a hurry, as husbands who've been kicked out of their homes often are, the availability of apartments made it a predictable choice.

Terry Messenger opened the door. Georgia had only seen him briefly on the news the day Molly was released. He was better looking in person. Bald by choice—he couldn't have been much older than forty—the shape of his head was pleasing. His eyes were hazel, with dark lashes that gave him a slightly feminine cast. Unlike his wife and daughter's freckled skin, his was ruddy, and he looked like he'd been out in the sun. He was a doctor, Georgia recalled, which meant his time in the sun was probably due to tennis or golf. Maybe sailing. He was wearing a soft-looking yellow t-shirt, jeans, and sandals.

"Thanks for coming." He ushered her in, his expression tight, as though he was struggling to control his emotions.

Georgia looked around. He hadn't invested much in decorating. A black leather couch—what was it about men and leather? A left-over childhood desire to play cowboy? A dining room table with four chairs. But no rug or carpet, and nothing on the walls. This was where he slept, not where he lived.

"How's Molly doing?"

Messenger looked puzzled.

"I met her a couple of days ago at your—ex-wife's house."

"Oh, that's right." He swallowed. "She's—she's in bad shape."

"I'm so sorry." Georgia's voice caught.

Messenger's eyes filled. Then he pulled himself together and cleared his throat. "She can't sleep, she can't eat, and she's sucking her fingers again. She hasn't done that since she was four."

"Is she here?"

He gestured toward a hall leading away from the living room. "She's taking a nap. Or trying to." He sat at the dining room table and motioned Georgia into a chair.

"Have you considered getting her some help? A therapist or counselor?"

"What are they going to do? Feel her pain? Tell her it's going to be okay? Molly's mother is gone. She's never coming back."

He had a point.

"I don't mean to belittle your suggestion. I just haven't had time to think about anything. The past twenty-four hours have been surreal. I keep thinking the other shoe is going to drop, but I don't know where or when or even what size it is."

"The police are investigating, aren't they?"

"Yes, but they don't seem to have any—any passion for it, if you know what I mean."

"Are they aware that Christine's boss died in a car accident too?"

"Yes, but they're not prepared to say the two incidents are linked. At least not yet. They're not ruling it out, but they say they need evidence."

"Do you know if they have Emerlich's accident report from the Illinois State Police?"

"I don't."

"Well, I do. And from what I can tell, it looks like the brake fluid in his car was too low. If the same was true in Christine's car, it could indicate something."

"You see? That's what I need. Someone who's willing to make those connections. Christine was sure something weird was going on. She called me, you know. The night before she—she died."

"And?"

"She said—she said, 'I screwed up.'"

"Screwed up? How?"

She wouldn't tell me. Believe me, I asked. But she sounded terrified. For her, that's saying a lot."

"Because she was always—so controlled?"

He grimaced. "That's the nice way of saying it. A rock showed more emotion than Chris. That was one of the reasons—well, we won't go there. She wasn't that way with Molly, of course." He lapsed into silence. Georgia waited. He seemed to forget where he was and what he was talking about. The guy was still in shock.

Georgia said softly, "You were explaining Chris's call the night before the accident..."

"Right." He snapped back. "She wanted me to take Molly for

the weekend. She sounded scared. She kept saying she thought something bad was going to happen."

"Did she say what? Or why? Or who was behind it? Anything?"

He shook his head. "I asked, but she wouldn't tell me. Just asked me to pick Molly up. She was on her way out to a meeting. I went right over. Molly was next door with a neighbor. We were on our way back here when the police called."

"Do you think that 'meeting' might have had something to do with the accident?"

"I don't know." A burst of pain shot across his face. "I'm a cardiologist, you know. I deal with specific symptoms that can be diagnosed, then treated. But this—this is so—I'm way out of my league. I don't even know if the police know what they're doing."

Apparently Christine Messenger wasn't the only control freak in the family. Then again, the man had just faced one crisis and was in the middle of another, either one of which could profoundly affect a person. She should lighten up.

"What you're feeling isn't unusual. You've suffered two tremendous shocks. In quick succession. I'd be surprised if you weren't disoriented."

His eyes fired with shame. Doctors were taught to perform under pressure, no matter what the situation. To play God. Was he just now realizing that he wasn't?

"Did you tell the police about Chris's phone call?"

"Of course."

"And?"

He shrugged. "The detective took notes."

Georgia pictured her former partner, Robbie Parker, sitting in the same chair as she, interviewing Messenger. She suppressed a stab of annoyance. She recalled something Christine said at their first meeting. "You said your wife—I mean Chris—was good with Molly."

"That's right."

"Would you call her a good mother?"

"She was super. I never had any complaints. She was doing a great job raising her."

Georgia frowned. Christine had said Terry accused her of being a bad mother. Of putting her career before Molly. She'd been afraid to tell him about Molly's abduction for fear she'd lose custody. Should she bring it up? No, not now. She was about to ask him about Christine's car when she heard footsteps in the hall. Molly shuffled into the room.

"Daddy?"

Georgia couldn't believe it was the same child. Molly was wearing a pink bathrobe with brown stains smeared across it. Her feet were bare, and her hair was matted and tangled. Her skin was so pale it looked translucent. She was clutching a scruffy stuffed Beagle. She squinted and blinked rapidly, as though the light in the room was too strong.

Terry held out his arms, and Molly ran over. He scooped her up into his lap. She settled herself, then stuffed three fingers in her mouth and turned to stare at Georgia. She showed no sign of recognition.

Georgia wished she could take the girl in her arms. Instead she said, "Hi, Molly. Do you remember me? I was at your house the other day."

Molly sucked on her fingers without replying. Then her lips puckered and she buried her face in her father's chest. The girl had only met her once, then her life had collapsed. Even if Molly did recognize Georgia, she would probably always associate her with grief and tragedy.

"It's okay, freckle-face," her father said softly. "Georgia's here to help."

Molly burrowed deeper, as if she wanted to climb into his pocket and stay there. Georgia knew that feeling.

"Molly is the only important thing in my life," Terry said. "She must stay safe," he went on. "Do you understand? I need to know what's going on so I can take appropriate measures. I'm prepared to compensate you to ensure that. Will you help me?"

Georgia looked at him, then Molly. She explained her terms. He'd pay her a retainer. She would work on an hourly basis and keep track of her time. When she got close to an agreed-upon amount, she'd let him know so he could determine whether to proceed further. He agreed to everything.

"Molly, honey, you have to get up for a minute. I need to write Georgia a check."

Georgia held up her hand. "Don't worry. I can get it later."

"Thanks." He tightened his hold on his daughter. "What do you see as your first step?"

"I'll need to get the police report on her fatal—I mean, accident. Then I'll start making inquiries. Because of the similarity with Emerlich, I'll probably start at her office." She thought for a moment. "What about family? Does—did Chris have any siblings, cousins, who might talk to me?"

Terry shook his head. "She was an only child, and her parents are gone. My sister was close to her—wait. She has a cousin. Lives on the East Coast. I'll get you her name and number."

"That would be great."

"In the meantime, is there anything special I should do—with her?" He brushed his fingers over Molly's hair, tucked a lock behind her ear.

Georgia knew she'd have to talk to Molly about the kidnapping, but now wasn't the time. She wanted to reassure her that she would survive. *Georgia* had, although she wasn't sure how. She'd let the days and nights spill over her like waves in the ocean. Eventually enough breakers washed over her, and the wound wasn't as raw. She could even smile and laugh again. But the pain and regret never faded entirely. Even after twenty-five years.

"Just keep her close."

Terry nodded. Molly must have sensed the conversation drawing to a close. She squirmed, then turned around and looked at Georgia. Slowly, she took her fingers out of her mouth.

"Peaches," she said softly.

"What was that, freckle-face?" Terry asked.

But Georgia knew. She remembered how Foreman had teased Molly about Georgia's name when they met. She leaned across and drew her hand down the girl's cheek. "That's right, Molly. That's my name. Georgia Peaches."

CHAPTER 11

Monday morning Georgia emailed the report she'd written about More-than-Friends to her client. Technically, her job was finished—unless her client opted not to go to the police. Then Georgia would have a decision to make. But that was still a ways off.

Next she called O'Malley. He wasn't there, so she left a message and went to work out. She'd discovered a gym on the second floor of an older building in Evanston. It was a smelly, barebones place with wood floors and fluorescent lighting, frequented by guys she'd never want to meet in a dark alley. But it had all the equipment she needed, and she liked getting in and out in under an hour.

Back home she showered and dressed and slathered a piece of toast with peanut butter and jam. She was just biting into it when her phone trilled.

"Davis..."

"I would hope so..." A gravelly voice cracked.

"Hey Dan." O'Malley. "Thanks for calling back."

"You considered my offer and want to come back on the force."

"Er... not today."

"Business must be good."

"That's why I'm calling. I'd really like to get a copy of the accident report on Christine Messenger."

"You and every reporter in Chicago."

"I'd never leak it."

"I know you won't, but what about the gremlins who come in every night and steal things off your computer?"

"If you're going to be a hardass, I can get it another way. I just thought—"

"Look. Parker's team is working this thing the right way. I don't want it to get fucked up."

That was only part of the truth. As Deputy Chief of Police, O'Malley had a stake in it, too. His reputation as a boss and manager was on the line. She sighed. "I get it. But you should know I got the report on her boss from the Staties."

OMalley was quiet for a minute. "You gonna tell me who your client is?"

"You gonna get me the report?"

"Now who's being a hardass?" He laughed. "Got to be the father."

Georgia kept her mouth shut.

"Listen. If you have the State Police report, just substitute the name of the victim, and you'll have the general idea."

"The circumstances were that similar?"

"You know I can't answer that."

She didn't need him to.

"Actually, there's been an interesting development," he said softly.

"I'm listening."

"Because the mother's 'accident'..." he emphasized the word "... was so close to the time the daughter was snatched, we convinced the county to do an autopsy."

"That *is* interesting."

"The ME did it yesterday."

"That was fast."

"One of the assistants owed me a favor."

What kind of favor, Georgia wondered. She didn't ask.

"You didn't hear this from me."

"Of course not."

"Christine Messenger was two months pregnant when she died."

* * *

Georgia thumped the heel of her hand on the steering wheel as she drove downtown. She *knew* it. Christine Messenger was hiding something. Her behavior said it all. She'd been guarded. Secretive. Doling out information in tiny bits. This had to be the reason why.

The case had just exploded. Messenger had a man in her life, but she didn't want anyone to know. Did that mean the guy was married? Or otherwise unavailable? More important, did that relationship—or the fact she became pregnant—have anything to do with her death? Or Molly's kidnapping?

Georgia ran down a list of possibilities. Messenger was sleeping with her boss at the bank. The wife found out, threw a shit fit, and came after them. Or she'd taken up with her ex-husband. Ex-sex happened, especially when one partner starts a relationship with someone new. And Terry Messenger supposedly had a girlfriend. Or she was sleeping with a friend or a neighbor's husband. Or it was someone else altogether—a mystery man no one knew about.

Two months pregnant. Did Messenger know? Georgia decided she probably did. By eight weeks, there are plenty of signs, and Messenger had been pregnant before.

O'Malley said they'd requested a DNA sample from the fetus. Depending on the results, the police might crack the case faster than she could. Good for them. Not for her. The thought that Parker, her former partner, might ace her sent a spurt of irritation up her spine. She forced herself to remember this wasn't a competition. The important thing was Molly's safety. She'd been hired to make sure the little girl wasn't at risk.

The skies were hazy and gray, with humidity thick enough to punch a hole through. She parked in a garage on Dearborn and walked the few blocks to the Midwest National Bank building. A sixty-some story skyscraper, its stark white exterior sizzled against the gunmetal skies.

The lobby was a mass of cool marble. Off to the right was a glass-walled room almost as large as a football field. On one side was a row of teller booths; on the other a group of desks surrounded by an ocean of thick blue carpeting. A woman in a two-piece suit but no blouse sat at one of the desks. Her hair and make-up was perfect. She could have been moonlighting at More-than-Friends. Georgia shook it off. This was a bank, for Christ's sake.

She scanned the lobby directory for the IT department, but it wasn't listed. Neither was Arthur Emerlich. But Christine

Messenger's name was still posted. Not surprising; she'd died Friday. Just three days ago.

Messenger had worked on the fifty-first floor. Georgia took the elevator up. Glass doors flanked both ends of the hall, but they were locked, and a card swipe box hung beside each door. She peered through one of the doors and saw a series of beige cubicles that looked more like an animal warren than an office. She went to the other door. A receptionist's desk stood in front. Vacant. Was the receptionist off on an errand, or had the bank, in a cost-cutting mood, eliminated the position? Behind the desk was a gray carpeted hallway leading to a string of offices. At the end of the hall she could just make out another glass-walled room. Probably for the computers that ran the bank's business.

She went back to the door that opened onto the cubicles. Where were the corporate worker-bees? She'd been there at least five minutes but hadn't seen a soul. The entire floor seemed empty, as if everyone had abandoned ship. Were they out to lunch? At a staff meeting? Maybe the computers were secretly running everything, making humans obsolete. She crossed the hall and checked the other glass door. No one.

She returned to the elevators, flummoxed. If she tried to go through channels, she wouldn't get far. People were often reluctant to talk to the cops during a crisis, and a private detective carried even less weight. Still, Christine Messenger had worked on this floor. Maybe Arthur Emerlich's office wasn't far away. Someone had to show up eventually. She would wait.

Ten minutes later an elevator dinged. The doors opened, and a woman came out. Short gray curls framed her head, a slash of red lipstick covered her mouth. Thick glasses gave her a no-nonsense, intelligent look. A floral scent swirled in her wake. Georgia hated florals.

She cocked an eyebrow at Georgia. "May I help you?"

Was it that obvious she didn't belong? "I hope so," Georgia replied. "I'm looking for Christine Messenger's department."

The woman's eyebrow arched higher. "For what reason?"

"I'd like to talk to her colleagues. Get a better picture of her."

"Are you with the police?"

Georgia played it straight. "Her ex-husband hired me. I'm an investigator."

"We're not supposed to talk to anyone, unless it's the police."

"I understand." Georgia was pretty sure the fact of Messenger's pregnancy was still under wraps. But Molly's kidnapping wasn't. "Molly's father wants to protect his daughter—that's why I'm here. He wants to rule out any possibility that his ex-wife's death and his child's kidnapping are related."

"I wish I could help you." The woman looked sincere.

"Do you have... a daughter?" Georgia almost said "granddaughter" but changed her mind at the last minute.

The woman's brow furrowed. "We're under strict orders to report any strangers to security. You're going to have to leave."

"Tell me one thing. If I did want to talk to someone, if I could clear it through the police, who would you suggest? All I need is a name."

A sympathetic smile came across the woman's face. Georgia dared to hope. Then the woman shook her head. "I'm sorry. I can't help you."

Georgia fished out a card. "I'm sure you know how devastating something like this can be to a parent. If you change your mind, give me a call. I'll keep whatever you say confidential."

The woman took the card. That was something. But she waited until the elevator came and Georgia stepped inside.

There was a man in the car. Tall, mid-thirties, with raggedy brown hair that looked like it hadn't been styled since the seventies. Four pens poked from a pocket protector in his short-sleeved shirt, and a plastic card hung from a cord around his neck.

"Is the staff meeting over?" the woman asked.

"Yup. Just going down for a Coke."

She nodded. As the doors closed, he shifted nervously.

Georgia spoke up. "Weird times, huh?"

He looked up, startled.

Georgia smiled.

He started to relax. "You can say that again. I've never worked anyplace where so many people died so suddenly."

"Not to mention the little girl being kidnapped," Georgia added.

He nodded. "Everyone in the department is talking about it. Forget about getting any work done."

He had to be talking about the IT Department. Still, she needed to tread carefully. Any wrong move would reveal her outsider status.

"When I signed on," he went on, "I never thought I'd be in middle of *CSI*."

"Yeah?"

"You know, cops and detectives in and out. Checking her desk, her computer. Emerlich's too. They took 'em away." He shook his head. "It's getting crazy."

"What's your take on it?"

"Man, I don't know. A lot of people think they had something going on the side, but I see—saw—them every day, and I never picked up on it."

Georgia glanced at his left hand. No ring. That didn't mean much these days, but it was a hopeful sign. She smiled again, hoping it looked like she found him attractive. "How come we've never met?"

Again he looked surprised, as if he didn't expect a woman to come onto him. Then he flashed a broad smile. Unfortunately, the elevator doors opened at that moment, and a man and woman got on. The man was scowling, and the woman looked angry. The chill they brought with them was just enough to make the tech guy clam up. The elevator sped up, descending from the forty-fifth floor to the lobby. Georgia couldn't continue to chat without sounding forced.

At the lobby, the guy stepped off but made no effort to continue their conversation. He'd probably remembered he wasn't supposed to talk to anyone. She sighed as her golden opportunity picked up a soda and candy bar at the newsstand then headed back to the elevators. Georgia exited the building and perched on the edge of a concrete planter. It was still hot, humid, and gray. But there was no rain yet.

She thought for a moment, then pulled out her cell.

CHAPTER 12

Ellie

"What do you mean, you need me?" When Georgia called I was in my office plowing through promotional materials from Voss-Peterson. Critics were charging that contrary to popular opinion, ethanol actually contributed to greenhouse gas emissions. They cited the carbon dioxide released while the corn was growing, as well as nitrous oxide. They also criticized the corrosive properties of the ethanol. Naturally, Voss-Peterson challenged the assumptions. I was weighing how—or even whether—to address those issues in the video.

"I... help me out... not so bad... a drink... Madison and Dearborn. Okay?" The reception from Georgia's cell faded in and out. It must be the coming storm.

"You're breaking up. Georgia. Are you saying you want me to come downtown?"

"... drink with someone."

"Georgia, you know I'm involved with Luke. I'm not on the market."

"No... need information."

"You're still breaking up."

Her next words were clear. "Get here before three. Wear a skirt. And make-up."

* * *

I met her at the corner of Madison and Dearborn at two forty-five. There was no sun, and the air was as sticky as cotton candy. My shirt clung to my neck and back. "So, what's up?"

Georgia cast an appraising eye over me. "You clean up okay."

"Thanks," I said dubiously.

"I met a guy in the elevator—I'm pretty sure he works in the IT department."

"Which means Christine Messenger was his boss?"

"Right. We started talking, and it seemed like he wanted to say more."

"Great. Why do you need me?"

"The police ordered them not to talk to anyone." She explained how she was practically thrown out of the building. "By now the guy has probably realized I don't work there. And he knows my face. You, on the other hand—"

"I get it. What do I want to talk to him about?"

"Turns out Christine Messenger was two months pregnant when she died."

I let out a breath. "Oh boy."

"Yeah."

"And you want me to find out whether she was fooling around with her boss."

"Something like that. Plus anything else you can pick up."

"Like why two people who both work for the same company die within days of each other?"

She just looked at me.

I sighed. "Who's this guy you want me to talk to? Where do I find him?"

"He's inside. Should be out soon."

"And you want me to lure him to a bar, ply him with alcohol, and then pump him."

"Come on Ellie. You know how to do this. It would really help me out. Not to mention Molly."

I swallowed. She'd said the magic word. "When does he come out?"

"I assume he's on the day shift—which usually means seven to three or eight to four. It shouldn't be long. I'll point him out. You do the rest."

"Sure. I'll just put my lips together and blow."

Her response was a saccharine smile.

There were two exits from the building, one on Madison, one on Dearborn. The concrete planter on the corner gave a view of both. Using it as a base of operations Georgia studied everyone who emerged from the building. I sat on the edge of the planter, dangling my legs and pulling my dark curls, which were coiled by the humidity. I looked enviously at Georgia with her ironing-board blond hair.

By three-twenty, the man she was waiting for hadn't come out. Georgia checked her watch. "Sorry. I guess he doesn't get off till four."

"I'm not really fond of hanging around street corners."

Georgia ignored me.

By four, rush hour traffic was already clogging the streets. The heat pressed down, and a sheen of perspiration glazed my face. Droplets of sweat dribbled down my back. Lifting my hair, I fanned the back of my neck. "I'll give it another ten minutes. Then I'm outta here."

Georgia leaned forward. "There he is." She scrambled off the planter, ducked behind it, and squatted down. In other circumstances it would have been funny. "The tall guy," she whispered.

I squinted. A tall young man exited onto Dearborn. His hair looked like something from the last century. Pens sprouted from the pocket of his shirt. The only modern accessory I spotted was a satchel—a cross between a backpack, briefcase, and purse—worn across his chest. He turned south on Dearborn.

"Pen-pocket?" I asked.

"That's him."

"Jesus, Georgia. I'm old enough to be his mother."

"Which is why he'll appreciate you picking him up."

I scowled. "Where are you going to be?"

She looked like she was thinking about it. "Not sure yet. But you'd better get going."

As I started to trot after him, the skies darkened, and the first few drops of rain spattered the sidewalk. Pen-pocket was probably headed to the subway at Monroe and Dearborn. Which meant I only had a block before he disappeared. And though the subway was well-lit, I wasn't anxious to ride the Blue Line out to O'Hare.

A flash of lightning and roll of thunder made people accelerate like Energizer bunnies. The rain started in earnest. Pen-pocket reached the corner of Monroe and pulled an umbrella out of his satchel. I was still half a block behind. Fortunately, the light changed to red and he stopped. Unfortunately, the rain became a downpour, and my skirt and tank top promptly got soaked. I was ready to call it a wrap—I had no desire to be left out in the rain, even for Georgia. Then I remembered I wasn't doing this for her. I was doing this for Molly, a girl whose universe had been shattered.

I hurried over to Pen-pocket and tapped him on the shoulder. He turned. I tried to look pathetic. It wasn't hard. The rain, lashed by the wind, was now sheeting sideways. Even some streetlights had come on.

"I beg your pardon," I said breathlessly. "I would never do this, but I'm—could I share your umbrella? Just across the street to the bus stop." I hoped there was a bus stop nearby.

Pen-pocket looked me over quickly then tilted the umbrella my way. "Sure."

I tried to smile. "You are a very kind man." I grabbed the base of the umbrella. A sudden streak of lightning and clap of thunder made me jump. Our arms touched.

"It's okay," he said. "It'll blow over."

"I hate thunderstorms. Especially when I'm out in them." That much was true. Rachel was worse. Whenever a gust of wind blew in on a dark day, she was convinced a tornado was imminent, even though they're pretty rare in Chicago. It was my fault—I let her watch the *Wizard of Oz* repeatedly when she was little.

"Which bus do you take?"

I was afraid he'd ask that. "Er... the one that goes up Dearborn."

"Where's the stop?"

The light on Monroe turned amber. In a few seconds we'd cross.

"I'm not sure." I spotted a bus a few blocks away. It was heading north on Dearborn towards us. "Caddy corner, I think. I—uh—don't take it much."

"You drive?"

"I—um—usually work out of my house." That was true. "I was just downtown for a meeting. What about you?"

The light changed. Huddled under the umbrella, we started across. Rain lashed the exposed side of my body.

"I work at Midwest National Bank."

"Oh." I hoped I sounded impressed. "What do you do for them?"

"I'm a programmer in IT."

The noise from the storm combined with angry motorists leaning on their horns made it hard to hear.

"Oh." I repeated, louder this time. We crossed Monroe. One more street to cross. "I'm Ellie."

"Cody."

The light turned green.

"There's the bus stop," Cody said. A bus shelter hugged the curb about fifty feet south of the intersection. The bus I'd seen approaching was only a block away. We headed over.

"Cody, thank you so much. For your chivalry. You really are a savior." I was laying it on thick, but he didn't seem to mind. He even smiled. "Hey..." I hesitantly placed my hand on his arm. "Are you in a hurry?"

He looked puzzled.

"Oh, forget it. You probably need to get home. I was just thinking I could maybe buy you a drink. To thank you for being such a gentleman."

"Well... actually..."

* * *

Ten minutes later Cody—his last name was Wegman—and I sat on barstools in Bailey's, a quiet café across from the old Shubert Theater. Concrete planters with red petunias edged an arrangement of empty—and now wet—tables outside. Inside were the requisite dim lights, small tables, and metal-backed chairs. After reapplying my make-up and running a brush through my hair in the ladies room, I half expected to see Georgia when I came out, but there was no sign of her.

I hurried over to Cody and picked up my glass of wine. "So..." I smiled. "A toast to the last of the courtly gentlemen. Thanks again."

He took a swig from his draft and laughed. It was a loud, crude, goofy laugh, the kind that calls attention to itself. A couple at a nearby table looked our way. For an instant I was taken aback. Cody must have realized it, as well—someone probably told him his laugh wasn't socially acceptable—because he abruptly closed his mouth.

I recovered quickly. "Oh, don't be embarrassed. I like it."

"Really?"

"It's—distinctive. No one will ever mistake you for someone else."

Color came into his cheeks, and the look in his eyes deepened. I got the feeling he was trying to come up with a suave reply.

"So..." he said, "... what do you do?"

If that was the best he could come up with, this would be a tough conversation. "I'm a video producer. Mostly industrials—you know, corporate and training videos."

He looked impressed.

"It's a living. But you... you have to be pretty smart to be a programmer. Where did you learn?"

"It's not that you have to be smart. You just need to understand how code is written. I get a lot of help."

"How long have you worked at the bank?"

"About five years."

"That's a lifetime in corporate-speak."

"Sometimes it seems like twenty."

"Why is that?"

He shook his head, and a distant look came over him. "Nothing."

I peered at him. "You're at Midwest National, right?"

"That's right."

I sat up straighter. "Hold on. Isn't that the place where the woman worked? The one who died in the accident a few days ago? The one whose daughter was kidnapped?"

"How do you know that?"

"Um..." I fumbled for a response. "Actually, she lives—lived near me. On the North Shore. A good friend of mine is her neighbor. Christine Messenger." I frowned. "Did you know her?"

"She was my boss."

"You're kidding." I pretended to shiver. "How creepy."

"You live in the suburbs?"

"That's right. I told you, I came downtown for a meeting."

"Then, how come you were taking the bus?"

"I—I'm supposed to meet a friend for dinner. She lives near North. I parked my car there earlier. Of course, I had no idea it would be coming down like this." I made a sweeping gesture.

"Oh."

"How about another?"

"Not yet."

I drained my wine. "So Christine Messenger was your boss. You must be devastated."

"I didn't see that much of her. She was on one side of the floor. I was on the other."

"Was she a good boss?"

He cocked his head. "I never had any complaints."

"What a tragedy. Especially for the daughter. To go through something like a kidnapping, and then to have your mother die." I shivered again, for real this time. I looked over, then paused as if a new thought struck me. "You don't think... I mean... you don't think the two events are related, do you?"

"What do you mean?"

"I mean the newspaper said it was an accident. But the little girl was taken just a week or so ago. The timing is—weird, you know what I mean?"

He leaned forward. "It gets even weirder," he said softly.

"How's that?"

"Her boss, the COO, Mr. Emerlich. He's dead, too."

I feigned shock. "You're kidding."

"His car smashed into a truck on the Eisenhower last week."

"Oh man." I signaled the bartender. "I need another. You?" This time he nodded.

"Another round, please." I ordered. "And a glass of water."

He hesitated. "Look. I'm not supposed to talk about this. The police told us not to."

"My lips are sealed." I picked up my napkin. "It's just so strange. First her kid is kidnapped. And released. Then her boss dies.

Then she does." I paused. "Do you think they were having an affair? You know, Christine and her boss?"

"I wouldn't know."

"You never noticed if they came in or went out together or within a few minutes of each other?"

"No. Chris was always all business—at least with me."

Our drinks came. Plump beads of sweat rolled down my glass of water. I pushed his draft toward him. "So you *don't* think they were having an affair?"

"Like I said, I don't know." His guarded look came back. "Why are you so curious?"

I had to be careful. Cody's brain might be mired in bits and bytes, but his antennae were sharp enough that he realized I was grilling him. "It's just—like I said, it's creepy. And to think we both knew her. I mean, these things just don't happen to me. I live a boring life."

"Me too." He cocked his head and appraised me. Then, as if he'd made a decision, he leaned forward. "There's something else."

A wave of anticipation rippled through me "What?"

"I shouldn't be telling you this."

"Who am I going to tell?"

He took a long pull on his beer. "One of my friends is a supervisor in accounting. Turns out the bank started getting complaints from some of our customers last week."

"What kind of complaints?"

"There was some kind of mysterious service charge on their statements." He leaned forward and lowered his voice. "After a few calls Sandy—that's my friend—decided it must have been some kind of computer glitch. So she went up to talk to Christine about it, but Christine wasn't there. It was just about the time her daughter was released, and she was at home." He paused. "So Sandy went to Emerlich instead."

"Chris's boss."

"Right. And the next day Emerlich was dead."

I mulled it over. "Do the police know about this?"

"I wouldn't know."

My brain was flying off in twenty different directions. Before I realized it, I blurted out, "What's Sandy's last name?"

Cody straightened up. "Why? What I told you is highly confidential."

I tried to cover. "You're—you're right. I don't need to know."

He eyed me suspiciously.

"It's just so eerie."

He kept his mouth shut.

I backed off, and we chatted idly for another few minutes while we finished our drinks. Glancing through the window, I saw the skies had cleared and the sun was peeking through the buildings in the western sky. It was suddenly one of those perfect Chicago summer evenings that made you forget about the *sturm und drang* just moments earlier.

I pulled out some cash from my wallet. "Well, Cody, this has been a lot of fun, but the storm's over, and I ought to get going. My girlfriend probably thinks I drowned."

He leaned close to me and covered my hand with his. "You're really nice, Ellie. Can we get together again? I'm a mystery shopper, and I get all these free coupons to great places, like Applebees, and TGIF. Places like that."

"What's a Mystery Shopper?"

"Oh, man. It's great. You sign up online to rate these places, and they pay your way. Or reimburse you. It's a great way to go out. For instance, I have some coupons for—"

I stammered, flustered. "Um... uh... Cody, that's really flattering, and I think the shopping gig is cool, but I'm old enough to be your mother."

His expression said the idea had already occurred to him and he was okay with it.

I felt heat on my cheeks. "But I'll tell you what. You just made my day."

He shot me a look that was both longing and reproachful. I didn't know if his distress was because he couldn't use his coupons, or if he was truly saddened by my answer. In any case, I melted. "Tell you what. Give me your card. You just never know."

That was the truth, too.

CHAPTER 13

Georgia

While Foreman was in the bar with the bank guy, Georgia drove to Arthur Emerlich's house. Located in Hinsdale not far from Interstate 294, the house was part of a block of stately homes with trees tall enough to have been planted a generation ago. A large red brick colonial with cream trim and black shutters, it was recessed from the street and accessed by a circular driveway. Sedate landscaping suggested substance, not bling. So did the Camry and Buick on the driveway. Georgia got out of her car and shaded her eyes. The snarl of rush-hour traffic, slowed even more by the storm, had doubled her travel time, but now a cheerful sun was shining.

"Yes?" The woman who opened the door had to be somewhere in her sixties. Although petite, her body was all sharp edges and angles, and her short hair was too black. A bad dye job. Despite the heat, she wore heavy gray slacks and a black sweater. A pair of black ballet slippers were on her feet.

"I'm sorry to disturb you, Mrs. Emerlich, but I wonder if I could have a few words." Georgia held out her card. Dierdre Emerlich gave it only a passing glance, as if reading was too much effort. "Who are you?"

"Georgia Davis. I'm an investigator, and I've been hired by Christine Messenger's family to look into her death."

The voices from a radio talk show whispered out from another room. A baby cried, followed by the murmur of a female voice. Mrs. Emerlich frowned in a way that said she was trying to be polite but that Georgia's presence was a distraction. "I heard. What a tragedy."

"You knew her?"

"Of course."

Georgia was surprised by the forthright response. If she'd been suspicious her husband and Messenger were fooling around, wouldn't she be more cautious? Even reluctant? "May I come in?"

"Miss…" Dierdre checked her watch. "We're just about to have dinner. It's a difficult time…" Another cry from the unseen baby. "My daughter and grandson came in from Kansas. If it weren't for him…" Grief was etched into the lines on her face, but at the mention of the baby, her expression smoothed out.

"It took almost two hours to get here. I'll only take a few minutes of your time."

"I don't want to be impolite, but I—"

"This is important, Mrs. Emerlich. It might lead to some answers about your husband's death."

Dierdre hesitated, but a spark of interest caught on her face. She opened the door and led Georgia into a living room. The décor, circa 1960, had the feel of time in a bottle. Dignified but dull furniture. Faded beige carpeting. The only unusual—and colorful—objects were two framed collages of theater playbills on the wall. Georgia remembered Emerlich was on the board of a local theater company.

"Your husband was a supporter of the arts."

Dierdre followed Georgia's gaze. "We both were. I'm an actor, and Arthur produced. It was our passion."

Georgia scanned the frames and found playbills for *Our Town*, *Macbeth*, *The Music Man*, and other dramas she hadn't thought about since high school. If they were theater people, were they the free-spirited types? Not bound by convention? Could Emerlich be sleeping around with Dierdre's tacit permission? The house didn't look bohemian, but physical décor didn't necessarily indicate behavior.

"Mrs. Emerlich, do you have any reason to believe your husband's death was not an accident?"

The woman didn't look surprised. She seated herself on the sofa. "The police asked the same thing. Whether he had any enemies. I kept telling them no. Arthur was beloved. By everyone." The baby cried again. She swallowed. "The baby keeps asking where PopPop is."

"So you don't think it was an accident?"

She looked down at her ballet slippers, flexed her feet, pointed her toes. "Arthur bought a Mercedes two years ago. It was his baby. He took care of it—well, like Carol takes care of Sam. I can't believe he would have let the brake fluid drain out."

Georgia nodded. She hated to ask the next question. She eased into it. "How well did your husband know Christine Messenger?"

"You mean was he having an affair with her?" Georgia's pulse sped up until she saw the shadow of a smile cross Dierdre's face. "If he was, more power to him. Arthur had prostate surgery last year. He wasn't—the straightest fork in the dishwasher." She clasped her knees and rocked forward. "He enjoyed attention, of course. All theater people do. My friends used to call him a flirt. But that's as far as it went. He knew where to draw the line."

"Can you remember any comments he made about Chris?"

"Actually, we talked about her quite a lot. He was concerned. In a paternal way. Being divorced. Having the child. She used to bring Molly out here every once in a while. She called us Molly's surrogate grandparents." She paused. "I think she was grateful we were there."

Georgia's skepticism must have shown on her face.

"Look, I know where you're trying to go. The other detective tried, too. But Art wasn't that way. I never saw any hints of it, and believe me, I know. I'm an actor. I recognize the tics, the looks, the body language when you're hiding something. Arthur didn't have any secrets. We were married nearly fifty years, you know."

"Were *you* ever unfaithful?"

Dierdre's mouth opened. "What kind of question is that?"

"I'm sorry. You're right. You don't have to—"

"You know something?" She cut in. "I'll answer that. Because it might prove something. The answer is yes. I was unfaithful. Art and I had been married six months, and I thought I'd made a horrible mistake. I started seeing a man I used to go out with. He was also married, but we had an affair. I pulled all the tricks you pull when you're involved with someone. About two months later I realized I'd made the right choice after all and that Art was the man I wanted to spend my life with. So you see, I know what unfaithful spouses do. Art wasn't capable of deception. There was no way he was having an affair with Chris."

* * *

"So where do we find the accounting supervisor?" Ellie asked the next morning.

"*We* don't. I do," Georgia said.

They were in Foreman's kitchen. When Georgia had climbed back into her car in Hinsdale, she found three messages from Ellie on her cell. They discussed what Ellie had learned. The next morning, Georgia drove to her house. Cruising up Green Bay Road, she had the eerie sense that someone was following her. She slowed, hoping to catch a glimpse of whoever was tailing her, but she saw no one. When she arrived at Foreman's, she even searched under the carriage of the Toyota for a bug or GPS locator. Nothing.

Inside, Ellie held up a pot of coffee. The rich aroma filled the room. "How do you take it?"

"Black." Georgia sat at the table.

Ellie poured and slid a mug toward Georgia. "So what do you think?"

"I'm trying not to make any assumptions."

"Apparently there were a lot of complaints about this service charge. If someone slapped—say a ten dollar charge on 10,000 accounts—that would add up to serious money. Money that could have been used for a ransom."

"Are you saying Chris was putting one over on everyone? That there was a ransom demand after all? And she somehow paid it with these service charges?"

Ellie nodded.

Georgia frowned. "I don't know. It's too soon to connect the dots. I have to find out more. When the charges were levied. How much. On which accounts. There could be a perfectly legitimate reason."

"What if you find out the service charges were levied on the same day or the day before Molly was released? Wouldn't that clinch it?"

Georgia shrugged and sipped her coffee.

Ellie set the coffee pot down. "Hold on. She *did* go down to the office, remember? To pick up her laptop. Didn't you tell me O'Malley said—"

"I'm way ahead of you. If—and that's a big 'if '—ransom money changed hands via the bank, the internet, or any other means—why was Arthur Emerlich killed? Messenger either, for that matter?"

"Because the accounting supervisor figured out what happened and told Emerlich?"

Georgia raised three fingers. "Three problems. Assuming the kidnapper got what he wanted, why would he care how Chris came up with the money? It'd be her neck on the chopping block, not his. Second, how would the kidnapper have figured out Emerlich knew about them? And third, it's rare for a kidnapper to come back once he's negotiated a successful ransom. Almost never happens."

"Maybe the accountant found where Chris parked the money."

"That would have been pretty stupid, wouldn't it? I mean, Chris was the director of IT. Wouldn't she know how to hide money so it wouldn't lead back to her—or the kidnapper?"

"Maybe that was her way of letting people know who did it."

"They had her daughter, Ellie. They were going to kill her if she didn't meet their demands. If it was Rachel, would you take the time leave a clue so people could figure out who did it?"

"You're right." Foreman sighed. "You think the police are asking the same questions as we are?"

"Hard to say." Georgia closed her hands around the mug. "If they are, they might even be farther along. They have resources we don't."

"I could call Cody back. Maybe get Sandy's last name."

Georgia shook her head. "I appreciate it, but you've done enough. For now."

Ellie pursed her lips. "Just tell me one thing, Does that mean you're dropping the pregnancy angle? Her secret lover and/or a jealous wife or girlfriend?"

"Everything's still on the table. Why?"

"Because I spoke to my friend Susan and found out who Terry Messenger was dating."

Georgia sat up straighter. "Is that so?"

"The woman's a pathologist at Rush. I can arrange to bump into her if you want."

"Not right now. If I need more help, I'll let you know."

CHAPTER 14

Back in her apartment, Georgia picked up the phone and called Midwest National Bank. A recorded greeting offered her a laundry list of options. Normally Georgia would be irritated by the antiseptic, depersonalized, and largely useless nature of business communication, but today, that was exactly what she was counting on. She pressed "4" for the bank's departmental directory, then "8" for Accounting. The system prompted her for an individual, but she didn't know Sandy's last name, so she punched "o." Eventually a real person came on the line.

"Hello. I'm trying to find Sandy in accounting. She's a supervisor. The problem is I don't know her last name. Can you help me?"

The operator's voice was cool. "We don't release employees' names as a matter of policy."

Georgia sighed audibly. "In that case, what would you suggest I do?"

"I really couldn't say." The voice was frigid.

Georgia forced herself to remain polite. "Then, perhaps you could connect me to the general accounting extension."

"One moment."

A series of clicks ensued, followed by a female voice. "This is Laura. How may I help you?"

"Hello, I'm one of your customers, and I got a call from someone named Sandy in accounting. But my secretary must have written her last name incorrectly because I couldn't find her on the automated system. Can you help me?"

"Oh. Are you calling about the service charges?" Laura sounded friendly.

"Um... as a matter of fact... I am."

"You want Sandy Sechrest. Her extension is 4397. I'll transfer you."

"Thank you." Georgia smiled to herself as the transfer proceeded. Sandy Sechrest's phone rang four times, then went to voice-mail. Georgia hung up without leaving a message, and went online to a White Pages Directory. No Sandy Sechrest. Or S. Sechrest. She sighed and checked one of her subscription databases. Nothing. Finally, she went to Kroll and entered the paltry information she had. S. Sechrest was listed on the 4800 block of North Claremont, Ravenswood. She jotted down the address and the phone number.

That evening, she drove down from Evanston. Sechrest's block was a tidy residential area made up of sturdy row houses and small apartment buildings. A construction dumpster was wedged between parked cars at one end of the block. Georgia remembered hearing how Ravenswood property values had skyrocketed since the neighborhood had taken on the more fashionable name of "Lincoln Square." But the area still had a homey feel, and as she got out of the Toyota and slammed the door, a squirrel scurried up a nearby tree.

Sechrest's home was a small, older brick row house with a porch in front. The home looked neat and in good repair, but it hadn't been renovated. The porch, with latticed slats below it, reminded Georgia of her childhood home on the West side where she used to play hide and seek. One day she'd hidden herself so well that her mother couldn't find her. She remembered her mother's frantic yells, and how, when she finally revealed herself, giggling at her subterfuge, her mother had seized her and held on much too tight. "Never hide from Mommy again, Peaches. Mommy gets scared when she can't find you."

Ironic, given that her mother walked out a few years later.

Now she mounted the steps and pressed the doorbell. A thin buzzer sounded. No response. She rang again. Nothing. She knocked. Still no response, Georgia wondered if she had the right Sechrest. Or whether Sechrest might be living elsewhere, with a boyfriend for example, and used this place only when they had a fight. She tried to peek through the blinds but couldn't see anything.

She clattered down the steps and strode to the house next door. Although the layout looked like a carbon copy of Sechrest's, it wasn't in very good shape. The steps up to the porch were rickety, the exterior needed a coat of paint, and the eaves above the door sagged. The windows, double-hung with an old-fashioned lock, looked about a hundred years old.

Georgia rang the bell. A buzzer identical to Sechrest's sounded, and she heard feet shuffling almost immediately, as if whoever was there had been expecting her. The door remained closed, but a thin male voice called out.

"Who's there?"

If he'd been spying on her, he already knew, but she played along.

"Sorry to bother you, sir," Georgia said. "I'm a private investigator, and I'm looking for Sandy Sechrest."

"Name?"

"Georgia Davis."

"How do I know you're who you say you are?"

She pulled out a card, bent down, and slid it under the door. "Here's my card."

There was silence, then a phlegmy cough.

"You're Davis?"

"Yes sir."

"How do I know you didn't just get those cards made up so you could get me to open the door?"

"Sir, I'll be happy to show you my driver's license, but I won't slide it under the door."

"Show it to me through the window."

Shaking her head, she fished for her license and took it out of her wallet. The glass was covered by a dark curtain, but a bony hand appeared and lifted the material. She could just make out a frail, elderly man with pale skin. He was wearing a striped bathrobe. She pressed her license against the glass. Squinting, he took his time examining it. Then he looked her up and down. "Anyone with you?"

"No, sir. Just me."

More coughs. He gestured to the front door. Georgia stepped toward it.

He opened it. "Can't be too careful these days, you know."

"I understand." She slipped her license back in her wallet and extended her hand.

"And you are?"

"Guy Lasalla. Lived here over fifty years."

Lasalla looked to be in his eighties and was bald except for a soft gray frizz on the sides of his head. His nose was red and bulbous, his eyes rheumy, and he needed a shave. Georgia smelled alcohol on his breath. Although she couldn't see into the house, it smelled of too many cats and too few litter boxes. She stepped back. She didn't like cats.

"Thank you for speaking to me, Mr. Lasalla. As I said, I'm looking for Sandy Sechrest. Do you know where I can find her?"

He cackled an old man's cackle. "Join the club."

"What do you mean?"

"You're not the first person to come lookin' for her. But you are the first 'un I opened the door for."

She smiled gratefully, although she wondered who else had been here. But first things first. "I take it Sandy's not here."

"Hell no. She took off like a bat outta hell a couple days ago."

"When, exactly?"

"Over the weekend."

A striped tabby cat suddenly appeared and rubbed himself against the man's bare leg. Lasalla scooped it up and started to massage the back of its neck. The cat blinked disdainfully at Georgia as if to say, "See what I can get anytime I want?" Arrogant creatures, Georgia thought, not for the first time.

"Do you know where Sandy went?"

Both man and cat stared at her. Georgia had the sense they didn't think her worthy of being told. But she needed information. "You said someone else came looking for her. Did you get as good a look at them as you did me?"

The cat jumped down and streaked back into the gloom.

"Mr. Lasalla, I think Sandy might know something—something important. I need to find her. Before whoever else is looking for her does."

"It's about her job, isn't it? Those two bankers who died."

"It could be."

Lasalla rubbed the grizzled hair on and under his chin. He pulled a few folds of loose flesh in the process. "She did look pretty scared."

"Who else came here?"

"Don't know. A man."

"What did he look like?"

"Only saw him from a distance. A ball cap hid his face."

"Tall? Short? Fat? Thin?"

"Average."

"What about his clothes?"

"Jeans. Black t-shirt, I think."

"Do you remember what kind of car he was driving?"

"Dark. Black maybe."

"A sedan?"

"Dunno. It was practically dark when he drove up."

"When?"

"Last night."

"Any license plates you could see?"

"Sorry."

It wasn't much, but it fit O'Malley's description of the car Molly came back in when she was released.

"You didn't talk to him?"

LaSalla hesitated. "I didn't say that."

Georgia felt a spit of irritation. "I thought you said I was the first one you talked to."

"I said you was the first one I opened the door for."

"What did you talk about, with the other guy?"

"He came over. Same as you. Asked where she was."

"You talked to him through the door."

When Lasalla nodded, she asked, "Did you card him, too?"

"Sure I did."

"So what was the name on his license?"

"Hell if I know."

Georgia blinked.

"I can't see a damn thing without my reading glasses. Just wanted to let him know I know what I'm doing."

"Same as me," Georgia said dully.

"Right."

"So what did you say?"

"Same thing I told you. That she left two days ago."

"Over the weekend."

"Right."

"Does Sandy have a boyfriend? Or any family members she might have gone to?"

"Her father lives in Cicero. About my age, he is. But he's in a nursing home."

"His name would be Sechrest?"

"No. That was her married name."

"She was married?"

"For fifteen years. She's divorced now."

"Do you know her maiden name?"

"Sorry." He shook his head.

"Did you tell the man who came looking for her everything you just told me?"

"Pretty much."

Georgia blew out a tired breath. This was a disaster. She wound up the conversation and was on her way back to the car when LaSalla called after her. "Hold on, there, miss. There is something I didn't tell the other guy."

CHAPTER 15

The smell of pine mingled with the stink of skunk as Georgia drove up County Road G near Necedah in central Wisconsin. She rolled up her window. It was after eleven, and the journey had taken four hours. She would have been there earlier but for the construction on every possible roadway leading out of Chicago. Barrels, cones, and concrete barriers had overrun the expressways, like some alien creatures invading Earth.

She'd prodded Guy LaSalla until he admitted that the Sechrest family had a summer cabin on Castle Rock Lake. The chances were good Sechrest was either there or close by. Georgia raced home, threw a few things into her Toyota, and set off. She hoped to arrive before midnight. Not a good time to drop in unannounced, but, given the fact that someone else was pursuing Sechrest, Georgia had no choice. She hoped she wasn't too late.

She rolled down the window. The skunk smell had dissipated, and a late night breeze rustled the leaves. She drove through a thickly wooded area with hardly any road signs. Luckily, she'd bought a portable GPS a few days ago. Although it was pricey, buying it had been a smart decision. No more worrying about how far the next turn was or overshooting her mark. It was especially helpful at night, when a brightly illuminated screen pointed the way.

According to Cody Wegman, Sechrest was investigating the service charges that had been levied. What kind of service charges? How many accounts were charged? What was Sechrest supposed to be doing about them? Georgia knew next to nothing about banking. She parked her money in a checking account. Sometimes she made a few dollars in interest, although they were usually wiped out by ATM charges. She also had a few thousand dollars in a CD. Mad money, her mother used to call it. But that was the extent of her financial planning.

The GPS indicated a right turn ahead. She glanced at the screen. She was ten miles from Castle Rock Lake. A quick Google search before she left told her Castle Rock was the fourth largest lake in Wisconsin. About forty miles northwest of the Wisconsin Dells, it was shaped like the letter "V." In between the V was Buck-horn State Park. To the north was Lake Petenwell, the second largest lake in the state, but aside from a few towns ringing the lake, civilization was sparse.

As she headed east, the trees thickened, and a canopy of leaves closed over her. The moon, which had been over her shoulder for most of the drive, disappeared. The only light was the throw from her headlamps. Georgia preferred flat terrain and wide open spaces. Limited sightlines and inky darkness made her uneasy. She tried to imagine pushing the trees apart like Moses parting the Red Sea.

There weren't many cars on the road, which at first surprised her. It was the middle of summer; shouldn't she be passing families on vacation, fishermen, other lake-lovers? Then again, it was late. Maybe everyone around here went to bed early and rose at the crack of dawn to fish. She slowed to make a curve in the road. Over the chirp of crickets, she heard a lower-pitched bleat. Frogs. She must be near the lake.

The sudden ring of her cell phone pierced the silence. Georgia pulled to the side of the road. She checked the incoming number. She didn't recognize it.

"Davis." She kept her voice low, as if loud noise would disturb the nocturnal landscape.

"Georgia, it's Terry Messenger."

She'd tried to reach him before she left Evanston but had to leave a message.

"Thanks for calling me back."

"What's up?"

A mosquito or two or ten hummed near her ears. She swatted at them and rolled up the window. "I thought you should know. Someone is still prowling around the edges of this—situation." She explained about Sandy Sechrest, her sudden disappearance, and the man who'd shown up at her house.

"Oh, Christ." His voice was raw. "I can't—I mean, Molly—should I hire some protection?"

"I don't think they're after Molly this time. I think it has to do with something at the bank."

"Which involved Chris?"

"Yes."

There was a pause. Then he said, "What the hell was she doing?"

"I don't know." She paused. "Look, I called because the case is going into a new direction, and I need to ask if you want to pursue it. Officially, the cops are still saying Chris's death was an accident, and I'm not sure they'll change their opinion, despite their investigation. So, here's the thing—you have a choice. I think it's safe to say they've gotten what they want from Molly. And Chris. I doubt they'll be coming back. I can understand if you want to get out."

"If I did, would you drop it?"

She hesitated again. Two people were dead, a little girl was traumatized. The kidnappers, whoever they were, were now rich. And free. And might do it all over again to someone else's daughter. "No comment."

"Where are you now?"

"In central Wisconsin. Following a lead."

Terry's voice was harsh. "My daughter may be safe, but some asshole took her mother away. Molly will never know what it's like to have a mother help her plan her wedding, babysit her grandchildren. I want to find the bastards who did it. They need to pay."

Georgia realized that's what she'd hoped he'd say. "Okay. You got it."

But—Georgia?"

"Yes?"

"Be careful."

Georgia looked across the car. Her Sig Sauer lay on the passenger seat. She'd cleaned and oiled and loaded it before she left.

"You can count on it."

* * *

When she reached Castle Rock Lake, she drove around the western prong of the "V." Guy Lasalla had told her Sandy Sechrest drove a red Honda Accord and that her family's cabin was on the southwest shore of the lake. Most of the cabins ringing the water were set back from a narrow road. Georgia slowed as she passed several driveways.

It was almost midnight when she found the Honda. A silvery shaft of moonlight flickered through the trees, turning the red purple, but the Accord had a distinctive shape that was easy to recognize. She drove past a dirt driveway that was studded with stones and pulled to the side of the road. Then she reversed and turned the Toyota around so she was facing the direction from which she'd come.

She slipped her Sig into her holster, grabbed a small but powerful flashlight, and got out of the car.

The cabin was a small log structure with two tiny windows on either side of the door. Behind it was a dark expanse of yard that Georgia assumed led to the lake. She stood next to the Accord, getting the feel of her surroundings and letting her night vision adjust. Despite the late hour, the air was warm. Tomorrow would be a scorcher. The sound of frogs had ceased, but the whine of insects and other creatures hummed. An image of Pete, her neighbor, flashed through her mind. He loved the woods and the lake and the wilderness. But Georgia was a city rat. This felt unfamiliar.

She made her way toward the cabin, trying to decide how to approach Sechrest. Most people would be scared shitless if a stranger showed up at their home in the middle of the night. Georgia would be. But someone else was looking for Sechrest, and Georgia had no way of knowing when he would find her. Or if they already had. She couldn't wait.

A high-pitched shriek made her freeze in her tracks. She grabbed the Sig from her holster. She couldn't see anyone or anything. Nothing seemed to be moving. A series of short screeches followed. An owl. She let out her breath and reholstered the Sig. Then she shivered. She couldn't help herself.

Three feet from the door to the cabin, a branch snapped under her foot. She stepped around it and continued up to the door. A light automatically flashed on, startling her at first. The chirr of insects grew louder. She lifted her hand and knocked.

"Sandy, are you in there?"

There was no response.

"I know it's late and I don't want to scare you. My name is Georgia Davis, and I'm an investigator working for Christine Messenger's family."

Nothing.

She knocked again. "Sandy, I know you're in there. Please talk to me."

Still no response. Was Sechrest that sound a sleeper? Or was it something else? The flashlight was in her left hand. She wondered if she should turn it on and look through a window.

"Sandy, I know you ran because you're scared. I would be too. And I want to help, but time is running out. Please, if you're in there, talk to me."

Georgia thought she might have heard a floorboard creak inside the cabin. Adrenaline streaked through her. She let her right hand brush against her holster.

"Sandy?"

Suddenly a voice rang out from inside. "Drop your weapon in front of the door. Along with some ID."

Georgia froze.

"Did you hear me? Drop the gun. And let me see your license."

Georgia slid the Sig out of her holster and laid the flashlight at the door. Then she reached for her back pocket and extracted her driver's license. She put that down by the door. With her other hand she leveled her Sig at the door.

A moment later, the door opened a crack. An arm snaked out and grabbed the flashlight and her license. The door closed. Then it opened again, just wide enough for Georgia to see the barrel of a shotgun aimed at her chest.

CHAPTER 16

Time slowed down, softening the edges of Georgia's awareness. All that was real was the night, the barrel of the shotgun, and her Sig. "Drop the fucking gun," Sechrest ordered, "or I'll blow your head off."

Despite the harsh words, the woman's voice was high-pitched and full of fear. And frightened people do irrational things. If she didn't lay down the gun, Sandy Sechrest might do exactly what she threatened. And while Georgia might get off a shot herself, a bloodbath wouldn't serve anyone's purpose. She chose her words carefully.

"Okay, Sandy. Let's not either of us do anything we'll regret. I'll put down my gun if you'll do the same. Like I said, I'm not here to hurt you." Georgia bent over to lay down her Sig.

"Hands up," Sechrest said.

Georgia straightened, her hands in the air. "You've got to be pretty freaked out, Sandy. I understand. I'm here to help." She wanted to get a look at her, see what her face showed, but the door was ajar only about eight inches, and all she could make out was the outline of Sechrest's body. She looked to be about as tall as Georgia, but heavier by twenty soft pounds. Her cop instincts told her she could take Sechrest if she had to. But she wasn't a cop. She was a PI, following a lead. She prayed the woman didn't have an itchy finger.

How much time had passed? A second? A minute? An hour? If the woman didn't back down in another second, she'd have to act.

"Sandy, I did what you wanted. Now put the shotgun down. We have to talk, and we don't have much time. Someone else may be coming for you."

"Who are you working for?" The woman asked.

"I told you. Terry Messenger. Chris Messenger's ex-husband."

There was an intake of breath. The owl screeched again. Georgia heard small creatures scuttling deep in the woods. Suddenly the woman's face collapsed. The shotgun pointed at the floor. Sechrest's shoulders started to heave, and Georgia heard repetitive, wrenching sobs that were oddly similar to the owl's cries. "I knew it wasn't an accident. Oh god."

Georgia sagged in relief. "I'm coming in now, okay, Sandy?"

The woman nodded and turned away from the door. She was still carrying the shotgun. Georgia walked in, but not before slipping her Sig back in her holster. "Sandy, do me a favor. Put the shotgun down. I'm a former police officer. I get nervous around guns."

"But what if... what if we need it?"

Georgia smelled fear on Sechrest's body. Was the woman still rational? "Just put it somewhere safe while we talk."

The woman hesitated, looked around, finally laid it on the kitchen table.

"Now, can you turn on a light?"

"No way!" Sechrest's voice was laced with panic. "There aren't any curtains on the windows. Anyone can see in."

"Did you forget your Honda's out front? How do you think I found you?"

"That's just a car... it doesn't mean I'm here too." But she sounded less certain.

Georgia forced herself to remain calm and not tell her how naïve she was. "Listen. You heard me drive up, right?"

"Of course. Heard you way down the road."

"So if we hear anything, we'll douse the lights before they get here."

"I don't know."

"Sandy, I know you've been alone. But I'm here now, and I'm on your side."

This time it seemed to work. Sechrest moved heavily to the couch and switched on a small lamp. Georgia blinked. The room was a combination living room, dining area, and kitchen. A narrow hallway led to an open bathroom door and a bedroom. A cracked leather couch was draped with a plaid tartan blanket. Beside it was a Lazyboy that had seen better days. The kitchen table was not much bigger than a card table, with four folding chairs around it.

Georgia sat on the couch and patted the seat beside her.

Sechrest sat. Her long blond hair was dirty and disheveled. She was dressed in flipflops, sweat pants and a black t-shirt with the outline of a panda bear on the front. She started to rock back and forth. Tears streamed down her cheeks.

"I can't do this any more," she sobbed. "It's like a horror movie. I keep wondering when I'm gonna wake up. But I never do."

Georgia gave her time to pull herself together. "Start at the beginning."

Sechrest looked up and wiped a sleeve across her face, then settled back against the cushion. When she spoke, her voice was stronger. "Right before the Fourth of July people started complaining about the service charges."

"How did you get involved?"

"I get computer generated logs of most of the bank's transactions. My job is to look them over and check for any unauthorized entries. After the calls came in, the CFO of the bank asked me to look into the matter."

"And what did you find?"

"It took me a while to find the right log. But once I did, I discovered that every account in the bank had been assessed a ten dollar service charge."

"Which is unusual."

"Highly." A look of impatience paged across Sechrest's face.

That was good, Georgia thought. She was regaining her bearings.

"It just doesn't happen that way. The thing is, the amount was so small. Only ten dollars." She sniffed. "Our commercial accounts, which are on analysis, probably never even saw it. But all the little old ladies who bank with us have eagle eyes. You wouldn't believe the calls we get. They always think the bank is out to screw them. Then again, any unexpected charge does have an effect if you're on a fixed income."

"What day were the charges levied?"

"Wednesday, June twenty-fifth."

Molly Messenger had been released by her kidnappers that afternoon.

"At first I thought it was a computer glitch. You know, someone in data processing was tinkering with some software, and it got screwed up."

"Right."

"So I called Chris Messenger. She's—she was the IT Director."

Georgia counted back the days. Christine's fatal "accident" was on Friday, July fourth. "When was that?"

"On Tuesday, July first. When I checked the Daily Transaction Journal for the twenty-fifth." It came out quickly, as though Sechrest had already done the math and knew the two events were connected.

"A week after the charges first appeared."

"Sometimes it takes that long for the customer to notice things. Especially when they only get a statement once a month."

"Go on."

"I called Chris, but she wasn't there. She was at home with her daughter. After that horrible..."

"Kidnapping." Georgia finished.

The knowing look in Sechrest's eyes intensified.

"Did you leave Chris a message?"

Sandy swallowed. "That was the problem. I left my name. My extension. My title. Why I was calling. Everything."

Georgia winced. If Chris—or anyone else—had listened to Messenger's voicemail on that Tuesday, they'd know everything too. "Then what happened?"

"Well, like I said, the CFO was on me to get this thing cleared up. He was getting flak from the chairman. She shook her head. "Everyone was getting into the act. So I called Mr. Emerlich."

"Arthur Emerlich."

"He was the VP of Operations. The COO."

"And Chris Messenger's boss."

Sechrest nodded.

"When did you call him?"

"The same afternoon. I couldn't reach Christine. He didn't know anything about it but said he'd try to get to the bottom of it." A haunted expression crept across her face. "He died the next day." She tensed. "But, here's the thing. I came in early the next morning to work on the problem. Before I knew Emerlich was dead. That's when I found it."

Georgia found herself tensing, too. "Found what?"

"Any time you go into bank records, you leave a trail—your fingerprints, really—of what you do and when you do it. It's supposed to be that way, so if there's ever any questions or irregularities, we can track them and see who or what went wrong. Usually, it's just carelessness. Someone enters the wrong numbers, so the totals are off, stuff like that." She stopped and she tilted her head. Her face took on a fearful expression. "Did you hear something outside?"

Georgia was concentrating so hard on Sechrest's words she hadn't been paying attention. She quickly got up, turned off the light, and went to the window. Nothing was moving. Even the breeze had died.

"What kind of noise did you hear?"

"Something crunching on gravel."

Georgia squinted. "I don't see anything."

"You sure?"

Nodding, she returned to the couch and turned the light back on. "So, you were saying…"

Sechrest hugged her knees and rocked forward. "Every employee has their own ID number. Whenever you log in—whether it's to do a transaction, or even just to review them, it shows up. Anyway, when I checked the Daily Transaction Journal, I saw an offset for a lot of money had occurred the same day the service charges were levied."

"An offset?"

"A credit to an account. Of course, that happens all the time, but this credit was exactly the same amount as the total of the service charges."

"Which was?"

"Three million dollars."

Georgia whistled.

"I was still thinking it was all just a mistake. But then I checked another log. Turns out the ID number of the person responsible for the credit to the account was Chris Messenger."

"What are you saying?"

"It seemed as if Chris put all the services charges into a dummy account."

"What's a dummy account?"

"It's basically just an electronic account. There are no paper files on record, no signature cards, no OFAC checks, no bank officer signature signing off on it. All that's there is the electronic account."

"And Chris opened it?"

"Not only did she open it, but she closed it, too."

Georgia frowned. "I don't get it."

"The account was opened around the beginning of June. By Chris Messenger. At least, her ID number was on the paperwork." Sechrest paused. "What's more, she authorized three million dollars to be withdrawn the same day."

"On June first?"

"That's right."

Georgia went quiet. That made no sense. Messenger couldn't have embezzled three million dollars for a ransom three weeks *before* her daughter was kidnapped. Unless she stole the money for another reason. "What happened to the three million?"

"Three cashiers' checks were issued from that account. Each for a million dollars. But, you see, there's a catch."

"What?"

"Technically, there wasn't any money in the account to pay those checks."

"No money? Now I'm totally confused."

"It gets complicated. Especially if you don't understand banking. Basically, what we had was an overdraft for three million dollars on the account that Chris opened."

"Did Chris know?"

"Absolutely."

"How can you be sure?"

"Because in order to *close* an account, you either have to eliminate the overdraft, or the bank ends up taking a loss. Which, for a bank of our size, would be catastrophic. It appears that Chris monkeyed around with the computer system—she was the head of IT, remember—and issued the service charges which totaled three million, put them into the account so it *looked* like the account had been funded. Then she promptly turned around and closed the account."

Georgia had so many questions she wasn't sure where to start. "When was the account closed?"

"Wednesday, June twenty-fifth."

"The same day the service charges were levied."

"Right."

The day Chris had been escorted downtown by the police, ostensibly to get her laptop. The day Molly was released. Is that when she'd "monkeyed" with the system? But why? None of it made any sense. "Who did the cashiers' checks go to?"

Sechrest shook her head. "I don't know. Recipients aren't on the reports I have access to. Just numbers. We scan all our checks, so I was planning to look up the scanned images, but I didn't have time." She ran her hand up her arm. "But, you see, that's not the end of it."

"There's more?" Georgia ran a hand across her brow.

"A lot more. But by the time I discovered the other pieces, Emerlich and Chris were both dead, and I knew I had to split."

"Tell me."

Sechrest rearranged herself on the couch "See, there was a—" She stopped short as a light flashed through the window. "Oh my god!"

CHAPTER 17

Georgia snapped off the light, pulled out her Sig, and dropped to the floor. "Get down. Now!" But Sechrest appeared to be frozen. "Jesus, Jesus," she moaned. "I told you there was a noise. Oh fuck!" "Did you hear me, Sandy?" She hissed. "Get down on the god-dammed floor." Finally Sandy rolled off the couch onto the floor. "I'm getting the shotgun."

"No. Let me handle it."

"Like you handled the noise? No way."

Georgia winced. Sechrest was right. She'd let down her guard. One of the first things you learn as a cop is to be aware of your surroundings. She'd been too interested in what Sechrest was saying.

Sechrest thumped over to the table and retrieved the gun.

"You know how to handle a shotgun?" Georgia asked.

"Are you kidding? My father taught me when I was a kid."

Georgia nodded, more to herself. It would have to do. She crawled to the window and stood to one side. Inclining her head, she cautiously peered out. Headlights were approaching Sechrest's cabin. A sedan, she thought. Dark. Like the car that stopped by Sechrest's house.

The car slid to a stop before turning into Sechrest's driveway, and Georgia realized they'd spotted her Toyota. Shit. She'd left it at the edge of the road in case she needed a quick getaway. Which meant whoever was in the sedan could see her plates and probably identify her.

"Can you tell who it is?" Sechrest sounded panicked.

"No."

"Christ. What are we going to do?"

Georgia thought about it. She and Sechrest both had a weapon. If only one or two people were in the car, they could give as good as they'd get. But what if there were four of them, not one or two? And what if Sechrest didn't really know how to shoot? And what would happen to Georgia if she got away but Sechrest didn't? The woman was just about to tell her something important about Chris Messenger and the bank. There were too many unknowns to make a stand. After expending so much effort to find her, Georgia couldn't afford the risk of something bad happening. "Is there a back door?"

"No."

"Is there any way out of here beside the front?"

"My little brother used to crawl out the bathroom window."

"Let's go."

"There's no way I'll fit," Sechrest said.

"I'll make sure you do."

The door to the sedan opened, and a figure slipped out of the car. Medium height. Burly. A man. But the dome light didn't come on—he must have disconnected it—so Georgia didn't get a good look at him. She could see he was carrying something long and narrow. A shotgun? A rifle? Georgia was torn: part of her wanted to take him, but every second she delayed meant less time to escape. "Let's go. Now."

Sechrest faltered as she got up. The shotgun was tilting her off balance.

"Maybe you should leave it," Georgia said. "I've got a gun."

"Not on your life." Sechrest's voice was resolute. "The bathroom's this way."

They stumbled through the dark to the bathroom. Georgia shoved aside the shower curtain. Her heart sank. The window, above the bathtub, sat behind a tiled ledge, but was only fifteen inches square. She wasn't even sure she could squeeze through. But it was their only option. Thankfully, it was square, not casement. She wouldn't have to detach the glass, a task that would cost precious time.

Georgia raised the window. A mesh screen was in the way. She pulled an army knife out of her pocket and slashed through it.

"Can you hear anything?" She whispered.

"No." Sechrest whispered back.

If Sechrest's heart was pounding as loud as hers, Georgia thought, it would be hard for her to hear anything.

Georgia hoisted herself up to the shelf and thrust her head through the window. It was only about six feet off the ground. If she could squeeze through, she could fold her arms and legs and drop into a roll as she fell. She might not hurt herself too badly. She stretched out her arms, using them as leverage to push herself through the small space, but her shoulders got stuck. They were broad, perhaps even wider than her hips. She wriggled and pushed and squeezed; shrugging one, then the other. Finally, her left shoulder jutted through, leaving a nasty scrape on the fleshy part of her arm. She'd be sore for a week.

Her torso slipped through but jammed at her hips. She swiveled and angled herself up forty-five degrees. Her hips wouldn't budge.

"Shit."

Straining, she tried to wiggle her hips through, using her arms for purchase on the side of the house. All at once, she burst through, but with so much momentum there was no time to curl up. She pitched forward and fell on the ground. She lay in the grass, trying to catch her breath. A sharp pain shot down her left arm. She got up carefully, levering it up and down. As she did, light flooded the back yard.

Georgia gasped. Her heart hammered in her chest. "What the—"

"It's a light sensor," Sechrest said. "It turns on whenever there's motion in the back."

"Great. Nothing like being sitting ducks."

"It'll turn off as soon we're out of range. You can't see it from the front, anyway. The trees mask it. That's how my brother was able to sneak out."

"I sure as hell hope so." Georgia shook it off. "All right. Your turn, Sandy."

Sechrest handed the shotgun down to Georgia, who propped it against the house.

"Arms first," Georgia said.

Sechrest promptly got stuck.

"Shrug your shoulders one side at a time. And try to angle your body. Even an inch at a time is progress."

Sechrest grunted with the effort but made scant headway. They were losing time. Georgia grabbed Sechrest's arms and pulled.

The woman wriggled and squirmed and moaned as the metal window frame scraped her skin. Finally, she managed to shove through the window. Like Georgia, she collapsed on the ground.

While Sechrest was pulling herself together, Georgia tried to come up with a plan. They couldn't escape in her Toyota—they'd run straight into their pursuer. Sechrest's neighbor's cabin was on one side, a densely wooded area lay on the other. Castle Rock Lake was directly ahead.

A gust of wind blew her hair across her face. She pushed it behind her ears. "What's on the other side of the woods?" Georgia asked.

"The main road. But not for a mile or so."

"What's down at the lake?"

"A dock. We share it with our neighbors."

A thump and rustle sounded from the front of the cabin. Then something jiggled. He was rattling the door knob.

Sechrest gripped the shotgun. "Shit!" She whispered. "He's trying to get inside!"

"Is there a boat?"

More rattling. "A dinghy down by the dock. Why?"

Georgia started jogging toward the dock.

"We can't take the boat. Talk about sitting ducks!"

"Come on." Georgia persisted.

As they approached it, she heard the crash of wood splintering. He'd broken in. They didn't have much time.

The dock was dimly lit by the light from the back of the house. Georgia made a quick visual sweep of the dock. She spotted a rusty life preserver and an old tarp crumpled against the edge. The dinghy lay upside down a few yards away. An idea occurred to her. She ran to it and started to turn it over. "Sandy," she hissed. "Help me."

"I told you. We can't go out. He'll come after us. Or shoot us from shore."

"Trust me." She didn't have time to explain.

Sechrest's fear must have been stronger than her need for clarity because she came over and together they flipped over the dinghy. As they dragged it down to the water's edge, Georgia turned around. A chill raced up her spine. The light at the back of the house had gone off, but the beam from a flashlight was bobbing and weaving through the bathroom window from which they'd just escaped. Another minute and he would be outside with them.

Sechrest turned and saw the flashlight beam. "Oh god! Oh god. Oh god!" Her frantic whispers sounded like a broken record.

"Sandy, get it together. We *are* going to make it." Georgia raced back to the dock, grabbed the tarp, and threw it into the dinghy. Suddenly light kicked on from the back of the house. The motion sensor. She turned around. The figure was outside, clearly silhouetted against the light. A man. He lifted his left hand and spread the fingers to shade his eyes against the glare. His hand looked like it was missing most of his index finger.

Her jaw clenched. Although she and Sechrest were far enough away to be out of the light, she could tell from the tilt of his head he was trying to figure out where they were. She veered across the lawn toward the cabin of Sechrest's neighbor.

"What are you doing?" Sechrest squeaked.

Georgia grabbed a fistful of gravel and threw it as far as she could toward the neighbors' cabin. The effect was instantaneous. The man sprinted in the direction of the sound.

Meanwhile, Georgia ran back down to the dinghy. Together she and Sechrest pushed the dinghy to the edge of the water. Too late Georgia realized she needed something to prop up the tarp. She didn't see any oars, and she didn't have time to look. A long tree branch would work, but there was no time for that either.

The shotgun. She could use that as a stake. "Give me the shotgun," she ordered.

"Are you crazy?"

"Sandy, it's our only chance. I've got a 9 millimeter."

"Yeah, but what does that leave me with?"

Georgia forced herself to remain calm. "A shotgun will only work if you're within range of your target. In a few seconds we won't be. Look, there's no time to argue. If you want to live past the next two minutes, hand it over."

Sechrest didn't move for a moment. It seemed interminable. Then she passed the gun to Georgia.

Georgia propped it up against the thwart seat. It was sturdier than she'd expected She draped the tarp over it. Maybe it would fool their pursuer into thinking a person—or two—was in the dinghy. At least for an instant.

As if on cue, the figure reappeared at the side of the house. Georgia pushed the dinghy into the lake. It started off at a sharp angle. She fished out her keys from her jacket pocket. "We need to split up. You run like hell through the woods to my car. It's facing the main road. Start it and get out."

"What about you?"

"I'll cut through and meet you on the main road."

"But what if—"

"No what-ifs." Georgia cut in. "Just go." She looked over her shoulder. The man had come back to Sechrest's yard and was making his way toward the water. "Now!"

Sechrest sprinted toward the woods faster than Georgia thought possible. Georgia cut across the yard away from the man, heading into the woods fifty yards away. She was quickly shrouded by trees and brush, and she knew she couldn't be seen. She started counting seconds, hoping Sechrest would make it to the Toyota before she reached sixty. One minute. That was all they had.

She was up to thirty when she heard a burst of machine gun fire. Fuck! The asshole had an assault rifle! He was shooting at the dinghy. If she and Sechrest had been on in the boat, they would be mincemeat by now. Which meant the diversion had been the right move. But how was she supposed to compete with an assault rifle? Compared to its firepower, her Sig was about as effective as a matchstick. She picked her way through the forest, trying to avoid tree roots and underbrush. Thorns and branches scraped her arms.

A car door slammed. An engine sputtered to life. Sechrest was in the Toyota. Georgia kept thrashing through the woods. Sandy needed to floor it. Their pursuer was undoubtedly headed toward the car.

The engine noise swelled. Another burst of machine gun fire. Georgia heard the clang of metal on metal. He was close enough to shoot at the car! The Toyota barreled down the dirt road. Forty-eight, forty-nine, fifty. She kept counting. By fifty-seven there were no more shots, and Georgia could barely hear the car. Did that mean Sechrest was out of range of the assault rifle? Was she safe? She wouldn't consider the alternative.

CHAPTER 18

Ellie

"There are issues," the woman said. I watched her pick up her drink and take a dainty sip. "Financial issues." "Really?" Her companion leaned forward. The woman nodded. She was wearing too much lipstick and mascara. "Bob is very active with the church. We know too much."

Mac came back to the table, interrupting my eavesdropping. He was carrying a pitcher of beer and two glasses, neither of them all that clean. When I pointed that out, he set them down with a thud. I poured.

It had been a long day. We started at dawn with some B-roll of cornfields, their tender stalks swaying in the morning breeze. Things deteriorated, though, when we taped at the Voss-Peterson ethanol plant. The oven-like heat not only made us slow and sluggish but triggered worries over the equipment. When video gear feels hot to the touch, and more alarming, soft, it's time to take precautions. We covered the gear with towels and hurried through the set-ups in record time. Sweat poured down my back, plastering my t-shirt to my skin. Luckily, I keep a change of clothes in the car.

We were ready to wrap when Fred Hanover horned in. He'd been with us most of the day, but had refrained from insinuating himself into the shoot. After lunch, though, he must have talked to a higher-up, because suddenly he started running back and forth, asking us to shoot here and there and everywhere. He reminded me of an ADD kid in need of Adderal. After about his tenth suggestion, Mac and I locked eyes, and I pulled Fred aside.

"Fred, I know you'd like us to shoot everything in the plant, but we don't have the time or money."

"But you're here," he said sourly. "Why can't you just point the camera at the holding and denaturing tanks, for example? They're a critical component, and they're right here."

"It doesn't work that way. You know that. For each scene we need to decide how to shoot it, set up the equipment, rehearse the shot, then tape. It all takes time. For example, we'd love to see them filling up or emptying, but you told us that wouldn't be possible. In that case, all we'd have are exteriors of the tanks, which, frankly, aren't very compelling visuals." I wiped my brow with the back of my hand.

He lower lip protruded below the sparse collection of hair he called a mustache. I was having trouble believing this was the same man, compared to his gregarious manner the first time we met,

Ultimately we added two set-ups, including exteriors of some tanks he begged us to shoot. It wasn't great video, but I persuaded Mac it was worth it. We were "clean and green" for a change.

This was a corporation engaged in something benevolent for the greater good of the planet. We could be accommodating.

By the time we finally did wrap around five-thirty, the dry t-shirt I'd put on was soaked. The crew headed north in Mac's air-conditioned van, but neither Mac nor I could face the ride home without a drink. We took my Volvo and headed towards Funks Grove and Shirley. North of the towns, not far from the place where we'd had lunch, was Tom's Bar, a one-story shack with wood siding and dirty windows. We parked in a diagonal space next to a pickup.

The sun was still high in the sky, but inside the shades were drawn, and it took time for my eyes to adjust. There was a battered bar in front, and a juke box ground out country music. A sour smell hung in the air, as if years of alcohol fumes had saturated the few tables and chairs in the room.

Aside from the two women immersed in church gossip, only a couple of young men hung out at the bar. They were wearing fatigues and dark t-shirts, and their hair was cropped close to their skulls. The table behind us was occupied by another group of men in t-shirts and jeans, some with suspenders. They looked like farmers.

I swilled my beer. Usually I drink wine, but I figured Chardonnay was too pretentious for this crowd—even the Churchies were tossing back what looked like shots of bourbon. "We got a lot of good stuff today, Mac. I really liked the dolly shot you did past the vats."

"It should cut well."

"Don't forget we have the Voss-Peterson CEO interview on Thursday."

"Do we come back here to shoot?"

"No." After deciding the plant manager with the taciturn expression wouldn't be the best spokesperson, I'd set up an interview with Voss-Peterson's CEO. "He'll meet us at VP's Chicago offices. "It should only take half a day."

"Where are their offices?"

"In Deerfield."

"Halleluiah."

I lifted my glass in a toast. "And no Fred Hanover."

"Amen." We clinked glasses. "He has the hots for you, you know."

I almost spit out my beer. "I don't think so."

Mac rubbed it in. "He does."

"It will be a cold day in hell—"

I stopped as the two women's voices drifted over. "What are you bringing to the church supper?"

"I guess I'll do macaroni salad."

"I'm bringing fried chicken."

"That sounds good," I whispered to Mac.

Mac sniffed.

"Hey, we're downstate. Farm country. Pitchers of beer, wholesome food and people."

"These wholesome people are probably ethanol millionaires," Mac said. "Do you know what's happened to the price of corn?"

"After decades of farmers surviving on subsidies, not knowing if they were going to make it year to year, they deserve a break, don't they?"

Mac shook his head. "What do you get when you cross an optimist with a liberal?"

"I don't know. What?"

"Someone who can't wait for Big Government to screw them."

I rolled my eyes and got up.

"Where are you going?" Mac asked.

I gestured to the men behind us. "I'm thinking we ought to talk to some of these millionaire farmers. Maybe interview them for the show. You know, happy farmers give thanks to Voss-Peterson because they're finally getting top dollar for their crops."

Mac looked over. "Those particular guys don't look much like millionaires. And now that I'm noticing, not very happy either."

"Let's find out."

It was Mac's turn to roll his eyes, but I ignored him. Five men and a boy of about sixteen were at the table. I went over and put on what I hoped was an amiable but professional smile. "Hello. I'm sorry to disturb you, but I wonder if I could talk to you for a minute."

Blank stares were my response. I turned around to Mac. His eyebrows rose. Everyone in the bar was watching me. I took a breath, introduced myself, and told them about the video. "I thought it might be interesting to have some comments by farmers who grow corn. I'm looking for statements about the effect of ethanol production on your business. And Voss-Peterson's role in it, if it's relevant."

When I mentioned Voss-Peterson, they traded surreptitious glances, and their bodies stiffened. I started to get nervous, and when I'm nervous, I talk too much. I kept blathering about the video, Voss-Peterson, ethanol, and finished by saying, "I'd love to buy you all a round while we talk. If that's okay."

More glances, this time directed at a man with long silver hair and a spider web of reddish veins on his nose. He seemed to be the leader of the group. He twirled an empty shot glass, looked at his friends, as if to say, watch this, then shifted his gaze to me. "Who are you again?" His voice was cool.

I repeated my name.

"And why are you here?"

I repeated what I'd said about interviewing them.

Then, "I don't think we got much to say to you. It'd probably be best for you to leave."

I couldn't have felt more rejected than if Luke had turned away from me in bed. I swallowed my pride and sheepishly made my way back to Mac. The men at the table shot sullen looks my way.

Mac said, "Great job, Ellie. You really know how to get people to spill their guts."

"Oh, shut up."

Mac poured me more beer. As I reached for my glass, one of the church ladies leaned toward me. "Miss, I couldn't help overhearing what you said."

"It wasn't one of my finest moments."

"Well," she paused dramatically. "There's a reason why they don't want to talk to you."

"Beyond just being rude?"

She fluttered her eyelashes. "See, when Voss-Peterson decided to build that plant, they went around and asked the farmers if they'd be interested in selling their land."

"To Voss-Peterson?"

She nodded. "Things were pretty depressed around here. We had floods, then droughts, and you could never really count on anything from year to year. Kids were leaving home in droves. People eked out a living. Barely scraping by."

"So a lot of them sold?"

"They got good money."

"Why are they still here?"

"Most of 'em made management agreements with VP. You know, to raise corn like they did before. Maybe take a little to sell on the side."

"So basically they're sharecropping their own land?"

Another nod. "They used to be landowners. Now they're just employees. But Voss-Peterson took all the risk. At the time, it was a godsend."

I made the connection. "But now the market has turned around, and the demand for corn-based products is going through the roof."

The church lady shrugged.

"And, with the price of corn today, Voss-Peterson must be raking in astronomical windfall profits."

"You got it." The woman gestured to the men. "They sold their souls as well as their futures to Voss-Peterson. Now maybe you can see why they're not real anxious to talk to you."

* * *

"I can't believe how I was taken in," I groused when Mac and I were back on the road.

Mac didn't answer.

"My father always says if it looks too good to be true, it probably is."

"You didn't know."

"I should have. But I wanted to believe Voss-Peterson was on the side of the angels. Us, too."

"In corporate America? You should know better. You want to create a higher quality of living, they want to create a higher return on their investment. There's a fundamental difference in objectives."

I scrunched down in my seat and stared out the window. We were passing the field with the barbed wire fence and the "No Unauthorized Personnel" sign. "I guess that's some kind of military facility."

"Because of the men at the bar?"

"They looked like soldiers."

"There aren't any bases here that I recall."

"Well, maybe they built a new one. To keep the Heartland safe."

"Maybe." Mac's tone was noncommittal. "I wonder—"

Whatever he was going to say was cut off by a snippet of the Beatles singing "You say goodbye... I say hello." Rachel had programmed my cell to play it when I got calls from people for whom I don't already have ring tones. I checked the screen, but I didn't recognize the number. "Hello?"

"Ellie, it's Georgia Davis."

"Hi, Georgia. Everything ok?"

"Don't you have a friend with a place in Lake Geneva?"

"Um, yes. Luke lives there. Why?"

"I'm with someone, and we need a safe house."

CHAPTER 19

_____

Georgia

If Luke Sutton's home was any indication, Ellie Foreman had been holding out. Georgia wasn't usually intimidated by the overt display of wealth; she'd seen plenty of it on the North Shore. Usually, though, she didn't know the people involved.

This was different. Luke Sutton was Ellie's boyfriend, and the mansion he lived in, a twenty-room estate on Wisconsin's Lake Geneva, was beyond affluent. A red-brick structure, with four white columns supporting a large portico, it sat in the center of a circular driveway, well recessed from the road. A white dome sat on top of the house. As they trudged up to the front door, the glow from the setting sun enveloped the dome in molten gold.

Even Sechrest was subdued. "You know the people who live here?"

Georgia nodded.

Sechrest swallowed.

At least Ellie, who arrived a few minutes later, had the decency to act embarrassed. "Luke was going to sell the place, but then, at the last minute, he took it off the market." She led them inside and up a circular stairway.

"How come?"

"Long story." Which, from Ellie's tone, she wasn't about to tell. When she stopped in a carpeted hallway on the second floor and inspected Georgia and Sechrest, it was Georgia's turn to be embarrassed. She hadn't showered or changed clothes in over twenty-four hours. She knew she looked exhausted and disheveled. Probably smelled worse.

After she'd met up with Sechrest on the main road leading out of Castle Rock Lake, they'd driven like Nascar racers over rural Wisconsin roads. They seemed to have shaken their pursuer, but Georgia took precautions, in case the guy had police contacts and was somehow able to put out an APB on them. She thought about ditching the car altogether and renting one but didn't want to risk being seen. Instead she removed the license plate from the front of her Toyota and muddied up the back.

She considered calling O'Malley but decided against it, at least for the time being. She trusted him, but not Robbie Parker or the other cops in the village's chain of command. They might ignore Georgia's theories and buck it back to the Wisconsin police, anyway. Just your run of the mill attack with an assault rifle, they'd say. No connection to Chris Messenger or George Emerlich.

She and Sechrest grabbed a few hours sleep in the car, then made a furtive run for coffee. But it wasn't until late afternoon, after putting another hundred miles on the car, that she thought about Ellie and her Lake Geneva connections. Georgia didn't want to put Foreman in danger, but they needed a place to crash, and a motel was too risky. She persuaded herself it would only be for one night. Once she'd figured a safe place to hide Sechrest, she'd go home. And face whatever—or whoever—was out there.

Now, Ellie opened two doors across the hall from each other. "Both these rooms have their own bathroom. I'll grab some towels and extra clothes. Meet me down in the kitchen."

As Georgia showered, some of the stress of the past twenty-four hours circled the drain with the dirt. After toweling off, she padded across the thickly carpeted room. Foreman had left a pair of jeans and a t-shirt on the four poster bed. She put them on. They were probably Ellie's—they were a little loose on Georgia. But not much.

She looked around the room. It was bigger than her entire apartment. In addition to the four poster bed, the furniture included an antique-looking armoire and a white wicker rocking chair. Cheerful white curtains fluttered in the night breeze, and a chintz floral spread lay on the bed. She wondered whose room it was.

She made her way down to the kitchen. Sechrest was already there, her hair still wet. She was wearing oversized sweats, Luke's probably, and a yellow t-shirt. Her face was pale and drawn, but the tense, panicky expression was gone.

Luke came in carrying a large pizza box and two paper bags. Foreman kissed him, took the bags, and removed salads plus a bottle of wine and pop. She bustled around the huge kitchen getting plates, napkins, and looking—despite her apparent discomfort earlier—very much at home. They sat at a round table by a large window with a view of the lake. A silvery moon threw slivers of light on the water, the waves breaking white against the inky dark.

Georgia was ravenous, and it was all she could do not to grab the pizza and cram it all in her mouth at once. She polished off three slices, plus salad and bread, but passed on the wine. When she couldn't eat another bite, she sat back and took a breath. It had been a long time since anyone had fed her, clothed her, made sure she had a place to rest. She felt cared for. Her throat unexpectedly tightened. She eased it with a swallow of pop. "Thanks, Ellie. This was great."

"Don't mention it." Foreman started to clear the table. "So. Why are you here?"

Georgia glanced over at Luke, who'd been sitting with them while they ate.

Foreman followed Georgia's gaze. "He's trustworthy."

Georgia studied Luke. He had fair skin, reddish hair, and deep blue eyes that hinted both at laughter and sorrow. He was only two or three inches taller than Foreman, but his frame was solid, and she suspected he could take care of himself. It was because of his generosity that she and Sechrest had asylum at all.

The coffee maker beeped. Luke got out mugs and poured. Sechrest asked for sugar. Luke got it out along with the milk.

"So?" Foreman asked impatiently.

Georgia explained the bank service charges and the fact that Chris Messenger apparently opened and then closed an account into which the charges were deposited.

"How much was involved?" Foreman asked.

"Three million."

"That's not just spare change." Ellie's brow furrowed. "So Chris was embezzling money?"

"That's what I thought... but Sandy doesn't think so." Georgia looked at Sechrest. "Tell them."

Sechrest ran her tongue around her lips. "There's more to it."

Foreman gazed from Georgia to Sechrest. "Well?"

Georgia cut in. "Give her a minute. She's been pretty freaked out."

She explained about their escape from Castle Rock Lake. When she finished, Foreman got up and lowered the blind on the window, shutting out the view of the lake. Georgia telegraphed her thanks. She turned to Sechrest. "It's okay. You're safe here."

Sechrest nodded shakily. "Well, like I told Georgia, after I traced the service charges to the dummy account, I pulled up the account activity and saw the three cashiers' checks."

"Cashiers' checks?"

She nodded. "At first I thought Chris might have sent the checks to herself. You know, embezzling money, like you said."

"But?" Foreman asked.

Sechrest held up her hand. "The timing doesn't work. The checks went out at the beginning of June. She closed the account at the end of June."

"While her daughter was kidnapped," Foreman said.

"They let Molly go a few hours later the same afternoon," Georgia said.

"So," Foreman said, "if she wasn't embezzling money, somebody must have forced her to close the account, right?"

"But," Sechrest went on, "The thing is, Chris had to have known—even if she was being forced—that closing the account wouldn't make it go away."

"How come?"

"We have all these systems to make sure no one's engaging in any hanky panky. Plus, every time you go into the system to do anything, you leave your employee ID number. Chris had to have known her trail would be discovered. All she was doing was buying time."

"How much time?" Georgia asked.

"It took about a week for the phone calls to start. She had to know a suspicious activity report would be filed shortly after that."

"Who did the cashiers' checks go to?" Ellie asked.

Sechrest shook her head. "The names weren't on the reports I got. And I didn't have time to check the scans."

Foreman ran a hand through her hair. "Okay. Let's go through the chronology again. Three cashiers' checks for one million dollars each are paid to three John Does. Sometime in early June. Three weeks later Chris's daughter is kidnapped. Chris levies a service charge and closes the account the money came from—"

"Except there was no money in the account."

Confusion swam across Foreman's face. "Excuse me?"

Sechrest explained how Messenger created an overdraft in the account she'd originally opened.

"An overdraft for three million dollars? How can that happen?"

"It's not supposed to."

"But..."

"But sometimes there are—situations."

"Like what?"

Sechrest propped her elbows on the table. "Let's assume, hypothetically, that you're handling a customer's account. A large customer. Maybe even the biggest in the bank."

Foreman nodded.

"And let's say they have ten, twelve, maybe twenty-five different accounts for various activities. One day they come to you and say, listen. I need a favor. I need you to open a new account with the following name and EIN number." Sechrest paused. "Then I need you to draw three cashiers' checks on that account. And mail them out per my instructions."

Foreman cut in. "Isn't that when you ask where the money's coming from to pay for those cashiers' checks?"

"The customer tells you he understands the checks will overdraw the account. But, he says, the daily balance of all their accounts combined is over forty million. So there's plenty of money there. He asks you to approve the checks, and says that he'll cover the overdraft in a couple of days."

"Isn't that illegal?"

"Not exactly. A bank officer has the authority to approve overdrafts for a short period of time."

Luke broke in. "She's right, you know. It does happen. I've had similar accommodations from my bank once or twice."

"Did Chris have the authority to authorize that kind of overdraft?"

"Well, she was a Vice President, as well as head of IT. But for that kind of money, no way."

"Then who did? Emerlich?"

"No. The only person who could authorize that kind of overdraft would be our chairman, Thomas Pattison."

"And did he?" Ellie asked.

"His signature was on the cashiers' checks."

Foreman and Georgia exchanged glances. Georgia looked at Luke. "Do you know Pattison?"

He shook his head. "Sorry."

"So," Ellie picked up the thread. "Who is this very important customer that gets such royal treatment from your bank chairman?"

Sechrest turned back to Ellie. "That's where it gets creepy. The account was opened in the name of Southwest Development, Inc." Sechrest paused. "But we have no customer by that name. Their address and EIN number turned out to be fake, too."

"Jesus! This just gets better and better. Chris Messenger creates a secret account. With fake names. And no money." Ellie raised her palms. "Are you saying the bank is out three million dollars, and except for Chris Messenger—who's dead—and the chairman of the bank—no one knows whose account it was or what happened to the money?"

"Ordinarily, it would be difficult to find that out. Maybe even impossible. Unless the chairman of the bank chose to reveal it."

Georgia crossed her arms. "Which, given the situation, he has to do, doesn't he?"

"I can't speak for him." Sechrest let out a small smile.

Georgia picked up on it. "Why are you smiling?"

"Well, remember what I said about leaving your fingerprints in the system?"

Georgia nodded.

"Well, after I discovered all this, I did a search on Chris Messenger's ID number."

Ellie's eyes widened. "Clever."

Sechrest's smile broadened. "Turns out Chris Messenger was the clever one."

"How so?" Georgia asked.

"A couple of days after the three million in cashiers' checks went out, she put a hold on one of our customers' accounts."

"A hold?"

"Essentially, it freezes an account so it can't go below a certain level until the hold is lifted. It was clearly an insurance policy. In case the overdraft wasn't paid."

"Gee..." Ellie said. "I'll bet the hold was for three million dollars."

Sechrest nodded. "Bingo."

"So, whose account was the hold on?"

Sechrest looked around. Then she shivered. "It's a company called Delton. Delton Security."

Luke sat up as if a hot poker had been rammed up his butt.

CHAPTER 20

D elton Security began during Desert Storm by providing certain kinds of equipment and services to the military," Luke said.

"What kind of equipment?" Georgia asked.

"Nothing exciting. I remember hearing about them when I was over there."

"You were in the military?"

"I flew BUFFS for the Army."

"BUFFs?"

"Big Ugly Fat Fellows. A B-52 Stratofortress. They carry cargo."

Georgia wanted to ask more, but Luke cut her off. "Delton supplied tents, cooking equipment, portable galleys, stuff like that." He paused. "But after 9-11, everything changed. Now they provide protective services for government functionaries in high-risk areas. Diplomatic security contracts, they call them. They have corporate contracts, too."

"So, basically, they're mercenaries?"

When Luke nodded, Ellie said, "Like Blackwater?"

"Similar. But Delton isn't as big. Or well known."

"Or infamous?"

"No, but they're a major player."

"Is there a Delton?" Georgia asked.

"Geoff Delton," Luke replied. "They say his best friend was killed during Desert Storm because of faulty armor. Delton's company didn't supply it—they didn't provide things like that back then—but he was supposedly torn up about it. He vowed never to let that happen again. To anyone."

"What—is he some kind of bleeding heart?" Foreman asked.

"I always thought of him as a grown up Boy Scout," Luke said. "You know, loyal to God and country and all that. Anyway, he took over the company from his father and rebuilt it. Daddy had ties to the Bush administration, and things percolated along nicely. Especially after 9-11."

"You know the guy?" Georgia said.

Luke shook his head. "But his story is well known in military circles. And he's local. From Iowa originally, I think. Now he lives near Chicago."

"And Delton is a customer of Midwest National Bank?" Ellie asked.

Sechrest nodded.

"Well, that answers one question," Foreman's smile was ironic.

"What?" Georgia asked.

"The chairman of the bank gets a call from some former high-up in the last administration," Foreman went on, "asking him to do Geoff Delton a favor. It's a matter of national security. A contribution to the war on terrorism. How can Pattison refuse? He'd look un-American."

Sechrest nodded energetically. "Plus, he knows Delton has the money to cover the checks one way or another."

Georgia frowned.

"What's the matter?"

"We don't know why Messenger closed the account three weeks after the fact," Foreman said.

"Careful," Luke warned.

Foreman shot Luke an irritated look. "I get that there could be a perfectly legitimate reason, Luke. But an innocent little girl was kidnapped. Her mother closes the account while her daughter is a hostage. Then her daughter is released. At the very least the timing is suspicious."

Luke kept his mouth shut.

"I hear you, Luke," Georgia said. "But kidnapping wouldn't be a stretch for these guys. Mercenaries are known to be ruthless."

"But why?" Ellie said. "What would they be hiding—or trying to prove?"

"Bear in mind that at the time the account was closed," Sechrest said, "nobody knew it was Delton's."

"Except for Chris. And the chairman," Georgia said.

Sechrest nodded. "But as far as the books were concerned, it was an account with a fake name, fake address, fake everything. All we knew was that it had paid out three cashiers' checks."

"Are we talking money laundering?" Georgia asked. "Or embezzlement?"

"I'm not sure yet," Sechrest said.

"And what about Arthur Emerlich? "Georgia asked. "Wouldn't he have known that Delton was behind the cashiers' checks?"

"I don't know that, either. I was going to brief him on the whole thing, but he died before I could."

"And what about Pattison?" Foreman asked. "He knew Chris opened the secret account for Delton. Did he know she closed it, too?"

"If he didn't then, he does now," Sechrest said. "My guess is he's pretty unhappy about the situation. First, he authorizes a hefty overdraft on a secret account. Then the account is suddenly closed, two of his officers are dead, and he's out three million dollars."

"But they'll get it back, won't they?" Georgia asked. "I mean, isn't that why Chris put a hold on their other accounts?"

"That's true," Sandy said. "But it's embarrassing. And Pattison is in the middle of it. I'd be surprised if he doesn't suddenly 'retire.'"

"Hold on a minute," Foreman said. "We're forgetting something."

"What?" Georgia asked.

"Three million is a lot of money, but it's not as if a company like Delton doesn't deal with large sums every day. Whether it's for supplies, salaries, training facilities, three million can't be all that much to them. The question is what was so special about *this* three million." She turned to Sechrest. "How can we find out who the cashiers' checks went to?"

"Ellie," Luke cut in sternly. "Don't mess with these people." He turned to Georgia. "What does this have to do with Molly Messenger, anyway? You're supposed to be protecting her. How does tracking down missing cashiers' checks fit in?"

Georgia was quiet for a moment. Early in her career, she'd found the corpse of a little girl named Sharron White. Sharron's uncle had raped her, strangled her, and tossed her body in the Skokie Lagoons. By the time she and Matt found her, the body had decomposed so much she was almost unrecognizable. Still Georgia could tell she'd only been about ten.

Now, she leaned forward. "Molly Messenger was kidnapped. Her mother was killed. Her life has become one big fucking tragedy. She'll never be the same. If that happened because some assholes wanted to launder or steal three million dollars, I want to nail them."

Nobody spoke.

"So, how can we find out where the money went?" Foreman asked Sechrest. "Aside from getting someone to go online—which you say would leave a trail?"

"Well, there is one possibility," Sechrest volunteered. "The teller department keeps a log of all the cashiers' checks issued by the bank."

Ellie's eyebrows widened. "A paper log?"

Sechrest nodded. "But I don't know how long they keep them. Maybe a few months."

"Where would they be?" Georgia asked.

"In a locked drawer somewhere."

"Sounds promising." Georgia turned to Ellie. "In the meantime we need to keep Sandy safe until things calm down."

A knowing look passed between Ellie and Luke.

"I already called him," Luke said quietly.

"Called who?" Georgia asked, alarmed. "Who else knows we're here? You shouldn't have—"

"Calm down. It's Jimmy Saclarides." Ellie answered. "He's the Chief of Police in Lake Geneva.

"Shit! The last thing I need are more cops on this thing."

"Jimmy happens to be a close friend of Luke's," Ellie went on calmly. "He has ways of getting things done."

"And keeping people alive," Luke added.

* * *

Sechrest went to bed a few minutes later, but Georgia, fortified with a can of Red Bull, paced the kitchen while Ellie cleaned up.

"I think Luke has a point," Ellie said. "Have you considered just dropping the case?"

"Of course," Georgia said.

"But you can't."

Georgia didn't answer.

"I know you're concerned about Molly, but her father—from what Susan says—is taking good care of her. Isn't that enough?"

Georgia shrugged.

Foreman dried her hands on a towel. "How much do you know about companies like Blackwater and Delton?"

"Only what I read and see in the news."

"So you know Blackwater killed a bunch of innocent people in Iraq—"

"In Bahgdad, wasn't it?"

"Right, and that's only what we know about. Some people think they averaged four to five shootings a week."

"I wouldn't be surprised."

Foreman turned around. "And do you know that some weapons that belonged to Blackwater ended up with Kurdish rebels in Northern Iraq? And that they found Blackwater guns in New Orleans? And that the government, except for Iraq, hasn't done a damn thing about any of it?"

Georgia kept her mouth shut.

Foreman must have mistaken her silence for acquiescence.

"When you outsource your military to private contractors, you give up a lot of power. Companies like Blackwater—and Delton—think they can get away with almost anything. It's pretty damn scary. You don't go up against these people. You—"

"Ellie, stop." Georgia threw up a hand. "I didn't say I was going up against them. But that's beside the point. Neither of us were in Iraq. We don't know what it was like. You're talking about a fucking war zone." She stopped pacing. "Look... even here on the North Shore, you have no idea what people are gonna do. Take a car bust in Hubbard Woods, for example. Penny ante stuff, right?"

Foreman cocked her head.

"As a cop, you still have to wonder whether the guy in the car has a weapon. And if so, what kind? A knife? A gun? What caliber? How many magazines? There's no way to tell, so you prepare for the worst. And if you see something—even a flash of something from the corner of your eye—well, it's either you or them." Her jaw tightened. "Shit happens. It's not fair to judge. Even mercenaries."

Foreman rubbed her hand across her chin. "There's a big difference. As a cop, you're accountable for what you do on that bust. Blackwater isn't. They're not subject to military law because they're private. But they claim they're not subject to civilian law either, because they're part of the military. So basically you have a bunch of guys who do whatever they want. Or whatever's the most lucrative. And the government is subsidizing them."

Georgia stared at Foreman. She couldn't believe how different they were. "Chaos is unacceptable. These guys are trying to restore order."

"But at what cost?"

Georgia was rattled. She crossed her arms. "Look. I don't keep up with what's going on in the world like you. But I do know that when there's a threat, large or small, somebody's got to protect people. Get rid of the bad guys."

"What happens if the protectors turn out to be the bad guys?"

Georgia's nerves were stretched raw. She hadn't counted on having to defend her beliefs to Foreman, who'd led a privileged life. Sometimes the woman seemed to enjoy arguing for the sake of it. Fortunately, their conversation was cut off by Luke, who hurried out of his office waving some paper. "Hey... I was just searching online."

Georgia spun around.

"They're saying that companies like Blackwater are pretty much done with Iraq."

"Why am I not surprised?" Foreman said dryly.

"According to the articles, they see domestic issues as their next challenge."

"Good. Now they can wreak havoc in our part of the world."

Luke leveled a hard look at Foreman.

She held up her hands. "Sorry."

"Here's the interesting part," Luke went on. "Geoff Delton lives in Barrington. He built a big mansion he calls the 'Fortress' because of all the security systems on it."

Ellie and Georgia exchanged glances.

"And get this," Luke went on. "Delton has two training camps. One's in California, but one's actually in Illinois."

"Where?" Georgia asked.

"Downstate. North of Funks Grove and Shirley."

Ellie gasped.

"What?"

"I know exactly where it is." She explained how she and Mac

had driven past the fenced off land while shooting a video on ethanol. "I thought it was a military base." Her eyes got a faraway look.

"Don't even think about it, Ellie." Luke warned.

Ellie went over to Luke and brushed her fingers against his cheek. "Don't worry, love. I have no intention of getting involved."

Luke pulled her fingers down to stroke his neck, and they shared an intimate smile. Then Luke turned to Georgia "And don't you try to be a hero, either. A live coward is better than a dead hero."

Georgia met his cool gaze with one of her own.

* * *

Later as she drifted off to an exhausted sleep, she thought about the way Luke and Foreman had touched each other. Maybe it wasn't a good idea to spend so much time with the two of them. It reminded her of what she was missing.

CHAPTER 21

———————

Dawn broke with a watery sunshine that leaked through a pale layer of clouds. Georgia stood at the bedroom window, gazing out at the green lawn, blue lake, and flowers in red, orange, and yellow. Nothing horrible could happen in such a beautiful place, she thought. Then she recalled that horrible things had happened here. Luke Sutton's sister had been killed—accidentally some said; purposefully, said others—by his brother, and it had been covered up by their father. The brother was serving a life sentence. The father, also in prison for life, had passed away last year. She turned away from the view. That would teach her to get too comfortable in rich peoples' homes.

Throwing on a pair of borrowed shorts and t-shirt, she went for a run along the banks of the lake. Thirty minutes later she was jogging back when a nondescript white Impala pulled into Luke's driveway. She spotted an antenna poking through the trunk. An unmarked. A man in a white uniform shirt and black pants with a gun belt around his waist got out. He slipped off his sunglasses and hung them on his shirt.

"Morning. You must be Ellie's friend."

Georgia slowed. "Who are you?"

"Name's Saclarides. Jimmy."

"You're the one. Lake Geneva's Chief of Police."

"Guilty as charged."

She almost smiled.

"You used to be on the force yourself, I believe."

She nodded. "I'm private now."

"So I gather."

He was deeply tanned, and slim, with straight dark hair receding from his forehead, a long, thin nose, and widely spaced brown eyes. She suspected those eyes could turn cold, but right now they were kind. He filled his uniform nicely, she thought. Very nicely. Suddenly she was aware of how sweaty and smelly she must be. She ran an awkward hand over her hair, then changed her mind and dropped it. She was what she was.

Jimmy's glance seemed to take it all in. His voice softened. "I understand we have business to conduct."

Georgia was grateful for his discretion. "Can you keep her safe?"

He smiled. It was a good smile, warm and kind, like his eyes. "I think that can be arranged. How long?"

"I'm not sure. A week or two. Until I get to the bottom of this. Unfortunately, it just got deeper."

"I'll handle it."

"Where will you take her?"

He shook his head. "You shouldn't know. Better for both of

you. But take this." He slid his hand in his pocket and fished out a card.

She glanced at it briefly. Two numbers. His office and probably his cell. "Thanks."

"What's your next move?"

"I'll be going back to Chicago. I need to check on a few things."

"You need help?"

She focused on his face. Did he want to wrest control of the case and hand it to the Illinois police? Contact O'Malley and Parker himself? She didn't think so. He looked sincere. Concerned. Maybe even a little worried. He was a friend of Luke's. And Foreman had vouched for him. "I appreciate the offer. I'm okay for now."

He nodded and motioned to the card, which was still in her hand. "Keep that. You never know... down the road..." His voice trailed off.

"No. You don't." She closed her hand around the card.

* * *

The rain started on her way back to Chicago, a gentle summer rain. Georgia imagined thirsty crops and flowers opening up, drinking it in. For some reason that put her in a good mood. By the time she was back in her apartment, it had mostly subsided, leaving only a few drops to plunk on the metal downspouts near her windows. She checked her answering machine and saw the blinking red light. She skimmed the messages, then picked up her phone and dialed.

"Davis? Where the hell have you been?"

"And hello to you too, Dan."

O'Malley sounded annoyed. "I've been trying to call you. Don't you check your messages?"

"Sorry—I was—out of town. What's up?"

"You're okay, right?"

"Why shouldn't I be?"

"Davis, I thought by now we could stop playing games."

A momentary quiver shot through her. Was Jimmy Saclarides playing her? By now the cops had to know something about the account that Chris Messenger opened and closed. But how much? Had they connected it to Delton? And what about Sandy Sechrest? Did they know she was in Lake Geneva? She wanted to ask but knew O'Malley wouldn't tell her. At least not directly. Despite their friendship, he was loyal to the Blue Brotherhood. She forced herself to stay cool. She could fence and parry as well as the next guy. "No games, Dan. I'm just working the case. Trying to figure things out."

"Course. Well, I have something for you."

"Yeah?" She braced herself.

"Yeah. The DNA tests came back. Prelim, of course."

Christine Messenger's fetus.

"And?"

He sighed. "What you'd expect. No match to anyone in our database. Or any of the Feds', either."

She relaxed. "Which narrows it down to about four billion people."

"Only two, if you leave out females."

So whoever Christine Messenger was sleeping with didn't have a record. Or any reason to have surrendered his DNA to a government organization. She filed the information. What she really wanted to know was how far down the money trail the cops were. At the same time she didn't want to tip her hand. She took a roundabout approach. "Where are you on Chris Messenger's death investigation?"

"So far, we're still calling it a motor vehicle accident." She heard the hedge in his voice.

"You know it's a homicide."

"We know. You know. Everyone knows. But there's not enough evidence."

"So?"

"So Parker stays on it until he finds some. Which..." O'Malley cleared his throat, "is another reason I called."

Here it comes, she thought.

"By the way," O'Malley added, "you can cut the crap about being on vacation."

Georgia stared at a bare spot on her living room wall. Pete had suggested getting some paintings or prints, but she hadn't gotten around to it. Her apartment was comfortable, but spare. "I didn't say I was on vacation. Just out of town."

"Whatever. We really need to talk to the little girl, but her father won't let us. We offered to bring in a kid shrink, a doctor, whatever he wanted, but he won't budge. Says she's too traumatized. He can't go there. *You*, on the other hand, are working for him. And I know you've got a way with kids. And I'm betting the father would let you in. So..." He paused as if he knew what he was about to say was the last thing she wanted to hear. "Would you be willing to have Parker there with you when you talk to her? We figure she's got to remember something about the kidnapping. It could really help us out. You too."

"Are you kidding, Dan? You want Parker to tag along with me on an interview? Is that even allowed?"

"It is if I say so."

She mulled it over. "I don't think so."

He was quiet for a moment. Then, "What about someone else? I've got more than one dick working the case."

She mulled it over some more. "No. I'm not taking anyone with me."

"That's what I thought you'd say."

"I'm sorry."

"Well, will you at least brief us afterwards? We're all on the same side here, you know that, right?"

"Does that mean you'll share your information with me? You and Parker?"

He kept his mouth shut.

"That's what I thought *you'd* say."

"What do you want to know?"

"What about the link to the bank? Emerlich was an officer. Messenger, a Director. Assuming they weren't having an affair, which I'm sure you already know, you've got to be looking pretty carefully at bank operations."

"As a matter of fact, the Bureau is lending us a hand. They've got a forensic accountant going over a shitload of records."

Which meant they'd probably found the cashiers' checks. Maybe even who they went to. And, despite his promises, Georgia doubted Parker or O'Malley would share that information with her. She had to move fast if she wanted to get to the bottom of things before they did. It wasn't a race, but being a cop meant having power—the power to interrogate, imprison, and prosecute— all powers Georgia no longer possessed. And while she wasn't a vengeful person, she had to admit that a piece of her ego—maybe more than a piece—was wrapped up in the case. She wanted to resolve it first. O'Malley knew that. Still, she should let him think she was a team player.

"All right, listen," she parried. "*If* I get in to see Molly, and *if* I get anything from her, I'll let you know. In return, I want to know what that forensic accountant finds."

"You got it. Thanks, Davis."

She didn't believe him for a minute. She stared at the spot on the wall again. She decided she didn't want a picture or print.

CHAPTER 22

The oversweet smell of food just beginning to rot emanated from Terry Messenger's kitchen. Georgia tried not to notice as he led her into the condo that afternoon. It had only been six days since Chris Messenger died—barely enough time for a funeral and memorial service—but time enough to be swimming in casseroles, platters, and baked goods brought by concerned friends. Most of the dishes, uneaten and still wrapped in plastic, were crammed on counters and the tiny table.

Terry saw her eyeballing the food. "You want to take some? We'll never eat it all. Neither of us is hungry."

Georgia shook her head and resisted the urge to start putting things away. "How's Molly?"

Terry winced. "I think it's starting to sink in that her mom isn't coming back."

"Where is she now?"

"She's sleeping. At last." He flopped down in one of the easy chairs in the living room and let out a sigh. Georgia studied him.

His crisp appearance, which she recalled from their earlier meeting, had wilted: his chinos were wrinkled, and she spotted a stain on his shirt. His bald head and face needed a shave, and the dark half-moons under his eyes were pronounced. If Molly wasn't sleeping well, neither was her father.

She sat on the couch. "I want to fill you in on what I've found." She summarized Chris's actions surrounding the cashiers' checks, services charges, and secret account, the incident at Sechrest's Wisconsin cabin, and the link to Delton Security. As she explained, Terry's eyes widened. By the time she finished, he was leaning forward. "This is—unbelievable. Mercenaries? Cashiers' checks? Are you sure?"

"Why do you say that?"

"It's just—so alien from the life she and I led together." He brushed his hand across his forehead. "We were just your average, normal family, you know? A doctor and a banker. A little girl. But this—this sounds like something out of a movie."

He looked like he was telling the truth; nevertheless, Georgia was careful. "So, nothing rings a bell? Nothing you can add?"

"Like I said, Chris and I haven't lived together in three years. I had no idea her life was this—extreme."

"There's something else..." Georgia bit her lip. She didn't want to mention it but knew she had to. "Chris was pregnant when she died."

Terry's expression grew weary. "I know."

Georgia frowned. "How? Oh. The police."

He nodded. "I wasn't surprised."

Georgia remembered Chris's reluctance to call Terry when Molly was first kidnapped. Her fear that he would blame her, accuse her of being a bad mother. "Why not?"

"She'd been leaving Molly with baby sitters a lot. When I'd call, Molly would say she was out. So I figured she was seeing someone." His jaw tightened.

Georgia caught it. Was there some truth to Chris's fears after all?

"Do you know who it was?" he asked.

"I was going to ask you."

He spread his hands. "I have no clue."

"Would Molly know?"

Terry's face hardened. "What does Chris being pregnant have to do with Molly's kidnapping?"

"I'm not sure. But until we know who took Molly and why, everything is on the table."

"Molly's still not talking much. About anything. She's definitely regressed. I talked to one of the kid shrinks at the hospital. She says that isn't unusual."

"Terry, I really need to talk to her."

"About her mother being pregnant?" He scowled. "I don't think—"

"About the kidnapping."

"No. It would be too much of an ordeal."

Was he just being a concerned father? Or was his unwillingness motivated by something else? Georgia pressed. "You asked me to find out who was behind Molly's kidnapping. Especially in light of Chris's 'accident.' That's what I'm trying to do. Molly might be able to tell us something that will move this thing forward. But if you're denying me access, I don't really know how much more I can do."

"It's not that. But you, the police, everyone wants a piece of her. I just can't risk it. Not yet. When she's stronger."

Georgia clasped her hands around her knee, trying to think of a way around the stand-off. She decided Terry wasn't trying to stall. Or throw her off the trail. He seemed sincere. And he had a point. Molly had been traumatized. Her recovery would take time and patience and love. Even then she would always bear scars. At the same time, following up on bank records could only tell Georgia so much. It wouldn't prove the events were connected. She needed more.

She rocked forward and took in a breath. Another odor overlaid the food smells—the musty smell of humans who've been cooped up too long. The air conditioning kicked on with a steady hum. As cool air began to circulate, Georgia dropped her hands from her knee. "I have an idea."

* * *

The temperature had to be just right. Georgia knew. Her grandmother had tried to give her baths, but she'd invariably make them too hot or too cold. The only one who ever got it right was her mother. Georgia tested the water with her fingers. Never mind the elbow—that was an old wives' tale.

The water was perfect. She went back into the living room where a sleepy Molly sat on her father's lap, sucking her fingers.

"Okay, I think we're good to go, Goldilocks."

When Molly frowned, Georgia reminded her of the story. "This is your chance to play Goldilocks. If it's not exactly right, you say so, and I'll fix it."

Molly cocked her head, as if the idea was intriguing, but she wasn't convinced. Terry Messenger played it well. "I bet you and Goldilocks would have been good friends, don't you think?"

Molly, still sucking her fingers, didn't answer.

"Just give it a try, okay?" Georgia said. "If you don't like it, you can get out of the tub right away. Deal?"

Molly looked Georgia up and down. Then she reluctantly detached herself from her father. Georgia held out her hand. Molly took her fingers out of her mouth, slipped her hand into Georgia's, and they walked into the bathroom. Georgia hoped the water hadn't cooled too much.

Georgia had found Barbie bubble bath on the rim of the tub and dribbled it into the water. Now a mass of fluffy white bubbles floated across the surface. Molly's face registered approval, but you couldn't really call it a smile. Georgia helped her take off her bathrobe and Disney princess nightgown. Her ribs protruded. She *wasn't* eating enough.

"In you go..." she lifted Molly into the water.

Molly sat down, stretched out her legs and studied the bubbles. She scooped some of them up and deposited them on one arm.

Georgia smiled. "Is that a new blouse?"

Molly's eyes narrowed, as if considering the idea. Then she scooped up more and coated her other arm. She looked over at Georgia. Georgia smiled more broadly. Molly's expression smoothed out, her mouth twitched, and she cracked a tiny smile. Georgia's heart flipped. This had to be the first time in a week.

"It's gorgeous," she said. "And just your size."

A sly look came across the girl and she wiped the bubbles off her arms. She lowered her hands into the water, but this time, instead of scooping up more, she started to slap them. She glanced at Georgia then swatted more forcefully, creating waves of white foam that sloshed against the side of the tub. As the waves gathered steam, the water spilled over the top and onto the floor. She giggled.

Georgia dipped her hand in the water and gently splashed Molly. Molly splashed back. Then Georgia scooped up a handful of bubbles and smeared them on her chin. "See my beard?"

Molly giggled and mimicked her.

"You too?"

Molly nodded.

"I guess we're two bearded ladies."

"Girls don't have beards."

Georgia feigned surprise. "They don't?"

"No, that's just silly."

Georgia shrugged. "Oops."

That made Molly laugh. A real laugh.

Georgia let her splash a while longer, then asked, "Would you like your back soaped?"

Molly nodded. Georgia found a washcloth on the towel rack, dipped it in the water and scrubbed Molly's back.

"Up here," Molly said, snaking her hand around her back.

Georgia rubbed the spot Molly pointed to.

"Now down here." Molly moved her hand down.

Georgia complied.

"Now over here." Molly placed her other hand on her back.

"I bet down here, now," Georgia said, moving the cloth.

"No!" Molly ordered. "Not till I say so."

"I'm sorry, your majesty."

When the water finally cooled, Georgia lifted her out, wrapped her in a towel, and dried her. She examined Molly's bathrobe. It needed laundering.

"You have another one?"

Molly shook her head.

"No problem." Georgia went back out to the living room and asked Terry for a clean t-shirt. Returning with one, she put it on Molly. It hung to the middle of her calves. "Now that's a perfect fit."

But Molly didn't say anything, and she stuck her fingers in her mouth, as if she somehow understood that her bath had been just a respite, a special but temporary moment of happiness in the midst of grief.

Again Georgia held out her hand. "How about we put some food in your mouth instead of your fingers?"

When they came back into the living room, Terry was on his laptop. Georgia told him she was going to fix Molly something to eat. She bypassed the food on the counter and scrounged the cabinets. She found a can of chicken soup, bread, and in the refrigerator, sliced cheese. She started the soup on the stove, got out a pan, and prepared three grilled cheese sandwiches.

Molly watched carefully. She took her fingers out of her mouth. "I can't eat all those."

"One's for me. And another for your Dad."

Molly blinked as if she needed time to process the information. "I don't like crusts."

"Then you shall not eat them."

Ten minutes later the three of them were at the dining room table with soup and crustless sandwiches. Georgia watched as Molly slurped down soup, glad the girl was eating something. Terry seemed relieved too. Georgia didn't really need a sandwich, but she pretended to enjoy it. Determined to keep the mood light, she made small talk about the Taste of Chicago, which had just ended, all the while wondering how to—or if she even could—bring up the subject of Molly's abduction.

When Molly finished her sandwich, she put her fingers back in her mouth. Georgia was disappointed. But Terry, who must have cottoned to the idea of keeping things light, laughed. "You keep sucking your fingers, baby, you might suck them right off."

Molly dropped her fingers. "Like the man who stole me."

Georgia froze. Terry Messenger paled. His smile vanished. After a moment he managed to ask, "What was that, freckle-face?"

Molly looked at Terry, then Georgia. "The man who stole me. He sucked his finger off."

"How do you mean, sweetie?" Georgia asked softly.

Molly held up her hand. "This finger." She pointed to the index finger of her left hand. "There wasn't anything there. Just a lump." She cast her eyes down. "He got mad at me for staring at it."

CHAPTER 23

A slanting sun brushed the evening sky with rose and orange and purple as Georgia drove back to her apartment. One of Molly's kidnappers was missing the index finger on his left hand. The man at Sechrest's cabin looked as if his finger was missing. It might not be compelling, but it was a solid connection. Missing fingers weren't common. If she'd been on the force, she could search the criminal databases. They'd spit out any man with a missing finger right away.

At the next red light she pulled her cell out. She'd told O'Malley she would call. It was the right thing to do. Otherwise, she'd be looking forever. And hoping for divine intervention. But. She stared at her cell until the light turned green.

"Second strike out for Lilly in two innings..."

The Cubs game was on the radio. She listened sometimes in the car. She wasn't a rabid fan, but the announcer's chatter, the swell of the crowd, even the organ music were white noise; comfort food for her soul. Her father used to listen to Cubs games when she was little. Those were the only times that he seemed happy. Or at least not angry. He'd sit in the old recliner, a bottle of beer in one hand, eyes closed. He'd smile when the Cubs did something right, but more often he'd yell and curse. Still, the few hours that the games were on provided an oasis of safety and security for Georgia. He was distracted, not focused on her. She'd come to believe the world couldn't be too bad a place, that things couldn't go too far wrong if a baseball game was still on the air.

The day's colors were fading and the shadows lengthening by the time she parked two blocks away from her apartment and walked back. It was quiet: fireflies blinked; her shoes thudded softly. The kids who lived across the street usually peppered the street with screams and shouts. But the rain had left an uncomfortable sheen of humidity on everything. They were probably indoors playing computer games, and driving their mother crazy.

Suddenly she felt a weight behind her, a charged mass of air. She automatically reached for her Sig until she realized she wasn't carrying. She spun around anyway. Nobody was there. She squinted into the dusk. She searched the hedge of waist-high yews bordering her neighbor's yard. No one, and no place to hide. She went back to the corner and checked the street in both directions. Nothing. An uneasy feeling came over her. Her instincts were usually right on. Then again, she'd been under a lot of stress in Wisconsin. And while Lake Geneva was safe, it had its own tension. Maybe she was imagining things.

She jogged the rest of the way back to her building. Whoever had tracked Sechrest to her cabin in Wisconsin had seen Georgia's license plates. They could easily trace them back to her. She looked into the deepening dusk one more time. Was Sechrest's pursuer coming after her?

Unless it wasn't an enemy. She wouldn't put it past Robbie Parker or one of his men to tail her. Just to figure out how much she knew.

She hurried to the front door of her building. Pete's apartment was on the third floor. His light was on. She climbed the stairs to his place, wondering if her pursuer was missing a finger on his left hand.

* * *

Steps sounded in the hall outside her apartment the next morning. They stopped at her door. She crept to the door and looked out the peephole, which she'd had installed after the fire last year. It was Pete. She reached to open the door, then stopped. Their conversation last night hadn't ended well.

She'd gone upstairs to talk about the case. She'd done that with other cases, and Pete didn't seem to mind. He was a good listener, and talking out loud helped clarify her thinking.

"I think Molly's coming out of it." She sat on his couch and curled her legs under her. "And assuming her father doesn't push her, she'll probably recall more as time goes on."

"That's a lot of pressure to put on a little girl," Pete said. He was wearing a t-shirt and cut-offs. He looked tan, rested. Good.

"Depends on how it's done. We need to know what the kidnappers looked like, what they did, what they said. Any nugget she might drop. Like the man with the missing finger. I think it can be done with sensitivity."

"You hope."

"Well, yes." She peered at Pete. He didn't normally offer opinions, particularly with a bite. She uncurled her legs.

"It also makes you more dependent on Terry Messenger's good will."

"I don't think he's a bad person. Or untrustworthy."

"He was reluctant to let you talk to his daughter."

"He has his hands full. But you could be right. I get the feeling he wants to cross this off his 'to do' list."

"He's a busy doctor. Can you blame him?"

"I guess not. The problem is I still need to find a stonger link between Molly's kidnapping, her mother's murder, the bank account, and Delton Security. The man with the missing finger isn't enough"

"Are you sure there is one?"

"Common sense says it's there."

"I don't get it, Georgia. Isn't that the police's job? Shouldn't you let them make the connection?"

She bit her lip. "I will. Eventually."

"Why not now?"

"What I give them has to be air tight."

"Why? They've got detectives to connect the dots."

"I want to make sure there's no chance the case will go away."

"What do you mean?"

Georgia was surprised to find herself arguing what Ellie Foreman said just last night. "Delton Security is a government contractor, and the government doesn't want to bite the hand that feeds them. Or in this case, protects them. There's a precedent of investigations stalling. Getting watered down. Going dry. The police have concluded Chris Messenger's death was accidental. At least publicly. It would be easier all around to keep it that way.

Maintain the status quo. I have to make sure my case is so tight that no one, neither the police nor the Feds, can sweep it under the rug."

Pete nodded but he wasn't really paying attention, Georgia thought. He looked preoccupied.

"There's something else," she went on.

"What?"

"Someone came after Sechrest in Wisconsin. They know my license plates. I don't have a lot of time."

"You need to be careful." Pete went into the kitchen, got a beer from the refrigerator. He popped the top, came back in the living room, and sat down next to her. "Georgia, I know you're wrapped up in this case, but there's something we need to talk about."

She fidgeted. She didn't like conversations that began that way. She thought she knew what was coming, and she realized she dreaded it. Please, she begged silently. Don't, Pete. Not now.

"I need to tell you something."

Her heart sank, and she scolded herself for getting too close to a man, even platonically. Why was this relationship thing so difficult? Why couldn't they just be friends, share time together, enjoy each other's company? Men always wanted more. On the other hand, if they thought you were coming on to them, they ran in the other direction. Which made it tricky. After her own rocky history, she wasn't anxious to get involved. She thought Pete felt the same way. She turned toward him, searching for the right words, any words that would preserve their friendship.

"I've been talking to Kelly."

Georgia was shocked. Kelly? Then it registered. "Your ex-wife."

"She's not exactly my ex. We haven't signed the papers yet."

Georgia's spine stiffened. "I didn't know that."

"There's a lot you don't know about me, Georgia. And it's pretty clear you don't want to."

She found herself feeling defensive although she wasn't sure why. "That's not true. It's just—"

"You don't have to explain. I know it's a bad time for you. You're focusing on your career. You're still getting over Matt. There's always something."

Was she that transparent? "You don't know that." It sounded lame, even to her.

He smiled. "I don't have to. The point is, Kelly and I have decided to give it one more try before—"

She cut him off. "You and your ex-wife are getting back together."

"We're going to try."

Georgia's stomach twisted. She felt lost. She didn't know what to say. She rose from the couch. "I think—that's a great idea. Good luck."

She was almost to the door when he said, "Georgia, wait. I'm not getting good vibes here. Let's finish the conversation."

She shook her head. When she got to the door, she opened it.

"Georgia, please."

"There's nothing more to say." She made a speedy exit.

* * *

Now, the next morning, she knew she should open the door. Talk to Pete. Explain it wasn't that she wanted him for herself. Just that she couldn't help feeling abandoned. It was woven into the fabric of her life. She leaned against the door but didn't open it.

Eventually, Pete's footsteps retreated. She heard the front door of the building slam shut.

CHAPTER 24

Ellie

Mid-July. The peonies were long gone, the roses were just hanging on, but the day lilies were about to bloom. I was making the rounds of my garden with weed killer, trying to control nature in my little corner of the universe. With me was my friend, Fouad al Hamra, who was targeting crabgrass for demolition. Fouad owns his own landscaping business, but unlike some business owners, he still does most of the work himself. Although I only see him during the growing season, Fouad is one of my closest friends. Indeed, I owe him my life, a fact which he, with his characteristic sense of modesty, refuses to concede.

He leaned over the day lilies. "You have not been tending your garden, have you, Ellie?" Fouad was tall and dark, with eyes that could pick out deception a hundred yards away. His once lean frame was just a bit doughy these days. His hair, once black, was mostly silver now, and there was less of it. He'd shaved off his mustache a year ago—his wife Hayat said it was getting too bristly. He straightened and wiped a handkerchief across his brow.

He was right about the garden. "I haven't had much time," I answered guiltily. Now that he was chiding me, I kicked myself for not mulching, composting, and trying to reduce my carbon footprint a degree or two. At least I wasn't turning farmers into indentured servants like Voss-Peterson.

"Tell me something, Fouad."

"What is that?" He was now over by the mums, examining the tightly furled buds, as if sheer concentration could coax them into bloom.

"What would you think about a corporation that buys up farmers' land, hires them back to raise the crops, then takes all the profit?"

He stroked the skin above his lip where his mustache used to be, then stopped, as if he'd just now realized it wasn't there. "What crops are we talking about?"

"Corn."

"Ahh..." His eyebrows arched. "Corn is the new global currency. In some quarters it's as valuable as gold."

"Yes, but does that entitle a multi-national to rob farmers of their share of the pot?"

Fouad tends to remind me when I'm grandstanding, and he was smiling now. "I suppose it depends on what the situation was before. As one of your presidents used to say, are they better off now than they were?"

"The farmers sold the land for a bunch of money. And they get a salary now. Plus an acre or two to keep for themselves. But that's barely enough for a truck farm," I added.

"Still, it sounds like an honest deal."

"But the corporation took advantage of the farmers when they were down."

"Some might say they saved them. No more worrying about next season or whether there will be enough money to feed the family." Fouad frowned. "And do not forget, the land is still being farmed."

"What do you mean?"

"It could have turned into a condo development."

I was surprised at Fouad's attitude. I wouldn't have pegged him as so Adam Smith.

He gave a little shrug, as if he could read my mind, then bent over the mums. "These plants, Ellie. You must take care of them."

"They're not in bloom."

"Unless you fertilize now, they may not bloom at all. And if they do, the blossoms will be tiny and sparse."

I nodded and looked impatiently at my watch. I'd rushed back from Lake Geneva so I could cook Shabbos dinner tonight for Rachel and Dad. Rachel had invited her new boyfriend, and I wanted him to know that Rachel came from a family that still gathered round the table for a home-cooked meal. At least on Shabbos. He didn't have to know it only happened once in a while. I started making a mental shopping list. Brisket was my father's favorite, but in order for it to cook its allotted four hours, I had to drive to Sunset Foods now.

Fouad went back to the daylilies. "It seems as if the deer are already finding the lilies."

The deer wander over from the Forest Preserve every year to snack on my daylilies, but this was early, even for them. I peered more closely. Sure enough, I saw a few naked stalks that looked like they'd been chewed.

Fouad wiped his brow again with his handkerchief. He was sweating more than usual. Fouad was probably somewhere in his sixties, but he'd always seemed ageless in the way men of wisdom often are. But now that I was noticing, his olive skin tone looked pale, and he was breathing hard.

"Fouad, is something wrong? Are you ill?"

He didn't answer.

"Fouad?"

He wouldn't look at me.

"When was the last time you saw a doctor?"

He waved away my concern. "I am fine."

Typical. I drove to the grocery store, still worried. I thought about calling his wife, Hayat, but decided not to. If he didn't seem better the next time he stopped by, I would. I ran into Sunset and hurried to the meat department. I was waiting for my brisket when my cell trilled.

"Ellie, it's Georgia."

"Hey, Georgia. How are you? Did you get back okay?"

"Do you remember the IT guy from the bank you took for a drink? The one who first told you about the service charges?"

"Cody. Cody Wegman."

"Do you still have his number?"

I remembered the card he'd shoved into my hand when we left the bar. I still had it somewhere. "Yes. Why?"

"I need you to call him."

"Oh? And what am I going to say?"

"You're going to convince him to help me get into the teller department so I can find out where Delton Security's three million dollars went."

* * *

Cody Wegman, Georgia, and I met outside Midwest National bank on Saturday, a morning so hot and humid the office buildings looked like they were sweating. I'd called Cody when I got home from Sunset. He was surprised to hear from me. His surprise turned into shock when I made my request.

"Are you kidding? You want to break into the teller department?"

"Technically, I wouldn't call it a break-in."

"Okay. I know you were bullshitting me when you bought me a drink, but now you need to tell the truth. What's going on?"

I'd been half expecting him to tell me where to go and then hang up, so I was cheered by his response. I told him the truth. Or as much of it as Georgia allowed. "Cody, a private investigator I know is looking into Chris Messenger's death. A critical part of that investigation involves three cashiers' checks the bank made at the beginning of June. We need to know who those checks went to. We were told the teller department keeps hard copies of every cashiers' check the bank issues."

"Maybe."

"Please. We need to find out. And we can't ask you to go online to track them down. It's too risky."

"You can say that again." He went quiet. Then, "I could get fired for helping you. Maybe even go to jail."

"That assumes we're going to get caught."

He blew out a breath. "And what makes you think I even know anyone who could help?"

I hesitated. "Sandy thought you might."

"Sechrest? How is she?"

"How would I know?"

He cleared his throat. I recalled how he'd given me the information that led Georgia to Sandy in the first place.

"She's safe," I said after a pause.

"The bank thinks she's on sick leave."

"In a way, she is."

He was quiet again. "If I help, am I going to have to disappear, too?"

I wasn't sure what to say. I hadn't wanted to take advantage of Cody, but I'd overstepped that boundary when I bought him a drink. And it was clear someone wanted to stop us from uncovering information and was willing to kill to keep it hidden. When you added Delton Security to the mix, there was no guarantee any of us would stay absolutely safe. I had to be honest. "I don't know, Cody."

Silence. Then, "Chris was my boss."

"I know."

"I liked her."

"I know."

He sighed. "The teller operation is high security. For obvious reasons."

"Do you know anyone?"

"The only person I know is Joan Hiller."

I held my breath.

"I'll call her."

Now, as we waited for her outside the bank building, Cody said, "You're lucky, you know. We just started having Saturday hours. Lobby's open until noon."

I checked my watch. It was ten-thirty.

"We should have plenty of time."

Georgia frowned. "We?"

Cody shifted his feet. "Well, uh, yes. You need us to help you go through the log, right?"

Georgia had her shades on, which was good. I didn't want Cody to see the expression I knew was there. "Cody, you've been really helpful, but this isn't 24. It's a murder investigation."

Cody slung his hands in the pockets of his shorts. His shoulders hunched.

"You won't be coming in, either." Georgia turned to me. "Just Hiller." She turned back to Cody. "Are you sure she's coming?"

Cody shifted again. "She said so."

Ten minutes later, Georgia said, "Why don't you call her? See where she is." She paused. "You do have her number?"

A flash of irritation came over Cody, but he made the call. "Where are you? He listened, then turned his back on us and walked away, but I could hear him pleading. "You've got to. You can't leave me hanging. Come on, Joan." Then he grunted and snapped the cell shut. As he walked back, it looked like a two hundred pound weight lay on his shoulders. "She's not coming. She's too scared."

Georgia's lips tightened so much they almost disappeared.

CHAPTER 25

Georgia

"I'm really sorry," Cody Wegman apologized to Georgia at the Starbucks near Midwest National. Ellie covered Wegman's hand with her own. "Relax, Cody. You tried."

"Yeah, but I'd thought she'd have more *cojones*, you know?"

Georgia tried not to react. This wasn't some caper with macho language and attitude. And Ellie was right. It wasn't the kid's fault. He'd risked his job to help them. Still, when you rely on amateurs...

Ellie and Wegman both peered at her, as if waiting for her to come up with another solution. The problem was she didn't have one. She sipped her drink. Icy cold and sweet. Small compensation.

"What's so important about those cashiers' checks?" Wegman asked.

Ellie glanced at Georgia. She nodded.

"Chris Messenger authorized them," Ellie explained,

conveniently leaving out the part about the bank chairman's signature. "Then closed the account they came from while her little girl was kidnapped. We think they might be related to her death."

"Whose account was that?"

Georgia cut in. "That's something I don't think you should know. It's—"

"But he might be able to help," Ellie interrupted.

Aside from baseball, Georgia didn't like team sports. Which was part of the problem when she was a cop. Being paired with Robby Parker had dragged her down. She preferred working alone. It was safer that way. But Ellie Foreman had become a major part of the investigation. The kid, too. He had a right to know. "You don't know this," she said softly. "And you damn well didn't hear it from me."

"Of course." A self-satisfied look unfolded Wegman's face. Georgia forced herself not to wipe it off with her napkin.

"It's Delton Security," Ellie said.

His face lit with recognition.

"You know who they are?"

"Everyone does. They're one of our biggest customers."

"So we understand," Georgia said. "How did they come to be a customer of the bank?"

He thought for a minute. "I think Delton was the result of one of our new business campaigns."

"What campaigns?"

"About a year ago, the bank launched an outreach effort. Senior officers would visit potential customers and pitch them with all sorts of perks to give us their accounts. Teams of officers—marketing, investment guys, IT—would do a dog and pony show. You know."

Georgia leaned forward. "You mentioned IT. Was Chris Messenger on one of those teams?"

Wegman nodded. "She sure was. I remember the days she'd go out. She'd kid around about wearing her new business suit. Usually we didn't dress up."

Georgia took in his faded t-shirt, shorts, and flip-flops. That was the truth.

"Was she on the team that went to Delton?"

"Are you kidding? She was the reason we got it."

Georgia sat up. "How did that happen?"

"They wanted to work with someone who could put all their operations online. Synchronize the bank's stuff with theirs. Chris was the natural choice for Account Manager." "That explains why she authorized the cashiers' checks," Georgia added. "And brought the matter to Pattison," Ellie said. "Maybe even helped convince him to go along." Wegman looked from Georgia to Ellie. "What's the chairman got to do with this?"

Georgia and Ellie exchanged a glance. Georgia shook her head.

"Nothing, Cody," Ellie said hurriedly. "Forget it."

"So, Cody," Georgia jumped in. "If you were looking to find out who the cashiers' checks went to, how would you do it?"

His features relaxed, as if realizing he was still part of the team. He drained his Frappuccino. "We're talking about June twenty-fifth, right?"

"No," Georgia said. "That's when the account they came out of was closed. The date the checks went out was early June. The first or second."

"Oh. I thought..." his voice trailed off. Then he sat up, a puzzled look on his face. "That's weird."

"What?"

"I think June twenty-fifth was the day the elevator went crazy." He looked at Georgia.

"Hold on." He pulled out his wallet, extracted a tiny calendar card, and squinted at it. "Yup. That was the day."

"What are you talking about?" Georgia asked.

"It was the strangest thing. There was a power failure in our bank of elevators. They just shut down for a few minutes."

"What do you mean 'your bank of elevators?'"

"IT is on the fifty-first floor. The elevators go from the lobby straight to fifty and then up to sixty-two. Five people were trapped inside. No lights. No electricity. Nothing. It only lasted about a minute, but one woman still hates to get on the elevator. She walks up most of the way."

"What happened?" Ellie asked.

"They don't really know." He tapped his glass against the table. "It was a hot day. Lots of AC all over the Loop. Best guess is that it was a Com Ed brownout."

"But it was only your bank of elevators," Ellie said.

"I know." He looked meaningfully at Ellie. "Kind of weird, you know?"

Georgia didn't bother to keep the irritation out of her voice. "Listen to me, Cody. I'm not into long, meaningful looks or half-assed insinuations. If you think there's a connection between the power failure and what Chris Messenger did, tell me. Otherwise don't waste my time."

Ellie pursed her lips. She looked like she wanted to defend Cody, but kept her mouth shut.

"Okay." Wegman rolled his mug. "Here's the thing. In the early days of computers, in order to make something permanent, you had to power down. You know, reboot the system."

"Restart your computer," Ellie murmured.

"Right. That's not the case anymore, at least with the kind of systems we have. But if someone didn't know that—say they were ten years out of date—they might think the only way to make something secure was to shut down the system."

"Could Chris Messenger have done that?" Georgia asked. "Powered it down?"

"Absolutely. She was head of IT. She could do almost anything online."

"And if the computers and the elevators were somehow on the same power line, the elevators would shut down, too."

"That's right. But, like I said, in the five years I've been here, that's never happened. Or, if it did, it happened late at night when no one was using the elevators."

"But aren't there back-up generators," Ellie asked, "to prevent that from happening?"

"There are, but if someone disabled the back-ups..."

"But why would Chris have powered them down?" Georgia said. "She's up to date on computers. She'd know it wasn't necessary."

"Maybe it was a signal. You know, 'mission accomplished,'" Ellie said.

"Shut down the elevators for a signal?" Georgia looked at them. "You watch way too much TV. Look, it was a hot day. Com Ed is known for rolling brownouts. Especially in the Loop. Maybe that's all it was."

"Or maybe she was forced to." Ellie pulled out a scrap of paper.

"Write down the name of the woman who won't get on the elevator. If you don't mind."

Cody scrawled down a name. Ellie folded the paper and slipped it into her bag.

Georgia shook her head. "I guess you like chasing your tail, too."

Ellie's cheeks reddened.

"Sorry. It's been a bad day." Georgia held out her hand for the paper. "I'll do it."

"Apology accepted." Ellie fished the paper out of her bag. "You sure?"

"It's part of the package," she deadpanned. "Okay. Let's talk about something more important. I need a look at that log. It shouldn't be that big a deal. It's not like hacking into someone's system. Or," she smiled wryly, "hijacking elevators. I mean, how much skill does it take to read a few sheets of paper? All I need is access."

Ellie looked thoughtful. "So, how do we get you that access?"

Georgia flicked her eyes to the barista behind the counter. He was cleaning the expresso machine with a white rag. "Tell me about the door to the teller area. Do they use swipe cards to get in and out?"

Wegman nodded. "All the doors use them. But even if you can get in, the drawer it's kept in is securely locked."

"That won't be a problem." Georgia had learned how to pick locks years ago. Larry, an elderly locksmith in the neighborhood, had taught her. And sold her a set of picks. "Will your swipe card get me in?"

"No. We're all keyed to specific areas."

"So how would you get into the teller department if you needed to?"

"Someone would have to let me in."

Georgia watched the barista wipe down the drink counter. When he looked up and saw her watching him, he smiled. His earrings—he must have been wearing three or four—sparkled in the light. He finished wiping the counter, folded the rag, and hung it on a hook behind the counter. His shift must be ending, she thought. He was cleaning up for the next. Georgia looked back at Cody and Ellie and smiled.

CHAPTER 26

Sunday evening Georgia drove back down to Midwest National to wait for the cleaning crews. Shafts of light from the setting sun spilled between buildings, casting elongated shadows on the streets. The heat from yesterday had broken, and a cool breeze whistled through the concrete canyons. Georgia felt lucky to find a parking spot near the bank's entrance.

The cleaning crews started filtering in around eight. Most were Hispanic-looking women and were dressed in blue uniforms. Georgia had studied Spanish in college but hadn't had much opportunity to use it since. She hoped she could make herself understood.

A few minutes before nine she crossed at the light and went to the front door of the bank. She'd asked Cody Wegman who the cleaning company was. It took him a while, but eventually he came up with "Corporate Enterprises of Chicago." When she got home, she Googled the company and found their website. She copied their logo, printed it, and created a fake badge, adding her name as "Supervisor." She did the same with a business card. Then she went to Kinko's where she laminated the badge and printed a few copies of the card. Now, armed with those, and her driver's license, she pushed through the revolving door.

She probably could have dispensed with the preparations. The security guard, a beefy man with red-rimmed eyes and wiry gray hair, was absorbed in a Sox game on a tiny TV that sat on the desk. He barely glanced at her badge. Georgia wondered how he'd managed to wire the Sox game into the building's security system.

She clipped the badge to her shirt. She'd purposely worn an old denim work shirt, khaki slacks, sneakers, and had pulled her hair back into a pony tail. "Excuse me. I'd like to start in the lobby. Should I just go through the door?"

The guard didn't look up but nodded noncommittally. "I'll buzz you in. The crew's already there."

She headed toward the glass doors that led to the lobby and teller areas, thanking her lucky stars for his inattention. She remembered the lobby: a huge room with thick blue carpeting, desks and chairs, and plants that actually looked healthy. She also remembered the perfectly tailored woman at one of the desks who could have worked at More-than-Friends. There was no woman now. No one at all. But the lights were on, and she heard faint strains of music.

She heard the latch release and pushed through the door. The music, a bouncy salsa, was louder now. To her left an alcove of teller booths stretched the length of the room. It was closed off with doors at both ends. To the right were clusters of desks and a grouping of sofas. So people could count their money in comfort? A supply cart stood about twenty feet from one of the teller booth doors.

"Hello?" Georgia called out. "Anyone there?"

A dark-haired woman stuck her head out of the alcove. Georgia beckoned. The woman looked both ways, hand on her chest, as though she wasn't sure Georgia meant her. Georgia waved again and held up her badge. "Supervisor," she said, giving it a Spanish accent. She hoped she had the right word.

The woman reluctantly came through the door. Georgia wanted to follow her back into the teller booths right away, but she had to play it cool.

"*Buenas Tardes,*" Georgia said. "*Soy la supervisora nueva. Hace una semana.*"

The woman nodded. Up close, she looked young, maybe under thirty. But her brows knit together and her expression was worried. Georgia wondered if the woman was an illegal and thought Georgia was there to check her papers.

"Es okay?" The woman asked in a small voice.

Georgia gave her a reassuring smile. "*Si.* Okay. I am here just to watch. *Estoy observando. No mas.*"

"Ahh." The woman's face smoothed out.

Georgia smiled. So far so good. The woman went back to her supply cart. Georgia followed. The music grew louder. Perched on top of the supply cart was a radio. It looked old, like the transistor radio her parents owned when she was a little girl. When the woman saw Georgia gazing at it, she snapped it off.

Georgia shook her head. "*No es necessario.* It's fine."

The woman shot Georgia a quizzical glance.

"*El radio. No problema.*"

The woman's lips approximated a smile, revealing crooked teeth. She nodded as if she understood but left the radio off. Then she started to roll her cart across the room. Away from the teller booths. Wrong direction.

A female voice from the back of the room called out in Spanish. Georgia looked. A second supply cart stood beside a desk, and another woman was dusting its surface. She finished and rolled her cart toward them. She looked remarkably like the first woman, but older. Were they sisters? A rapid conversation ensued in Spanish. All Georgia could make out were the words "supervisor," and "observer."

Georgia put on her most disarming smile. The second woman dipped her head. "I am Isabella Santiago," she said in accented English and pointed to the ID card clipped to her waist. When Georgia looked, a spark of fear shot up her spine. It was altogether different from the one she'd made. Would the woman notice? She pretended to read the woman's ID.

"*Gracias, Isabella. Me llama Georgia Davis.*"

The woman gazed at Georgia's ID. From her attitude Isabella appeared to have more seniority than the first woman, and she seemed to register the difference between the cards. Georgia was about to launch into a rationale about corporate always changing things, trying to improve, not leaving well enough alone, but decided against it. She was supposed to be a Supervisor. To Isabella she *was* corporate. She didn't need excuses.

"What's your colleague's name?" Georgia asked.

"Maria."

"Does she speak English?"

"Not much," Isabella said.

Georgia nodded. "Please tell Maria not to be afraid. I'm not here to check up on you. I'm just here to find out what you do. See if you have everything you need. We want to help you do your job better." She motioned with her hand. "So you both just go ahead with your work. I'll follow along, okay?"

Isabella's eyes narrowed. Georgia didn't blame her for being suspicious. Her own bullshit meter was off the scale. But then Isabella's shoulders lifted slightly, as if she'd decided Georgia was either telling the truth or it wasn't a big enough deal to worry about. "Okay."

The pressure in Georgia's chest loosened. "You divide up the floor?"

"Si. She does the front, I do the back."

And who does the teller booths, Georgia wanted to ask.

The two women starting talking in Spanish again. Their voices were hushed, but Georgia thought Maria was asking how long Georgia would be tailing them.

"*No se.*" Isabella pushed her cart to the back of the room.

Which meant Maria would be cleaning the front. Good. If Maria had secrets of her own, she'd probably be less inclined to wonder why Georgia wanted to go into the teller booths. Maybe less observant, as well.

Maria went to the first desk at the front of the room. She worked methodically but slowly, emptying the waste basket, dusting the cabinet and desk, spraying Windex on glass surfaces. Then she moved to another desk and started all over again. Rather than stand there with nothing to do, Georgia pitched in. Maria didn't say a word, but by the third desk, they'd achieved a steady rhythm. Maria would dust and spray, while Georgia would empty the trash.

Still, it took another six desks and a long thirty minutes before they met up with Isabella who'd been working back to front. Maria detached an industrial vacuum cleaner from the supply cart, plugged it in, and started to run it across the carpet. They would be finished soon and would be going to another floor. But Georgia hadn't seen the teller booths yet. Her pulse sped up. She grabbed the vacuum from Maria.

Surprise chased across Maria's face. "No, Mees. I do."

Georgia held up her hand and shook her head. "No. *Yo trabajo* too. *Qiero trabahar tambien*."

Maria and Isabella exchanged glances. They must have thought she was crazy. Still vacuuming, Georgia worked her way to the closest teller door. She motioned to the door.

Maria held up her swipe card.

Georgia nodded.

Maria slid her card through the card reader. A green light flashed on, and the door opened. Georgia followed Maria in. The room itself was long and narrow. On one side were about ten teller booths separated by partitions. On the other was a long counter with file cabinets and drawers underneath.

Both Sechrest and Wegman said the log was kept in a drawer, but there had to be over twenty drawers and just as many file cabinets. Each one had a tiny lock under the handle. Georgia felt for her picks in her back pocket. Drawers like these only had two or three pins and were notoriously easy to pick. But how could she proceed without Maria seeing what she was up to? And which one held the cashiers' check log?

She turned around. Maria was right behind her. Georgia pointed to her watch. "You look tired. *Quieres descansar?* Do you want to take a break? *Un break?*"

Maria grinned. "*Un descansco?*"

"*Si. Un descanso.*" Georgia nodded energetically. "I'll finish in here."

"'Es okay? *De veras?*"

"Absolutely. You go. *Vete.*" Georgia waved her out of the teller area.

Maria gave her a toothy smile and left. Georgia pushed the vacuum cleaner to the side but left it running. As she did, she checked the ceiling for cameras. She didn't see any. Which was odd. There had to be cameras watching the tellers. Maybe they were in the individual booths, rather than the general work space. She hoped to hell she was right.

She slipped on a pair of rubber gloves and pulled out her lock picks. There were no identifying labels on any of the drawers, and for a horrified moment, she thought she might have to open each one to find the log. Which, of course, wouldn't be possible in the few minutes she had.

She edged down the side of the room past the drawers, searching the counters for any clue that the log was close by. She spotted in-trays and out-trays, all empty; thick three-ring binders, which she assumed specified tellers' procedures, and, farther down, a small safe. She frowned. No way could she crack a safe. But they'd said drawer, not safe.

She'd completed one pass down the side of the room and was starting back up when she noticed a drawer underneath the manuals. It was a little longer and wider than the others. She went to it and slipped her tension wrench inside. She gently levered it, then inserted her rake, decided she didn't need it, put in the hook instead, and worked it a few seconds. The lock popped, and she opened the drawer.

Pamphlets and brochures about the bank's services. No log.

Dejected, Georgia closed the drawer and moved past a stack of smaller drawers. Another larger drawer lay beyond them.

Followed by a stack of smaller ones. Then a large one. So there was a pattern. She went to the second large drawer and used her locks to open it. This time she found a thick red three-ring binder, with tabs for each month. On the cover someone had written in marker, "Cashiers' Checks."

A buzz skimmed her nerves. She pulled it out and paged through. Each sheet of paper was separated into six columns: the date the check was cut, the check number, the payee, the remitter and their account number, the bank officer's authorization, and, in some cases, the address where the check was sent. There were typically two to three hundred entries a day. With all the online banking processes, software, and other high-tech practices, Georgia was surprised any bank information was still recorded in something as low-tech as a three-ring binder. But here it was. She flipped through entries for March and April—there were a slew of them in April, related to taxes, she guessed—then May.

Finally she reached the June entries. She scanned June first, focusing on the remitter column, looking for Delton Security. She was half-way through the entries for that day before she remembered she should be checking "Southwest Development," not Delton. She started over. Nothing for June first. She was just starting June second when she realized the whine of the vacuum cleaner, which was still on, would effectively mask the sounds of Maria and Isabella returning. She had to hurry.

Paging down the list for June second, she saw two entries for cashiers' checks remitted by Delton Security. Ironic. One was for $45,000 and the second for $22,459. Both were authorized by Chris Messenger. She was halfway down the second log for June second when she found the words "Southwest Development." She checked the amount. One million dollars. Authorized by T.

Pattison. With an asterisk by his name. She looked at the next entry and the one after that. Three cashiers checks. Each authorized by Pattison. Each for one million dollars. She read the names of the people to whom the money was sent:

Edward Wrobleski

Kirk Brewer

Rafael Peña

Her stomach pitched. She scanned the log to see if there were any addresses indicating where the checks were sent. Wrobleski's went to a bank in Cherry Hill, New Jersey. For Brewer, a bank in Oklahoma City. For Peña, there was nothing. She copied everything down, stuffed the log back in the drawer, and closed it. At the same time the door to the teller area opened. Georgia looked over her shoulder. Both Maria and Isabella stood there. Maria was holding a bottled water.

Georgia felt the blood rush to her head. Her cheeks started to burn. Had they seen her? Could they tell? She whipped around to face them, quickly sliding her notepad in her back pocket. The women looked curiously at her. Georgia pushed the vacuum, still blowing at high speed, toward the door. She made herself take slow, deep breaths.

The women continued to stare. They knew. They had to.

Georgia unplugged the vacuum, took it back into the lobby area, and stowed it on the cart. The two women followed her out. Georgia frantically tried to come up with a plausible reason why she was ransacking the drawers. But when she turned to face them, they started chatting in Spanish. Maria said something about Montrose and *el lago*. Isabella mentioned Great America and McDonalds. They both laughed.

Georgia shifted her feet. If they had seen her messing with the drawers, apparently they weren't going to do anything about it. The tension drained out of her. "Well, I think I'm pretty much finished here. *Finito. Termine.*" She held out her hand. "You both do excellent work. I'll make sure the boss knows."

The two women shook her hand and smiled. Georgia smiled back. Then she headed to the glass door. She could hardly contain her elation.

CHAPTER 27

It was after one in the morning when Georgia got home, but she was pumped. She booted up her computer, took a quick shower, and threw on some sweats. This called for a celebration. She'd accomplished her mission. Neat and clean, so to speak. How often did that happen? She wished she had a beer. Too bad she didn't drink anymore.

She got a pop instead, took a sip, and carried it to the computer. She got out her notepad. Starting with an online white pages directory, she entered Cherry Hill, New Jersey, then Edward Wrobleski. The website promptly spit out an address and phone number. It couldn't be that easy, could it? She wrote down the number; she'd call first thing in the morning.

She went back to the directory and entered Kirk Brewer and Oklahoma City. Five Brewers came back, but none of them Kirk. She wondered if one of the five was a relative. She printed out the page, just in case. Then she went into one of her subscription databases and entered his name. Two addresses came back. The first was in Oklahoma City but wasn't one of the five from the directory. The other was in Tallahassee, Florida. She wrote them both down and clicked onto a reverse directory for the phone numbers. Nothing came up for Oklahoma City, but the Tallahassee address yielded a number. She wrote it down.

Next she tried Rafael Peña. She searched across half a dozen public and private websites, but nothing came back. One website indicated that Rafael Peña was in their database, but unlike the more reputable websites she paid money to, this one was just a come-on. Without more information, she was stuck.

Then, just for the hell of it, she Googled Thomas Pattison. Pattison had served in Vietnam with the 101st Airborne in '68 and '69. After being awarded two Purple Hearts, he went back to college and graduate school, earning an MBA from UNC. Surprisingly, Pattison went into the public sector and worked at the Treasury Department during the Reagan administration. Which meant he probably had some heavy-duty clout. Once Reagan left office, though, Pattison went private, working for Chase, First National of Chicago, and Harris Bank. He'd taken the chairman's position at Midwest National five years ago. Georgia clicked on more links. Apparently Pattison had a sterling reputation and was highly respected both in and out of government. Midwest National had hired a big deal.

She picked up the pop—she'd only had the one sip—and poured the rest of it down the drain. She needed a few hours of sleep.

* * *

By seven-thirty Monday morning, armed with a strong cup of

coffee, Georgia was ready to make her first call. She disabled her caller ID, then punched in Edward Wrobleski's number in Cherry Hill. She heard a faint swish as the call connected. It rang once. Twice. Then again. On the fourth ring, it went to voice-mail. "Hi. This is Eddie. You know what to do."

Georgia hung up. There could be all sorts of reasons why Wrobleski wasn't answering. She'd try again later. Still, after her success last night, she couldn't help hoping she was on a streak. She went back to her notes, found the Tallahassee phone number for Kirk Brewer, and dialed.

After three rings she was about to disconnect when the phone was picked up.

"Hello?" A woman's voice. Low-pitched, smoky. A Southern drawl.

"Is this Kirk Brewer's residence?" Georgia asked.

"Who is this?"

"My name is Georgia Davis. I'm calling from Chicago. Is this Mrs. Brewer?"

"Why are you calling?"

"I'd like to talk to Mr. Brewer. Please. It's a financial matter."

"Financial? What do you mean by financial?" Georgia picked up something in her voice besides the drawl.

"Are you Mrs. Brewer?" She repeated.

The voice hesitated. "Who'd you say you were?"

The woman was playing cat and mouse. Georgia didn't want to divulge anything, but she needed information. She had to give her something. "Georgia Davis. I'd really like to talk with Mr. Brewer, if that's possible."

Another pause. "It isn't."

"Excuse me?"

"Kirk isn't here." Her words were slurred. Now Georgia got it. The woman was drinking. Georgia automatically checked her watch. Barely nine in the morning in Florida.

"When do you expect him?"

"I don't."

Georgia forced the edge out of her voice. "Ma'am, this is an important matter. Do you know how I could get in touch with him?"

The woman didn't answer for a minute. Then, "I s'pose you could, if you can communicate with the other side."

Georgia gripped the phone. "What are you saying?"

"I'm saying that Kirk is dead. That's what I'm saying."

Georgia felt like she'd been punched in the gut. "I—I'm sorry. I didn't know."

"Yeah. Well."

"Was—I mean—when did this happen?"

"I think you'd better tell me what you want."

Georgia realized she had to come clean. "I'm a private investigator. I'm working on a case in which Mr. Brewer's name has come up. Apparently, he received a large sum of money recently. I'm trying to understand why."

The woman's sudden intake of breath told Georgia she knew something.

"What's your name, ma'am?" Georgia asked.

"I'm Mary Louise. Kirk's fiancée."

"Mary Louise, I'm sorry for your loss. But could I ask you a few questions?"

"You can ask."

Mary Louise might be drinking at nine in the morning, but her brain was still functioning well enough to be cautious. "How did Kirk die?"

"They say it was an accident."

"An accident? Where?"

"Kirk was working a job out in Arizona."

"Who was he working for?"

"Delton Security."

Georgia sat up. "What did he do for Delton?"

"He was a security specialist."

"Can you be more specific?"

"Don't know. He wouldn't never talk about it."

"Where in Arizona was he?"

"Place called Stevens. Near the border."

"He was there how long?"

"Couple months. Maybe three."

"Mary Lou, did you know he'd received a lot of money recently?"

There was silence. "Lady, I don't know who you are. Who you're working for. So I don't think that's any of your business."

She knew. Georgia thought about it, then decided to approach it from another way. "You said he died in an accident?"

"I said *they* said it was an accident. A training accident."

"You don't believe them?"

"I don't know what to believe."

"Why? What happened?"

"It was about three weeks ago. They were working with explosives. Something went wrong. They said he just—blew up. Didn't even have enough body parts to send home."

Georgia winced but pushed on. Three weeks ago would have been the end of June. "Who's 'they'?"

"Delton."

"Mary Louise, do you doubt what they said?"

"Look, Davis? That's your name, right?"

"Right."

"Well, Davis, let me tell you something. My Kirk knows—knew—what he was doing in the field. He did two tours of duty for the Army, both of them in Iraq. He knew about explosives, IEDs, land mines. All of that. He quit the Army 'cause Delton said they'd pay him ten times what he'd been making. A year later he's dead because of a 'training' accident? You say you're some kind of investigator. You figure it out."

Georgia frowned. "Mary Louise, could you tell me—"

"No. I don't got nothing more to say. We're done here."

"Wait. Just one more question. Have you ever heard of Edward Wrobleski?"

"Eddie? He was Kirk's buddy. They met in Iraq. Both of them went to work for Delton."

"What about Rafael Peña?"

"Never heard of him. And now we *are* done. And please, don't call here again." Georgia heard a click followed by the hiss of empty air.

* * *

The white pages directory for Cherry Hill had a listing for Milos G. Wrobleski on Chestnut Street, but Georgia couldn't bring herself to call. It was a hazy, hot July day, but she felt chilled. She stood and went to her window. The glass was new—it had been replaced last year after a bullet pierced it, hit a candle, and set her apartment on fire. She peered out. The house across the street had kids' toys scattered across the lawn. The walkway up to her apartment had two cracks in the concrete. The yews flanking the walkway were thriving. Everything looked normal.

But it wasn't. A little girl was traumatized, three people were dead, and Georgia had a feeling the body count would be going up. Mary Louise, Brewer's fiancée, knew something but was holding back. Was she being paid to keep her mouth shut? Or was she just afraid? Too bad Georgia couldn't go to Florida to find out, but she wasn't sure it had anything to do with Molly Messenger's kidnapping.

Still, she should find out what Brewer—and Delton—were doing in Arizona. Delton had sent Brewer a million dollars from a secret account. And then tried to close the account in a clumsy, ultimately unsuccessful, maneuver. Now, Brewer was dead and his fiancée, for one, thought the reason for his death—a training accident—was suspicious.

What about Eddie Wrobleski, Brewer's "buddy," who also got a million dollar check from Delton? Was he in Arizona? And what about Rafael Peña? He got the third million. Why couldn't she get a handle on him? Georgia turned from the window and glanced at her computer. Before going back, she lowered the blind.

* * *

The man who answered Milos Wrobleski's phone sounded curt and impatient. "What is it?"

"Hello, Mr Wrobleski. My name is Georgia Davis, and I'm calling from Chicago. Do you have a son by the name of Edward?"

An irritated sigh confirmed she had the right person. "What do you want now?"

"I beg your pardon?"

"Everyone keeps calling, sending me these fucking forms, telling me they need this and then that and who knows what the fuck else. And it's all gotta be done yesterday. Can't you assholes let us mourn in peace?"

Georgia went rigid. She found it hard to catch her breath. "I'm—I'm so sorry."

"What the hell do you want?"

She forced air into her lungs. "I'm an investigator, and I'm looking into the money your son received a few weeks ago."

She heard a hollow laugh. "Yeah. You and everybody else."

"What do you mean?"

"I mean the bank, lawyers, even the IRS has been dogging me about it. Well, fuck you all. It's ours. Eddie's will was crystal clear."

"He put it in his will?"

"He changed his will right after he got it. Even faxed me a copy. Not that anyone believes me, of course."

"When was this?"

"Who'd you say you were?"

"I'm a private investigator. We think the money that was sent to your son may be related to other cases here in Chicago."

"Well, I don't know about any case in Chicago. And I don't give a shit. All I care about is that a million dollars went into my boy's bank account. Less than a month later, he's dead. I don't need to know any more."

As long as you can keep the money, Georgia thought. But aloud she said, "Was he in Arizona working for Delton Security when he—died?"

"So? What if he was?"

"Mr. Wrobleski, how did he die?"

"It was an accident. Some explosives he was working with were screwed up, and they blew. Took him along. Look, lady, I don't want to talk any more."

"I understand. Just one more question. Have you ever heard of Rafael Peña? He might have worked at Delton with your son."

There was a long sigh. "The only one Eddie ever talked about was Brewer. Kirk. They were buddies from the military."

Georgia blinked. She should tell him about Kirk Brewer's death. It would be the right thing to do. It might change his attitude. She kept her mouth shut.

"Thank you, Mr. Wrobleski. I won't bother you again."

CHAPTER 28

The Liberty Club owned a stately greystone in the middle of the Loop on Jackson. Three flags—the U.S., Illinois and Chicago's—flapped in the breeze out front. The club had been around forever, at least since the Civil War. Georgia wasn't sure how you became a member or what you got when you did, but its roster included the top echelon of Chicago's political and business establishment, so apparently there were benefits. Like the series of speakers they brought in Tuesday mornings.

She went inside and climbed a set of marble steps. To her right were about twenty-five people in a huge room with windows that spanned two stories. The windows were covered in long green drapes. Two enormous chandeliers showered light on the room. The smell of coffee with chicory floated through the air. Georgia stood at the back of the room.

"Rule number one in my family was pride and loyalty to our country," the speaker was saying. "My father never let any of us forget it." Geoff Delton aimed a dazzling smile at the group. Tall, fit, and handsome, his blond hair looked almost white. Which made his dark eyes seem black. Dressed in a light khaki suit, blue shirt, and yellow tie, he cut a vigorous, electric image, forceful enough, Georgia thought, to power the chandeliers by himself.

"So when my time came, I was proud to enlist in the Marine Corps. As you know, I was deployed to Iraq during Desert Storm, where, in addition to fighting for our country, I had a unique opportunity to observe how our military works. It was there I realized the armed forces could be much more efficient if the private sector was involved."

He went on to discuss the redundancies and inefficiencies of the military and how it could be faster, lighter, and smarter. Several audience members, all men, nodded. Former military types, probably.

"We now have over a thousand men in five countries," Delton said. "We're not as big as Blackwater, of course, but we don't want to be." He smiled. "We are the ones you call when you don't want publicity." That got a ripple of laughter.

A flash of light exploded. Someone was taking a picture. Startled, Delton took a step forward and shaded his eyes. "Excuse me. I must insist. No pictures. Ever." He paused for a moment to let it sink in, then nodded to someone at the back of the room. Georgia craned her neck but didn't get a good look at whoever it was.

Delton stepped back behind the podium and launched into a discussion about the security issues faced by corporations and business leaders. He explained the types of services Delton Security offered, from protection and body guarding to something he called Delton's "Special Operations Division."

"Depending on the need, Delton men... and women... are

prepared to serve you efficiently, thoroughly, and at a reasonable cost."

The impression he gave was earnest, open, trustworthy. How much of that was calculated, she wondered. He concluded with a flourish, asking his audience to consider their security needs. He took a few questions, which he answered mostly by offering to talk one-on-one with the questioner. Finally, he held up some business cards. "Feel free to call any time. I still answer my own line."

After watching him glad-hand and pass out cards for a few minutes, Georgia approached.

"Good morning," he said. "I saw you come in."

"I wanted to meet you."

His smile broadened as if he'd expected her to say that. It made her uncomfortable. He was too interested. She cleared her throat. "I'm an investigator. I've been looking into the deaths of Chris Messenger and Arthur Emerlich at Midwest National. I understand you're one of the bank's customers."

His gaze flitted away for an instant. Then it returned. His smile faded. "What a tragedy. We're still reeling."

Georgia nodded. "From what I understand Chris was your personal banker, is that right?'

"I'm not sure what you mean by 'personal.' She was the point person on our accounts. Much of our banking needs are online, and she was the director of IT. It was a good fit." He cocked his head. "Are you with the police? If so, I've already given a statement."

Good information to know. It meant the police had already made a connection between Delton and the bank. Did that mean they knew about the service charges and cashiers' checks too? "I'm private," she said.

"Did the bank hire you?"

He was pumping her. She sidestepped the question. "I saw you handing out business cards. Mind if I have one?"

"Not at all. I'm always happy to take a call from an attractive woman." He smiled again, but this time, it didn't reach his eyes.

"I won't take up your time here, but I have some questions about one of your contracts out West. In Arizona."

His expression didn't change. "Not sure I can tell you anything. Much of what we do involves national security."

"I understand completely. I'll be in touch."

"I'll be waiting." Again he broke eye contact, his gaze searching out someone or something at the back of the room. She spun around. She didn't see anyone, but she had the impression someone had just left the room. She turned back to Delton. An elderly man who'd been in the audience had approached and was pumping his hand.

"Thank you so much for making time for us this morning, Geoff. You gave an excellent presentation."

Delton dialed up the wattage on his smile. "Glad to be of service." He glanced over at Georgia and winked.

* * *

"I just can't take it any more," the woman whispered that afternoon in the bank's cafeteria. "I'm asking for a transfer."

Benay Weiss looked like she might topple over if you blew on her, but Georgia suspected her appearance belied a tough core. She had mousey brown hair streaked with gray, a nose too small even to call "button," and owlish eyes that rarely blinked. She wore a flowered skirt, white blouse, and green cardigan draped over her shoulders. It was well after lunch, and most of the tables in the cafeteria were empty. The few people still there didn't appear to have the slightest interest in the two women, but Georgia kept a watchful eye on her surroundings.

"That's confidential, of course." Benay said, losing the whisper. "I haven't told anyone yet. Including Cody." Her voice had that irritating fifth-grade teacher squeak.

"Because of the elevator incident?" Georgia asked.

The woman nodded. "It was—how shall I put it..." she paused theatrically, "... something I will never forget."

"Can you tell me exactly what happened? If it isn't too difficult."

Weiss flashed a ghost of a smile, as though she'd heard her cue and was ready to play her scene. Georgia wondered how many times she'd repeated the story. "Well, I was on break—I'm an administrative assistant in the bank's Commercial division. Equipment leasing. On the sixty-second floor. And I'm always cold. Even on a day like today.

"So I drink two cups of tea: one in the morning, one in the afternoon. I usually get my afternoon cup down here. It's a nice break."

Something about the woman made Georgia's teeth itch. She almost wished she'd let Foreman do the interview. "Lily was waiting for the elevator, too. She's a manager in asset-based lending. A different department." She sniffed, as if Lily's department was second-rate. "The elevator arrived. We stepped on. It made a few more stops. One or two people got on."

"Do you remember what floors it stopped on?"

"I couldn't say. Not with any authority."

"Are you sure?"

"Positive. Except for Lily, who I didn't know at the time, there was a messenger, two other men, and then a man with sunglasses."

"Go on."

"Everything was fine until we started down to the lobby. After fifty, it's supposed to be an express. Anyway, the elevator started to speed up, the way it always does. But then, without any warning, it jolted to a stop. Just like that!" She snapped her fingers. "It bounced hard, and I was thrown up in the air. Then I fell. I still have bruises on my legs." She stared at Georgia, as if daring her to challenge her. "The lights went off, and everything just stopped. The cab was dangling in mid air. I mean, you could feel it. No one knew what was going on." She shivered and pulled her cardigan closer. "You know, I hate to fly. I have nightmares about crashing. This was like that. But real. I really thought I was going to die a violent, horrible death."

"What about the other passengers?"

"What you'd expect. It was pure bedlam. People were on the floor. One man thought his leg was broken. Everyone was screaming. Me, too, of course. I was praying out loud." She shivered again and took a sip of tea. "This is still so hard."

Georgia knew she was supposed to comfort Weiss. Encourage her to go on. Which, after an appropriate pause, Weiss would bravely but reluctantly do. Georgia couldn't do it.

Weiss waited for Georgia's cue. When it didn't come, she frowned slightly and drew herself up. "Eventually the gears started to grind. Lights flashed on, off, then on again. The elevator lurched once more—again, we thought this was the end—but then it started to descend. Nice and slow. As if nothing had happened. When we got to the lobby, we piled out. A crowd had gathered. Of course, security said it was a brownout." Her eyebrows arched as if to say no sane person could believe such a bald-faced lie.

A fast-paced movement in the corner of the room caught Georgia's attention. She squinted but couldn't make out anything. Then it disappeared. She dragged her gaze back to Weiss. "How long was the car suspended without power?"

"It seemed like an eternity. But it probably wasn't more than a minute or two."

"And you don't believe it was a brownout?"

"I don't know what to believe," Weiss said.

"I'm sure elevator inspectors have come in to go over the system."

"Yes, they did. But I haven't heard any explanations. Oh, Midwest National was very sensitive. They sent flowers, and gave me a week off with pay." She laughed in a practiced tone. "They were afraid I'd sue. Actually, someone is suing, I understand. The messenger, I believe. But I've worked here over ten years. I don't want to be a troublemaker." She sighed audibly. "I just want to work in a place where I don't have to take an elevator. I shiver every time the doors open."

"Is there anything else you can remember?"

Weiss frowned. "Why do you want to know?"

"Cody told you I'm an investigator, right?"

"He said you were looking into Christine Messenger and Art Emerlich's deaths."

"That's right."

"Everyone's still reeling. I don't think it will ever be the same. Which is another reason it's time for me to move on. My sister, who lives with me, wants me to work out in the suburbs. She's out there. Much safer, she thinks."

Georgia nodded. "Back to the elevator. Anything else?"

Weiss looked blank.

"Have you talked to any of the people on the elevator since the incident?"

"Well, Lily and I talk. After something like that, there's a bond, you know? She's still considering whether to take legal action." She slapped her hand over her mouth. "Oh my god. That was highly confidential. Forget what I said."

Again Georgia scanned the corner where she'd seen the flash of movement. Nothing. "No problem. What about the others?"

Weiss got a faraway look. "As I said, I didn't know the messenger. The man from sixty-three I've seen a few times, and the man whose leg was injured. He's doing a lot better. But the man who was missing part of his finger, I haven't seen since—"

Georgia was instantly alert. "What did you say?"

"I said, the man from sixty-three..."

Georgia cut her off. "No. The man who was missing part of his finger..."

Weiss pursed her lips, as if she thought Georgia didn't get it. "The man with the sunglasses who got on at fifty-one was missing part of his finger."

"Which finger?"

"Let me see." Weiss sipped her tea. Slowly. Then she closed her eyes. She was milking the moment, damn her. Finally, "It was his left hand. Index finger."

"Describe it."

"Just that. The top half of his finger, down to the knuckle, wasn't there."

Georgia nodded imperceptibly. "You're sure."

"Of course. He was bracing himself against the steel railing. When the lights came on, I saw it clearly."

"What floor did he get on?"

She sighed impatiently. "I already told you. Fifty-one."

"Isn't that the floor IT is on?"

"Yes."

"But you didn't see him afterwards?"

"No."

"Did security talk to him? After the elevator got to the lobby?"

"You know, now that I'm thinking about it, I don't believe they did." She said. "I think he just sort of disappeared."

* * *

As Georgia drove back to Evanston, dirty gray clouds pushed across the sky, and fat drops of rain splattered her windshield. Then the storm started in earnest, rain and wind lashing the street. She flicked on her wipers, barely conscious of the weather. Benay Weiss said a man missing part of the index finger on his left hand had been on the elevator that got stuck. The man who kidnapped Molly Messenger was missing the same finger, and Sandy Sechrest was stalked by a man missing his finger. Cody Wegman thought the power source for the IT Department and the elevators servicing those floors might be linked. And the elevator incident occurred June twenty-fifth—the same day Christine Messenger closed Delton Security's secret account. This could be the connection she'd been hoping for.

Georgia swung onto Lake Shore Drive. The Kennedy would be faster this time of day, but the Drive was prettier. Today, though, angry waves pummeled the beach and the rocks. Sheets of gray water swept across her windshield and pooled in potholes.

When she got home, she'd call Terry Messenger. The next step depended on him. They could go to O'Malley with what they had. Even though the police had already questioned Geoff Delton—a fact he'd conveniently let slip during their conversation—at the very least Georgia could give them a new angle. But until they could identify and apprehend the man with the missing finger, Molly wasn't truly safe.

Traffic was thickening as she headed north. She was glad she'd taken the opportunity to meet Geoff Delton. He'd dodged her question about the Arizona contract, which, while not surprising, fueled her suspicions. Two Delton Security specialists in Arizona were a million dollars richer but were now dead from a "training accident." How much did Delton know about it? Was he in some way responsible? Somebody was going to great lengths to eliminate people—the count was up to four now, plus a kidnapping.

And what about Rafael Peña, the third Delton contractor, who seemed to have gone off the grid? Was he alive? Maybe he'd taken his money and skipped. Unless *he* was the man with the missing finger.

As she approached the curve near Hollywood and Sheridan, she saw that orange and white pylons blocked the outside lane. Damn construction. She instinctively eased off the gas pedal to move into the middle lane. She coasted for a few yards, then braked. Nothing happened. She pumped the brake. The Toyota didn't stop. She jammed her foot down. Still nothing. Blocks of silver and black flashed by. She was going to slam into another car, which was also trying to merge. At the last minute she wrenched the wheel toward the pylons. At least she wouldn't plow straight into the car. She did anyway. She heard the hideous crunch of metal smashing metal. The impact jarred her and threw her backwards. She wanted to fly, but she was strapped in her seat. Something exploded and hit her face. Everything went black.

CHAPTER 29

Ellie

Y ou might not see Puck, Oberon, or Titania, but our village's "Midsummer Days and Nights" Festival is just as whimsical. A four-day fundraiser, "Days and Nights" combines bands, carny booths, rides, and an auction. Its best feature is the lighting. Strands of multi-colored lights are woven through the trees of the Village Green, and at night the sparkles and twinkles are as dazzling as a troupe of fairies in the forest.

"Days and Nights" is also known for its food. Almost a dozen village restaurants cook up their favorite and most portable entrées, like lemon grass soup and chicken satay. The less sophisticated booths are a paradise of junk food: cotton candy, pizza, brats, and funnel cake. The smells alone are a contact high.

A fierce storm had battered the village earlier, but the bruising clouds and rain vanished as suddenly as they came, and by evening bright sunshine streamed down. Even the grass had dried. Dad, Rachel, and I spread a blanket in front of the main stage. We'd come to hear a Beatles tribute band, and, of course, eat. We rounded up what I call the Foreman Family Sampler: ribs, sweet corn on the cob, hot dogs, gyros, curly fries, and lemonade. For dessert we ate "Dippin' Dots," tiny little beads of flash-frozen ice cream first invented at Southern Illinois University.

I kept an eye out for Doug and Susan, who'd be joining us for the music. My father won't eat ribs—he never eats pork—but he seemed to enjoy his gyros, and Rachel was inhaling a plate of fries. A cool breeze, more like fall than midsummer, kicked up as we finished, and I detoured for coffee. When I returned, Rachel suddenly seemed fascinated by the weave of the blanket.

"What's wrong?" I gave one coffee to my father and set the other down carefully.

She spoke softly, not looking up. "There's a guy here I don't want to see."

"What guy? And why not?"

"Paul Mishkin. He owes me money."

I picked up my coffee, took a sip. "He does?"

"I lent him twenty dollars a couple of weeks ago to—um—buy his girlfriend dinner." Rachel wouldn't meet my eyes.

I frowned. Her story sounded as fishy as a bait shop in high season. I wondered if she was fronting him cash for weed and whether I should call her on it. I decided to let it go. I'd weasel the real story out of her when Dad wasn't around. "I'm glad you're so wealthy."

That earned me a quick but hostile glance. "He swore he'd pay me back."

"When?"

"What, when did he swear?"

I nodded.

"About a month ago," she confessed.

"And he hasn't come through."

She picked at a thread on the blanket.

I tried and failed to ignore my welling self-righteous anger. "Rachel, there's no need for you to feel embarrassed. He owes *you*. For whatever reason you lent him the money." Another irritated glance. "He should be ashamed of himself. How was he raised? That's just not right. Morally or ethically." I pulled a yellow packet of sweetener out of my purse, tore the top, and sprinkled it in my coffee. "I have half a mind to talk to him myself. He's ripping you off."

My father stared at me. Rachel did too, her embarrassment temporarily forgotten.

"What are you staring at?"

"How many of those yellow packets do you have?" My father asked.

"I don't know. I always pick up a few in the..." My voice trailed off.

"How much do you pay for them?" His voice was stern.

I knew where he was going, but pride made me mount a half-hearted defense. "Have you seen how much a box of sweetener costs these days? Even at Costco it's nearly ten dollars."

My father's eyebrows arched so high they knit together. Both he and Rachel cast glances at the empty packet still in my hand.

"Well, Miss Moral Majority," my father said, "Congratulations on the fine ethical example you're setting for your daughter."

Rachel shot me one of those insufferable teenage I-told-you-so looks. Crumpling the packet, I dumped it back in my bag and slouched on the blanket.

Relief finally came when the band trotted out on stage. The

four guys were dressed in those collarless matching suits the Beatles wore when they were still innocent, asking nothing more than if they could hold my hand. One of them even looked like John Lennon.

They promptly rolled out a brisk rendition of "A Hard Day's Night." The crowd whooped and hollered and applauded. Some people were already dancing. My eyes were drawn to a woman wearing a gaudy print blouse and slacks, with heavy make-up and hair in a French twist, who was grooving to the music. She looked like she had a few stories to tell.

A few minutes later, Doug and Susan joined us and settled on our blanket. Susan was wearing her mint julep sundress and looked like she'd just stepped out of *Gracious Southern Living*. Doug was in golf shirt and chinos.

"How's it going?" She rummaged around the woven basket she'd brought and extracted a home-made pecan pie, plates, and forks.

While she sliced the pie into eight perfect pieces, I filled her in on Rachel's college preferences. She distributed the slices. My father dipped his head in thanks. Rachel grinned as she took hers. "This looks great. Thanks, Mrs. Siler."

Susan nodded. "My pleasure, Rachel." She handed me a plate. "Any idea what Terry Messenger's going to do with their house? It's just sitting there empty, and the not-knowing has cast a pall over the block."

I tried the pie. The brown sugar maple-y filling was overkill, but the pecans and crust cut the sweetness a bit. "How would I know?"

"Isn't your friend still looking into Chris Messenger's death?"

"You mean Georgia?" I nodded and tuned out the music, not

an easy task since they were playing "I've Just Seen a Face" from *Rubber Soul*. I took another bite of pie. "You know, there is something. Since you live a few houses away, and since you know everything that happens on the block, did you ever hear or see anything to indicate Chris was seeing someone?"

Susan bit her lip. She hadn't taken any pie for herself. "If she was, she was discreet. She never talked about it with me, and I never saw anyone. In fact, I offered to fix her up once with Fred Rea—he's divorced now—but she wasn't interested."

Doug was keeping himself busy with his pie.

"Doug?" I asked.

He wouldn't look at me.

"Um, Doug?"

Now Susan was looking at him oddly. "Honey, what's the matter?"

Doug's face colored, and he shoveled in more pie.

"You know something," I said.

Finally, he looked up. "I don't know."

"Come on," I urged. "There's something you're just dying to tell us."

"It may be nothing. And you know how I hate gossip."

"This isn't gossip," I snapped. "It's a murder investigation."

He still looked uncertain.

"Doug..." Susan's voice held a warning note.

Doug nodded imperceptibly. "Okay." He turned to me. "You know I'm a car buff, right?"

Susan gave him a fleeting smile. "Another lesson on the brake hydraulics of a Porsche?"

Doug ignored her. "One of the finest cars I know is the Aston

Martin. It's so beautiful you could put one in the Art Institute. And it performs so well it'd have any Nascar racer eating its dust."

"Bond. James Bond," I cracked.

He threw me a disdainful look. "I've thought about getting one." He glanced at Susan. "Someday." He put his pie down. "Anyway, I was up late one night working online, when I noticed an Aston Martin pulling out from Chris Messenger's driveway. A DBS, I think. You can just see her front yard from the window in the study," he added.

"When was this?" I asked.

"I don't remember exactly. But the window was open, and I heard the engine turn over. That's why I looked."

"So within the last two or three months."

"Definitely."

A pulse of excitement ran up my spine. "You didn't happen to see a plate, did you?"

"No."

"What color was it?"

"Hard to say. It was dark, though. Black. Maybe dark green."

"What about the driver?"

"Sorry."

"You never told me about that," Susan said to Doug.

"You never asked," he replied.

"I didn't know our relationship was on a 'don't ask-don't tell' basis," she said primly.

"Damn," I cut in, as much to head off any unpleasantness as to bring the conversation back on track. "So close and yet so far."

"Maybe not," Doug said after a pause.

"You've got no plate, no color, and you don't even know if a man or a woman was driving."

"You still might be able to track it." A tiny smiled curled his lips.

"How?"

"There's only one Aston Martin dealer in the entire Chicago area."

"You're kidding."

"People come from all over the Midwest to get their cars serviced there. It's in Lake Bluff. Which isn't so far away. And given your powers of persuasion..."

I stared at him, then recovered, and blew him a kiss.

Susan smiled. "I knew I married well."

My father polished off the rest of his pie. "Susan, my dear, that was the finest pecan pie I've ever had."

"Thanks, Mr. Foreman."

"Tell me, did you use sugar or sweetener?"

* * *

I was on the phone going over the rest of the production schedule with Mac the next morning when my call waiting beeped. "Hold on, Mac."

"Ellie, it's Georgia." She sounded distant. Weak.

"What's going on?"

"Can you pick me up at Evanston Hospital?"

* * *

I've never liked hospitals. My mother died in one. As I parked at in the Evanston lot thirty minutes later, I recalled how everyone had tried to cushion the inevitable with quiet footsteps, soft voices, and sympathetic faces. It didn't work.

The lobby looked more like a piano bar than a hospital. It

boasted an atrium with a two-story ceiling, abstract art on the walls, and soft music, no doubt intended to provide spiritual balm. I hurried past to the bank of elevators, feeling claustrophobic.

The third floor looked more like a traditional hospital. I walked down a hall with linoleum floor and fluorescent lights. I passed men and women in scrubs. The odor of antiseptic, alcohol, and cleanser brought back unwanted memories. I found my way to Room 345.

Georgia looked like she'd gone ten rounds and lost. Her left arm was in a sling, and underneath her denim shirt was some kind of brace around her middle. Her right eye was swollen shut, and a gauze dressing was taped to her forehead. One foot was wrapped in an ace bandage. I tried to keep my expression neutral but the nurse, an elderly woman who could have been my grandmother, picked up on my distress.

"She refused to stay another day," she said disapprovingly. "She claims her insurance won't cover it."

Georgia raised one eyebrow just enough to let me know she didn't care what excuse she'd given.

"Are you family?" The nurse asked.

I snuck a glance at Georgia. "Um... I'm her sister."

"Then you should talk her out of it. She broke her wrist, cracked two ribs, and sprained her ankle. Not to mention the scrapes on her face. She needs another day here."

"I wouldn't have much luck," I said ruefully. "She's so stubborn she makes a mule look reasonable."

"Well, make sure she does nothing for at least a week," the nurse sniffed, handing me two slips of paper. "Here are two scrips.

One's for antibiotic ointment, the other for pain. And she needs to come back to the clinic next week for a follow-up."

"Yes, ma'am," I said meekly. The nurse handed me Georgia's discharge papers and arranged Georgia in a wheelchair an orderly had brought in. All of us knew she wouldn't be coming back

I stopped at a drugstore on the way back to fill the prescriptions. I picked up more bandages and some magazines, as well. After she directed me to her apartment, I helped her out of the car. She was barely able to close her good hand around the handle bar of the crutch they'd given her, but somehow we hobbled inside and up the stairs. I opened her door with her key and guided her to her couch. Then I filled a glass with water and gave her two Darvocets. She gulped them down.

"Do you have any food?" I asked.

She shrugged. I wandered into the kitchen. There was nothing in the refrigerator except moldy cheese and a jar of mustard.

"I'll be back."

I returned a half hour later with three bags of groceries. I sliced down a cooked chicken, put salad in a covered bowl, and made sure it was all within reach. Then I threw together a tuna sandwich and soup and carried it out to the living room. I pulled up a chair. "Your place…," I said, looking around, "… it's nice."

She caught my hesitation. "For a barracks, you mean."

"Well," I confessed. "It is spare. But it's nice."

"Thanks, Ellie. For all of this."

I waved it away. "First, I want you to eat your sandwich. Then I want you to tell me what the hell happened."

She obediently took a few bites, then told me about the accident.

"Thank god for airbags," I said when she finished.

She nodded. "That's what knocked me out."

"The brakes didn't work at all?"

"Nope."

"You know what this means."

She glared at me. "I may be down, but I'm not brain dead."

I almost smiled. "You file a police report?"

"Couldn't not. Lots of blue around. It's a major intersection."

"Which means O'Malley knows. Or will soon."

"He already called."

"So maybe now they'll take the homicides seriously."

"Maybe," she said.

I paused. "And maybe you'll let them do their job."

Georgia went quiet. Then, "There's something you should know. I'm going to Arizona."

I crossed my arms. "Pardon me?"

"I'm going to Arizona." She repeated. "Place called Stevens."

"You're not going anywhere for a while," I said with more authority than I felt. "But—well, let's say hypothetically—you *were* healthy enough to travel, why Arizona?"

She explained who'd received the cashiers' checks and that two of them were now dead after working for Delton in Arizona.

I frowned. "Where is Stevens?"

"It's a border town in the southeastern part of the state. The town on the Mexican side is Esteban."

"A border town? Georgia, have you lost your mind? Do you know what goes on there?" I shook my head. "Drugs. Illegals. Violence. I don't like it."

"You don't have to." Her voice was firm. "But the best lead we have points to Stevens."

I processed the word "we." So nice of her to include me in the mix. "If what you say is true, and I don't disbelieve you, whatever is going on out there is clearly bigger than you or me. I think it's time to bring in the cavalry."

She hesitated. "We *are* the cavalry."

"Huh?"

"Just because the police suspect foul play doesn't mean they're gonna do much about it. They've been trying to back-burner the whole thing since it started. Plus, I know something they don't."

"What's that?"

"Remember how the elevator in the Midwest National building suddenly stopped the same afternoon that Chris closed the Delton account?"

I nodded.

"The man who kidnapped Molly Messenger was on that elevator."

I sat back in surprise. "How do you know?"

"I tracked down the woman on the elevator. You know, the one Cody told us about. She distinctly remembers a man in there who was missing a chunk of his left index finger. So does Molly." Georgia spooned soup with her good hand. "The asshole who came after us at Sandy Sechrest's cabin was missing part of the same finger."

I swallowed.

"Which means the kidnapping and the bank job are definitely related."

"You suspected that was the case. At least, Cody Wegman did."

"I'm starting to think this missing finger guy is behind a lot more."

"The brake tamperings?"

She nodded.

"All the more reason to let the cops go after him."

"I told you. They've already decided this isn't a heater case. George Emerlich isn't even in their jurisdiction. Neither is the bank. And I don't see Parker doing much to connect the dots. Even with the Arizona connection, he'd just make a few phone calls and call it a day."

"What about the FBI?"

She shook her head. "The kidnapping's over. Finished. There's no need for them to come in."

"Aren't they looking over the bank records?"

"Possibly. But they're here in Chicago. Not Arizona."

I tried one more time. "Georgia, you can't even walk to the corner of Ashland and Ridge. How are you going to manage a trip to Arizona?" I fumed. "And what about Terry Messenger? Is he going to finance this little jaunt?"

"He already agreed."

"You talked to him?" I eyed her warily. "If that's true, he's as crazy as you."

"Actually, it might be more dangerous for me to stay here."

"What do you mean?"

"Whoever tampered with my brakes, whether it's the guy who's missing a finger or someone else, isn't gonna stop just because I've been in the hospital. It's probably safer for me to disappear for a while."

"Yeah, but what if the missing finger guy, or whoever's behind this, is doing the heavy lifting out in Arizona, too? You'd be walking into a trap."

"If that's the case, then it doesn't matter where I am."

Despite my irritation, I marveled at her courage. Or was it foolhardiness? Whatever it was, there was clearly no way I could talk her out of it. "If you are crazy enough to fly out there, you're going to have to check in with me every day. We'll set a time. If I don't hear from you, I call O'Malley. Or Parker. Or whoever I need to."

"Yes, Mom."

"I mean it." I took the tray back into her kitchen. I washed the dishes, helped her change the bandages on her face, then left. On the drive home, I made a call.

CHAPTER 30

Georgia

Tumbleweeds hugged the desert floor as Georgia headed south from Tucson two days later. The sky was vast and cloudless, the sun blazed. Shimmering waves of heat rose from the road, making her eyes ache. She drained the bottle of water she'd bought at the airport and squinted through her sunglasses. There was no subtlety to the high desert.

By Friday she'd no longer needed the crutch, and the contusions on her face were healing. Her left arm was still in a sling, and she liked the support from the brace they'd given her for her ribs, but she couldn't delay her trip. She made a reservation, rented a car, and packed a small bag with t-shirts, extra jeans, her blazer, and her Sig. She made sure both her PI license and tan card were in her wallet. She'd have to check the gun in Chicago, but there'd be less red tape at the other end with the proper ID. Not that she had any plans to use the Sig—she was on a fact-finding trip, no more—but Arizona was an open carry state. Better to be a Boy Scout.

She hesitated when she considered who to tell she was going. Pete? Not any more. O'Malley? He'd try to talk her out of it. Her friend Sam was on vacation in Italy. The truth was the person she was closest to these days was Ellie Foreman, and Ellie already knew. She felt a flicker of a smile. She wouldn't have considered Ellie a friend a month ago.

She turned south off Interstate 10 onto Arizona Highway 80. A few minutes later, as she passed a billboard for Tombstone advertising a daily "gunfight at the OK corral," a memory of her father surfaced. He'd liked to watch old westerns on TV between ball games. Wasn't Tombstone near that hole-in-the-wall the outlaws always fled to after fleeing the sheriff and his posse? She'd worshipped the lawmen in those movies. They were heroes, always risking their lives to fight the bad guys, regardless of the danger. They would never come home from work, toss back a belt of bourbon, and knock their kid around.

Her ears started popping as the elevation rose. A few miles farther south, rugged mountains sparsely covered with brush closed in on both sides of the road. As she passed through Bisbee, an old mining town with tiny houses dotting its hills like some low-rent Italian village she'd seen in pictures, she saw the remains of a huge copper mine carved into the rock. Bisbee was the seat of Cochise County, which she'd read was one of the ten most economically depressed areas in the country. She believed it. She'd been passing abandoned churches, car dealerships, even empty trailers the whole way.

After Bisbee, the desert suddenly flattened out as if a giant boulder had smashed down on it. She pulled into Stevens a short time later. The Stevens Hotel was a six-story building that took up the entire block on the main drag, but its peeling shingles and crumbling stucco façade said it had seen better days. She followed the signs to a ragged parking lot in back and parked. With her good hand she pulled her bag out of the rental, a blue Ford Escort. She headed in, skirting broken glass and trash.

The lobby was cool and dark. Gilt-edged columns flanked the room, and wide marble steps led up to a series of stained-glass panels depicting desert scenes. When she'd booked the hotel online, the website called it the "grandly elegant Stevens Hotel." On closer inspection, though, the marble was scuffed and the carpet threadbare. Underneath the smell of furniture polish was the musty odor of decay.

A lonely grouping of brown leather furniture took up the center of the lobby. An old man sat on the couch, grasping a cane with both hands and staring vacantly ahead. The man was pale enough to be a ghost, which, she recalled from reading the website, wasn't so far-fetched. Like the Gadsden in Douglas, the Stevens was supposed to be haunted by the ghost of Pancho Villa, the famous Mexican revolutionary general from a hundred years ago. Apparently he had stayed here on one of his forays across the border.

The desk clerk couldn't be bothered to stop clacking her gum as she checked Georgia in. So much for "grandly elegant."

Georgia took the elevator to her room on the third floor. Spider-web cracks laced the ceiling, and brown streaks, water damage probably, stained the wall. She found rust stains in the bathroom tub, and the mirror above the sink was permanently fogged. She thought about checking out and finding a Motel 6—it had to be in better shape. But her broken wrist was throbbing, her ribs were sore, and fatigue was climbing all over her. She took a pain pill and fell onto the lumpy mattress.

When she awoke it was nearly dusk, and she was famished. She took a quick shower, relieved to find plenty of hot water. Then she rinsed out her tank top and underwear, and changed into clean clothes. She put on the brace and tried to cover the bruises on her face with make-up. Because of her cast, everything took twice as long.

She flipped through the yellow pages scanning the listings of bars and restaurants. But the phone directory covered Cochise County, not just Stevens, and it was impossible to figure out where anything was. Then she remembered the hotel had a restaurant.

It was small, maybe fifteen tables, most of them empty. She took a seat in the corner. A middle-aged Latino man with salt and pepper hair and a bristly mustache put down his newspaper and brought her a bi-lingual menu listing a good number of Mexican dishes. She ordered a hamburger—rare—and fries. Before he left, she asked whether she could borrow the newspaper.

"Sure."

While she waited for her food, she scanned the *Stevens Star*. Stevens was only about ten thousand people, and the paper was full of the stories you'd see in a small town: an article about the upcoming school budget, a new stoplight, a neighborhood fair.

She flipped back to the front page. The lead article was a response by police to a bogus bomb threat at a neighborhood bank. The reporter, Javier Garcia, quoted a police spokesperson as well as the bank's president.

Georgia tapped her finger, then checked her watch. It was well after five, but journalists generally didn't work bankers' hours. She pulled out her cell.

CHAPTER 31

After finishing her dinner, Georgia headed slowly down seventh Street, testing her ankle with progressively more weight. Not bad.

Light was fading, but she could see that the parkways were filled with rocky red dirt, not grass. The absence of green gave a primitive feel to the block. Most of the buildings were generally one or two story structures and featured Spanish signage. Some of the buildings were close together, while others were separated by long gaps. Clearly space, not height, was the architectural directive in Stevens. Though it was evening, a hot wind still gusted as if eager to blow the town back to its desert roots.

A sidewalk chalk board with several missing letters proclaimed she had reached Chevy's Cantina. As she walked in, a gust of cool air slapped her. She tried not to think of the westerns where the bad guy swings through the saloon door. To her left was a bar that wasn't much more than a slab of splintered wood. Cheap looking tables and chairs sat on an uneven floor. The overhead light was dim and the adobe walls were bare except for a Corona sign, a dusty mirror, and an Arizona map with Cochise County outlined in black. No guitars, serapes, or sombreros here. A radio blared out Mexican pop music. Several people sat at tables, nursing drinks and playing poker.

A stocky Latina woman lounged behind the bar. Georgia caught a glimpse of her reflection in the mirror. With her blond hair and pale skin, she had *Gringa* written all over her. She stepped up to the bar. "I'll have a beer."

The woman stared at her sling, then fished a longneck Corona out of a cooler. She held up five fingers. Georgia dug out a five, knowing she'd been ripped off. The woman stuffed the bill inside a drawer. Georgia tipped back her head for a swig, rinsing the grit that seemed to have settled in her throat. She took her beer to an empty table.

Five minutes later, a young man came in. Olive-skinned, with a razor haircut that was probably intended to make him look older, he wore jeans, a denim shirt, and cowboy boots. A small object poking out of his shirt pocket—a recorder or Blackberry, maybe—identified him as Javier Garcia. Georgia waved him over.

"Thanks for coming. I'm Davis."

He nodded. His thick eyebrows furrowed in what looked like a permanent frown. "Friday's a good day. I'm not on deadline."

She motioned toward the woman behind the bar. "Get what you want and tell her to start a tab."

Garcia ordered a Pepsi. The woman nodded, popped the top off, and filled a tall glass with ice. Garcia dropped a dollar tip on the bar, pointed at Georgia and told the woman to start a tab.

"Sure thing, Javier," she said. She cast a quick glance towards Georgia.

He brought his drink to the table. "This is a treat. It's not every day I get a call from a Chicago PI."

She took a sip of beer, wishing she'd ordered a Pepsi. But she'd wanted to fit in. "You cover the Stevens police beat, right?"

Surprise flickered across his face. "My reputation's that widespread?"

She smiled. "I'm working on a case in Chicago that has ties to Stevens. I need someone who knows what's going on."

"And is willing to talk about it."

Garcia couldn't be much older than thirty. How much did he know? She almost said something to that effect but changed her mind. "So, tell me about Stevens."

"The town or its secrets?"

"Both."

He sipped more Pepsi. "Stevens used to process copper from the Bisbee mines but most of the mining operations are gone. We still have a good number of cattle ranchers."

"I thought the land was barren."

"Not exactly. This part of the country is a series of small mountain chains with basins and valleys. Stevens sits in the high desert grasslands between the Sonora and Chihuahuan deserts. A lot of the land's gone to scrub, but we have our moments. Especially during monsoon season."

"Tell me about the people."

"It's heavily Hispanic," he said. "Most of the whites, ranchers mostly, or rich people, live outside of town. And we have a prison."

A man at the next table started to deal out cards. Five card stud.

"Isn't there an Army base nearby?"

He nodded. "Fort Huachuca's about fifty miles away, near

Sierra Vista. Been around forever. Since the days of Pancho Villa at least. It's a major base for the Signal Corps. The Thunderbirds train there."

Georgia recalled the Thunderbirds from Chicago's annual Air and Water Show, their jets diving and corkscrewing in tight sequence a few feet above Lake Michigan. She loved feeling the rush of the jets as they tore through the air.

Javier drained his Pepsi. "Fort Huachuca's one of the Army's centers for military intelligence. Lots of training, classes, and field work. People think the guys who interrogated prisoners at Abu Ghraib got their training there." He paused. "They've also got an aerostat."

"A what?"

"A radar-equipped dirigible. DEA uses it to detect low-flying aircraft flying across the border."

She pointed to his pop. "Another?"

"I'll get it." He stood and gestured to her Corona, which she'd hardly touched.

"No, thanks." Her wrist ached, her ankle was sore, and she wanted another Darvocet. But she had to remain sharp.

He went over to the bar and came back with another bottle of pop. He glanced at her sling. "So I've been dying to ask. How'd you break your arm?"

"Plowed into some pylons and a car in Chicago."

He winced. "What happened?"

"Brakes failed."

He arched an eyebrow.

She shrugged. He didn't need to know more. "Back to Stevens. You said it's heavily Hispanic."

"A typical border town." He propped his elbows on the table.

"Lots of traffic back and forth. Plenty of us have family on both sides. For example, my parents and siblings are here, but my grandparents live in Esteban."

"Do they visit?"

He nodded. "You used to be able to go back and forth at will. Now you need proof of citizenship, but my grandmother still crosses to go the supermarket once a month. They operate a bus from the border to the store."

"Who runs the town?"

"Why?"

"I told you. I'm working a case that has links to the town."

He cocked his head. "I need more than that."

"All I'm asking for is public information. I thought it would be easier—and more pleasant to buy you a drink than go to the library. But if you're not willing..." She let her voice trail off.

He shot her a skeptical glance. "Okay. We have a mayor. A city council. A small police department. The prison. And the Sheriff's Department of Cochise County. You know, all the requisite civil institutions."

"Yes, but who runs the town?"

"Ahh." A faint smile curled the corners of his mouth. "That would be the Grant family. Lionel Grant."

"What does he do?"

"He owns pretty much everything around here. The family settled here almost a hundred years ago and built the biggest smelting operation in town. Ever hear of Grant Copper Works?"

Georgia shook her head. The men at the next table placed their bets. One of them seemed to be taunting the others.

"Over the years the Grants built the town hall, the library, the hospital. You can't miss it—the family logo's plastered on almost everything."

"Logo?"

"A crouching lion. You know, for Lionel."

Georgia rolled her eyes. "But then, after the copper mines closed down, this Lionel—there's a Lionel in every generation—moved to Elgin, about sixty miles away, and built a vineyard. Now he makes wine."

"Why did he leave Stevens?"

"You'd have to ask him."

Georgia stared at Garcia.

"Okay," he laced his fingers together. "There are two theories. One is that he stripped the town of everything he could get and moved onto greener pastures. Literally."

"And the other?"

Javier lowered his voice. "This is off the record, okay? He owns the newspaper, and if—"

"No problem."

Javier looked both ways before he spoke. "The man is a racist. As the town got more heavily Hispanic, and as the UDA problem worsened, they say he didn't want any part of it."

"UDAs?"

"Undocumented Aliens. Illegals. Grant can't stand them. Won't hire anyone of color. Always harping about border crossings. Lobbying for more agents. Tighter control. Deportations."

"From what I've read," Georgia said, "Arizona does have—uh—let's say, the most porous borders. Compared to Texas and California."

"Like I said, it's tougher now, but illegals only get caught about half the time. There's a steady stream. Especially since the cartels have Mexico by the throat."

"How serious is the drug problem?"

The man at the next table who'd been taunting the others threw down his cards, stood up, and started to shout. A second man shot his hands in the air as if trying to calm the first.

Javier checked them out. "This place can get a little wild. But it's authentic. I meet some of my sources here. You know, people who otherwise don't want to be found."

She nodded.

"As far as the drug problem, it's getting bad. Mexico is becoming a failed state. The cartels own the courts, the police, the Federales, and everything in between. And Stevens is a border town." He rubbed his chin in a way that made Georgia think he used to have a beard. "They've started to make inroads here, too. Kidnapping. Blackmail. Extortion. At one point there was a rumor that the mayor's brother had a drug tunnel running through his property."

Georgia took a sip of her beer.

"All of which infuriates Grant," Garcia went on. "He makes the *Star* publish editorials all the time."

"Even though he's not here?"

"He still owns most of the town."

"Must be a popular guy,"

"People didn't shed tears when he left," Garcia admitted. "But you gotta give the man some credit. He's a true believer, and he's ponied up a lot of money for the cause. Anyone, local or national, who takes a stand against drug trafficking and illegal immigration can count on a generous contribution."

"Including the Minutemen?"

Garcia laughed. "The Minutemen are a joke. They drive down from Ohio in their SUVs wearing camo jackets and fatigues, but all they do is sit around and mouth off. Grant's the real thing."

More raised voices at the next table. Other patrons in the bar were starting to stare. Georgia ignored the furor. "What made him so—passionate?"

"Don't know. He mouths all the platitudes about Latinos stealing jobs from "real" Americans, the burdens on health care and education, the destruction of the American character. And now, with the escalating drug violence, he's got more ammunition."

"Maybe that's why he took his family north."

"His son is still here. Lionel Kenneth. They call him Ken. He's on the city council."

"Carrying on the family tradition?"

Javier rubbed his chin again. "Actually, Ken never worked in the smelting business. He owns a crafts company. Goes around to villages and reservations, here and in Mexico, buying up stuff. You know, blankets, jewelry and crap that he sells at flea markets and tourist shops."

"Interesting. You wouldn't think the son of a mogul—" An image of Luke Sutton came into her mind and Georgia cut herself off. "What's he like? Ken?"

"Whatever Dad isn't. Liberal. Rebellious. A friend to Latinos."

A flash of lightning followed by the roll of thunder startled Georgia. She turned toward the window.

Javier chuckled. "It's monsoon season. We get violent storms. From now through the end of August." He rolled his empty Pepsi bottle on the table. "Okay. Your turn. Why all the questions?"

"I told you. I have a case—"

"You'll have to do better than that."

Georgia ran her tongue around her lips. "This is off the record."

"Go on."

She lowered her voice. "Do you know someone named Rafael Peña?"

Javier shook his head.

Georgia leaned forward. "If—and this is purely hypothetical, if a Blackwater type security team was operating here, what would they be doing? Would Grant be financing them?"

Javier hesitated.

"What's with the hesitation?"

"Nothing."

Georgia felt a flash of impatience. "Would they be connected to the army base? The police force? Border Patrol?"

"It wouldn't be the Army. And border patrol would be the Feds. But I haven't heard a word about any security force in the area, local or Federal."

"You sure?"

"Not a whisper." He paused. "But there is something you have to remember."

"What's that?"

"Despite the appearance of civilization, this is still the Wild West. People like to take the law into their own hands. So you can never be sure who's doing what. Until..." His voice trailed off.

"Until what?"

"I was going to say 'until it's too late.'" His expression was solemn.

"I'll take that as a warning." Georgia picked up her bag and set it on her lap. "Listen, Javier. What I just told you has to stay off the record."

"Don't worry." He pulled out a card, handed it to Georgia. "If it turns out to be true, though, I'd appreciate a call."

The barmaid brought the card players another round of drinks. The man who'd been shouting at the others grinned. All was forgiven. Georgia slipped Javier's card into her pocket and paid the tab. A moment later they emerged from the bar into a torrential storm. Dark low-hanging clouds were backlit by constant lightning. Thunder crashed overhead. The rain pummeled her like bullets. So much for the image of a western sky with stars so plentiful and close you could practically touch them.

"I don't get it," she shouted to Javier over the din. "An hour ago the air was so dry my lips were cracking."

"Like I said, from now till September we get storms so violent you think everything is gonna float away. Half an hour later sometimes, you'd never know it rained."

"Like Chinese food."

Garcia laughed. "I like you, Georgia Davis. So take what I say in that spirit. Don't hang around this place too long. You're a *Anglo*."

"I'll remember that." She gave him her good hand, and they shook. Then she ducked back inside to wait for the rain to stop. The woman who'd ripped her off for the beer was wiping down the bar.

Georgia approached her and cleared her throat. "I'm looking for someone," she said in a low voice. The woman didn't look up. "His name is Rafael Peña."

The woman still wouldn't look up, but the brisk circles she was making with her rag slowed.

"Have you ever heard of him?"

The woman kept wiping. Then she looked up. "*No hablo Ingles*."

Georgia remembered her talking to Javier in perfect English.

She waited. Nothing happened. She turned around and headed back to the door. The barmaid began talking to a man who'd just come out from the back. He had an apron around his waist, and a small towel was slung over his shoulder. Just like Owen Dougherty, Mickey's owner back home. He must be Chevy. He checked his watch and nodded to the barmaid. She untied her apron and disappeared through the back. A moment later, Georgia saw her hurrying down the street—without an umbrella.

Georgia waited until the rain subsided, then walked slowly back to her hotel. She thought about what Javier said about people taking matters into their own hands. Luke Sutton had said Blackwater's next mission would be in the U.S. Is that why Delton Security was here, if they were? And if they were, what were they doing and who were they working for? And why did the barmaid leave in such a hurry?

Georgia wondered just how wild the West really was. And whether she was up to finding out.

CHAPTER 32

"Drug trafficking? Illegal aliens?" Ellie said when Georgia called the next day. Ostensibly it was to check in, but also to talk through what she'd learned. "Jesus, Georgia. I told you. This is way over the top. You need to get your ass back to Chicago."

"Relax, Ellie. It's not as bad as you think. Yes, this is a border town, and yes, there are issues, but people here kind of take it in stride, you know? They don't make a big deal out of it."

"Until the bodies pile up. Including yours."

"First of all, there's no evidence that's what's going on. I told you, there's an Army base nearby, and the man who owns most of the town hates Latinos. There's Border Patrol, local cops, and a big Sheriff's Department. There could be plenty of reasons why Delton is here that have nothing to do with drugs. Or illegals."

"I'll bet you still believe in Santa Claus, too."

Georgia sighed. "Look. I just want to find out why those three guys got a million dollars and two of them turned up dead. And what it has to do with Molly Messenger."

"I don't like it," Ellie said.

Georgia ignored the comment. She wasn't used to having someone fuss over her, and she wasn't sure how she felt about it. "Tell me, what would make someone hate an entire race of people?"

Ellie didn't answer right away. "That's probably not a question you want to ask me, considering my family history. But the way I see it, what matters is whether the people in question controlled the hate, or it controlled them."

"Latinos have lived in Arizona and New Mexico longer than the Grants. Why build an empire if you can't stand the people who inhabit it?"

And it was an empire. She'd spent the morning touring the town, including the Grant Library, Grant Hospital, Grant Town Hall, even the old Grant Copper Works warehouse. Garcia was right—the damned lion logo figured prominently on all the buildings. Then she'd driven down to the Stevens Port of Entry, an array of stone arches and columns flanked on one side by the Grant Immigration Center. She drove as far as she could within the city limits, passing fences and border patrol stations that bisected Stevens and its sister town, Esteban. She was surprised the name of the town wasn't Grant, until she discovered that "Stevens" was the middle name of the first Lionel Grant to settle here.

Ellie changed the subject. "How's the arm?"

"Better. I'm thinking I can dump the sling soon. What's going on there?"

"With all the commotion about your accident, I forgot to tell you I might have a lead on Chris Messenger's boyfriend." She explained how Susan's husband, Doug, had seen an Aston Martin in Chris's driveway and that there was only one Aston Martin dealer on the North Shore. "Although from what you're saying now, it may be irrelevant."

"Nothing's irrelevant. Are you going to check it out?"

"Monday." Ellie cleared her throat. "What about Rafael Peña? You find anything on him yet?"

"Not yet. But I haven't been dropping his name all over town. For obvious reasons."

"Georgia—"

"Enough, Ellie. I'm on a fact-finding trip. If I don't find any, I'll be home in a couple of days."

* * *

But she *had* dropped Peña's name at Chevy's Cantina last night, and the barmaid's reaction was suspicious. After she disconnected, she went to her hotel window. A high noon sun blazed down, stunting the shadows of fences, walls, and cars. This morning she'd noticed people bustling around. There were still people outside now, but they moved more slowly.

She spent the afternoon in her room with the air conditioner cranked high. Except for an occasional drop of water that fell onto the carpet, it was tolerable. She read for a while but then must have dozed off because an explosion of thunder woke her. She went to the window. It was almost dark, and another monsoon was pounding the town.

By the time she'd showered and dressed, it was after nine, and the storm had passed. Her wrist felt stronger, so she dispensed with the sling. Already grateful for the added mobility, she put on her blazer with the deep pockets. She slipped her Sig into her holster underneath.

Outside the rain had swept the heat away. She drove her rental back to Chevy's Cantina, but instead of going in, she pulled into a paved lot on the side. It was Saturday night, and the music was louder, the people more boisterous. She slid out of the car and went to the front door. The door swung open, and a couple came out. The smell of booze was all over them. The woman was in a tight red dress and giggled like she'd had a few. Georgia peered inside. The barmaid was delivering a tray of drinks to a group at a table. Georgia went back to the Escort, prepared for a long stake-out.

She was surprised, when, two hours later, the barmaid slipped out through the side door. She looked both ways, then walked north. Georgia let her get half a block ahead, then pulled out. The barmaid picked up her pace but didn't seem to realize she was being tailed.

Eight blocks later, she was still walking, but the neighborhood had changed to barrio. Buildings that looked more like small huts than houses occupied crowded blocks. Street lights were farther apart, spilling pools of weak light on cracked sidewalks. It seemed hotter here, as if the barrio was in a valley bereft of crosswinds. Passing cars were scarce, and Georgia slowed to avoid calling attention to herself. She thumbed down the window, trying to keep the woman in sight.

The barmaid stopped at a corner bodega, its lights still on despite the late hour. She exited ten minutes later clutching a loaded grocery bag. As she headed down the street three young men materialized from the shadows. They closed in on the woman, making wolf whistles and kissing sounds.

The barmaid, who had to be older than the boys' mothers, ignored them and kept walking. They pretended to be insulted and dogged her down the street. The barmaid sped up, but a forty-something waitress was no match for three teenage assholes. They ambushed her against a brick building. The barmaid gripped her bag. Her body language screamed fear.

The boys taunted her in Spanish. Georgia couldn't make out the words, but she stiffened at the tone. She inched the car forward. As she did, one of the boys lurched toward the barmaid and snatched her bag. The barmaid's face went white. She tried to hold on, but the paper ripped, spilling fruit, milk, and cereal. A carton of eggs smashed on the sidewalk. Two large pop bottles fell, too. One shattered on impact, releasing a flood of orange liquid on the ground. The other rolled into the street.

Georgia threw the car in park and got out, leaving the engine running. The boys were still haranguing the woman. Georgia pulled out the old police badge she'd neglected to turn in when she was suspended.

"Hey!" She yelled, waving the badge. "Stop right now and get your hands where I can see them!"

The boys spun around. Shock and surprise swept across their faces. The barmaid's eyes widened too. Although the streetlamp's beam was dim, Georgia could tell the woman recognized her.

"The fuck you think you're doing?" Georgia barked at the boys.

They looked at each other, then at Georgia. No one answered. Despite the cooler night air, sweat beaded her brow. She hoped to hell none of them had a gun. "I told you to get your hands in the air."

They exchanged glances. Then one slowly raised his hands.

The others followed suit. Georgia dared to breathe. She pointed to one. "You. Pick up the food and put it back in the bag."

He looked at his buddies, then drew himself up. "Who the fuck are you?"

"Do what I say, or I'll book you for assault."

His look was challenging. "We ain't done nothing to the old woman."

Georgia narrowed her eyes. "Pick up her groceries. Now."

He stared at her. She stared back. Then he bent down and started picking up the food.

Georgia motioned to the others. "You two, help him."

They glared defiantly. Georgia stood her ground. One of them picked up an apple. When he straightened up, he wound up like he was going to pitch a fast ball in her direction. She dumped her badge and felt for her Sig.

"You don't want me to pull out what's in my pocket. Because then, I really will take you all in."

Apple Boy planted his hands on his hips. "If you're a cop, how come you're not in uniform?

"Not your problem. Just finish the job."

Slowly, they collected the rest of the food and put it back in the bag. They sat the bag down on the street.

"Now take out some money for the eggs and the pop you broke."

"Hey man, that ain't our fault."

Her hand went back to her pocket. "Do it."

Reluctantly, one of the boys took out a couple of dollars.

"Good. Put it in the bag."

He did, then muttered to the other two. She heard the word

"José." The other two ponied up a few bills each and dropped them in the bag.

"Now get out of here. And don't let me find out you've bothered her again."

"You don't even know who we are."

"You want to put money on that, José?"

The boys exchanged another look. One of them, presumably José, screwed his eyes shut and shook his head. Then he thrust the torn bag at the barmaid. She grabbed it from the bottom.

A moment later the woman and Georgia were alone on the street. The only sound was the hum from the streetlights.

Georgia felt the stress trickle out of her, leaving a bone-deep exhaustion. She hadn't realized how much effort it took to be brave, especially when she was still on injured reserve.

The barmaid didn't say anything, but Georgia caught a mix of gratitude, shame, and fear on her face. Finally she spoke. "Thank you."

Georgia nodded. "You need a ride?"

"No. I just live down the street." She hefted the bag in her arms.

"What's your name?"

"Carmelita Herrera."

"Well, Carmelita, we need to talk."

* * *

Carmelita Herrera lived in a small adobe cottage that Georgia learned had once housed workers for Grant Copper Works. The house consisted of three small rooms, all with wood floors except the kitchen. Carmelita had tried to spruce up the place with braided rugs, colorful throws, and curtains. Despite an air conditioning unit, the windows were open, and Georgia heard canned laughter from a neighbor's TV. An overhead ceiling fan rotated slowly. Georgia wondered how many weeks' salary that had cost. The smells of peppers, grease, and sweat hung in the air.

An elderly woman was dozing on the sofa, but snored awake when they came in.

"¿Mama, como te sientes?" Carmelita asked.

A whiny response was the answer. Carmelita rolled her eyes and spoke rapidly in Spanish. The old woman heaved herself off the couch, and trudged into another room. Carmelita gestured for Georgia to sit in her place, then went to the window and drew the curtains.

"Your arm? It's going to be ok?"

Georgia rubbed her hand up and down the cast. "Soon."

Now that she could study her close-up, Georgia realized Carmelita wasn't much older than she. Her skin was a smooth buttery caramel, and her dark eyes were fringed with long lashes. Thick black hair fell softly to her shoulders, and a long straight nose hinted at Native American ancestry. She'd been a beauty once upon a time.

She started to put the groceries away. "You want a drink?"

Georgia shook her head. "I want you to tell me about Rafael Peña."

"I don't know him."

Georgia raised her eyebrows and waited. Carmelita carefully folded the empty grocery bag, stowed it under the sink, then came and sat next to Georgia. "It is true. I do not know him. My brother does. They call him Raffi. He comes from around here. He was a migra."

"A what?"

"A border agent."

"But now he works for Delton Security."

Surprise swept across Carmelita's face. Followed by suspicion. "How do you know?"

"I'm a private investigator from Chicago. His name has come up in a case I'm working on."

"You come all the way from Chicago for Raffi?"

"Are you surprised?"

Carmelita slumped against the couch and looked around, as if the walls had ears. "I guess not."

"Because?"

Her voice was almost a whisper. "Because many bad things are happening here."

"What bad things?"

Frown lines creased Carmelita's forehead. Georgia kept absolutely still, as if the slightest move would influence what the woman said. Georgia was acutely aware of the slight breeze from the ceiling fan. She wished she could shut it off. After a long moment Carmelita hugged her legs and leaned forward. "You know many people here have ties to Mexico." She pronounced it "Mehico."

Georgia nodded.

"Things there are desperate. No jobs. No food. No safety. The drug wars are destroying the country. People want to come here. So their children will have a better life." She rocked forward. "You have seen the fences, no? And the patrols?"

Georgia nodded again.

"So they try to sneak across. But that is hard. They spend many hours in the desert. With little water." She stopped, seemingly reluctant to go on.

Georgia prodded. "So?"

"Everyone knows someone who has tried to cross. Some make it. Some do not."

"Because they're caught," Georgia said.

Carmelita shook her head. "No. There is more."

"What?"

She crossed herself. "There are stories. Trucks in the night. Men and women who disappear. No one sees them again. Ever."

Georgia kept her mouth shut.

"The ones here are afraid to talk about it because they are UDAs. They are supposed to meet coyotes who will bring their relatives or friends across, but when they arrive, no one is there." Her eyes flashed. "At least when Border Patrol or Customs get you they send you to deportation center. You are a prisoner, but you are alive."

Georgia stood and started to pace. She'd heard stories about coyotes capturing illegals and smuggling them into drop houses where drug traffickers extorted money from their families back in Mexico. If the families didn't pay, the consequences could be fatal. She stopped pacing. "These coyotes—who do they work for?"

"I do not know."

Georgia sat back down. "And what does Rafael Peña have to do with this?"

Carmelita hesitated, then blurted it out. "He is the one who makes them get in the truck."

CHAPTER 33

Georgia's thoughts swirled. Rafael Peña worked for Delton Security. And yet, according to Carmelita, he was smuggling illegals across the border, forcing them into trucks, and taking them god knows where. Was that part of his work for Delton? Or was he moonlighting? Was Peña even still alive? And what about the other two Delton men, Edward Wrobleski and Kirk Brewer? They had been killed in "training accidents." Were they smugglers too? All three men had received a million dollars from Delton. Money for which Chris Messenger had been killed and her daughter kidnapped. Whose side were they on?

She didn't know enough about drug trafficking, illegal aliens, or human smuggling to form any theories. But that wasn't her job. Her job was to follow a lead. Uncover evidence. She eyed Carmelita. The woman looked like she was telling the truth. Still.

"If what you're saying is true, I'm going to need proof."

Carmelita shivered. "I cannot."

"Can't or won't?"

The woman ran a worried hand through her hair. "You do not understand. You cannot fly here from Chicago and fix everything. Just like that." She snapped her fingers. "I must live here. After you go. There is danger."

"From what quarter?"

Carmelita didn't answer. She just shook her head.

Georgia remembered what Javier Garcia, the reporter, said about frontier justice. She wasn't taking matters into her own hands. Or was she? She chose her words carefully.

"My client's wife was killed, and his eight-year-old daughter was kidnapped. She's safe now, but he wants to make sure she stays that way. Everything we know points to Stevens. And Peña."

"A child?" Carmelita murmured.

Georgia nodded. "Two of the men who were working with Peña are also dead. For all I know, Peña is too. I'm not looking to put you in harm's way, but I need to find out what's going on."

Carmelita pressed her hands together for such a long time Georgia thought she was praying. Then she dropped them and looked at Georgia. "Raffi is not dead."

Georgia tilted her head. "How do you know?"

"I—I have seen him. With my brother."

"When?"

"Maybe... two weeks ago?"

"Two weeks is a long time. I need to find him."

"He is—not here." She looked down.

Frustration thickened Georgia's throat. "Damn it, what game are you playing? Either you know this man or you don't. And if *you* don't, I want to talk to your brother."

Carmelita wrung her hands. "My brother disappeared two weeks ago. I do not know where he went."

"Is he with Peña?"

"I do not know."

Georgia's voice was ice. "Not good enough."

Carmelita looked down. Georgia could sense the woman's mind working. Running over the pros and cons. Making a decision. Then she slumped against the couch. "Come back tomorrow. In the evening. I will show you."

* * *

The next night Georgia zig-zagged through the barrio with Carmelita riding shotgun. The woman directed her to a block even shabbier and more ramshackle than her own. Georgia parked and they got out. Carmelita rounded a corner and led the way to a dim street. Tiny buildings—you couldn't really call them houses— flanked the street. In front were garbage cans, with yellow twist-ties and white plastic peeking out. The stench was so strong Georgia had to breathe through her mouth.

Carmelita stopped halfway down the block at a small yard enclosed by a chain link fence. The gate was unlocked. They walked up to a small adobe shack. Light filtered through a yellowed shade. Tapping lightly, she called out in a quiet voice. There was no response. A cat streaking across the lawn startled Georgia, and she stepped back. The cat disappeared. Carmelita tapped again.

A long moment later, a shadowy form blocked the light inside. Carmelita talked hurriedly through the door. The person on the other side shook her head, which prompted more conversation. Then the shade lifted, and the door opened. Carmelita beckoned to Georgia.

The woman who let them in was stout and wrinkled and much older than Carmelita. She wore bright pink polyester pants and a frayed t-shirt with an Arizona State U logo. The two women clearly knew each other, and their conversation was intense. At one point the older woman stared at Georgia. Carmelita raised her palms, as if in supplication. The woman grunted, glanced at Georgia again, then left the room.

"What's going on?" Georgia asked. "Who is this woman?"

"She is our aunt," Carmelita replied. "She doesn't want no trouble."

"Why are we here?"

Carmelita hunched her shoulders. "You will see."

They waited in the tiny kitchen. Georgia noted the cheap formica counters, small table, and shabby linoleum floor. The refrigerator would fit easily into hers back in Chicago. And yet the sink was spotless, and the drainboard empty—all the dishes and silverware had been put away. A crucifix hung on the wall.

Carmelita's aunt came back out, shaking her head. "He will not come." She glared at Georgia. "He is afraid."

"Who?" Georgia asked.

Carmelita and her aunt exchanged glances. The aunt shot Carmelita a grim look, then disappeared. A door closed. Georgia followed Carmelita into a hall with two doors. One was partially open. Carmelita opened it wider and stepped into a tiny room. The windows were closed and the odd, paste-like smell of little boy filled the air. A bed, its covers askew, took up most of the space, but there was also a three-drawer chest. The top drawer was open. A Spanish comic book and an X-men action figure lay on a scuffed table.

Carmelita pointed to the bed. On one side the rumpled covers hung to the floor.

Georgia nodded, crossed to the bed, and squatted down. She cleared her throat. "Hey there, pal," she said quietly. "My name's Georgia. What's yours?"

"He doesn't speak English," Carmelita said.

"Will you translate?"

Carmelita took a breath and obliged.

There was no response, but Georgia didn't expect one. She looked around and spotted the X-men action figure. Something about it looked slightly off. She wondered if it was a bootleg. "Hey. I really like your X-men guy. Is that the Iceman? I'll bet he's really brave."

Carmelita translated. No response.

"Just like you."

After Carmelita translated, the sheet hanging over the bed rustled, as if the boy was shifting. "His name is Diego," Carmelita whispered.

"Do you think I could play with Iceman, Diego? Would that be all right?"

More bedcovers rustling.

"I'm not going to take it from you. It's yours. I just want to play. And talk." She nodded at Carmelita who translated. When nothing happened, she said, "Does Iceman have another name? A special nickname or something?"

A muffled sound came from under the bed.

Georgia cocked her head. "Sorry. I didn't hear you."

"No." This time his voice was distinct. High-pitched. Fearful.

"Well, I think we should give him one, don't you, Diego?"

Carmelita translated. A moment later a tiny hand lifted the

sheet a few inches, and Georgia was looking into the large, frightened eyes of a little boy.

"Hello, Diego." She smiled.

Diego stared at Georgia but made no move to come out from under the covers. She felt as if she were being examined like a toy truck.

"He is scared they are coming back for him," Carmelita said.

"Who?"

Carmelita bent down and spoke in soothing tones. His muffled responses were monosyllabic. Carmelita turned to Georgia. "He says I should tell you."

Georgia swallowed. "Tell him he is very brave." She straightened up, retrieved the Iceman, and slid it under the bed. "Tell Diego we'll come up with a name together. When he's ready."

Carmelita translated, then spoke in English. "A neighbor brought him here several weeks ago. He was barely alive. He had not had any food or water in two days. He would not talk." She rubbed a hand across her forehead, as if trying to erase the memory.

"My aunt, well, she appears angry, but she has the heart of gold. She could not turn him away. She fed him, bathed him, and put him in here. He slept most of two days, and when he woke up, he told us what happened."

"Which was?"

"His parents were trying to cross the border. They were in a group, maybe twenty or so, from their village in the Sonora. Besides Diego, there were two other children. They thought the numbers—you know—would protect them." She went quiet. The rustling under the bed stopped.

"They were to meet a *coyote* who would help them get to northern Arizona."

"*El otro lado.*" Georgia heard from under the bed.

"*Si. Entiendo,*" Georgia said.

"So they go to the appointed spot. And they wait. For a long time. They ran out of food. And they were starting to run out of water. Diego said his mother was crying." She took a steadying breath. "Finally the *coyote* came."

"Was it Peña?"

"I do not know. Diego can not tell. But the man was driving a truck. He made the people get in. Some did not want to, but he has a shotgun. Diego had been playing behind a large rock near his mother. He hears people shouting. Arguing. There is a blast from the shotgun. One of the women, his mother's best friend, falls to the ground. She does not move. His mother knows something is wrong and whispers to Diego. She tells him to stay behind the boulder. And run away after the truck leaves. She leaves him the rest of her water. Then she is forced into the truck. It drives away. He has not seen his family since."

Georgia's skin went cold. "What did Diego do?"

"What his mother told him. He waited until the truck left. Then he ran."

Georgia heard a shuffling noise, and Diego slid out from under the bed, clutching the X-men action figure. Georgia guessed he was only a year or two older than Molly Messenger. Unlike Molly's solid frame, though, Diego was all head and face and so skinny his ribs were visible through his shirt. His hair was tousled, his cheeks pasty, and his eyes held a knowing expression, as if he already knew how hard life was. Georgia opened her good arm, and he slipped into her lap. She smoothed down his hair. He wriggled closer. Her eyes and throat ached.

"Somehow he made it to Stevens," Carmelita continued. "He was wandering around the downtown, not far from the border, when my aunt's neighbor saw him and brought him here." Carmelita shrugged. "That is all."

Georgia bent over Diego and kissed the top of his head. "*El camion...* the truck that picked you up... what color was it? Was there any lettering on it? A picture or logo?"

Carmelita translated.

Diego looked up at Georgia. "*Si*," he said clearly. "*Había un dibujo de un león con unos racimos de uvas al lado del camion.*"

A lion. With bunches of grapes on the side.

CHAPTER 34

After dropping Carmelita off, Georgia wound back through the labyrinth of Stevens streets to the hotel. Someone was herding Mexican illegals into trucks and making them "disappear." That someone may have been Rafael Peña, and the truck he was loading them into could belong to Lionel Grant.

Was Peña working for Delton Security while he was abducting Mexicans? If so, why was Lionel Grant's truck involved? If Grant hated UDAs as much as Garcia said, it made no sense for him to transport them from the border to Northern Arizona, if that's where they were headed. Presumably Delton's mission was to help *stem* the flow of immigrants and drugs, not help it. So, what exactly were they doing? Who was financing them? And why?

Unless Peña was moonlighting, without the knowledge of Grant or Delton. Maybe he'd been exposed. That could make Delton angry. But angry enough to kill? And what about Wrobleski and Brewer? Were they moonlighting with Peña? Is that why they died in "training accidents?" Or did Peña kill them himself?

She turned back onto Seventh Street. Nothing felt right. She had no explanation for the million dollar cashiers' checks that went to the three men. No hint why Chris Messenger manipulated the bank accounts or why she and Art Emerlich were dead. And no solid evidence as to who kidnapped Molly Messenger. She bit her lip. Maybe Ellie Foreman was right. Nothing she'd learned in the past three days was getting her closer to the truth. Maybe she should take what she had to the cops and let them run with it.

* * *

Bright sunshine streamed through the windshield the next morning as Georgia drove east on Tenth Street. A tall latte steamed nicely in the cup-holder, reminding her that even in a border town Starbucks was ubiquitous. After pulling into the Walmart parking lot, she went in and bought two pairs of little boys' shorts, three t-shirts, and a pair of kid's gym shoes. In the toy department she picked up an electronic Transformers table-top pinball machine and two X-men action figures. She finished with bubble gum and candy.

She drove back to the barrio. No one answered when she knocked at Carmelita's aunt's home, so she dropped the shopping bags at the back door. As she pulled away, she saw Diego cautiously creep out and examine the bags. When he saw what was in them, his eyes widened.

She headed downtown. She'd decided to give it one more day. Whoever had tried to kill her in Chicago probably killed Chris

Messenger, Art Emerlich, and the two Delton Security men. She owed it to them to stay on the case until all her leads dried up.

She squinted against the glare of the sun and slipped on her shades. If some kind of deal was in place between Delton Security and Lionel Grant, there had to be people who knew about it. But except for Javier Garcia, the people she'd met in Stevens were pretty far down the economic and social ladder. They might not have direct knowledge of the decisions and machinations of the guys at the top. On the other hand, Georgia thought she knew who would.

* * *

Grant Copper Works occupied most of a converted warehouse a mile or so east of downtown not far from the border. From a distance, it looked like a shabby industrial brick building, the type you might see on Chicago's West side. As she drew closer, though, she saw a freshly painted "Grant Copper Works" logo—replete with crouching lion—hanging over the entrance. Georgia parked in a gravel lot and went to the door. It looked like reinforced steel and was securely locked. She pressed the buzzer mounted on the side. A few seconds later, a man's voice cut through static.

"Yes?"

"My name is Georgia Davis. I'd like to talk to Ken Grant."

"Do you have an appointment?"

"I won't take much of his time."

She sensed a silent sigh. "Just a minute."

The man who opened the door looked to be in his late fifties. He was bald on top but had a steel gray ponytail. His cheekbones were surprisingly high, and he had a lantern jaw. Deep set blue eyes checked her out. "I'm Ken Grant."

Georgia took an involuntary step back. "I didn't expect you to answer to the door yourself."

"Most people don't." He was dressed in a denim shirt and jeans, and had a turquoise bolo around his neck. A silver belt buckle flashed at his waist, and he wore cowboy boots. Javier Garcia was right. He did look like an aging hippie. "What can I do for you?"

"I'm an investigator from Chicago. I have a few questions about a case I'm working on."

He flicked his index finger up and down under his nose. "What sort of case?"

Georgia looked around. "You're on the city council, right?" He nodded. "It could be city business. Can we go inside?"

"City council?" He dropped his finger and flashed her a cool smile. "I'm very busy. You should have made an appointment... I suppose I can spare a few minutes." He led her in.

Part of the warehouse had been renovated to look like a living room rather than a workspace. A large central area was filled with comfortable-looking sofas and chairs. Woven rugs covered the floor, and splashy art hung on walls. Colorful masks, dolls, and silver objects sat on small tables. The central area was ringed by four or five offices, but only one of the doors was open. The walls cordoning off the central area looked to be about fifteen feet high and blocked the view of the rest of the warehouse.

Georgia was aware Ken Grant was watching her. "You seem surprised."

She turned toward him. "I am. From the outside..."

"I like to confound people's expectations." Again the cool smile. "Coffee?"

"No thanks."

He pointed to her arm. "What happened?"

"Car accident."

"Sorry to hear it. Well, let's go into my office." He led her through the open door. Following, she picked up a distinct musky smell, not as strong as Patchouli, but sensual, almost erotic. She felt uneasy.

The office was larger than she'd expected. Warm brown on the walls, a stained oak desk, leather club chairs. Old Wasp, not old West. Grant sat down behind the desk and kicked his feet up. He seemed to be waiting for her reaction. When none was forthcoming, he said, "So, what can I tell you?"

"I'm trying to find a man who was working for Delton Security. Does that name mean anything to you?"

He hesitated for an instant, then said, "I'm afraid it doesn't. But I'm not in the security business."

"What business *are* you in?"

"My interests are more—well—populist." He waved a hand. "You saw some of my inventory in the other room?"

"You have some lovely objects."

"I try to buy the best. Everything I acquire is in some way hand-crafted. One of a kind. I want to support indigenous crafts-people." He paused a beat. "It's the least I can do."

Georgia felt a twinge of impatience. "What do you mean?"

"I want to improve peoples' lives. This is one of the most economically depressed areas of the state. Perhaps the entire country. Buying original artwork helps local artisans keep a roof over their heads and food on their tables. It's not much, but it's something."

"I'd like to ask you about—"

He cut her off. "Actually, I split the profits with them. As you may know, I am fortunate—I don't need the money. So I can indulge my social conscience."

"Like being on the city council?"

He flicked his index finger again just below his nose. "Yes. It allows me to press for better schools, more resources. Literacy programs. Controlled development." He paused. "And they said we would never work through the system." He grinned. "But this has nothing to do with your case, does it?"

"Does Stevens have a serious drug trafficking problem?"

Grant laced his fingers together. "I won't lie. Like any other border town, it is an issue. But we're dealing with it. The Cochise County Sheriff's Office and our local police work closely with DEA and ICE—that's Customs—and Border Patrol. Even the FBI." He spoke with authority. "We have sniffing dogs, high-tech monitors, and, of course, the fence. And there's one other thing."

"What's that?"

"The supply of drugs that comes across the border here doesn't remain here. It's intended for other cities. So while Stevens might be the first stop on the distribution route, traffickers generally don't hang around."

"What about illegal aliens?" Georgia asked.

"What about them?"

"Could the city have hired a private security firm to reduce the stream of illegals?"

"With public money?" He laughed. "On our budget? That's a joke, right?"

"What if I told you there are rumors about exactly that kind of thing?"

Grant leaned forward. "Then I'd question the people who are spreading them. What ax do they have to grind?"

"And if I heard that people were being taken away in trucks in the middle of the night, you wouldn't believe it?"

"Taken where?"

It was an odd answer, Georgia thought. She leaned back, remembering what Javier Garcia said about Grant's relationship with his father. "Okay, maybe there's no public money involved. What about private?"

Grant glanced down. After a moment, he looked up. "You're referring to my father, of course."

She didn't answer.

He sighed. "It's true that he has the deepest pockets in town. But that makes him a target. Especially whenever something comes up that's not easily explained."

"So you're saying he wouldn't finance any such activity?"

"Look..." He cleared his throat. "My father and I are very different people. In fact, we rarely speak. But I won't allow him to be villainized by people who don't know us—or the town we live in."

Which meant Georgia, of course. Still, he hadn't answered her question. "Tell me how you're different."

"He's an old man. With old ideas."

"Old ideas that include an eye for an eye?"

"There's no pretense about him." He shifted. "And, at the risk of earning your scorn, I understand his side. Although I am diametrically opposed to it. I think illegals play a necessary role. Not just because the cost of their labor helps keep prices in check. Too often we forget that immigrants pay rent. And electricity and cable bills. They buy groceries and clothes. And TVs. If we deported every illegal, some of the things we take for granted wouldn't survive. Landscape companies, cleaning services, restaurants—"

Georgia cut him off. "But, as you said, your father doesn't see it that way. And you're not the first person to tell me how—determined—he is."

Grant held up his hand. "Georgia—you don't mind if I call you that, do you—you need to understand something. The issue just isn't as clear cut as you'd like to make it. It's true that some immigrants *are* drug traffickers. But others aren't. Makes it hard to distinguish the good from the bad."

"So you'd rather let them all in and look the other way?"

"Of course not. I'm just trying to point out there are shades of gray. On both sides."

Georgia felt the conversation slipping away. "Getting back to my question, if I had proof that someone was kidnapping innocent people and making them disappear—"

It was his turn to cut her off. Again. "I would be shocked."

"And you would report it to the authorities."

"Of course."

"I have reason to think it might be happening here, and that someone is trying to cover it up. Four people have died, and in each case, their deaths were made to look like accidents."

He tilted his head. "How many people?"

"Four. And a fifth man who may be involved has disappeared."

"Who is this man?"

"Rafael Peña. You know him?"

"No."

"Will you help me find him?"

Grant spread his hands. "What can I do?"

"You're on the city council. You have influence. You could ask the police. Maybe even make them put some muscle into it."

Grant grew quiet. Then he flicked his index finger below his nose. "If someone is trying to cover their tracks, it's usually because they're afraid."

"Your point?"

"Fearful people are dangerous. I'd advise you to be careful."

Georgia stared at him. "I need to find Peña."

Grant folded his arms. "If what you're saying is true, I would, too."

CHAPTER 35

_____

Ellie

Only on the North Shore would the floor of an auto mechanic's shop be clean enough to eat off. When I showed up at North Shore Motors in Lake Bluff Monday morning, I marveled at the spotless floor and shiny equipment. The Lake Bluff village board must have outlawed every drop of grease north of the county line.

The car dealership sprawled across several acres on a private street off Green Bay Road. On one side of the street was the showroom, where gleaming sports cars with unpronounceable names seduced customers. On the other was a cavernous hangar where sports cars occupied a dozen bays. Hydraulic lifts had raised the cars to different levels, revealing their undercarriages, and some of the wheels were detached. A car door leaned against the wall. Even those cars looked clean, and there were no grease spots, dirty tools, or oily rags to be seen.

At one end of the shop was a counter, behind which was an

office of several desks, chairs, computers, and phones. Five or six men in striped shirts and painters pants drifted in and out. A couple wore billed caps. Their shirts, emblazoned with their names, were immaculate.

As I approached the counter, a man named Greg was checking off a form. I remembered a mustard stain on my shirt and unobtrusively put my hand over the offending spot.

"Good morning," I chirped.

Greg looked at me with a puzzled expression. "Are you all right?"

I realized he was staring at my hand, which was draped across my stomach, as though it ached. I slipped my hand into my pocket and smiled. "Are you the manager?"

"Naw." He yanked a thumb toward the back and called out, "Hey, Tim. Some lady to see you."

A man who'd been leaning over a computer printer looked up. I smiled at him. He scooped up his printout and ambled toward the counter. He was wearing the same striped shirt as the others, and it, too, was immaculate. Did these guys change clothes every fifteen minutes? As he drew closer, though, I thought I saw a smudge on his pants. I felt a little smug.

"What can I help you with, Miss?"

"Good morning, Tim," I said and launched into my cover story. "I'm a writer, and I'm working on a spec article for *North Shore Magazine* about luxury sports cars."

"You came to the right place."

I smiled gamely. "You bet. I just wish I knew what I was looking at. Now, my husband loves sports cars. He talks about Aston Martins, Lamborghinis and Lotuses"— I'd boned up on the names last night—"all the time. Anyway, I'm looking to find a couple of owners to interview for the article. You know, why they love their cars. How they feel and handle. I could even include something about this place. It's the only one in Northern Illinois, I understand."

"That's right," Tim's face relaxed. Not quite a smile, but I'd take it.

"And you service customers from all over the Midwest?"

"I just got an Aston Martin from St. Paul the other day," Greg was hanging around, eavesdropping.

"That's exactly what I mean." I looked around admiringly, hoping a little ditz would be disarming. "Of course, St Paul isn't our target audience. Our readers are, well, from the North Shore." I paused. "Anyway, I was wondering whether you might have a list of North Shore customers I could take a look at."

Tim's eyes narrowed, on their way to a frown.

"Of course, I don't want their phone numbers or addresses," I added. "That's confidential, I realize. But if I could check the names and the type of car they have, it would really help. Who knows? Maybe I already know them. Or maybe you could recommend someone from the list. You know, whether they'd be a good interview."

Tim shook his head. "I don't know. We have thousands of customers."

"Hmm." I furrowed my brow and pretended to think. "Well, what if we generated a list by car instead? Wouldn't that narrow it down?"

Tim and Greg exchanged a glance.

"It would be great to get a couple of names for each car."

Tim's face assumed a pained expression.

"Oh, I'm sorry. That would take too much of your time,

wouldn't it? I wasn't thinking." I hesitated, then smiled brightly. "Well, let me ask you this. If you could print out a list, say, of your customers who have an Aston Martin, I might be able to track them down myself."

Tim and Greg exchanged another glance. Tim shrugged. "I guess."

"Hey, that's great!" I dug out a business card from my wallet. "By the way, I'd be happy to give you a plug in the article."

Tim examined it, then handed it back. He elbowed Greg. "Get her what she wants." He turned around.

"Thanks again, Tim. I really appreciate it."

He waved and headed out to the shop floor.

"So," Greg asked. "What kind of cars are you looking for?"

"Well, why don't we start with the Aston Martin? You know, the names of people who own them."

He nodded and went to one of the computers. I waited at the counter trying to contain my excitement. It was a safe bet that anyone who spent fifty grand on an Aston Martin would probably spend more to maintain it. It was also a safe bet that they'd bring it here to be serviced. With a list, I could start to winnow them down to see who knew Chris Messenger.

I watched as Greg pulled up a couple of screens. Then a few more. He scowled. "I'm having a hard time separating out Aston Martin customers on the North Shore from our entire Chicagoland database."

Damn. In my haste I hadn't considered that Chris Messenger's boyfriend might not live on the North Shore, but in Oak Park or Hinsdale or even downtown. Greg didn't realize it, but he had just saved me. "Um, that's all right," I stammered.

"It could be over four hundred names."

"I'll deal with it."

He shrugged and went back to the computer. I hoped I wasn't cutting off my options—what if the boyfriend lived in Indiana or Wisconsin? I chased the thought away.

Eventually, ten sheets of paper spooled off the printer. Greg scooped them up and brought them to the counter. "Here you go. Have fun." He grinned. "What did you say your name was?"

"Ellie Foreman." I hurriedly whisked the sheets off the counter, in case he had second thoughts. "Thank you so much. I really appreciate it. I'll send you a copy of the article when it's done."

* * *

I scurried out to my car clutching the print-outs. Before starting the engine, I scanned the sheets. There had to be close to five hundred names, mostly men, listed alphabetically. I started skimming the first page. At the top of the second I saw the name that made me gasp.

I rummaged in my bag for my cell and punched in Georgia's number. It rang once and went to voice mail. Tapping my toes impatiently, I listened to her message. When I heard the tone I said, "Georgia, call me right away. I'm at the Aston Martin dealer and I found out who Chris Messenger's boyfriend is. It's—"

My call-waiting clicked in. "Shit. Hold on. No, I'll call you back."

"Mom?" Rachel's voice sounded close to panic.

"What's wrong, Rach?"

"It's Fouad. He was here working in the yard, and he collapsed. I called 911 and they're coming to take him to the hospital. Please come home right away!"

CHAPTER 36

Georgia

A big sky, relentless sun, craggy mountains dusted with green. With an occasional sagebrush, tangled mesquite tree, and cactus thrown in. This was what the Old West was supposed to look like, Georgia thought, driving to Elgin that afternoon. She half-expected John Wayne to gallop up on horseback.

But as she got closer to Elgin, the terrain changed to rolling grasslands. Patches of green appeared more often, and the sand-colored soil turned dark. Exiting the highway onto a country road, she passed a green sign with three arrows pointing in different directions towards "Winery." For an instant she thought she was in a Monty Python skit. Fortunately her GPS, which she'd programmed for the Grant Winery, indicated a left turn.

A few miles later, a giant chartreuse meadow opened up on one side of the road. Georgia slowed. Fields of grapevines, bathed by sunshine, stretched as far as she could see. The rows were spaced much farther apart than Midwest cornfields, which had sharply delineated rows of tilled dirt between them. Most of the grapevines were supported by trellises, but a few runners sprawled across the dirt.

Set back from the fields were two long narrow adobe buildings. She pulled into a gravel driveway in front of one. A sign said she'd arrived at the Lionel Grant Winery. Open 10 to 5. Tours welcome.

It was only three. She parked next to an old Woody station wagon and slid out of the Escort. A surprisingly loamy smell hit her nostrils—she'd been expecting the dusty smell of sun-fired dirt. It felt slightly cooler here, too.

The door to the closest building was open. She walked up and peered through the screen into a gift shop, stocked with cases of wine, a revolving greeting card rack, wheels of cheese, and stuffed lions, among other things.

She went in, letting the screen door slam. A woman was working at a computer behind a counter, her back to Georgia. She wheeled around. She was wearing jeans, a yellow t-shirt, and cowboy boots. Her salt and pepper hair was stiff, her face brown and leathery, but her smile was welcoming. "Howdy."

Georgia nodded. "Hi."

"What can I do you for? You here for a tour?"

Georgia considered it. She couldn't admit she was there to spy on Lionel Grant, and she didn't think he'd see her without an appointment. But she might pick up some useful information. "I don't know much about wine-making. When's the next one?"

The woman laughed and glanced at her watch. "Whenever you're ready. We don't get a lot of visitors on Mondays."

Georgia glanced in the direction of the computer. "I don't want to interrupt your work."

The woman gave a dismissive wave. "The books can wait." She

stood up and wiped her hands on her jeans, although Georgia wasn't sure how tapping keys on a computer made them dirty. "You ready? I'm Sarah. Sarah Byrne."

"Georgia Davis."

Sarah lifted up a section of counter and came to the front of the shop. "Well, I reckon if you don't know anything, we'll start at the beginning. In the fields." She guided Georgia back outside, then closed and locked the door.

"What if someone else comes?"

"Probably won't be no one. Like I said, around here Mondays are our Sunday. Even Mr. Grant's gone." She waved toward one of the fields of green, and they headed over.

"Mr. Grant is Lionel Grant?"

"Yup. Owns the place."

"I've heard the name."

"He used to live in Stevens. Moved up here maybe ten years ago. He's done real well."

Georgia wasn't surprised. By all accounts Lionel Grant was a man who got things done. She continued to pick around the edges. "I'm staying in Stevens. That's where I heard about the winery. And Mr. Grant."

Sarah stopped, turned around, and studied Georgia. She looked as if she might say something.

Georgia, playing it safe, changed the subject. "I was amazed how much the scenery changed as I got closer to Elgin."

"Most folks are." Sarah must have reconsidered. "You're on a plateau that's up about five thousand feet. So if you need to catch your breath, that's why."

She led Georgia to the edge of the field. From one angle, the vines seemed like a vast sea of yellow-green, quiet and serene. But moving closer she could make out a world of subtle stirrings that belied the calm. Leaves rustled, insects buzzed, and a light breeze hummed. In reality the field was in constant motion.

"It all starts here. We have acres of vines, just like this."

"I imagine they need a lot of care."

"Not as much as you'd think. We have an irrigation system, if we need it. But the soil is nearly identical to that of Burgundy, France."

"Really?"

"Turns out the Arizona climate is pretty good for certain kinds of wine. There are over a dozen wineries out here." Sarah leaned over and grabbed a handful of grapes. "We have several varietals."

"Varietals?"

"Different kinds of grapes. We do pinot noir, syrah, and chardonnay. Of course, we're small. What you'd call a boutique producer."

"How much wine do you make?"

"Maybe about six thousand cases a year." Sarah straightened up. "Where are you from?"

"Chicago."

"I never been to the Windy City." She smiled. "Come over here." She led Georgia over to a gleaming metal bin that looked like a giant laundry room sink. "After the grapes are picked and sorted and cleaned, they go into a hopper like this."

"Who does the picking?" Georgia asked.

"Machines mostly. Sometimes we hire day laborers."

"Mexicans?"

Sarah's smile faded. "Mr. Grant doesn't want to get in trouble with undocumented workers." She paused. "Anyway, after the grapes are sorted and washed, they go into the crusher." She showed Georgia several structures that looked like wide slides attached to more hoppers.

"I guess you don't crush grapes with your feet any more."

Sarah grimaced. "You really *don't* know much, do you?"

She went on to explain how red wine differs from white, depending on the grapes and whether the juice stays in contact with the skins. Then they went inside the building where rows of stainless steel tanks flanked the walls.

"The juice from each grape and vintage goes into its own tank where it's fermented. Sometimes we mix them if we're doing a vintage blend. It all goes into oak barrels after that, and they're aged for a while. Then bottled. Back there." She gestured to another room. "Here. I'll show you."

"Oh, that's okay."

But Sarah insisted. "Go ahead. Take a peek."

Georgia peered into a dark, musty room filled with rows of wine bottles and wooden casks stacked on top of each other. "How long do you age the wine?"

"Depends. Six months or more. Sometimes it ferments for years. Till the content of the alcohol and the sugar is just right."

"Would your wines be available in Chicago?"

Sarah shook her head. "Like I said, we're tiny. Just local. We ship up to Tucson. Phoenix. Flagstaff."

"How does the wine get there?"

"We have trucks. We drive 'em north. And south. Down to Bisbee and Douglas. Sierra Vista, too."

"So you have a fleet?"

Sarah tilted her head back, as if she was trying to figure out why Georgia was asking. "Just four. But one of them is—well, not in operation."

Georgia's spine straightened. "It's in the shop?"

Sarah frowned. "Not exactly." She led Georgia back outside. "It was leased out." She wiped her hands on her jeans again. "Well, that's about it. Now we go back to the gift shop for a tasting."

Georgia raised her good hand. "Oh, that's okay."

"No?"

"I—I'm not much of a drinker." She smiled. "Tell me. Who leases the truck?"

Sarah's eyes narrowed and she planted her hands on her hips. "Time for you to level with me. You're no wine lover. You don't even like the stuff. And you're asking me questions that have nothing to do with making wine. So, who are you and why are you here?"

Shit. She'd been too obvious. Maintaining her cover, she replied smoothly. "I told you. I'm a tourist with some extra time, and I wanted to see the countryside."

Sarah folded her arms. "You know, we get a lot of reporters up here. They pretend to be tourists. Want the 'inside scoop' on Mr. Grant. Why he left Stevens, why he's producing wine, why he's the way he is. You wouldn't happen to be one of them now, would you?"

Georgia's tension eased. A reporter she could deal with. "I'm not a reporter."

"We also get a lot of competitors. Mr. Grant's won awards for his pinot noir. Folks come around and play dumb, thinking they're gonna find out his secrets. Maybe you're one of them."

Georgia met Sarah's cool gaze with one of her own. "I'm not a reporter. And I'm not a spy. But I will get out of your hair. Thanks for the tour." She headed for the door. Then she stopped. When she turned around, Sarah hadn't moved. "Actually, I have a friend back in Chicago who loves wine. If you don't mind, I'd like to buy a case of your Chardonnay."

CHAPTER 37

As Georgia drove back to Stevens, an uneasy feeling broke over her. Lionel Grant had four trucks. One of them was "leased out." Diego said a truck with a lion and grapes painted on its side took his parents away. Which meant whoever leased the truck could be connected to Rafael Peña and Delton Security and the kidnapping of illegals. To be fair, though, it was also possible someone with no connection to the case had leased the truck. Or borrowed one of the other three.

Lionel Grant had deep pockets, and no love for illegals. Still, a contract with a security firm like Delton, if he was underwriting it, was one thing. Human smuggling and murder were another. The reality was that unless she camped out in the desert and waited for the truck to show up, she probably would never know who was driving it. But hanging out in the desert near the border—alone, and outgunned—wasn't a good idea.

Georgia was close—she could feel it—but time was running out. Someone in Chicago had gone to a lot of trouble to make sure she didn't put the pieces together. That had been one of the reasons she'd come to Arizona in the first place—to fly under the radar, buy herself some time and safety. But it wouldn't last forever. If someone wanted her out of the way, they could already be on to her.

She was back on Route 90 heading south when her cell phone beeped. She pulled over and checked. A message had come in an hour ago. Elgin must have been out of the cell's service area. She clicked to her voice mail and listened. Then she hit redial.

"Ellie? It's Georgia. What's going on?"

"I'm just leaving the hospital." Ellie sounded distracted.

"What happened?"

"My friend, Fouad, had a heart attack. It was awful. He collapsed in the front yard. They're saying it was a—"

"Are you okay?"

"I'm okay."

"Sorry. I hope your friend recovers."

"They're saying—well, it doesn't matter right now."

Georgia cleared her throat. "So who was it?"

"Who was what?"

"Chris Messenger's boyfriend. You left a message with everything except the name."

"Right. I went to the Aston Martin dealer this morning, and—"

Georgia cut her off. "Who, Ellie?"

Ellie hesitated. "It's Geoff Delton."

Georgia blinked. "Fuck! Geoff Delton's Aston Martin was parked at Chris Messenger's house?"

"Looks that way."

"Isn't he married?"

"With three young children." Ellie paused. "Georgia, don't you see? It's classic. They have an affair. Chris gets pregnant. But he won't leave his wife. Chris goes bonkers and screws up his bank accounts for revenge. He decides she's too dangerous and has her hit."

Georgia kept her mouth shut.

"Come on." Ellie's voice was edged with frustration. "Say something."

Georgia still didn't answer.

"You know a guy like Delton could pull it off. And we know Chris had the IT knowledge to do anything she wanted with the bank accounts."

"I don't know," Georgia finally said. "It sounds too convenient."

"But it fits. Chris was on that new business team at the bank that landed Delton as a client, remember? She was even the face person on the account. So one thing leads to another, and they start sleeping together. And then the rest happens." Ellie took a breath. "You know to never underestimate the wrath of a woman who's been rejected."

Georgia flashed back to Matt. She'd been in love with him, and he'd rejected her. She hadn't been vengeful. Or had she? "I don't know, Ellie. What about the elevator? The man with the missing finger? And what about Art Emerlich? He didn't have anything to do with their affair."

"Maybe Chris told Emerlich about it. Maybe Emerlich confronted Delton. And the man with the missing finger could be the hit man." Ellie said. "About the elevator, I don't know, but I have a feeling we'll find out."

"How do you figure that?"

"I called O'Malley."

Georgia went rigid. "You did? When?"

"While I was at the hospital. I couldn't reach you. And you said if something broke, I should."

Ellie was right. But that didn't do much to lessen Georgia's disappointment. Still, she tried to suppress it. "You—you did the right thing. What did he say?"

"He's bringing Delton in. And he wants to talk to you ASAP. Georgia, it's time for you to come home."

* * *

It made sense, Georgia thought after she disconnected. An affair gone bad put a new spin on the case. Especially when a surprise pregnancy was factored in. Now Geoff Delton would be under tremendous pressure. And while he probably considered himself a soldier of sorts, putting loyalty to his men and his mission above all else, it wouldn't take the cops long to discover whether he'd engineered Chris Messenger's death and her daughter's kidnapping. There was always the chance that the other answers she'd been looking for would surface, as well. Ultimately, the four days she'd spent digging in Stevens probably *didn't* matter. Ellie was right about that, too. It was time to go home.

She stopped at the hotel restaurant for dinner, but by the time she went up to her room after dark, she felt deflated and fatigued. She pulled out her card key and was about to slip it into the lock when she stopped. Each time she'd left her room, she'd used the old trick of placing a hair in the door jam. If the hair wasn't there when she returned, she'd know someone had been inside. The hairs had been there each time she'd come back. Until now.

It wasn't the maid, who'd cleaned the room before Georgia

stuck today's hair to the jam. It couldn't be room service or the laundry, either. She hadn't ordered or sent anything down.

When she heard a muffled thump on the other side of the door, her heart banged in her chest. Someone was in her room. She slipped her Sig out of her holster and gripped it in her good hand. Slowly she lifted her other arm and inserted the key. The latch unlocked. Grabbing the door handle, she twisted and opened the door an inch. She dropped the key in her pocket, brought her Sig up, and stepped inside.

She tried to wedge the door open with her foot, but operating with just one arm was problematic, and the door closed behind her. The shades were drawn, and the lighting was dim, but she could make out a man sitting on a chair. He was pointing a gun at her. She aimed her Sig at him. Neither of them moved. The window was open a crack. A car radio barreling past on the street below blared out a Latino rap.

She kept the Sig trained on the man, but she hadn't chambered a round. Could she bluff her way through?

Before she could start, the man spoke. "Well now," he said lazily, "I guess this is what you'd call a Mexican stand-off."

"Drop the gun and get on the floor, asshole," she said sharply.

"Or what? You'll shoot me?"

"Do you really want to take that chance?"

"I think the more important question is 'do you?'" He leveled his pistol at her. It was a semi-automatic. Maybe Heckler and Koch.

"The way I see it," he went on, "We can both fire. Assuming you can rack your slide. Which, with your bum wrist, could be a problem. But even if you could, you'll die. See, you don't have a vest on. Or any other kind of protection I can see. I, on the other hand, am wrapped up in Kevlar where it counts."

He had her.

"This might be a good time for *you* to drop *your* weapon," he added.

Georgia had no choice. She went down on one knee and placed the Sig on the floor. He side-stepped over and picked it up, the barrel of his gun never wavering. He slipped her Sig into his vest and straightened up. "Normally, I'd cuff you. Stuff something in your mouth. But I'm guessing if you were going to scream, you would have done it already. And since you're already incapacitated...," he motioned to her cast, "... I'm willing to forego those things." His voice hardened. "I haven't miscalculated, have I?"

She stared at him as if it might illuminate the man's soul. "You're Raffi Peña."

"And you're Georgia Davis."

He watched her with a curious expression. Georgia had the feeling he was assessing how much of a threat she posed, even with her broken wrist. Still, the fact that she was alive, at least for the moment, gave her some hope. "I've been looking for you."

"I know."

Carmelita or her brother must have contacted him. "I have questions. About a case I'm working." She wanted to keep him talking while she figured out a way to stay alive.

"Nice try, but I'll ask the questions. Who are you and why are you here?" His gun was inches from her chest.

He wasn't going to give. "I'm a private investigator from Chicago. I'm looking into the kidnapping of a little girl and the subsequent murder of her mother. She was a banker, and she issued three cashiers' checks, each for a million dollars. One of them was made out to you."

He grunted.

"I know you work for Delton Security. I know your two buddies are dead. And I know you're on the run. I want to know if that's because you killed them. Kidnapped the little girl. Killed her mother."

"And I should tell you these things because..." His voice was laced with irony. "How do I know Delton didn't send you?"

Georgia frowned. Something was off. "Why would Delton be coming after *you*?"

He hesitated a moment, as if he realized he'd said the wrong thing, then pulled back the slide and chambered a round. "Give me a reason not to take you out."

Georgia took a breath, wondering if it might be her last. "Because if you do, we'll have both failed in our missions."

He seemed to ponder that. "Why did you get a phone message about Delton from someone named Ellie in Chicago?"

"How did you know about that?"

"Answer the question."

She thought fast. Ellie must have called the hotel at some point when she couldn't reach her cell. It was probably on the room's answering machine. Which Peña had obviously listened to. "Ellie's my—partner. She's working the case in Chicago."

"And?"

Georgia shook her head.

"What?"

"Nothing more until we deal."

He almost laughed. "Deal? What do you have to deal?"

"Intel. About Geoff Delton."

Now he did laugh. "You're willing to risk your life in a flea-bag hotel in Stevens, Arizona, over some intel you think I need?"

She wondered if there was any way to gain an advantage but decided there wasn't. Better to stand her ground. She wouldn't beg for her life. "That's right."

He didn't reply, but he didn't shoot, either. After a moment he motioned with the gun. "Sit on the bed."

Georgia went to the edge of the bed, sat down, and flicked the switch of the lamp on the bedside table. She wanted to see her killer.

"You shouldn't have done that." He growled.

She ignored the comment and took stock of Peña. Under the black Kevlar vest he wore a black t-shirt and jeans. Desert boots on his feet. Thick black hair tied back in a ponytail. A well-trimmed goatee. But his most striking feature was his eyes—dark pools that captured and gave off light as if a fire raged behind them. Right now they were focused on her like a laser. She could tell he liked what he saw.

"You shouldn't have done that," he repeated.

"I have the right to see the man who's going to kill me."

He inclined his head toward the window. "The light tells them you're back."

She weighed his comment. It could be a ruse, to trick her into giving him what he wanted. Whatever that was. "Who?"

He didn't answer.

"Peña, the least you can do before you kill me is tell me why you got a million dollars from Delton. Why Wrobleski and Brewer are dead. And what you've been doing for Lionel Grant."

A lazy smile crept across his face. "Those are fair questions."

She was waiting for his answer when the room exploded. The

shade billowed out, then fell off its track. The window shattered, and shards of glass blew onto the floor. Another explosion tore through the window. Georgia dropped to the floor

"Davis!" Peña hissed. "Are you all right?"

Adrenaline surged through her, rendering her momentarily speechless.

"Answer me, Davis!"

"I'm—I'm okay." She stammered.

"Then turn off the fucking light!"

Georgia crawled over, stretched up her good arm, and snapped off the light. Once again dark shadows cloaked the room. Warm air gusted in, scented with rain. She tried to peer out of the space that used to be the window, but all she could see was the black of the building next door against a deeper black that was the night sky. A hazy glow came from the street below. "Who's the shooter?"

He didn't answer.

Her anger mounted. "How do I know they're not after *you?*" More silence. "Who the fuck are you, Peña? What game are you playing? If you—or your goons—are planning to kill me, let's just get it over with, okay?"

She heard rather than saw his grin. "All in good time."

Another shot screamed through the window. Georgia ducked. She thought she smelled cordite. "Fuck it!"

"They're just trying to scare you. If they really wanted you dead, they wouldn't be firing randomly into the room."

"How do I know you didn't set me up?"

"You don't." He paused. "But I'm thinking now might be a good time for us to make our exit."

Us. He said us. "How do you plan to do that? As soon as we show ourselves, they're going to use us for target practice."

"I might have a trick or two left up my sleeve."

"Well, this would be a good time to pull them out."

CHAPTER 38

T en minutes later Peña peeled out of the lot in a battered Dodge Ram with Georgia in the passenger seat, rigid and tense. They'd crept down an unmarked staircase she'd cased when she first checked in. By the time they got to the ground floor, a storm had blown in, and the pounding rain made it impossible to see in any direction. There was no hail of bullets when they ran from the building, and they sprinted safely to his pickup.

While Peña sped through the streets of Stevens, Georgia twisted around looking for a tail. She couldn't spot anything. "I think we're clear."

"The monsoon helps."

The feeble beam of the truck's headlights dissipated in the dark, but Peña drove confidently. It was only through brief flashes of lightning that Georgia could see where they were. Once they reached the outskirts of town, Peña drove toward Bisbee, and a moment later climbed into the hills. As they ascended, the storm grew more violent. Rain drenched the pickup, lightning crackled, thunder exploded. Peña hunched over the wheel and squinted through the windshield. Georgia gripped the edge of her seat.

After what seemed like an hour but was probably just ten minutes, Peña turned off the paved road. The truck jounced down a dirt path, made several turns, and finally slid to a stop in a muddy clearing.

Except for the exchange about the tail, they hadn't spoken. Now he said, "We're here."

When Georgia climbed out of the pickup, her feet promptly sank into mud. She tried to slog through it, but the muck sucked her down so deep her shoes disappeared. Over the thud of rain she heard a rushing, flowing sound. "What's that?"

"Water filling the gulleys. It'll dry up after the rain stops."

Peña trudged to a small cabin with a corrugated metal roof. Georgia followed, her steps plodding and heavy. Rain soaked her clothes. A makeshift window near the door trickled light from inside.

"Where are we?"

"An abandoned mining cabin. Kick off your shoes."

Georgia did and followed him inside, shaking herself off.

The cabin was even smaller than Carmelita's place: two rooms separated by a primitive bathroom. In the main room was a table, two chairs, a hot plate, a sink with a couple of cabinets underneath, and a five gallon gas can. An M4 assault rifle was propped up against the table, and a small arsenal of hand guns, along with accessories for the M4, lay in a duffel on the floor. Another duffel contained a Mag Lite, a grenade launcher, a knapsack, night vision goggles, binoculars, and a video camera with a Mini DV label.

Peña walked past the gear into the other room. Georgia thought about helping herself to a couple of guns while he was gone, but he returned with a towel before she could. He dried his face and arms, then tossed the towel to Georgia. She caught it with her good hand and waved it in the direction of the gear. "Christmas presents for the family?"

He glanced over. "Things are not always what they seem."

"Why are you hiding out here?"

"My mission isn't finished." A sudden crash of thunder seemed to emphasize the point.

Georgia faced him. "Did Lionel Grant pay you to kill illegal immigrants in the desert?"

He seemed to sense her mood. A strange light came into his eyes. "Yeah, it's time. You deserve some answers."

She hung the towel around her neck and waited.

"I am Mexican. My family is from the Sonora. That is where many who cross come from. Do you think I could kill my own people?"

He seemed sincere. Still. "Why should I believe you?"

"Who do you think teaches them to take a brush to erase their footprints? To make sure they bring plenty of water? To sleep during the hottest hours and walk at night?"

"I thought you were working for Delton Security to *stop* illegals from crossing the border."

He smiled at her confusion. "I was a *migra*. After Delton got the contract from Grant, they recruited me from Border Patrol."

"To do what?"

"To interrupt the supply of drugs."

"Because what's being done isn't enough?"

He nodded and gestured to the window. "Drugs flow just like water in those gullies, if you know what to look for."

"So you weren't there to kidnap and kill illegals."

He shook his head.

"Then why did Carmelita say you were the one who made them get into Grant's truck?"

His face turned grave, even a bit sad. "It was not me. Perhaps someone who looks like me. Who has the uniform, the equipment."

"Wroblewski or Brewer?"

He ran his tongue around his lips, looking uncomfortable. Was he hanging on to some remnant of loyalty toward his fellow mercenaries? Was he unwilling to call them out, especially since they were dead? She'd seen that time and again in Chicago with the mob. And the cops. Whenever teams worked together against a common enemy.

"You expect me to believe Lionel Grant, a right-wing racist who's made a career of hating illegals, underwrites a contract with Delton to stop the drug trade, but not illegals?" she went on. "And then someone else—some rogue group—impersonates you and exterminates them?"

"It's the truth."

She wasn't buying it. "Why did three million dollars make its way to you and your men?"

Apparently he'd had enough of being challenged. "No more. Not now."

Georgia tried a different tactic. "Is Lionel Grant as crazy as they say?"

"No."

"No, he's not or no, you're not going to—"

"Stop!" He bellowed. "This conversation is over."

Georgia exploded. "No, goddammit, it's not! I've come over

a thousand miles to figure this out. Risked my life. More than once." She held up her cast. "Someone tampered with my brakes in Chicago. That's how this happened. Now someone's shooting through my hotel room. And you've got me pinned like a bug under a microscope. Until I know what's going on, this fucking conversation is definitely not over!"

"No more!" He raised his hands in the air and advanced toward her. Startled, she stepped back, but he kept coming. She braced herself. Less than a foot away, he suddenly stopped, as if he'd just become aware of his behavior and was surprised by the depth of his rage. He took a breath and aimed a finger at her. "Go dry off."

He turned away, opened the cabinet under the sink, and pulled out a bottle of bourbon. He looked around for a glass, found one, and poured a few fingers full.

Georgia stood her ground. "I need to know why Delton sent you a million dollars."

Peña tossed back the bourbon. He looked like he was going to start talking when a cell phone trilled. He fished it out of his pocket.

"Yeah?" He paused. "You got the package? Good. Keep it safe." Silence. "I'm still working on it. It'll be wrapped up soon. Okay." He disconnected and glared at Georgia, as if daring her to ask him about it.

She did. "What package?"

He didn't reply.

"Look..." She started over, trying to suppress her own anger. Trying to be reasonable. "I'm grateful you decided not to kill me. For the moment. But this cat and mouse shit—this drama— has to stop. I won't be played. Talk to me straight."

He tossed back more booze. Then, "Did you ever think I might be trying to protect your ass, which happens to be quite fine-looking, by the way?"

But Georgia was in no mood for come-ons. "Fuck you, Peña. I can handle my ass myself." She snapped. "Either you talk to me now, or—"

"Or what?"

"I'll leave. Head back into town."

His eyes flashed. "You won't get far."

"You want to stop me, you'll have to shoot me in the back." She threw the towel down.

He shrugged, a wry smile on his face.

Georgia grabbed her shoes and put them on, caked mud and all. Then she pulled open the door, half-expecting a slew of bullets to mow her down. Nothing happened. She exited the cabin. The wind shoved her across the clearing. Jagged forks of lightning sizzled the sky. The rain was now sheeting sideways. The storm had grown fiercer. There was no way she could hike ten yards, much less the ten miles she guessed they'd driven. She flattened herself against the side of the cabin, but there were no eaves or overhangs to protect her. She crept back to the window, now steamy with condensation, and peeked in. Peña was at the table refilling his glass.

She let out a breath, opened the door, and skulked back inside. She was sopping wet, humiliated, and angry. She refused to look at him. She watched puddles form at her feet instead. He didn't say anything. Finally, she glanced up.

His eyes held the same wry look as before. Amusement or arrogance? He rose and went into the other room. She heard drawers slide open. He came back out carrying dry clothes and dropped them on the floor next to her.

Georgia picked them up and walked into the room from which he'd come. Barely furnished, it had a double bed, a three-drawer chest, side table, and lamp. A small window was cut high into the wall.

She tossed the clothes on the mattress, kicked off her shoes, and started to take off her jeans. She tried to unfasten the button at her waist, but she was working with only one hand, and her jeans, soaked through, were rigid. After struggling unsuccessfully with the button, she gave up. She managed to shrug off her blazer and tried to lift her t-shirt over her head, but it, too, was water-logged and stuck to her skin. When she tried to use the casted arm to take off the t-shirt, she yelped in pain. It had been less than a week since her wrist was broken.

She struggled a few more seconds, then collapsed on the bed. It was all getting to her. The accident. The past four days in Stevens. The lack of progress. The shots through the window. She couldn't remember ever feeling this alone, this isolated. She covered her eyes with her hand but refused to cry. She wouldn't give him the satisfaction.

She'd lost track of time when she felt his presence behind her. How had he snuck into the room so silently? Was this the moment he'd decide to kill her? She waited for him to wrap his hands around her neck and snap it. He'd know how. She should move out of range. Put up a semblance of a fight. But she was too tired.

He rolled his fingertips over her neck. A chill shot through her. Was this it? Then his palms settled on her shoulders and he started to knead them. Tender at first, then firm. She bowed her head and gave him more of her neck. If this was the prelude to death, maybe it wasn't so bad.

Suddenly he stopped. She arched her back, fearing the worst.

A moment later, a gentle massage moved down her good arm. He was drying her with the towel. His movements were languid and soft. She felt hot and cold at the same time. When his hands reached the cast on the other arm, he slid the towel carefully over the plaster.

The stroking stopped. "You should put on dry clothes." His voice was husky.

She tried to speak but her voice cracked.

"Stand up," he whispered.

Wordlessly she obeyed. Part of her was surprised by how submissive she was acting. Another part of her was way past that.

"Turn around."

She did. He stood in front of her, breathing fast. His eyes glittered. She smelled liquor on his breath. Without a word, he put the towel down and caught the tail of her t-shirt with both hands. Carefully he lifted it over her head. She wasn't wearing a bra. He gazed at her breasts. Her pulse started to race. He caressed her cheeks and pulled her toward him. She didn't resist. When his lips found hers, she responded, first tentative, then eager. Heat welled up from someplace inside her. She wrapped her good arm around his neck.

He cupped her breasts in his hands, bent his head, and ran his tongue around her nipples. She shivered with pleasure and pushed against him. He fumbled with the button on her jeans, unfastened it, and pushed them down to her ankles. She lay down on the bed, letting him pull off one pant leg, then the other. He did the same with her briefs.

He stared as if he couldn't believe what he was seeing. She smiled. He tore off his clothes and got down on the bed. Again he cupped her face with his hands. She kissed him, tracing her fingertips along his cheekbone. He moved hard against her. Then he was inside. As he thrusted, she rose up to meet him, wanting him deep. She needed him deep. His hands went around her hips and pulled her close. She cried out. The storm closed in around them.

* * *

Maybe it was the silence that woke her. Or maybe it was that she was sleeping next to a man she didn't know. Or maybe it was because she'd been with a man in the first place. It had been too long. His touch, his smell, her blond hairs tangled with his black on the pillow; it was all good and right.

Pale bars of moonlight bathed the room in silver. Raffi was sleeping, snoring lightly. She remembered the call that came in on his cell. The package. She crept out of bed, taking care not to wake him. She wasn't too worried. Men always slept well after sex.

His jeans were crumpled on the floor. She picked them up, rummaged in his pockets, found the cell. She pressed the menu key for "Calls Received" and memorized the number at the top of the list. Then she went back to bed.

CHAPTER 39

The morning sun crept over a ridge high above the town of Stevens. A breeze sighed through the trees, carrying the scent of pine and cedar. Aside from that, it was quiet, and Georgia could almost hear the yucca growing in the thin rocky soil. It was cooler than she'd expected; she pulled her now dry blazer close. She looked over at the gullies. Javier was right: the water that had gushed through them last night was gone. The creek bottom was barely damp.

She went back inside. Her Sig, which Raffi had confiscated last night, lay on the table beside two coffee mugs. She threw him a grateful smile and slipped it into her holster. He poured coffee, which was surprisingly good. He'd dressed in a flak jacket over jeans and a t-shirt, and he was loading extra magazines for the M4, a knife, and pepper spray into the pockets.

She tried to make small talk. "What kind of training do you need to work for Delton?"

"They trained me."

"Where?"

"Somewhere in the Midwest."

Georgia remembered how Ellie had discovered Delton's private training facility downstate. "Central Illinois?"

"Maybe. Yeah. Sure."

"How long were you there?"

"Ten weeks. They put me in charge of a team."

She smiled. "You were that good."

He nodded

"Is that where you met Wroblewski and Brewer?"

Another nod.

"You weren't far from Chicago, you know. Where I live."

"If I'd known, I would have visited."

"Next time."

Raffi attempted a pained smile, then fell quiet. He looked at his watch, scooped up one of the duffels, and went out. She watched him throw it into the pickup.

"Where are you going?" She asked when he came back in.

"To a meeting."

"Where?"

He picked up his mug. His eyes were veiled.

"You're distributing weapons. Or getting more."

He didn't answer.

"Let me come."

"No."

"Why not?"

He stopped pacing and set his mug down with a thud. "Look, Georgia, I'm not your enemy. But there are others who are. Or will be if you hang around. Go home. This isn't your fight."

"Is it yours?"

He clenched his jaw. "I need to finish my job." He headed back out.

Georgia followed him. "Why are you working alone? Where is Carmelita's brother?" Again he didn't answer. "Doesn't he have the guts to help you?"

He opened the driver's side door and hopped up into the cab.

Georgia hurried to the passenger side. Time to hit him with her theory. "That cashier's check—Geoff Delton was paying you hush money, wasn't he?"

Raffi hesitated just a fraction too long. "What Delton was doing is immaterial."

"Is it?" She swung herself up into the passenger seat.

"Get out of my truck."

"Listen, Raffi. Delton was 'detained' in Chicago last night. The police are questioning him right now."

Raffi looked over. "Why?"

"He was sleeping with the woman whose little girl was kidnapped. The same woman who was murdered after she helped Delton set up the account your cashiers' check was written against."

Raffi looked like he was thinking. Calculating. Then he shrugged. "So? It has nothing to do with me."

"The woman was pregnant," Georgia paused, "with Delton's child."

He put the key in the ignition.

"Delton couldn't risk the fact that she sent out the cashiers' checks for him," Georgia said. "He had her taken out. Her boss, too. But it's all falling apart now. The cops have him. Which means you may not have any reason to—"

The engine fired up, cutting her off.

"Why was he paying you off, Raffi?"

He shook his head.

She persisted. "What was the package you sent your buddy?"

"You never quit, do you?" He looked exasperated. "You want to know? Okay, I'll tell you. It's a goddammed videotape, all right? Now get off my fucking back."

"Grant's on the tape, isn't he? He's got something to do with all of this. He and Delton realized your team wasn't doing what you started out to do. That you'd been corrupted by the drug traffickers. The cartels. So Delton tried to paper it over with the money so no one would talk. And now you're—"

"Fuck it, Georgia, stop. The less you know, the longer you'll live."

"Given that someone's tried to kill me twice, your advice is a little late, don't you think?"

"Everything I touch turns to shit, don't you see?" His voice was raw. "I don't want you to be part of the pile."

But she'd already slammed the door and fastened her seat belt.

* * *

He drove fast through the mountains, zigzagging around switchbacks and rutted roads. The road was flanked by dense woods of pines and aspens. Sunlight sneaked through the branches every so often, and she could almost taste the heat-baked air. Although Georgia had no idea where they were, the terrain was starting to look familiar. Even beautiful.

Their conversation had been sparce and insubstantial, like a meal you didn't eat enough of. It was ironic—she'd never tolerate that in Chicago; why did she here? Probably because, despite their intimacy last night, they were still strangers, checking each other out.

Eventually, the road wound around a narrow pass and Raffi stopped in a clearing. A faded hand-painted sign said they'd arrived at the Lanedo Camp. Behind the signpost were several wooden cabins, low and squat. A picnic table sat in front of the cabin. Georgia was surprised. The camp looked deserted. Who'd want to picnic here? She slid out of the pickup and shaded her eyes. The ground was studded with rocks, tumbleweeds, and tall grass. Across the clearing was a cliff with an outcropping high enough to look down on the twisty pass they'd just traveled. "Where are we?"

"An abandoned mining camp. Used to be bigger, but it was chopped into parcels when the mines closed."

"What were they mining?"

"Copper mostly, but a little gold and silver, too. Even turquoise. But nothing now."

"Which makes it a safe meeting place."

He looked over. "Who said this was my meeting place? This is the end of the road for you. You're staying here."

She stiffened. "You're—you're ditching me?"

"You'll be safe here." He went to the back of the truck and pulled out a smallish 40 caliber Glock and a pair of binoculars. He came back, handed her the semi-automatic, and draped the field glasses around her neck. "Do some bird watching. I'll be back."

"I can't believe this. I told you—"

"You're not coming."

She glared, making sure he felt her anger. "You're a piece of work."

He grinned as he made his way back to the pickup. "That's what they tell me."

"Why the Glock? I've got my Sig."

"You might run into a snake or two around the camp. You're supposed to leave them alone. It's illegal to kill 'em."

She called out. "But?"

"But I figure you're pissed off enough to want some target practice, and I wouldn't want you to waste your ammo."

"Is this a joke?"

"You can't kill gila monsters either. But they move pretty slow. You should be okay."

"You live in a state with monsters?"

His grin broadened. "Yup." He hoisted himself back into the pickup, keyed the engine, and put it into gear.

"Where's the ammo for the Glock?" She yelled out.

He stuck his head out the window. "You've only got the one mag. Use it wisely."

"Fuck you, Peña."

"I'll hold you to it." He saluted and drove away. As he accelerated, the truck kicked up a cloud of dust.

* * *

Georgia watched the truck disappear around a bend. The whine of the engine faded but resurged a moment later. He was rounding the switchback they'd driven on the way up. She went to the edge of the cliff and saw him a few hundred yards below. As the road straightened out, he picked up speed. She watched, caught between annoyance and amusement. Then she tucked the Glock into her waistband. She would poke around the camp. Maybe shoot a gila monster, just for the hell of it.

She was just about to turn back to the cabin when a dark-colored SUV appeared around a curve. It was heading toward Raffi. It wasn't traveling fast but it was hogging the road. Raffi would either have to pull over or brake.

As the SUV approached, it slowed to a crawl. Georgia went on alert. She grabbed the field glasses. Focusing in, she spotted a man in the passenger seat cradling something long and thin. A rifle. The hair at the back of her neck stood up. The SUV's passenger window lowered. A rifle barrel emerged.

Everything went into slow motion. The SUV stopped. The rifle angled toward the pickup. Georgia wanted to shoot, to yell out a warning, but she was too far away. Paralyzed and helpless, she screamed wordlessly.

Raffi must have realized what was happening because the pitch of his engine shifted, as though he'd abruptly downshifted. It was too late. Yellow muzzle flashes, visible even in the bright sun, spit from the rifle. Staccato cracks echoed through the hills.

For an instant, there was silence. Then a horn blast shattered the quiet. A flock of frantic birds lifted into the sky. Georgia started to call 911, then realized she had no cell service.

The SUV's driver door opened and a man got out, aiming a pistol in Raffi's direction. He jogged to the pickup. Georgia sharpened the focus on the binoculars. He looked vaguely familiar— compact, dark, wrap-around shades. As he drew close to the pickup, she prayed for a burst of rounds from Raffi's M4, but there was nothing. He was still hunched over the wheel, unmoving. His horn was still blaring.

The driver holstered his gun and gestured to the shooter, who got out and joined the driver at the pickup. Together they dragged Raffi out of the truck. The shriek of the horn ceased, replaced by a stony silence. Even the breeze was hushed.

Georgia tried to focus on Raffi, but all she could see was his black ponytail. The top of his head was gone. Her mouth went dry; nausea climbed up her throat. She watched the men carry him to a stand of trees at the edge of the road. The shooter lugged him by his shoulders, the driver had his legs. His body trailed blood on the road. She upped the glasses' magnification and watched. The man gripping Raffi's legs was missing part of his left index finger.

She dropped the glasses, turned away from the cliff, and vomited. When there was nothing left to come up, she brought the binoculars up again. The men were rifling through Raffi's flak jacket. Something flashed in the sun. His cell phone. They pocketed it. They took his hand guns, his ammo, and what might have been a grenade. Please, God, she prayed. Don't let them detonate it. She needed the pickup to get back to town. They didn't. Instead the men backtracked to Raffi's pickup and searched the bed of the truck. The driver and the shooter exchanged words, after which the shooter scooped up Raffi's duffel and threw it in the SUV.

The shooter got back into the passenger seat, but the driver halted at his door, looking around, as if checking to make sure he'd attended to everything. When his gaze swept up the hill, Georgia ducked and stepped back. For an instant, she thought he'd seen her. She dropped the binoculars and raced to one of the cabins. If they came this way, she'd pick them off one at a time from inside.

She yanked on the door, but it was locked. Her stomach

twisted. She ran to the back of the cabin, braced herself against the wall, and pulled out her Sig. Nothing happened. From a distance, she heard an engine cough to life. A moment later the noise subsided to a hum. The SUV was going back down the road. She waited until it faded altogether. The silence stung her ears.

CHAPTER 40

Georgia picked her way down to Raffi. His truck was where he'd left it, the engine softly running. Blood and bits of whitish matter were splattered over the seat, the steering wheel, the dash, even the windshield. The truck was infused with a coppery, still-warm smell. She turned off the engine and pocketed the keys. They'd dropped his body near the trees at the side of the road. They hadn't bothered to conceal it; any passerby would see it.

She knelt beside his body. The bullet had entered his temple. She imagined the force knocking his head back. The bullet exited at an angle, which probably caused him to slump over the wheel. There wasn't much left to his head. Georgia covered him with her blazer. She waited for a rush of sorrow to overwhelm her, but nothing came. The only thing she knew for certain was that she would never come to the mountains again.

She remembered Matt once telling her about the Jewish custom of placing stones on graves to symbolize the act of burial. She scrounged around, found a few small rocks, and laid them gently on Raffi's chest. She bowed her head. Someone should mourn him.

After a while, she stood up and headed back to the pickup. She'd drive it back to Stevens, but exactly where, she wasn't sure. She'd call the police when her cell kicked in, tell them about his body. She'd call the FBI and Customs, too, and tell them everything. It was time. Then, if they let her, she'd go to the hotel and get her things. Drive to the barrio to tell Carmelita what happened. Hopefully she or her brother could see to a proper burial.

She was breaking cover from the woods when she heard another vehicle chugging around the pass. Was the SUV coming back? Had they spotted her after all? Gone for reinforcements? She ducked into the woods. It sounded like another pickup. Raffi's truck was in the middle of the road—whoever it was wouldn't be able to pass without stopping. And when they did, they'd see his body. She hid behind a tree and pulled out her Sig.

The brakes screeched. The gears shifted; the pitch of the motor changed to an idle. A door squeaked open.

"What the fuck?" A male voice. High-pitched. Nervous. "Who is that?"

"Don't get too close, Tate." Another voice. Firm. Authoritative. "It could be a set-up."

Then there was silence. Georgia felt jumpy. What were they doing? Drawing their weapons, getting a bead on her? The high-pitched voice again, ragged and scared. "Oh Christ! It's Peña!"

He was only a few yards away. Blood shouted in her ears.

"Aw, shit!" He cried.

Footsteps crunched through the brush. They were close.

"Oh, fuck me! He was always so careful."

Once more there was silence. Had they spotted her? She heard a rustle. Then the snap of a twig. She considered trying to flee through the brush, bullets be damned. But the reality was she wouldn't get very far. To tell the truth, she wasn't sure she wanted to run. Something inside her had begun to rip, like a tiny tear in flimsy material. It could eventually split her apart. Better to face it head on.

She stepped away from the tree. One of the men was crouched in a shooter's stance. The other was beside him. Both had guns aimed at her, and both racked their slides. The man with the voice of authority barked. "Drop your weapon and put your hands up."

* * *

Propped up against the cab in the bed of their pickup, Georgia was only dimly aware of her surroundings. Chills alternated with sweat, and her brain was fogged with pain. They'd taken her Sig and the Glock, lifted her blazer from Raffi's body and fished through the pockets for her Chicago blue card and license. They tied her arms and legs, then threw her in the back of the truck. Her broken wrist was pinned behind her back, caught in a vise of pain so sharp she could barely breathe. As they drove, she bounced around the bed of the pickup, drifting in and out of consciousness.

One of the men followed in Raffi's pickup, the second drove the pickup she was in. Mercifully, it was a short ride. She couldn't see out of the truck but she heard the crunch of gravel. The pickup stopped. The sudden cessation of motion made her roll over onto her broken wrist. A fresh stab of pain shot through her. She screamed. Then everything went loose, and a soft black curtain descended.

* * *

When she came to, she was lying on a ratty sofa that smelled of stale cigarettes and onions. Her legs were still bound, but her arms were free. Her casted arm rested on her chest. She opened her eyes to a colorless blur. She blinked. Things slowly swam into focus.

She was inside a large room. It looked like the interior of one of the Lanedo cabins, maybe the one she couldn't get into earlier. Now, though, a transformation had taken place, as if someone had waved a magic wand and brought the scene to life. Several men milled around, all of them dressed in camo gear or fatigues. One was spooning beans from a tinned can. Most of the men had heavy beards and short hair. Two were bald. Two women puttered around a primitive kitchen. One stirred something into a pot. They wore fatigues, too. Everyone had pistols strapped to their waists.

Where had they been earlier? Were they checking her out from some unseen hideout? Georgia tried to sit up, but a wave of dizziness stopped her. She plopped back down. One of the women eyed her, then motioned to the man eating beans.

"Untie her legs, Rem. I don't think she's gonna run."

The man put down his beans and came over to Georgia. He needed a bath. He untied the rope around her legs.

Georgia swallowed. Her throat felt like it was full of sand. "Water," she croaked.

The woman filled a jelly jar with water from a barrel, brought it over, and held it against her lips. Georgia gulped it down.

"You want to sit up?" The woman asked.

When she nodded, the woman helped her wedge herself against the back of the couch. She was weak, but the dizziness had subsided. "Thank you."

The woman nodded and called out. "She's back, Whit."

The man with the authority in his voice came out from a room in the back. He wore camo gear and work boots. A large 45 was holstered around his waist. He was a tall brawny man with a fair complexion and sandy hair. Earlier he'd had on shades, but now he was wearing clear glasses.

Georgia usually had a thing for men in glasses. Matt had worn them, and she thought they gentled him. Not this man. Behind his glasses were icy blue eyes that held no warmth. But there was no hostility, either. He studied Georgia as if she was not quite human—at best a minor complication.

The man called Tate followed behind Whit. Wiping his sleeve across his mouth, he said, "We should have done her back on the road."

"Shut up, Tate," Whit said.

"She offed Peña."

"Why don't you take a couple of guys and make sure we got everything from his truck." When Tate didn't move, he added, "That's an order."

Tate blinked. He reminded Georgia of a fish that doesn't know it's been hooked. Then he picked up a shotgun propped up against a wall and headed to the door.

Whit pulled up a chair, flipped it around backwards, and sat. "So, your name is Georgia Davis and you're a PI from Chicago."

"What are you going to do with his body?"

"Why do you care?" He was matching her, question for question.

"I was hoping his friends in Stevens could bury him."

"And who might they be?"

She eyed him. "Who are *you?*"

"Did you shoot Peña?"

"No."

"Prove it." Tate called from the doorway.

Whit twisted around. "Tate, get the fuck out. You're getting on my nerves."

A flush crept up Tate's neck, but he exited the cabin.

Georgia waited until the door closed. "My Sig isn't powerful enough to do what they did to him."

"You had a Glock, too."

"It was Raffi's. He loaned it to me."

"Raffi?" He stroked his beard, as if pondering the fact they were on a first-name basis. Streaks of red ran through the blond. He dropped his hand. "Maybe you had an assault rifle but ditched it before we found you."

"Sure. And I was just hanging around the crime scene for a good time."

"What's your tie to Peña?"

She shook her head again. Her temples throbbed. Her wrist was on fire. But this was her last shot. "No. First we deal."

His eyebrows rose. "You're in no position to deal."

"Sure I am. I have nothing to lose."

He didn't say anything for a while. Then he smiled wearily, conceding the point. "Okay. What do you have?"

"The man who killed Raffi is missing part of his index finger.

He kidnapped a little girl, then killed her mother and her mother's boss in Chicago. He tried to kill me too."

"Why?"

"Because I was getting too close to Geoff Delton's secrets."

"Which would be?"

She sensed his interest. "No. Nothing more till you tell me who you are. And how *you* know Raffi."

Whit shook his head. "You haven't given me anything useful."

She sighed. She was tired of the games, the lies, the circles of suspicion. Becoming dependent on people, their contacts, even their weapons, was never a good idea. She'd thought—incorrectly, it turned out—Raffi was more or less a loner like her. Yet, whoever these people were, hiding out in the mountains, they weren't Raffi's enemies. And while she wasn't at all sure they could—or would— help her, her options had dwindled. Like it or not she was at their mercy.

So she told him about Molly Messenger's kidnapping, the bank accounts and cashiers' checks, the deaths of Chris, Art Emerlich, and her efforts to protect Sandy Sechrest. She told him she suspected that Raffi, despite working for Delton, was involved in drug trafficking and murder. Enough to have warranted a million dollars in hush money. In a way, it felt good to finally lay it all out. When she finished, she motioned to Whit. "Your turn."

Whit took off his glasses, polished them on his sleeve, put them back on. His face revealed nothing. Maybe that was why he was their leader. Finally he spoke.

"We are part of a movement to take back our country."

"Are you Minutemen? Some border watch group?"

"No. We are the front lines—the infantry. We are committed to securing the borders. Saving our society from destruction."

"Why are you hiding out up here?"

"Because we're prepared to go further than anyone else. At least the ones who haven't been corrupted by the cartels. And they— well, let's just say the authorities don't like our attitude."

Georgia's stomach knotted. Just her luck to be hooked up with some wacko right-wing group. But aloud she said, "So you're allies with Delton Security and Lionel Grant—is that how Raffi got to you?"

Whit tilted his head. "Oddly enough, I doubt Lionel Grant— or Delton—knows we exist. Peña came to us on his own."

Georgia frowned. "Raffi's Mexican. Most likely working at cross purposes from you. What could you possibly have in common?"

"There are times that diverse people have mutual goals."

Whit was obviously an educated man. He was also clever and charismatic enough to have fashioned a bunch of ragtag weirdos into some semblance of order. But that didn't mean he wasn't crazy. He could be a latter day Charles Manson. Or a Unabomber who was off the grid. She had to tread carefully.

"Those mutual goals—what would they be?"

"Raffi had had enough."

"Of what?"

Whit looked around the room and waved his hand. Without a word, the two women and the man who'd been eating canned beans left the room. She and Whit were alone. "What I'm going to tell you,' he said softly, "no one knows. No one. Except the players themselves." He paused. "And me."

Georgia nodded.

"Peña's team *was* compromised."

"How?"

"Delton started out doing what Lionel Grant wanted. Trying to stop the flow of drugs across the border. They were mostly backups to the border agents. After a while, they became more confident. They did some reconnaissance, intelligence gathering, even made some forays across the border.

"But cartels are powerful organizations. They effectively control the government of Mexico, and they've made inroads here as well. More people are killed along the border than in Iraq these days. The cartels are the biggest threat to the American way of life. To our survival. And no one's doing anything about it."

Georgia didn't need a political rant. "What does that have to do with Delton? Or Raffi?"

Whit gazed at her. "It doesn't take much to flip someone. You know that. No matter how strong or powerful they are, everyone is vulnerable somewhere. The cartels make an art out of discovering what those vulnerabilities are. Of course, if they can't find any, they create them. Once they do, they own you." Whit rocked forward. "It's happening in U.S. border towns all over the Southwest. The cartels have infiltrated the police, civic organizations, even political groups. It's the beginning of the Armageddon. But no one will admit it. The degree of denial is—"

Georgia cut him off. "How did the cartels infiltrate Delton?"

"Given their MO, I would imagine they bribed them. If that didn't work, they probably planted drugs, weapons, or other evidence that was conveniently discovered by authorities." He paused. "I heard rumors that the body of a murdered whore turned up in someone's bed."

"Jesus." She winced. "Are the Stevens police involved?"

"This is a major border crossing for drugs. They have to be."

She nodded, not surprised. There wouldn't be much help from that quarter.

He went on. "As far as Delton is concerned, deals were made. Money changed hands. Lots of it. They are, after all, mercenaries. Up to the highest bidder. After that it was just a case of how far and how high Delton jumped."

"And Raffi was one of the jumpers?"

Whit held up a hand. "I'm getting there." He leaned back. "There are four major cartels. Their names don't matter. What does matter is that they are always trying to expand their turf. Usually at the expense of each other. They've been at war for years."

"What does that have to do with Delton?"

"Many illegals who want to cross the border don't have enough money to bribe custom officials or pay coyotes. So they become mules. Ferrying drugs for one of the cartels in return for safe passage. When Cartel A wants to take down Cartel B, Cartel A's soldiers target Cartel B's mules. Round them up and execute them. As a warning."

Like Diego's parents, Georgia thought.

"Authorities have found mass graves on both sides of the border."

"And you're saying Delton was killing those mules?"

He nodded. "Once the cartels have infiltrated an organization, they can force it to do whatever they want."

"But Raffi refused?"

"He discovered that some of the mules who were targeted were people from his village in the Sonora. He called Delton and threatened to expose him if he—Delton—didn't do the right thing. Instead, twenty-four hours later, three million-dollar checks were sent to Raffi's team."

Why was Whit telling her all this, she wondered. What was *his* agenda? She wanted to ask but didn't want to risk having him clam up.

"Wrobleski and Brewer deposited their money," he went on, "but Raffi tore his check up. And told Delton he did. Two days later the other two were dead and their records were scrubbed."

"The 'training' accidents."

"It's the cartels' way. Assassinate the soldiers. Then go after the leader. So Raffi ran. To us."

Georgia thought about it. "That's why Chris manipulated the bank records."

"What?"

She held up her hand, thinking it through. After Raffi refused his bribe, Delton must have told the cartel he had a mess on his hands. So they sent the man with the missing finger to clean it up. He kidnapped Molly Messenger and forced her mother to close Delton's dummy account at the bank, thinking that would erase the evidence of the hush money. But Chris had to have warned Delton—maybe the man with the missing finger as well—that it wouldn't work. That someone at the bank would discover what she was doing. They told her to go ahead anyway, and since they had Molly, she had no choice. Sure enough, when Sandy Sechrest found the discrepancies and reported them to Art Emerlich, the man with the missing finger was forced to cover their tracks by killing Emerlich and Chris. And try for Sechrest as well.

Georgia fixed her eyes on the floor. Usually she loved this part of a case, the part when the pieces resolved themselves into a pattern so clean and yet so obvious that it couldn't have happened any other way. This time, though, she felt no satisfaction. For the cartels a rising body count was just a measure of progress. The cost of doing business. Killing men, women, even children, came easily. Even the mob in Chicago had more compassion. And Geoff Delton, too weak to control his own men, was complicit in the carnage. Lionel Grant, too, who'd underwritten Delton in the first place.

"Why didn't Raffi expose Grant, too?"

Whit shook his head. "Lionel Grant was not a part of this."

"But Grant hired Delton. It was his truck they used in the desert."

"It wasn't him," Whit said firmly.

Georgia spread her hands. "Why should I believe you? You and Grant have similar missions. And you said yourself diverse people can work together."

He stared at Georgia for a long minute. Then he said, "There is a tunnel under the border."

"A tunnel?"

"Drugs flow in one direction, arms in the other. The collaborator you are looking for is not Lionel Grant. Your collaborator is the man who manages the flow of 'traffic' through this tunnel. Raffi decided the only way to stop him—and the traffic going through it—was to destroy it."

"Where is this tunnel?"

"That I don't know."

Georgia didn't believe him.

"There are more than seventy-five tunnels under the Mexico-Arizona border," he explained. "More are built every day. Raffi didn't tell us where this one was."

"Why not? Was he protecting you?"

Whit nodded. "He was."

"Why?"

"Because we were going to give him the supplies to blow it up."

CHAPTER 41

Georgia spent the night at the camp. Although she was more or less under house arrest, they fed her, loaned her some bedding, even let her walk around the compound—albeit with a guard. Still, when it was time for bed, she tossed fitfully.

She had questions. For one, she recalled how Sandy Sechrest said that Delton's accounts at the bank, the ones Chris closed, were technically unfunded. That Delton had persuaded the bank to temporarily loan him the three million dollars. But Geoff Delton wasn't stupid—didn't he know the bank wouldn't let it slide? Unless he'd been planning to shift the blame to Chris all along. Her fingerprints were in the system. Maybe he thought he could convince the bank she'd embezzled the three million and written bogus cashiers' checks as retribution because he refused to leave his wife. He could slip in the fact that she'd become pregnant as proof.

Still, Delton should never have ended up in this situation. He should have anticipated his men would be tempted by the cartels.

They were mercenaries, after all. Did he think his men were immune? Rumors of arms smuggling by mercenaries were nothing new. Unless Delton, the former Boy Scout, panicked when he discovered his own men were involved. Maybe he was just plugging holes—or letting the man with the missing finger plug them for him.

But Delton's motivations would have to wait. Georgia's most pressing question was figuring out who Delton was collaborating with. Geoff Delton was in league—willingly or not—with someone who could run drugs overland across the border or underground through a tunnel. Which meant that individual controlled key pipelines along the supply chain. And that made him a powerful person.

Yesterday she'd been ready to go to the police. But according to Whit, the Stevens police had been corrupted by the cartel. And Javier Garcia thought the mayor's brother ran a drug tunnel underneath his property. Going to the authorities, civil or law enforcement, wouldn't get her anywhere. It might get her killed.

She thought about the lives that had been snuffed out. The men who'd turned from soldiers into murderers. The children like Molly and Diego, whose world had been blown apart. The people who'd been coerced or corrupted.

Raffi had wanted to strike a blow for the powerless.

What did she want?

* * *

She woke to the aroma of coffee and the clarity that comes from making a decision. One of the women was scouring the pot that held last night's stew. The other was rolling up sleeping bags, putting things away.

"What's happening?" Georgia asked.

"We're breaking camp. We rotate between three or four places," the woman said. "It's safer."

Georgia couldn't see herself living a gypsy existence. She liked having a home base, her apartment. Even if the walls were bare.

She poured coffee and waited for Whit. She realized now why he'd confided in her. She thought she had an idea where the tunnel was. And whose property it cut through. The problem was she needed proof. She sipped her coffee, remembering the call that Raffi got from his buddy confirming that his "package," a videotape, had arrived. Someone or something important was on that tape. Was it the proof she needed? If so, the man with the missing finger might already have it. He'd taken Raffi's cell and could trace the call. She didn't have much time.

At length Whit came into the room, dressed in black, smelling like soap. He was carrying something under his arm. Her blazer, which she'd used to cover Raffi's bloody body. Someone had washed it. He handed it to her, then went to the coffee pot and poured a cup.

She folded the blazer, then turned to him. "Let's go outside. We need to talk."

CHAPTER 42

Ellie

"I know you do not like coming to the hospital, Ellie. So I am grateful for your visit."

I tried not to squirm. This was the third time I'd visited Fouad in a hospital. The first was several years ago when he'd been shot saving my life. The second was when he collapsed at my house a few days earlier. I didn't want to make these visits a habit. "When is your surgery?"

"Tomorrow morning. At seven."

"They're doing four arteries?"

He nodded, looking pale.

"My father says the third day is the worst."

"It is what it is. The Koran says 'what Allah writes on your forehead, you will become.'" He smiled. "And what Allah doesn't write, I'm sure the doctor and Hayat will."

I smiled back. There aren't many people who can integrate the spiritual with the practical as well as Fouad. "I'll be back tomorrow then, just to make sure Allah did his part."

I waited until Hayat arrived, then headed home. The afternoon rush was just starting, but the traffic on Green Bay Road was slowed by what seemed like a permanent state of construction. I craned my neck out the window. It looked like a car was double-parked on the street ahead, forcing cars to pull around it.

I took a cleansing breath, determined not to stress about it and turned on NPR. *All Things Considered* was in the middle of a story about ethanol. Mac and I had finished most of the shooting, including the interview with Voss-Peterson's CEO, and Hank was doing his magic with the editing. I turned the volume up. Robert Siegel was interviewing Neil Plakcy, a consumer activist from EcologyNow.

"It's a scam," Plakcy was saying. "Next to credit default swaps, ethanol's probably the biggest con ever perpetrated."

"How so?" Siegel asked in his crisp public radio voice.

"Essentially, lobbyists and government have colluded to give exorbitant subsidies to companies for making ethanol, when there's no clear benefit to doing so."

"I thought—we've been told—the product extends the life of fossil fuels."

"Marginally, if at all. It uses more energy to produce than what you get out of the savings. And ethanol is bad for the environment. Distilleries run on coal, you see. Plus the fertilizer used to grow corn runs off to the ocean where it settles in areas called dead zones."

I tapped my fingers on the wheel.

Plakcy went on. "But here's the kicker. Today, one hundred fifty plants produce six billion gallons of the stuff every year. But we have no indication—none at all—that it's making any dent in consumption. If it weren't for the recession, demand, in fact, would be up."

"Well then, who is benefiting?" Siegel asked in a dead-pan voice.

"The corporations making the stuff. They get five billion dollars in subsidies to produce it, then sell it at inflated prices."

I winced. Not only was Voss-Peterson receiving massive ethanol subsidies, but they'd been buying up farms too, thus qualifying for more breaks as "farmers." Plus, they were selling the stuff for top dollar. That's what I call getting them coming and going. I snapped off the radio and decided to double my fee.

When I finally came abreast of the double-parked car, I saw a sign in the rear window that read, "Company Car—I don't care."

I didn't know whether to laugh or cry. My cell phone rang.

"Ellie? It's Georgia."

"Hey, Georgia." I'd been calling her cell for the past day and was starting to worry. "I'm glad you called. Are you back?"

"Not yet."

"What do you mean, you're not? You said —"

"Ellie, I need you to pick up something downstate."

"What?"

"You remember that facility you passed when you were making your video?"

"The place we decided was a training camp for Delton?"

"Exactly. Well, someone there—one of the instructors—has a videotape you need to get."

"A tape? Why? The police picked up Delton and, from what I hear, he's talking. O'Malley seems confident they can tie him to Molly, Chris, and the cashiers' checks. Plus, he said the FBI's about to move in. It's over. We won."

"No." Georgia's voice was hard. "It's not over."

"What are you talking about?"

"The tape you're going for will prove who's behind everything."

"We already know. It's Delton. And that guy Grant."

"Geoff Delton was just a pawn. And it's not Grant." She explained about the cartel, the tunnel, and how the Delton team was turned. "A man—an American—who's in league with the cartel is on that tape."

"How does Peña know that?"

"He shot the tape. Then sent it to his buddy at the training camp and told him to release it if he was killed."

"So?"

Georgia didn't say anything.

"Peña's dead?"

No answer.

"What happened?"

I heard the sorrow in her voice as she told me. It made me want to comfort her, but something else in her voice, a bitter edge, said to back off.

"What format is the tape?"

"What do you mean?"

I explained about tape formats, cassettes, and discs.

Georgia hesitated. "I don't know."

"Well, does—did Peña have a camera?"

Another pause. "Yes. He did."

"What kind was it?"

"Christ, Ellie. I don't' know. Can't you just—wait!" She cut herself off. "I remember. The camera was lying around in the cabin. It said Mini DV on the side."

"Perfect!"

"Why?"

"I have a Mini DV myself. Which means I can screen it right away."

"Good. Listen," she finished. "The guy you're going to meet will probably give you a hard time. He did when I called. "

"You spoke to him? What did he say? How did you get his number?"

Georgia hesitated. "It doesn't matter. Look. Do what you have to. Just get the damn tape."

"Gee, thanks for the warning."

* * *

I fed Rachel and left after rush hour, but it still took two hours to drive downstate. I got off I-55, then took what I thought were the right back roads, but I didn't find the camp. By the time I backtracked to Funks Grove and Shirley, it was dark. Rural nights are blacker and more menacing than the variegated shades of color in the city, and except for the beam of my headlights visibility was nil.

Georgia had given me the guy's cell, and when I called, he answered on the first ring. He said he'd meet me at a bar a few miles north of Shirley. From his directions, it sounded close to one of the places Mac and I had eaten lunch, and when I finally found it, I saw I was across the street from the restaurant.

We have dive bars in Chicago—they're my favorite kind—but this one wasn't up to that caliber. Just one room with a linoleum floor and a few shabby tables. The bar itself was formica; the place had probably been a dry cleaners or sandwich shop at some point. The air conditioning, such as it was, groaned and clanked, and occasional drops of water trickled from a pipe in the ceiling. Thankfully, the lighting was dim.

I ordered a Miller Lite and sat at a table that wobbled when I put any weight on it. A group of young guys in shorts, t-shirts, and billed caps at the next table eyed me when I sat down. I was already on edge, and it didn't help that their conversation, vigorous and loud when I entered, tapered off. I squirmed, feeling every bit the outsider I was.

Ten minutes later, a beefy bull of a man came in. Despite the heat, he was wearing jeans and a sweat shirt. His head looked too small for his body. Thin dark hair was parted on the left. His eyes were widely spaced, but he had no neck. There wasn't an inch of fat on him. Not a guy I wanted to be on the bad side of. After ordering a beer, he looked around. He dipped his head when he saw me and came over.

"Are you Brian Gilomen?"

"I told your friend I'd come because I wanted to see what you looked like."

Not a promising start.

He looked me up and down. "How do I know Peña's dead?"

"Have you tried to call him?"

"Maybe."

"The people who killed him took his cell. If you called and someone else picked up, you have your answer."

He took a swig of beer. "How do I know you and your friend didn't kill him?"

"I haven't been in Arizona, but Peña told my partner about the tape. He wouldn't have told her unless he trusted her," she lied.

"Maybe she forced him to."

"Someone tried to kill her a week ago in Chicago. Her wrist is broken. She's not in great shape. He could have easily overpowered her."

Gilomen grunted.

"Look. This case started with a little girl who was kidnapped. Then her mother was murdered." I told him what we knew and how it had led to Peña and Arizona. "It's clear now this is part of something bigger. My partner wants the right people to be held accountable."

Gilomen pondered that.

"Peña obviously felt the same way or he wouldn't have given you the tape for safekeeping."

"What proof do I have that you're who you say you are?"

My patience came to an end. "Jesus!" I spit out. "I know you need to be cautious, but what about my questions? If you're such a good friend of Peña's, why are you working at Delton Security? Don't you know what's going on? How do I know you still have the tape? Maybe you gave it to Delton."

He didn't answer directly. "Despite the road our founder might have traveled, I believe in the company. And its mission. What we do is necessary and right."

I stared at him, feeling suddenly uneasy. "Are you working with Peña... or Delton?"

He didn't answer for a moment. Then, "Peña was the best recruit I ever trained. If he failed, it was my fault."

I sensed he was telling the truth. I almost said he was being too hard on himself. "Then you must feel an obligation to finish his mission." I paused. "Georgia—my partner—feels the same way."

His eyebrows arched.

"Okay, here's what I think: You don't trust me, and, frankly, the feeling's mutual. But if you hand over the tape, we'll make sure your name stays out of it. We have contacts in the press and the police. They'll respect your privacy. Deal?"

He thought about it for a moment. "If Peña got it right, you're up against powerful forces."

"All the more reason to keep you out of it. Someone needs to keep an eye on Delton down the road. I would guess that's easier to do from the inside."

* * *

Ten minutes later I sprinted to the car with the cassette in my purse. I'd charged my camera before I left; now I slipped in the cassette, flipped open the tiny screen, and pressed Play. I wondered if I'd be able to see anything. The screen filled with snow. It turned to gray, then black. I frowned. A few seconds later a light appeared near the top of the frame. Then another. Someone was panning the camera. The shot was jumpy, as if the cameraman was walking. It was impossible to see anything clearly.

Finally, the shot settled down; the cameraman had stopped. We were in a dark place. The only resolution came from those lights at the top of the frame. I zoomed in. The image was tiny, but I could make out a group of men standing in what looked like a tunnel. Two had dark hair and looked Hispanic. Two were white guys in army fatigues. Wrobleski and Brewer? The fifth man was in a suit. I hit pause and studied the image. I'd seen photos of this man.

Geoff Delton. The sixth man was white also, and his arms were wrapped across his chest. He had long hair tied back in a ponytail, a lantern jaw, and was wearing a denim shirt and jeans. A silver belt buckle flashed at his waist. He looked like an aging hippie.

They were all talking, gesturing, and nodding their heads.

I was just about to call Georgia when a dark sedan pulled up outside the bar. The entrance was dimly lit by an overhead light surrounded by moths. Two men got out. It was dark outside, but they were both wearing wrap-around shades. They did not look happy. I started the car and made a speedy exit. Then I called Georgia.

CHAPTER 43

Georgia

"The problem is we don't know where the tunnel actually is," Georgia said as she and Whit drove past Grant Copper Works the next morning. They were in Georgia's rental car. The blush of dawn had surrendered to a heavy cloud cover, and the crouching lion logo over the front entrance swayed in the breeze.

"Ken Grant." Whit shook his head. "I should have known."

"Why?"

"Upstanding citizen. On the city council." He sighed. "Just what the cartel targets."

"It probably doesn't hurt that he goes back and forth to Mexico for 'business.'"

Whit nodded. "I wonder how many supply routes he controls."

"He obviously has the Sonora covered."

Whit gazed at the warehouse. "You take the high road, and I'll take the low road..."

"Excuse me?"

"Overland through the desert, or underground through the tunnel, it all gets to the same place."

Georgia swung the wheel and turned the corner. "And with the perfect cover."

Whit looked over.

"The truck. Grant Junior must have leaned on Delton to borrow Dad's trucks for their desert operations. That way Dad would be implicated if anything went wrong. It makes perfect sense. Dad's just a wacko right wing nut, anyway."

Whit's expression went flat.

Georgia realized she'd insulted him, too. She bit her lip and circled back around the warehouse. "I don't know much about explosives," she said, eager to change the subject. "How precise does the charge have to be? Wouldn't it be easier just to blow the warehouse?"

Whit spoke in a cool, clipped voice. "You could take out the warehouse, and yes, you'd do major damage. Maybe even to the mouth of the tunnel. But the tunnel itself would likely remain intact. They'd just shore it up and find another way through."

Georgia headed down the Pan-American Highway. A deep drainage ditch paralleled the road about ten yards away. "What's that?"

"A storm drain. It runs along the highway all the way to Mexico."

"Do you think the tunnel hooks up with it?"

"I wouldn't think so. It used to be a way to get across the border from Esteban. Illegals would crawl through the pipe and exit through manhole covers on the streets of Stevens. But during monsoon season, it overflows with water. That happened during a flash flood a couple of years ago just as a dozen people were inside. Most of them drowned and were swept away. It's been barred up."

Georgia blinked.

"But it's an interesting theory. The cartel could have angled off the main drain at some point," Whit said. "We may be able to get an engineering plan. Or blueprints. They're probably public record."

"We don't have time," Georgia said. "And we'd just be duplicating what Raffi already figured out." As they approached the border, traffic thickened and slowed. She turned off the highway just before they reached the guard booths. "What about the other end?"

"In Esteban?"

She nodded. "Maybe there's a way to for me to sneak in from there. Do you know where it is?"

"I don't. But even if I did, you'll never get through. It's got to be heavily guarded."

"I wonder if Raffi checked it out."

"I'm telling you," Whit said. "It's a waste of time."

Georgia pursed her lips. Then she smiled "Maybe not."

* * *

"Carmelita, I need to talk to your brother."

Georgia had driven to Carmelita Herrera's home in the barrio, hoping to catch her before she left for work. The woman answered the door, but when she recognized Georgia, her expression turned sour. "You should not be here. Please. Go away." She tried to close the door.

"Wait." Georgia wedged her foot in the space. "We need to talk."

From deep inside the house came the strains of a Spanish TV soap opera.

"Raffi is dead."

Carmelita's hand flew to her mouth. Her eyes registered shock. "What happened?"

Georgia briefly explained. Tears sprang to the woman's eyes. *"Madre de Dios!"*

Georgia let her grieve for a moment. Then, "The thing is, you knew exactly what he was doing, didn't you?"

Despite her grief, a knowing expression came into her eyes. "Come in."

Georgia stepped inside the home. "Why did you let me believe *he* was responsible for murdering people in the desert?"

The woman blinked fast, as if trying to regain her composure. "You were a stranger. I thought you were his enemy."

Georgia nodded. She understood. She'd shown up without warning, probing Carmelita about Raffi, illegal immigrants, and drugs. At that point, in fact, she thought Raffi *was* her enemy. Now, though, she needed help. She chose her words carefully. "Carmelita, I want to finish what Raffi started."

Carmelita's lips parted in surprise. "Why?"

"Because it's the right thing to do."

Carmelita paused, then shook her head. "Raffi was the best. If he did not succeed, what makes you think you will?"

"I don't know that I will." Georgia lifted her chin. "But I have to try." She told Carmelita about the tunnel. "I want to approach it from the Mexican side, and I believe your brother knows where it is. Can you persuade him to take me to it?"

Carmelita was quiet for a moment. Then a faint smile crossed her lips. "You do not need him." She cocked her head.

Now Georgia's jaw dropped. "You know?"

"How do you think I crossed?"

* * *

Georgia hooked up with Whit back at Lanedo that afternoon. He led her to the back room where several wooden crates lay on a bed. The labels on them were faded, but she could make out a few words here and there: fuse igniters, primacord, Comp C-4. Whit opened one of the crates and lifted out six small blocks wrapped in dark green plastic. They were about ten inches by four inches by two. He slipped them into a backpack. Then he opened a smaller crate and pulled out half a dozen objects that looked like nails. Attached to the top of the nails were cylinders about the size of large bottle caps. On top of the caps were miniature switches.

"Detonators," he said, holding one up. "They have tiny batteries inside. With a timer. You can set it up to an hour."

Georgia knew that state-of-the-art equipment like this was only available through the military. Fort Huachuca wasn't far away. "Must be nice to have a demolitions depot just up the road."

Whit grinned. "Things tend to fall into your lap when you're in the right place at the right time." He handed her the detonators. "Any questions?"

Georgia had taken a class on explosives at the Academy years ago, but technology had evolved since then. "C-4 is fairly stable, isn't it?"

"It's covered with a thin plastic coating, which makes it less sensitive to heat and shock. They used to use it to heat food over in 'Nam. But it packs a pretty nice punch when it's triggered by a detonator. A few bricks can destroy an eighteen wheeler." He showed her how to poke a tiny hole in the C-4 with a pen. "It's really not hard. You only need this big a space." Georgia squinted— it was only about a quarter of an inch. "Then you push the detonator in, set the timer, and run like hell."

She nodded. "How many charges will I need?"

"Depends how long the tunnel is. At least three bricks. Maybe four, equally spaced. But I gave you enough C-4 and detonators for six. Try to put them in inconspicuous spots, not too near each mouth. And give yourself enough time to get out."

"There's no way we can use a remote control detonator?"

"You know the answer to that."

She did. The charges and the detonators would be underground, which would make above ground wireless signals chancy. She sighed.

He threw a pair of night vision goggles, a knife, and a flashlight into the backpack. "Add ten to fifteen minutes to however long it takes you to get into the tunnel, so you have enough time to get out."

She nodded. "What about collateral damage?"

"What do you mean?"

"What if I'm ready to set the charge and somebody happens to be in the tunnel?"

He was silent. Then he shrugged. "That's your call. You know what's going to happen if they catch you."

She pressed her lips together.

He made her go through the steps one more time, then handed her the backpack. As she slipped the detonators into her blazer pocket, something occurred to her.

"Why don't you do it with me? It would help me out."

Whit seemed to consider it. "I thought about it. But this really isn't our agenda. Our targets are usually the people Raffi wants to protect. Like I said, this is an isolated case of mutually converging interests."

She wasn't sure whether to believe him. Maybe he just didn't have the guts.

"One more thing," he said. He drew out her Sig from a pocket and handed it back to her. "You're probably going to need this."

* * *

Later that afternoon Georgia picked up Carmelita, who'd called in sick to work. Georgia had showered, put on clean clothes and make-up. Carmelita was wearing make-up too, and her hair was swept back in a soft, sexy style. She wore a flowery sundress, which was just a little too revealing, strappy sandals, and dangly earrings. Again Georgia was reminded of the beauty she once was.

Georgia had stowed the backpack in the trunk and threw some underwear, bras, and tank tops over it. She was terrified the agents would search the car at the border, but both Carmelita and Whit said the chances of that happening were small. Cars were usually searched coming back to the States. They were just two friends crossing the border for some afternoon shopping and margaritas.

Still, when they reached the crossing, Georgia's heart began to race, and her palms felt sweaty. She lowered the window and smiled at the guard. An overweight, balding man in uniform and wraparound shades, he asked for her driver's license. She handed it over. Carmelita did the same. The agent examined them, then leaned his head in, and scanned the Escort's interior.

"You're a long way from Illinois."

She nodded and forced another smile. "Vacation."

He grunted. "Whose car is this?"

"It's mine. Well, it's a rental," she said nervously.

"The contract, please."

She leaned over and snapped open the glove compartment. Thank God she hadn't stashed her Sig in there. She fished out the rental agreement, hoping her hands weren't shaking too much, and handed it to the agent. He studied it. Beads of sweat popped out on her forehead.

Finally, he handed it back. "Have a good afternoon." He waved them through.

Relief poured over her. She put the contract back in the glove compartment.

The Pan American Highway cut a broad swath down the western half of both border towns, but Esteban was even shabbier and more crowded than the barrio in Stevens. Georgia drove past block after block of cramped homes and one-story structures, all standing on flat gritty ground. Both towns supposedly lay between the Sonora and Chihuahua deserts, but the sandy soil and relentless heat made it seem like they were seamlessly connected.

When they reached Calle 4, they turned east and spent a few hours shopping and eating until well past dark. At around ten Carmelita directed Georgia to a bodega on a crowded street a block from the border. There was no sign in front, and the only indication it was a store was a halfhearted display of lettuce, mangoes, and beans propped up on crates outside. Carmelita made Georgia drive past it, then circle the block to make sure no one was around. They found a parking place two blocks away. Georgia killed the engine.

"You sure that was the place? It looks so—"

"Down here it is an open secret. Everyone knows."

"How come the police or border agents don't raid it? Board it up?"

Carmelita rubbed her fingertips together. "The cartel makes sure no one has a need to." She pulled a tube of lipstick out of her purse and angled the rear view mirror her way. "And if that doesn't work, they kill them." She calmly applied her lipstick. It was bright red. As Carmelita blotted her lips, Georgia wondered how far she would go, if she was in Carmelita's place. She wasn't a prude, but she had never traded sex for power, professional or otherwise. In fact, the idea was repellent. But there didn't seem to be any other solution. At least one that wouldn't require time to put into action. Still, it was a risk. "Carmelita, maybe you shouldn't do this. We'll figure out something else."

The woman waved her words away. "Raffi was a good man. I think you are good, too. I want to do this. I do not want to find more little Diegos."

"Still—"

Carmelita raised her finger to her lips. "I know what men want," she said softly. "It will work."

Georgia swallowed. They both got out of the car. Georgia opened the trunk, pulled out the backpack, and hoisted it over her shoulders. Then she returned to the front and stowed the keys under the seat. She hoped the car would still be there when they got back.

"In case I don't make it."

Carmelita shook her head. "Do not talk that way."

Georgia closed the door. "Let's go."

CHAPTER 44

They'd agreed in advance that Carmelita would go in, ostensibly to pick up a few groceries, which would give Georgia time to case the neighborhood. If Carmelita didn't come out in a few minutes, it meant she was proceeding. If she did, they'd abort and try again later. Meanwhile Georgia would work her way around to the back of the building. Carmelita said she thought there was a back door. Maybe a window, too.

She rounded the corner of the building and came to a small, unfenced yard. A dumpster leaned against the wall, emitting a rancid smell. Georgia picked her way through beer bottles, rotting food, paper, and god knows what else on the ground. There were no alleys in this part of the world, which she found a little unsettling. Back home they provided sure-fire escape routes, so essential that people wrote entire books about them.

But there was a back door. And a dirty window six feet off the ground. She found a cinderblock, pulled it over, and stepped up. Through the window she could see two men playing cards at a table. A lamp cast a dim light on the cards. A bottle of booze—tequila she thought—sat on the table, and the men took turns taking swigs. A skinny band of light from the front of the store poured through a narrow hallway. Although the window, covered with layers of grime, limited her sightline, Georgia saw flashes of Carmelita's flowery dress moving back and forth.

One of the men looked up from his cards. Something had caught his attention. Had Carmelita called out? He muttered something in Spanish, got up. He was tall and brawny. He headed to the front of the store. His companion, who was wearing a billed cap, stole a look at his cards.

Georgia peered around the room, trying to spot the entrance to the tunnel, but the glass was so dirty and the room so dark she couldn't see much except two closed doors. One might lead to the tunnel. She was surprised at how casually it was guarded. Just two men. Did that mean it was a quiet night? Or did it mean the cartel was so powerful they knew no one would mess with them?

Georgia looked to the front of the store. The tall man's body blocked most of the light, but Georgia caught glimpses of Carmelita. She was cocking her hip, placing one hand on it, and flashing a come-hither smile. She'd decided to impersonate a working girl, new to town. To prove her worth, she was offering a free sample. Georgia hadn't liked the idea, but Carmelita was adamant. "It is the only way to distract them. You will see." Georgia finally acquiesced.

She watched, trying to listen, but the conversation was muffled, and in Spanish. Billed Cap, who was still at the table, swilled down more booze, but was watching Carmelita and his buddy. At one point, he let out a laugh, but there was a cruel edge to it.

The tall guard scowled. Billed Cap stopped laughing. The tall guard shuffled back to the card room. Carmelita followed, her smile never wavering. She gestured provocatively, and said something low and throaty. The man ran his tongue around his lips. Carmelita's smiled widened. She groped for his hand, and moved it to her breast. Both men leered. Damn if she didn't bat her eyelashes.

More conversation between the men. Tall Guard's voice grew loud and harsh. Billed Cap's tone was resistant, but Tall Guard was clearly in charge. He pointed to the back door.

"No," Billed Cap barked. "*No voy a mover.*"

Tall Guard launched into a diatribe of shouting and gesticulating. Billed Cap sank back in his chair, looking afraid. Carmelita stayed by the passageway, but her smile had lost some of its wattage. Tall Guard pulled out a gun and aimed it at Billed Cap. He shuddered and crossed himself. Carmelita threw up her hands, cried out, and waved in the general direction of the back door. Tall Guard grunted and waved his gun. This time Billed Cap got up, picked up the tequila, and lurched to the door. Georgia stepped down from the cinderblock, hurried around the side of the building, and flattened herself against the wall.

A moment later the back door opened, and Billed Cap stumbled out into the yard, cursing in Spanish. The door closed behind him. Georgia held her breath and peeked around. The man stopped just outside the door, tipped the bottle to his mouth, and took a long swig. Then he staggered in her direction. If he came around the corner he would spot her. To be this close and have it all fall apart... she quickly crept around another corner.

Billed Cap turned the corner to the side she'd been flattened against a few seconds earlier. She risked a look. He seemed to be wavering. Was he going back inside? Camp out here? She heard more cursing. He listed to one side, righted himself and took an unsteady step forward. Then another. Finally, he headed away from the bodega. Georgia waited until he was well away from the store then hurried back to the window.

Tall Guard had shoved Carmelita against a wall. His hands were groping, pushing, squeezing. She was laughing, resisting playfully. He pulled away long enough to unbuckle his belt. She gestured to one of the two closed doors. He shook his head. Carmelita gestured again. Georgia knew she was protesting. Telling him she wanted some privacy. The guard growled in response. His hands moved up her legs, bunching the material of her dress at her waist. As he humped her through his pants, Georgia was close to despair. It wasn't going to work.

Then, without warning, Carmelita pushed hard against him. He pulled back. She darted across the room, went to one of the doors, and threw it open. Georgia could see a ladder going down. A shot of adrenaline shot down her spine. The tunnel entrance!

Carmelita went to the other door and threw it open. It looked like a small closet or storeroom crammed with boxes and crates. Carmelita spun around, smiled, and beckoned him in. He came towards her and pushed the tunnel door shut. She snaked her arms around his neck, drew him into the storeroom. The door closed.

Georgia immediately went to the bodega's back door, which was unlocked, and slipped inside. In two steps she was at the door to the tunnel. She opened it, but paused before taking the steps down. She heard Carmelita's moans of fake passion, the guard's grunts in response.

She descended the ladder.

* * *

As she reached the bottom of the steps, she was accosted by the odor of human waste. She breathed through her mouth. It had to be twenty degrees cooler, and the chill contrasted with the sultry heat above. It was eerily quiet, except for an occasional plink of water, which meant the tunnel might well be a spur off the storm drain she and Whit had passed earlier.

Turning around, she tried to get her bearings. A wheelbarrow on its side blocked her way. She grabbed the handlebars and moved it to the side. She'd thought she'd need a flashlight, but bare bulbs were strung with wire every twenty or thirty feet. A slight draft told her it was ventilated, too. The tightly packed dirt floor was fairly flat, but it was pitted with stones. Which meant she'd have to tread with caution. The walls had been hewn from rock and were shored up at regular intervals with wood supports. The ceiling, about seven feet high, was a surprise. No need to bend over or crouch as she walked. Someone had spent a lot of time and effort engineering the tunnel.

She started forward. The tunnel curved, blocking her view, but once around the bend, it straightened out. Under normal circumstances, Georgia could walk a mile in about twenty minutes, but the tunnel had to be much shorter, less than a quarter of a mile, she guessed. Three to four football fields at most. Six minutes later, by her watch, the path curved again, and the floor seemed to rise. She must be nearing the U.S. end. Negotiating the curve, she saw an abrupt end to the tunnel. Another set of steps led to a ceiling hatch made of steel with two metal handles protruding. A wheeled dolly sat on the ground near the steps. She was underneath Grant Copper Works.

Backtracking about ten yards, she slid the backpack off her shoulders. She opened it, took out one of the bricks of C-4, and unwrapped it. It looked and felt like white putty. She threw the plastic into her backpack and fished out a pen. Remembering how Whit had done it, she carefully poked a hole in the brick. Then she pulled out a detonator and inserted it in the hole, setting the timer for thirty minutes. A green light on the tiny LCD display flashed red. It was armed. She placed the charge in an unobtrusive area behind a rock.

She jogged about a hundred yards back toward the Mexican side and repeated the process with another brick, this time setting the charge and timer for twenty-nine minutes. Loping another hundred yards she did it a third time, setting the timer for twenty-eight minutes.

Done. She tried to ignore the nagging thought that she was sealing the time of her own death.

Slinging the backpack over her shoulders, Georgia headed around the curve back towards the Mexican end. She froze when she heard a voice in front of her. Male. Spanish. Conversational. Another voice replied. Chatty. Relaxed. Her stomach flooded with fear. Carmelita should still be servicing the guard. Or interesting him in a do-over. These sounded like different voices, and their steps and shuffles indicated they were coming toward her. Fuck! Her mouth went dry. There was no place to hide. As soon as they rounded the bend, they'd see her.

With her good hand she drew out her Sig and began to sneak back to the U.S. side. The voices kept coming. She made sure to stay well in front of them. Even so, there was only a few seconds until they saw her. She darted a look at the ceiling and walls, hoping to spot a manhole cover or something. Some way out. But there was nothing. Just the two ends of the tunnel. Meanwhile, the first charge would explode in less than thirty minutes.

Georgia started to run towards the U.S. side, thinking she would upend the dolly and use it as a shield. But she wasn't paying attention to the ground, and she tripped on a rock. As she fell, an arrow of pain shot up her broken wrist. Shaking herself off, she managed to struggle to her feet. The voices were loud. A moment later she heard gasps, and the voices racheted up to shouts.

"*Quieta!*" Their voices were shrill. "*Ahora!*"

She kept going. She heard running steps behind her, the click of pistol slides being racked. Shots filled the tunnel with a deafening roar. Something whizzed by her ear.

"*Alto, no te muevas!*"

With her bad arm she didn't have time to rack the slide on her Sig. She stopped, threw down her gun, and dropped to the floor.

* * *

Three men. She didn't recognize them. One was pushing the wheelbarrow, which was now full of large burlap bags. The other two tied her hands behind her back and stuffed something in her mouth. A conversation in Spanish ensued. It seemed to last forever. Georgia was caught between anger and despair. Even if she could speak, she didn't know how to say they had to get out before they were blown away.

Finally, one of the three men headed back to the Mexican side of the tunnel. Probably to tell whoever was in charge that there was an intruder, and an *Anglo* at that. Georgia tried to inch forward, but one of the men aimed his pistol at her. She halted. Her pulse was pounding. Shit! They didn't have time to wait for directions from the boss. They had to get out.

She was acutely aware of time passing. Was it one minute? Two? She wanted to check her watch, but her hands were tied. Her skin felt sweaty and damp, and she choked back panic. She wondered how to disarm the charges. Whit hadn't taught her that. Could she just pull out the detonators? Assuming she could even reach them.

Another minute passed. Her chest heaved. She started to whimper. One of the men raised his gun and aimed. She shook her head and whimpered again, louder. She yanked her head to the side. The other man gazed at her with curiosity, but the one with the gun snarled and spoke sharply. Probably told his buddy not to pay any attention. Regardless, Georgia kept groaning and yanking her head.

The second man frowned. *"Ella quiere decirnos algo."* She's trying to tell us something.

The first man shrugged. The second man came over to Georgia and took the gag out of her mouth.

"We have to get out of here!" She croaked. "Right now! We're in terrible danger!"

He looked at her, not comprehending.

"Peligro!" She yelled. *"Ahora. Vamos! Ahora!"*

"Si, si, peligro..." The first man cackled. He looked amused.

"No!" Georgia's throat tightened. *"Aqui peligro!* There's a fucking bomb in here! *Vamos rapido!"* She lifted her chin toward the ceiling of the tunnel.

"¿Qué pasa?" The second man asked.

Christ, they had to move! Georgia didn't know the Spanish word for bomb. "There's a bomb in here, you assholes! Let's go!"

Another conversation. The first man waved a dismissive hand. "*No, No puede ser verda.*" More conversation. Georgia heard the word "*bomba.*" The second man gestured vigorously.

"Okay." The man with the gun sighed. "*Vamos.*" He threw Georgia a disgusted glance, as if he didn't believe her but was reluctantly obliging his buddy.

They half pushed, half dragged her through the tunnel to the U.S. side, but the hatch on the ceiling was closed. Georgia guessed nearly twenty minutes had elapsed. The first charge would detonate in about five minutes.

One of the men banged on the hatch. Nothing happened. He pulled on the handles.

"Please," she prayed to herself. "Be there. Even if it's Ken Grant. We need to get out of here."

They banged again. No response.

The men looked back at her. She couldn't remember the Spanish word for "again," but she nodded. They banged once more. Nothing. She was about to give up when the cover finally slid back, and a face peered down. Dark. Hispanic. She imagined him with wraparound shades. She knew him. The man with the missing finger.

* * *

She was on the floor of the cavernous warehouse, propped up against a wall. The air was warm and close, but the floor was cool. Most of the warehouse was in shadow, but she could see large pieces of equipment in the corners. A couple of them had giant arcing pipes that swept across the ceiling and hung over her head. The walls were cinderblock, and crates and boxes were stacked against them.

In front of her was another set of walls. Shorter and painted white, they were the walls surrounding the remodeled office suites of Ken Grant. The entrance to the tunnel was a few feet away. The hatch was open, but the two Mexicans who had brought her here had left. Had they gone back to the Mexican side?

Suddenly a bright light shone on her face, blinding her. She squeezed her eyes shut. The light bobbed to one side. She opened her eyes. The man with the missing finger held a mag light and was staring at her with hard eyes.

From the darkness behind him Ken Grant stepped forward. He looked the same as the first time they'd met: a gray ponytail, high cheekbones, lantern jaw. Dressed in denim. He gazed at her with mild curiosity, in contrast to the other man's ferocity. "Who sent you?"

"No one."

His eyes narrowed, obviously not believing her, but he kept his mouth shut.

Where was the fucking explosion?

"I was hoping you would give up and go back to Chicago," Grant finally said. "You've become a problem."

Georgia forced herself to control her body language and voice. She didn't know whether the Mexicans had told Grant she'd been babbling about a bomb, but in case they didn't, she didn't want to alert them to the C-4. "Why did you arrange for Delton to use your father's trucks in the desert?"

Grant smiled. "I am a businessman. I was simply taking advantage of an opportunity."

She inched away from the hatch. "You're a murderer."

"Semantics." His smile faded. "Actually, my father would understand. He'd have done the same thing, if he thought he could get away with it."

"Are you sure?" Georgia wanted desperately to look toward the open hatch. It was agony not to.

Grant studied her. For an instant, she thought he could read her mind. She waited for him to whip around and gaze at the tunnel, but he didn't. Instead he sighed. "It's unfortunate it's come to this."

He turned to the man with the missing finger, who ran his tongue around his lips, as if impatient to get to the killing.

"Suppose you start from the beginning. How did you locate the tunnel?"

Georgia squirmed. Did that mean Carmelita got away? Wouldn't Grant have mentioned they had her if she hadn't? There couldn't be more than a minute or two until the first blast. With any luck, the two of them would descend into the tunnel to investigate. A few seconds afterwards... she inched further away from the hatch.

The man with the missing finger squinted at her, then launched into a hurried conversation with Grant. When Grant nodded, Missing Finger turned back to Georgia.

"Why were you in such a hurry to get out of the tunnel?" He said in perfect, unaccented English.

She sank lower against the wall. She just had to hang on a little longer.

"Answer me. You don't want me to force you."

As if on cue, he crouched beside her, pulling out a knife with a six inch blade. It glinted in the light. Georgia looked at the knife, then back to him. How much longer?

The man lifted his chin. "Believe it or not, I don't like to see anyone suffer, especially a woman. But if you won't cooperate..." He laughed then, a cruel raspy sound that contradicted his words.

She didn't reply.

"Well, now," he said. "In that case, I think I'll start with your arm. Since your wrist is already broken, we may as well make it permanent."

She was under no illusions. The cartel was known for torturing their victims before burning, decapitating, or otherwise killing them. He cut through her cast and dug his fingers into her wrist. The pain was excruciating. Incoherent thoughts tumbled through her mind. An image of Molly Messenger. Then Ellie Foreman. Raffi. Pete. Even Matt.

He raised the knife. She felt hot breath on her face. It would only take seconds to saw off her arm. Her eyes darted to the tunnel entrance. Still no explosion. Had she set the charges incorrectly? They should have gone off by now.

He paused, his knife in the air. He'd caught her glance toward the tunnel. He followed her gaze, then looked back, as if disappointed by such an obvious tell. He shook his head, as if he would never understand the ways of the *Anglos*.

Then the room exploded. The blast screamed hot and hard, piercing her eardrums. A blowback of pressure burst from the hatch, throwing out dust and sand and bits of rock. The floor of the warehouse heaved and seemed to rise before settling back.

Missing Finger dropped the knife, raced to the hatch, and hurried down the ladder.

"Stop. It isn't safe!" Grant yelled.

"My men are down there!" Missing Finger yelled back. "I need to check! Cover her!"

Ken Grant picked up the knife and looked at Georgia, his features distorted with rage. If there was a face of evil, she thought, this was surely it. She tried to slither farther away from the opening, but couldn't without his noticing. She braced herself against the wall. What about the other blasts?

The other two came almost simultaneously. A wall of hot pressure swept across the warehouse. Georgia was tossed backwards. She slammed into something hard. Objects flew through the air and hurled themselves at her: dirt, rocks, pieces of schrapnel. The blasts must have punctured her eardrums, because the scene unspooled in a crazy-quilt of silence. Pinpoints of light and color danced before her eyes like Fourth of July fireworks. Then there was nothing.

CHAPTER 45

Blurry white walls, white sheets, white dust motes in the air. Even the venetian blinds were white. For an instant Georgia wondered if she was dead. Gradually, her vision cleared. A heart monitor machine stood beside her bed, its regular beeps comforting. She realized she was alive. And that her hearing was back. She felt unaccountably grateful.

A nurse came in, took her blood pressure and stuck a thermometer in her mouth. When she was done, she smiled approvingly. "Glad you're awake. You have visitors."

Georgia felt too weak to smile back. The door opened, and Ellie Foreman entered, wearing a worried, tense expression. When she saw Georgia, her face softened.

"You gotta stop doing this, Georgia. I hate hospitals."

Georgia just looked at her.

Ellie sat on the edge of the bed. "It's all over now. Everything."

Georgia's lips parted. Her throat was parched. Somehow Ellie knew. She picked up a glass of water, angled the straw between Georgia's lips, and supported her neck while she sipped.

"Ken Grant didn't make it." Ellie guided Georgia's head back down to the pillow. "Neither did the guy with the missing finger. His name was Pablo Lopez, by the way."

Georgia grunted.

"I feel the same way," Ellie said.

Georgia tried to prop herself up on one elbow. "Car—Car—"

"Carmelita's fine. She said she—um—finished the job and took off before the C-4 went off. She's been to see you, by the way. She'll be back. Now lie down."

Georgia lay back.

"Delton's singing to the cops in Chicago. Blaming it all on the cartel. They have Pattison too—you know, the president of the bank. For allowing Delton to walk all over him."

A dull ache throbbed against Georgia's temples. Her arm was in a new cast, but it didn't feel as sore as it should. She turned her head. An IV was dribbling something into her veins. She felt around her face and made out new bandages. But there wasn't a lot of pain. Just profound weariness.

It was as if Ellie had divined her thoughts. "The doctors say you need to rest for a long time."

She nodded.

Ellie ran her hand through her hair, and her lower lip caught between her teeth, both sure signs she was nervous. "Listen. Someone is here and wants to see you. Can you handle another visitor, just for a minute?"

Georgia rolled her eyes.

Ellie left but returned a moment later with an old man. He was probably in his seventies, but he carried himself ramrod straight.

His hair was silver, and there was a lot of it. He had a lantern jaw, and deep-set blue eyes that, at the moment, were full of concern. He was wearing a black suit and tie, and a crisp white shirt. Georgia didn't need an introduction.

Lionel Grant made one anyway. "I wanted to shake your hand," he said. "But I can see that's not possible." A ghost of a smile crossed his face. "Thank you for your service to your country."

Georgia didn't know what to say. She hadn't done it for her country. She'd done it for a little girl who'd lost her mother. The rest of it was just, as someone once said, commentary. But knowing the effort it must have cost Grant to show up here, she tried. She cleared her throat. "I'm sorry for your loss."

The muscles in his face twitched. "My son's activities were—unanticipated. You need to know that. I had no idea the Delton team had been subverted. Or that my son was at the root of it. Until Peña came to me."

Surprise rippled through her. "Ra—Raffi told you?"

"After his team was taken out, he came to me. He knew he had to disappear, but he wanted me to know he had a plan to stop them." He looked a little embarrassed. "I ordered him to go ahead. Said I would give him whatever he needed. But he was to say nothing to anyone about our 'arrangement' until such time as I permitted."

She thought about Whit. "You didn't know the group Raffi hooked up with?"

He shook his head. "I understand it was a white militia group." He hesitated. "They would not be my first choice as an ally, but I do believe it takes an army to fight the scourge we're facing."

Georgia didn't reply.

Grant's eyes reflected a deep sorrow. "I thought I was doing the right thing. Passing solid values on to my son. I don't understand where it went wrong."

Wasn't that the universal story, Georgia thought? Everyone trying to do the right thing. And failing. But when people were raised to fear and hate with the same passion as to love, the results weren't surprising. To be fair, it might not have started with Lionel Grant. Maybe *he* was raised to hate. Maybe it was a family trait, handed down for generations. At least this time, in this family, the chain had been broken. Sadly, tragically. But broken.

"The police won't be coming to question you for some time. And when they do, you needn't worry. It's all been—arranged."

She nodded. There was something to be said for owning a town.

"And if you ever need anything, young lady, anything at all..." he went on, "... don't hesitate to call me." He tried to smile, but couldn't quite make it. He turned and left the room.

Ellie came back in. "There's something else you should know. Cody Wegman was right about the elevator."

"How?"

"Lopez was the go-to guy for the cartel and Ken Grant. Not just a bi-lingual hit man. He used to brag how much he knew about computers."

Georgia's eyes widened.

"But he didn't know as much as he thought," Ellie went on. "When he forced Chris to close the accounts, he made her power down the system, which stopped the elevator, since they were on the same circuit. But it wasn't necessary. He was ten years out of date. The changes had already been entered." Her smile was just this side of smug. "Then again, if he hadn't screwed up, we—you—might never have identified him."

"I guess there's something to be said for incompetence," Georgia grimaced.

Ellie's face darkened. "One last thing." Her next words seemed to come out reluctantly. "Geoff Delton never knew Chris was pregnant."

"She never told him?"

Ellie shook her head.

"What was his reaction?"

"Apparently he fell apart. He'd been planning to blame the bank shenanigans on Chris's need to get revenge over their affair. Then he discovered he'd murdered his own child." Anger flared in Ellie's eyes. "He'll have to live with that forever."

Georgia went quiet. She'd been quick to pronounce judgment on Chris Messenger. She'd assumed the woman was using the pregnancy to force Delton to leave his wife. She'd been wrong. In the end, Chris had been as much a victim as Molly and the others.

Ellie cut into Georgia's thoughts, her voice more cheerful. "You, on the other hand, need to sleep. Get your strength back. I'm taking you home as soon as they let you out."

Georgia lay back against the pillow. Ellie seemed to know she'd had enough and gathered her things. She told Georgia she'd be back in a few hours.

"Open the blinds before you go, okay?"

Ellie nodded and raised them.

After she'd gone, Georgia let her gaze drift to the window. Through the glass she could see the sun full in the sky, searing the land with its fierce desert heat. But the monsoons would come soon. They would shove the heat aside and flush everything with a cool, whistle-clean wash.

That's all you could really hope for, she decided. A cleansing, a cooling off, before it started all over again. This time it would have to do. She was ready to go home.

If you enjoyed this book, would you please consider leaving a review on Amazon and/or Goodreads.com? Thank you. And if you'd like to sign up for Libby's email list go to libbyhellmannn.com

MORE ABOUT LIBBY
facebook.com/authorLibbyFischerHellmann
twitter.com/libbyhellmann

45751706R00239

Made in the USA
Middletown, DE
12 July 2017